JUST ONE...

&You Anthologies

Another Chance to Get It Right: A New Year's Eve Anthology

As the Snow Drifts: A Cozy Winter Anthology

Craving You: A Spicy Valentine's Day Anthology

Recipes for Romance: A Sweet Valentine's Day Anthology

Just One . . .: A Summer Romance Anthology

JUST ONE...

A Summer Romance Anthology

Edited by Nicole Frail

www.andyoupress.com

Contents

Introduction

Nicole Frail, Editor

YOU DON'T EVEN NEED TO leave your comfy reading chair to make long-lasting memories this summer thanks to the unforgettable adventures (and drama!) the authors featured in this collection of short stories have waiting for you.

The characters in *Just One . . .* are traveling across the country and around the world, they're looking for love (even when they *swear* they're not), and they're oftentimes being forced into situations where resources are lacking and—oh, no!—they have to share, adding a layer of tension that cannot be ignored.

Forced proximity is the name of this game, and it's a favorite trope of many, many romance readers. You may be familiar with the "just one bed" situation when it comes to this trope, and while that certainly does appear in this book, many of the selections for this anthology take a different route and provide their characters "just one" of something else that will interrupt their good times, turn the tables, or usher some simple sparks into full-blown fireworks.

See if you're able to identify the "one" item or situation in each story. I'll tell you right now: some stories have multiple "just one"s. So keep your eyes open!

In this collection, among many other places, you'll travel to Napa Valley in Caz Luan's "Vintage Love," and you'll (try to) pitch a tent in the Colorado Mountains in Mitchell S. Elrick's "Millennial Magic." You'll sip coffee and visit the healing hot springs in Iceland in Elizabeth Baizel's "Starting Again Under the Summer Sun," and you'll be stranded on a remote island instead of enjoying yourself in Cancun in C.S. Robertson's "Unexpected Destinations." You'll prep for a music festival with college friends, go whitewater rafting, wrestle a mountain lion, ride rollercoasters, kiss your crushes, and simultaneously dream of and fear what the end of such a wonderful summer will bring.

We hope you enjoy our book. Please review if you do!

POWER

OF

THE

PEN

Power of the Pen

Amy Hepp

AS COLE STIRRED HIS COFFEE in the breakroom of the magazine office, the scent of sweet jasmine with a hint of citrus filled the space. Dahlia.

When the young journalist was hired to expand the growing publication, she arrived toting a sunny personality as bright and open as the flower she was named after. Dahlia's easygoing attitude and confidence bounced around the office like the blonde curls on her shoulders.

"Morning," she chirped behind him.

He summoned the courage to glance at her as she measured cream into her coffee and smiled wide, her straight, white teeth gleaming at him between raspberry-colored lips. Words, as if they were wrapped in caramel, stuck in his throat. Lifelong anxiety had made it so that he'd never been able to talk to women, let alone someone like Dahlia.

Snapping his head down, he ran a hand through his black hair and grumbled under his breath: "Mornin'."

"Don't forget to sign Jeanne's birthday card. She's going to love the balloon bouquet we bought her."

Dahlia had volunteered to lead the defunct office social committee soon after she was hired, tracking colleague birthdays, hosting retirement parties, and organizing holiday get-togethers. He couldn't imagine dealing with that on top of work, but Dahlia handled it with ease.

He nodded and swiped his mug off the counter, hustling from the breakroom to the refuge of his desk. The heavy beat of his pulse pounded in his ears and sweat dripped down his back. Steady breaths normalized his heart rate.

Would he ever get up the nerve to speak with her? Ask her out? Today was a Friday; maybe he'd ask her to join him for a drink after work. His hand shook, jostling the coffee in his mug. Who was he kidding? Dahlia had worked for the magazine for six months, but he hadn't summoned the courage to ask her out yet. She was so far out of his league with her outgoing personality and confidence, but he couldn't deny his attraction. Going on a date with her was a pipe dream.

Dahlia's laugh drew his attention across the open-concept office. Her jeans clung to her shapely legs, and a loose blouse floated around her while pink toes peeked out of her summer sandals as she talked with a fellow journalist on the way to her desk. She shoved papers and notebooks to the side of her desk to make room for her coffee mug and a pastry box.

Cole shook his head, not understanding how anyone could work among such a mess. He returned his attention to the photo he was editing on his computer.

A moment later, the boss opened his door.

"Cole, Dahlia," said Jon while waving them into his office.

Cole glanced over at Dahlia as he rose from his desk. She held a donut close to her mouth, about to take a bite, but growled and set the treat back in the pastry box before snapping the lid closed.

Cole stood in front of the boss's desk, silent, a soldier waiting for orders. Dahlia scurried into the office and closed the door behind her. "What's up, boss?"

"A protest against the company hired to mine the minerals on the edge of the Boundary Waters is in its third day. My sources tell me it's significant. There's potential for a cover story here."

Cole shifted back on his heels. A cover story? He'd worked for the magazine for three years and hadn't managed a photo on the cover yet. He'd never been on assignment with Dahlia, either.

Jon continued. "Dahlia, interview the protestors and organizer. Talk to the locals and dig into the human-interest side of the story. Cole, support the story with photos of the rally and the clean, undisturbed water in the wilderness."

Cole's mind raced. The photos weren't a problem, but how was he going to spend four hours in a car with Dahlia traveling to the Superior National Forest? It was the absolute best and worst news of his life. No. He needed time to prepare—to practice what to say to her and make some notes. He couldn't jump into a car and spend the entire day with her, could he? He swallowed hard, resisting the temptation to throw up.

"Um, sir? This sounds like a great opportunity, but can't it wait till Monday?"

The tips of Jon's ears turned bright red, and he looked up over his glasses. "Today. You need to go now."

"Yes, sir," said Dahlia.

They hustled from Jon's office.

"Meet you in the parking lot?" said Dahlia.

Cole's tongue stuck to the roof of his mouth. He could only nod.

Back at his desk, his pulse raced while checking his camera bag and tossing in a notebook and pen. On the other side of the room, Dahlia shoved a notebook and voice recorder into her satchel, and a book tumbled to the ground. She gulped her coffee. Cole straightened his desk lamp before returning his mug to the breakroom sink.

On the elevator ride down to the parking lot, Cole's nausea flared. There was no way he was going to survive a four-hour car ride with Dahlia; he couldn't even work up the nerve to visit her at her desk.

As he loaded his camera bag into the backseat of his SUV, Dahlia burst through the door, her satchel bouncing against her hip while she cradled the pastry box in both hands. She flashed him another killer smile, dumping her bag on top of his.

"Oh, geez. Your car is clean. Is it new? Can I eat my donut in your car?"

"It's fine." He opened the passenger door and held her pastry box as she slid into the bucket seat. Once settled, she held out her hands for the box, accepting it with a small hum of appreciation.

Cole started the car, cranked the air conditioning, and rolled up the shirt sleeves of his button-down shirt. Was he hot from nerves or the stifling vehicle? He wiped his sweaty hands on his faded jeans before pulling out of the parking lot and merging onto the highway.

He battled thick commuter traffic through downtown Minneapolis as Dahlia opened her pastry box. A sweet, creamy chocolate smell encased the interior of the car. His mouth watered. Dahlia lifted the donut to her lips and took a big bite. Her tongue darted out of her mouth to swipe a bit of custard from her upper lip. Cole shifted in his seat.

She lifted the donut toward him. "Want a bite?"

Cole shook his head.

"My Friday guilty pleasure: Boston cream. Do you know how many Pilates classes I have to do to justify just one of these?" Dahlia laughed and ate more of the donut. She moaned her approval of the treat.

When she opened her mouth wide for another bite, a car changed lanes without a signal. Cole slammed on the brakes to avoid a crash, and Dahlia yelped.

He glanced over, noting the chocolate that had smeared across her cheek and nose. Shit. He was such a dumbass. "Sorry," he croaked.

Dahlia scooped the remaining piece of donut into the pastry box and licked her fingers. "No biggie. I just need a napkin."

He pointed to the glove box. Dahlia popped open the compartment and swiped a paper napkin from a stack. Cole refocused on the road, changing lanes to pass a slow semitruck. The action caused his writing notebook to tumble out of the open glove box and onto the floor.

"Oh—um . . ." said Cole.

Dahlia ate the last bite of her donut and wiped her hands before picking up the fallen book. She held the thick, scuffed, leather-bound volume in her hands. "Is this yours?"

"Y-Yeah." Beads of sweat broke out on his upper lip. His notebook was full of prose and poetry he'd written since high school. He kept the book in his car to capture thoughts after walking in the park or camping up north. "It's nothing . . . just scribbles. How about some music?" The words tumbled out of his mouth before he could stop them.

"May I read an entry?"

Share his journal with Dahlia? Did he want Dahlia to read his poetry? Part of him longed for her professional writer opinion. Another part of him worried she would laugh at or critique the entries. She held the book in her hands and waited for him to answer. It wouldn't hurt for her to read a few entries. "You can read one or two."

Dahlia placed the book on her lap and opened it slowly. She turned to a page in the middle of the book and read aloud.

> Lake
> blue, clear, crisp, clean, home
> fiercely protected, untouched
> sustenance for all

He'd written the short haiku after a weekend fishing and camping on a lake up north, mesmerized by the pristine water.

Dahlia turned the page. He concentrated on the road and couldn't see the piece. Dahlia sighed. "These are incredible. I love the free verse about the pine tree. I can almost smell it."

He nodded, remembering the fallen pine at the campsite the previous summer. The pungent Christmas smell was at odds with the hot August day, and he'd attempted to capture the scent on the page.

Cole cleared his throat. "Music?" He reached for the radio.

Dahlia placed a hand on his arm. "No, please."

Goosebumps broke out along his muscled forearm from her touch. His body heated as blood surged through his veins. Dahlia's fingernails grazed his skin as she pulled away. The car remained silent.

Dahlia turned the page, and a faded, thin, half sheet of paper fell out. She read the poem out loud. Cole winced.

"What's wrong? I love it. You're a beautiful writer."

He swallowed past the dryness in his throat before answering her. "I wrote 'Birdsong' for an English assignment in tenth grade. It didn't do me any favors in gym class."

"I bet the girls swooned."

Cole shook his head.

"Oh, come on. A tall, dark, and handsome guy who writes poetry? You're every girl's dream." She gushed.

What did she say? Dahlia thought he was handsome?

When he looked in the mirror, he didn't see a tall man with dark, wavy hair and gray eyes or strong cheekbones and muscled shoulders. He saw the shy kid from high school who never wore the right clothes, didn't play sports, and couldn't talk to girls.

"Why did you become a photojournalist instead of a writer?" Dahlia asked.

"I couldn't interview anyone. Ever."

She glanced over at him but didn't say anything.

He managed to focus on the road despite the raging inferno inside his body as Dahlia continued to read from the leather-bound notebook, handling the loose papers with care. Every now and again, she read a poem out loud. He chimed in with her, his low timbre balancing her high-pitched voice. Reciting the poetry aloud calmed Cole's nerves, and he fell into a relaxed banter with her.

Dahlia sighed. "You're a great writer. Every piece has a feeling, a purpose, and meaning."

"Thanks. It's just a hobby." He paused. "I've read all your work since you started at the office. Your articles are well developed and tight with a unique voice. You've been an asset to the magazine."

"Aww, thanks for reading my pieces. This is my first job out of college. I love interviewing people and hearing their stories, but pulling everything into an article is the challenge."

The traffic thinned while the pine trees tightened into a green channel as they approached the north woods. The speed limit dropped, and Cole slowed the car on the outskirts of town a couple of blocks from the rally. He parked on a side street while Dahlia closed the leather-bound notebook, trailing a manicured finger along the spine and holding the journal to her nose. Was she smelling his book? His stomach flip-flopped. She placed the book back in the glove box before gathering her satchel and joining him on the sidewalk. They fell into step as they walked toward the rally.

Cole and Dahlia reached an intersection. While waiting for the light to turn green, he said, "This is the first time we've worked together. What's our plan?"

"I'm going to talk to some people and get a feel for the vibe before I locate the organizer of the event," said Dahlia.

Cole nodded. "Sounds good. I'll capture some shots of the rally and in-dividual signs. If you need a photo of something in particular, let me know." The light changed, and they stepped off the curb.

People of all ages and sizes swarmed Main Street with signs, chanting about saving the Boundary Waters. Cole slipped his camera around his neck, attaching the zoom lens. He found a bench to stand on and snapped action shots of people portaging canoes in the street. A local rock band performed on a street corner. While Cole worked, he watched Dahlia talk with the peace-ful protestors and record the informal interviews on her voice recorder. She jotted down notes in a small, spiral-bound notebook, too.

As the day progressed, Cole discovered he worked better with Dahlia than any other journalist at the magazine. She didn't crowd him or tell him what to do. It was a refreshing change from the norm.

Cole and Dahlia grabbed a hotdog from a food truck midway through the day. They sat under the shade of an oak tree in the town park, eating lunch before Dahlia's interview with the organizer.

"After the interview, I want to get some shots of the lakes," said Cole, his confidence in talking with her boosted after their successful morning.

Dahlia swallowed a bite of her hotdog. "Sure."

Cole crumpled his hotdog wrapper in his hand. "I love canoe camping through the Boundary Waters. It's quiet and peaceful and tough and exhila-rating all at the same time."

"What do you mean?"

"Well, you know there are no motors or anything like that allowed on the lakes, right?"

"Sure."

"You don't realize how loud our world is until you escape it." He looked up at the sky, robin's egg blue on the hot July afternoon. "I love a star-filled sky at night, the only noise from crickets. It's peaceful. But portaging from lake to lake and schlepping your gear over land or paddling through a rainstorm while battling waves on a big lake is tough. A fresh, grilled fish at the end of a rough day is worth it, though."

"Wow. My dad canoed through the Boundary Waters every summer. He complained about the bugs but went back every year. I guess they didn't really bother him as much as he said they did."

Cole tilted his head back and let out a deep laugh. He couldn't remember if he'd ever sat under a tree and laughed with a woman. It wasn't so scary. Maybe he *could* ask Dahlia out someday. They sat in silence in the park while couples walked hand in hand on the path, children climbed on the playground equipment, and squirrels scampered up trees. Ten minutes before Dahlia's interview, he stood and offered his hand to her. She grabbed it, stood, and faced him, staring into his eyes, not letting go, her touch soft yet firm. A pink flush broke out on her cheeks, and her sky-blue eyes sparkled under long lashes. She flashed a smile and dropped his hand. He didn't have a ton of experience with women, but the shared moment relaxed the tension in his body, making room for his chest to flutter.

Dahlia asked pointed yet empathetic questions of the rally coordinator, and Cole snapped photos of the interview. After the conclusion of the rally, they walked back to Cole's car and drove ten miles north to a put-in site for the Boundary Waters. At the water's edge, Dahlia trailed her fingers through the lake. Cole watched as she slipped off her sandals and rolled up her jeans. She waded into the water, and a half a minute later, she pointed to a deer nosing around the shore. Cole slipped off his shoes and captured the thirsty deer in his lens. He showed her one of the photos on his digital screen. The tan-colored animal contrasted with the bright blue lake, and the deer's dark eyes gleamed. Again, Dahlia touched his arm, leaning against him in the lake. Electrical sparks shot up his arm, warming his body.

Cole checked the time on his phone. "If we leave now, we can make it back to the city by eight. I'm sure you have plans tonight."

She shrugged. "Nothing important. Let's hang here for a while. You're right. It's quiet. I love it."

They waded back to the shore and sat on the rocky sand, soaking up the sun. Dahlia crossed her legs, and her knee bumped against Cole's thigh. Did she mean to do that? She didn't move away. He didn't budge.

"Why poetry?" asked Dahlia.

Cole picked up a rock, ran his thumb along the smooth side, the curve fitting into his palm. He skipped it into the lake, the rock bouncing four times across the surface. Ripples fanned over the water. "I stuttered as a kid. The disability kept me from talking in elementary school until my third-grade teacher introduced me to poetry's rhyming, movement, and flow. I didn't stutter when I read poetry aloud. My parents thought it was a miracle. It took a long time, but I eventually became more confident speaking. I still stutter and sometimes shut down when I'm nervous."

"Is that why you didn't talk to me in the office the last six months? Did I make you nervous?"

It was Cole's turn to blush.

Dahlia touched his arm again. "I didn't think you liked me. I'm sorry. I love talking to everyone."

He chuckled. "It's not your fault. I've always struggled talking to pretty girls."

Dahlia smiled. "You think I'm pretty?"

Cole locked eyes with her and whispered, "You're beautiful."

The words hung between them, suspended in midair.

Cole broke the silence. "Let's get going. It's a long drive back."

They put on their shoes and loaded into Cole's car. Once they reached the highway, Dahlia touched his shoulder and said, "May I read more?"

Cole smiled. "Sure."

Dahlia pulled his journal out of the glove box. She read the prose and more free verse. One of his pieces highlighted a shoulder injury he'd sustained during a storm in the Boundary Waters while canoe camping solo. Dahlia wanted to know all about the storm and resulting injury, which led them into a fierce debate about canoe camping solo. When she read a sing-songy limerick about a skunk, her whole body shook with laughter. Conversation flowed between them like a lazy river, and Cole couldn't believe he'd wasted six months not getting to know Dahlia.

Hours later, the sun winked goodnight, and he swung into the deserted magazine office parking lot beside Dahlia's car. She closed his journal and set it in the glove box, the soft click signaling the end of their road trip.

Cole walked around the car. The weight of Dahlia's satchel pulled on her shoulder, causing her to lean left.

"I had fun today," said Dahlia.

Cole looked into her eyes and smiled. He didn't know what to say; he could never find the right words, but for once in his life, he gave into his feelings. He reached for her satchel and lifted the bag off her shoulder and placed it on the ground. Dahlia's eyes widened and her mouth was silent for a rare moment. Cole cupped her chin with his palm and bent to meet her lips. He closed his eyes, relishing every sensation of her soft touch, her smell, and her taste. Electric bolts ignited a firestorm between them until he finished the kiss and rested his forehead against hers. Their chests rose and fell with heavy breaths. When he garnered the courage to open his eyes, he found Dahlia with a wide, excited smile.

Her arms whipped around his neck, pressing her body tight against his. They molded into another kiss, deeper and longer with each passing moment. Dahlia angled her head and moaned against his mouth, pushing her hips against his.

Cole pulled back before he lost all control. "Will you have dinner with me tonight?"

She squeezed him tight. "Yes. I'd love to have dinner with you."

They shared stories and laughter over plates of pasta and glasses of wine in a dark Italian restaurant around the corner from the office. Their knees touched under the table, and their hands gravitated toward one another throughout the meal. Their parting kiss left him breathless with swollen lips. Dahlia waved and pulled out of the parking lot. Cole raced home to write in his journal—his poetic mind flooded with thoughts of Dahlia.

On the way to work Monday morning, he bought her favorite Boston cream donut and placed the pastry box on Dahlia's desk with a haiku he wrote on the inside of the lid.

    Dahlia
Road trip, a journal
Getting to know you better
Dinner and a kiss

His chest fluttered when she followed him into the breakroom, sliding an arm around his waist.

"I had a fantastic time the other night," said Dahlia. "Thanks for the donut, and I love the poem. Will you split it with me?"

"Love to."

On their way back to their desks, Jon called them into his office. "Great job on the rally piece. We'll turn it into the cover story for the next issue. You work well together. I have another assignment for you—in Chicago."

Cole questioned Dahlia with his eyes. She smiled and nodded.

"Sir, we'd love to take another road trip," said Cole.

About the Author

Amy Hepp writes romance from her screened-in porch among the birds and blue skies of Raleigh, North Carolina. She has published two novellas with the Fifth Avenue Press of Ann Arbor, Michigan. *Northern Woods* (2022) and *Ripple Effects* (2024) are contemporary romance novellas set in the Boundary Waters of northern Minnesota. "Tiramisu" (2025) is a short story published in *Craving You: A Spicy Valentine's Day Anthology* with And You Press. When she's not writing, she enjoys running, working jigsaw puzzles, gardening, and visiting her three young adult children scattered across North America.

You can find Amy on:
Instagram & Facebook: @amyheppstories

You can visit her website at:
https://amyheppstories.wixsite.com/my-site

UNEXPECTED DESTINATIONS

Unexpected Destinations

C.S. Robertson

IT'S HARD TO IMAGINE WHAT was going through my mind as I boarded that plane to Mexico, a one-way ticket in my hand and a loosely concocted plan in mind. But now that I'm here—sand caked in every crevice, saltwater nipping at my sunburned skin, alone with a couple of strangers—there's no place I'd rather be than back home, lying in bed, binging Netflix. This vacation was supposed to be about empowerment—a chance to prove to myself that I am a strong, independent woman. That divorce doesn't equal failure. Of course, I pictured myself relaxing poolside for a week, a good book in hand, handsome waiters serving me cocktails—the polar opposite of how it's turning out.

Cool ocean water washes over my toes, my hot pink polish glowing neon through grains of sand. The last time I had a view of turquoise waves like these was with Mark; Aruba's beaches were gorgeous for our five-year anniversary trip. That was before the problems between us began. Before love was no longer enough. Before the lying. Before the affair. My teeth clench as the once beautiful memories turn sour.

Compulsively, I pull my phone out of my small backpack and swipe open the lock screen to find *SOS* still looming in the top corner. There hasn't been a single ounce of signal since the moment I stepped foot on that boat. I stare hopelessly at the useless social media apps dotted across the home screen. It seems the only dopamine rush I'm going to get right now is from imagining the look on Mark's face as he inevitably creeps on the bikini picture I posted earlier today. I captioned it, "Soaking up the sun in Cancun!"

He'll be wondering who I'm here with. Maybe he'll post a few photos of his own to try and one-up me. But that's fine. Serves him right to be jealous. A cheater always gets what they deserve, one way or another.

What he doesn't need to know is that the joke is actually on me.

"Hey! Barbie!" The voice snaps me out of my Mark-infested daydream. "Dusk is setting in. Better come up here and help set up camp. Looks like we might be here a while."

I'd love to ignore the man's booming demands, but it's nearly impossible. We're the only four people here, after all.

"Coming," I call up to him.

It's a short walk through the sand up to the tree line. When I arrive at our makeshift camp, I'm greeted by the three people I arrived with, varying degrees of concern plastered across each of their faces. I wrap my thin, cotton cover-up around my waist and take a seat around the fire, the dry sand pressing uncomfortably into my bare legs. The four of us eye each other awkwardly. We've had quite a few hours to size each other up after disembarking from the resort, but sitting around the fire now, the daylight fading around us, realization dawns that we might not be leaving here tonight. Suddenly, we're all new versions of ourselves—fresh and vulnerable. It's like meeting the three of them again for the first time.

"So, uh, what did you say your name was?" The middle-aged looking man with a salt-and-pepper goatee speaks up first. He's clearly addressing the other man in the group, a thirty-something-year-old with an athletic build and an air of confidence that reeks of arrogance.

"Slater. Slater Johns. And you are?"

"Dave. Dave Edwards. And this is my wife, Julie."

Slater continues poking at the fire that he's managed to build with his "bare hands." Apparently, he's a regular Ranger Rick.

"Great to meet you both," he says, subtly raising his fire-poking stick in their direction.

A small snicker escapes my lips, and the three of them turn to stare.

"Sorry. I, um . . ."

"Problem, Hannah? Aside from the obvious one?" Slater gestures with his free hand at the miles of wide-open beach surrounding us.

I swallow hard. "'Nice to meet you' seems like a bit of a stretch, doesn't it?"

I let out a dry laugh, but apparently no one else sees the irony, their expressions unchanged. I clear my throat, attempting to brush off the faux pas while Julie buries her face in Dave's shoulder, and Slater rolls his eyes, poking away at the flames.

"Do you think they're coming back?" Dave asks, voicing out loud the question we're all thinking.

Annoyance flickers across Slater's face. "Don't think like that, man. For crying out loud." For the first time since I sat down, he turns his back toward the group. "Of course they're coming back. They have to. They won't just leave us here. What kind of a thing is that to even ask right now?"

Dave remains silent, offering only a subtle nod in response. I watch as Julie gives his forearm a gentle squeeze.

"You could be a little nicer about it, Slater," I pipe up.

He turns to face me now, his brows still knitted tightly together. "What's the point in talking like that? We've only just arrived here. Why start with the doom and gloom when it's not going to help anything? We've got to keep morale up. We've got to keep our heads."

There's no point in pushing the conversation further. I've known men like Slater Johns. In fact, I was married to one for seven years: alpha male, oozing with toxic confidence—likely overcompensating for his lack of emotional availability. If he's anything like he's already shown—both here on the island and back on the boat—I'd say I've got him pegged: Mark 2.0.

"Since you seem to have this situation all mapped out," I start, not bothering to hide the petulance in my tone, "then I think you'll see that it's quite clear we need to make a plan for tonight. We can't just sit here in a circle all night long. This wind is ridiculous. We're in swimsuits. I'm sure everyone's exhausted. So?" I cock my head, hands folded in my lap, waiting for him to share his heroic idea. As expected, he makes a grand show of it.

Slater shakes the sand from his long-sleeved sun shirt before slipping it over his head and shaking the fabric down over his trunk. The thin, white spandex hardly covers the sleeves of ink adorning both his arms. I watch as his biceps tense just long enough to be noticed as he takes the fire poker into his grip. See: pure machismo. It oozes from him. He just can't help himself, not even in a situation as dire as this.

"We should look for some shelter. Something to keep us out of the strong winds rolling off the ocean. It's the best way to keep warm and stay hidden. It's hard to say what predators there might be out here late at night. It'll be hot and humid offshore, but it's better than sitting out in the open. We can build a small fire to ward off any wild animals at the new campsite."

I want to argue, to come up with something better purely out of spite. But I don't have a better idea. The ocean air is becoming too much to bear in just this bikini and thin cover-up. I can already feel the sting of windburn on my lips.

"He's right," Dave speaks up. "It's what we'd do on the beaches of Hawaii during training drills. Best way to keep safe. 'Course, we were wearing full field dress and combat boots. Hotter than Hades," he says, looking down at his damp swim trunks and flip-flops. "Nothing like this getup."

"Fellow Marine?" Slater asks, straightening his posture.

"Army. Charlie Company, First Battalion, 21st Infantry Regiment, 25th Division. Best four years of my life spent stationed at Schofield." Dave clears his throat. "Aside from the years I've spent married to the love of my life, of course."

Julie pats his arm with a wry smile. "We're very proud of him, the boys and I."

"Ah, well, then it's settled. We should find a spot to shelter before the daylight's gone completely." With that, Slater turns and heads toward the tree line, not bothering to wait for the rest of us.

Dave extends a hand to Julie and helps her to her feet. Uneasiness grows in the pit of my stomach as I gather the few items I arrived with: my backpack, phone, and a now half-full stainless-steel tumbler. Hesitantly, I stand and follow the group into the Mexican wilderness. *If Mark could see me now.*

When I finally catch up with them, I find Slater staring at a spot between two gargantuan trees.

"Right here should be fine," he announces.

Panic spreads through my body like wildfire as a foul smell like rotting seafood overwhelms my nostrils. The area is buzzing with insects and choked with underbrush. Vines tangle mercilessly around my bare ankles as I attempt to move forward, and it takes everything I have to shove the image of coiling snakes out of my mind.

"You—you aren't serious?" I ask, frantically batting cobwebs from my face.

"Yeah . . . unless you were planning on finding a Hilton Inn on this island, then by all means," Slater replies, his sarcasm palpable.

As we attempt to set up camp, the sobs and sniffles coming from Julie's direction are hard to ignore, and I fight back my own tears as I lay my cover-up down on top of a pile of palm leaves—my feeble attempt at a makeshift cot. Mosquitoes as big as half dollars buzz around my arms and legs as I lower myself to the ground, leaving red, burning welts in their wake. Strange chirps and trills in the distance have me on edge, the threat of wild animals at the front of mind.

I focus on slowing my breathing, turning my focus to the sky, watching as the last bit of daylight fades into a deep mulberry haze through the small gaps in the trees. I picture myself back at the resort, sitting at the poolside bar in the tight, red cocktail dress I'd stuffed into my suitcase. I can practically hear the salsa music, picture the dancing, smell the delicious food. My empty stomach growls at the thought of fresh guacamole. Tamales. Ceviche.

I'm interrupted by loud grunts coming from Slater's area of camp. He's obviously working away at some type of elaborate shelter, although I'm not sure why since he's so convinced someone will be back for us any minute.

"Are you all right over there? You sound like you're having a coronary."

"I'm making a shelter. You could help, if you want."

"I'm perfectly fine right here."

Slater stops what he's doing and turns to me. "You're the only one out here without any type of shelter and it's almost completely dark. But hey, suit yourself."

I can't help but roll my eyes as he gets back to work.

"You can join us in here," Julie calls out from their tiny lean-to. "It's not much, but you can't sit out there all night."

"I'll be fine. Thanks, though," I reassure her.

"The offer stands," Dave adds.

Minutes crawl as I adjust my position on the ground. I'm contemplating my next move when the sudden crash of a falling tree limb sends my stomach roiling. I jump to my feet.

"Change your mind?" Slater asks wryly, not bothering to look up from his work.

"I'll help," I say indignantly, slapping another mosquito away from my leg. "But only because these bugs are eating me alive over here."

"Right. Just start putting some palm leaves on top. Like this."

My teeth clench at his delusions of authority. Where does he get off ordering me around? I weigh my options and decide to bite the bullet.

As I pick up the damp, gritty palm leaves, my mind wanders back to the years I spent appeasing Mark, choosing the high road rather than muddying the waters with opposition. Time after time I'd simply give in to his demands. And where did it get me? Here: divorced in my thirties and stranded on an island in Mexico, taking orders from yet another man. Some luck.

"Almost done," Slater huffs as he stacks another stick against the tree.

I stare at the nearly finished product, struggling to envision us both inside.

"It's a pretty small shelter, isn't it?"

He wipes the sweat away from his forehead as he lowers himself to the ground and crawls inside. "You're welcome to build your own then. But as it stands, there's only one. And I'm not moving out."

"No, no. It's fine."

"Come on then," he says, sounding exasperated.

I'm not sure what's worse at this point: being stuck here or being forced to share a shelter with this prick. I could take Dave and Julie up on their offer to bunk with them for the night, but their shelter is even smaller and less impressive than Slater's, and that would be just as awkward. I let out a sigh, swallow my pride, and climb into the shelter beside Slater Johns.

"Welcome to my humble abode."

I release a puff of air through my lips. I'm not at all impressed with this man. I just need to make it through this terrible ordeal and back to the resort, where I can get this whole thing sorted out. I can only imagine the lawsuit I could win from this.

"So, where are you from, Hannah? Tell me all about yourself."

I flash Slater a glare to let him know I'm not interested in small talk.

"Listen, we're stranded. There's nothing else to do, is there? Might as well talk."

"I'd rather not. Why don't we just sleep? Though, one of us should stay awake, in case the boat comes back," I offer dryly.

"Listen, is there a problem?"

"What do you mean?"

"I mean, is there a reason you don't like me?"

"I never said I didn't like you, Slater."

He scoffs. "You don't have to say it. It's written all over your face."

I press my lips into a thin line before plastering on a small smile. "I've just known plenty of men like you."

"Wow. And what's that supposed to mean?"

"It means, I know your type. And frankly, I'm over it. I came here, to Mexico, to get away from all that. And then I get stuck on a random island with you."

"Uh—I don't even know how to respond to that." Slater shakes his head, scratching the back of his neck.

"You don't have to respond. Like I said, we should rest. I'm sure we'll be picked up tomorrow."

A brief moment of silence passes before Slater just can't help himself.

"You know, I haven't done anything to make you think poorly of me. You don't even know me. How can you tell me you *know my type*? That's so . . . so . . ."

"So what?"

"So typical."

"Oh, so *you're* going to generalize *me* now?"

"You know what? Maybe you're right. Maybe we should just get some rest."

"I saw the way you reacted back there. On the boat. When the captain asked some of us to volunteer to get off so that he could get the boat back to shore. I saw what you did. You know, I volunteered right away. No questions asked. Why would I ask that sweet elderly couple to get off? Or that family with young children? It was obvious which four people needed to get off the boat. But still, you had to put up a fight. It just shows what kind of person you are."

"Excuse me? Were you even on that boat?"

"Of course I was, Slater! I'm here, aren't I?"

"Then you felt the engine die?"

"Duh."

"And you heard the captains tell us that there were too many passengers for the one remaining engine to make it back to shore?"

I don't bother answering this time. I just shake my head in a way that clearly says, *Obviously*.

"Then you heard when Dave started arguing with the captain about him and Julie staying aboard?"

"What? No. I—"

"Hannah, do you even speak Spanish?"

"Some," I say defensively.

Slater narrows his eyes. "If you were following the conversation, then you'd know that Dave was the one refusing to get off the boat. Claimed Julie was too afraid of the water to be left on the island. But I wasn't having it. Those elderly people and the children—of course they shouldn't have had to get off the boat."

"Then why were you shouting? No one else was shouting, Slater. You were throwing your hands in the air and making a fool of yourself."

"A fool of myself? Hannah, I told Dave that if he and Julie didn't do the right thing on their own, I would personally escort them both off the boat. I won't stand by and watch people do the wrong thing. You volunteered. I volunteered. Why not them? The captain said he would be back as soon as he possibly could—once the other engine could be repaired. Was it completely sketchy? Heck yeah. But I couldn't see another solution at the time. I'd rather us be here, on land, on this island, than floating in the middle of the sea, *Titanic*-style."

We sit silently as I let Slater's words sink in. It's true that I wasn't very good at speaking Spanish. The language barrier was definitely an issue for me, but this was a touristy resort. Most people traveling here probably couldn't speak the language. I didn't think much of it. I guess I could have interpreted the situation incorrectly.

"Do you really think the captain will come back for us?" I ask after a few minutes. "I was so sure when they first asked us to get off the boat. It seemed so . . . normal. But once we stepped foot on this island, watching the boat sail away without us was sickening. I'm honestly beginning to wonder if we made a mistake."

Slater pulls at his beard. "I think he'll come back. He seemed decent enough. I am starting to wonder if that charter was legit, though."

"What do you mean?"

"I'm wondering if it wasn't just a fisherman looking to take advantage of all the foreigners here on vacation. Just a man with a boat and a sign. I definitely don't think that was one of the resort's excursion boats."

My heart plummets as I realize he's probably right. The resort would have had a backup boat come rescue us—or even the Coast Guard. Numerous possibilities begin to flash through my mind. How could I have been so naive? My first solo trip—the very first day—and I've already made such a poor judgment call.

Slater's eyes fall. "I can't believe I bought into it. I was just so ready to go sightseeing. To get off the resort and explore. The guy only wanted a few pesos. I figured, why not?"

"We all bought into it," I reassure him.

For a moment, our eyes meet, and something unspoken passes between us. I can't quite place it, but just as quickly, we're interrupted by a low, rumbling noise.

"Is that the boat?" I ask, sitting up so quickly I nearly knock the palm-leaf roof off the shelter.

"I'm not sure. I'm going to go look. Stay here, just in case."

Slater cautiously ducks out of the lean-to, motioning with one outstretched hand for me to stay where I am. The sound continues steadily, growing louder and longer by the second. My heart races at the thought of the wild animals that could be lurking around our campsite.

"You guys okay?" I hear Slater whisper to Dave and Julie. "What's that noise?"

"Sorry, Slater. It's Dave. He's got sleep apnea. Needs a CPAP machine at night. He fell asleep."

Dave snorts and grunts awake, recognizing the presence of Slater standing near his shelter. "What's going on? Is the boat here?"

"No. Sorry. I was just checking on you guys."

"You were snoring so loud, you scared the poor people half to death," Julie says with the air of someone who's been married for a very long time.

When Slater returns, the look of amusement on his face tells me there's nothing to be worried about.

"Was that really just Dave?" I ask.

"Snoring to his heart's content," he confirms.

"Oh my god!"

We share a laugh as Slater climbs back inside our shelter. I do my best to make myself small, to give him ample room to exist without our bodies touching any more than necessary. But his arm grazes mine as he leans back, and no matter how much I want to pretend that it doesn't, his touch ignites something inside me. Something I haven't felt in a very long time.

"Sorry. There's not much room in here." He smiles apologetically.

"No, there's not." I smile back.

"But I don't mind if you need to move over. It won't bother me."

"Ah. So I was right about you," I quip.

"Here we go with this again." He shakes his head. "Listen. Ask me anything. Whatever you need to know in order for me to prove you wrong."

"Prove me wrong about what exactly?"

"That I'm not like all those other men you know."

"Okay then. What do you do for a living, Slater Johns?"

"I'm a veterinarian."

Interesting. I can't hide the satisfied grin on my face. That is certainly not what I was expecting. Not even close.

"Come on," he taunts. "What did you think I was going to say?"

"Um. Well . . ."

"Out with it."

"I was banking on personal trainer. Maybe life coach? Or professional athlete." I wrinkle my nose at him playfully.

"First of all, what's wrong with any of those careers? Second of all, I play hockey in my free time. Which is something I don't have much of. But I do enjoy playing when I can."

"*Hockey*," I repeat as a scene from one of my favorite romance novels begins to play in my mind, where it lives rent-free.

"Is there something wrong with hockey, too?"

I grin. "Not at all."

As we sit huddled together in our much-too-small shelter, the conversation flows. Slater and I ask each other twenty questions, and I'm pleasantly surprised to learn that he isn't quite as much like Mark as I'd originally thought. Slater likes books. He likes to travel. He likes sports and the gym, but not to the extent of self-obsession I originally had pegged him for. He loves animals and has a cat back home named Chester.

"I know this situation—this whole boat-ride nightmare—has just been awful. But I'm glad I met you, Hannah. You're pretty cool. Even if you did profess your hatred for me before even bothering to get to know me," he says, nudging me with his shoulder.

"I'm sorry about that. It's just . . . I just went through a divorce. It was finalized right before this trip, actually. It's easy to see my ex-husband's faults in other men. But that's not fair."

"That must be hard." Slater's voice is genuine.

"It was. But I've come out of it stronger. And I'm ready to prove to myself that I can stand on my own two feet. Make my own decisions."

"Solo travel to Mexico and get yourself stranded on an island kind of decisions?" A sly smile spreads across his face.

"Well that obviously wasn't part of the plan." I drum my nails against the hard steel of my cup. "I just hope I make it back in one piece. To start the next chapter."

"You will," he says, his voice growing deep and serious. "No matter what happens with the boat, we'll figure it out. We won't give up without a fight. You'll make it back for your next chapter. Promise."

Slater extends a pinky, waiting for mine to seal the deal. As we link our fingers together and shake on it, I feel the same surge of sparks that I felt earlier. This time, I think he might feel it, too, because he doesn't let go.

A rush of warmth burns in my cheeks. This was not supposed to happen. Not here. And not with someone like Slater Johns.

"You know," Slater starts, his voice smooth and comforting. "I never would have imagined this trip could have turned out this way. Heck, this is something you see in a movie, or read in a cheesy romance novel." He breathes a laugh. "But now that it has, and we're here . . . what I'm trying to say is that I'm glad it's you I'm stuck with, Hannah."

His gaze meets mine, and for the first time, I notice how stunning his green eyes are in the flickering light of the fire.

"It could have been a lot worse," I say with a flirtatious smile. "You could have been left here with all those kids."

Slater matches my playful tone. "Yeah, or the old silver set."

"Slater!"

"Well, I'm just saying. It could have been one of them snuggled up with me in this hut."

"Is that what we're doing? Snuggling?"

"Well, I mean . . ."

Through the dim firelight, I manage to make out a hint of crimson as it rises to his cheeks.

"Only kidding," I say, lightly tapping his thigh.

His eyes travel to the spot where my fingers grazed his bare skin, just below the hem of his Americana swim trunks. "We could be. I mean, if you want."

I bite my lower lip, averting my gaze.

"I mean, we're stranded. On a gorgeous beach in Mexico," he jokes, batting his hand toward a stray palm leaf dangling overhead. "Might as well make the most of our vacation. Unless . . ."

"Unless what?"

"Well, I wouldn't want to come across too forward. Wouldn't want you thinking I'm some kind of Don Juan."

I snort a laugh. "Oh, Señor Johns. Your Spanish is muy excelente."

"Wow. We'll have to work on that," he teases, flashing a bright smile that reveals a single crooked eyetooth.

"Will we?"

"Of course," he replies, his voice taking on a low, silky tone. "We've got plenty of time."

Slater's hand reaches up and grazes my cheek. I close my eyes briefly, leaning into his touch. I'm not sure what's happening, but whatever it is, it's too late to stop it now.

"You had sand on your face," he whispers into my ear, so close I can feel his breath tickling my neck.

I pull back sharply as every ounce of my dignity is sent packing.

"Just kidding," he breathes, closing his eyes and pulling me close once again.

The gentle pull of his hand in my hair brings me back to myself, and for a moment, everything else fades. His lips find mine, again and again, my body drawn to him like the pull of the sea.

"Is this okay?" he asks, catching his breath. His eyes are fixed on mine as his touch glides over my shoulder.

"Yes," I say, barely above a whisper.

His lips trace the outline of my neck as his fingers slip beneath the thin strap of my bikini. My focus narrows to the flame building between us in this small space we share. It's a feeling I haven't experienced in so long, one I hadn't realized I'd been craving. My breath hitches as I give in to every last desire, the rumble of ocean waves in the distance the perfect soundtrack as we claim this place, making it our own.

Early the next morning, the sky above the island is a delicate blend of blush-flecked blue and the sun is already kissing the sea with its warm, golden rays. Slater sits beside me on the shore, watching the seagulls dive in and out of the water, his hand planted firmly in the sand.

"When do you think they'll be here?"

"Soon," he answers just a little too quickly, leaning in to kiss the top of my head.

I don't bother to act like I believe him, and I decide to change the subject. "When are you supposed to return home?"

"Actually, my flight leaves Saturday, but I wasn't planning to return home just yet. My next stop will be Roatán, Honduras. To see the Barrier Reef. They have superb diving. Crystal clear water."

"Sounds amazing."

"Yeah," he sighs regretfully. "Hopefully I can still make it."

"You will," I say, though I'm not sure either of us are buying it. "Were you taking some time away from work?"

"Three weeks. It's tough to get away from the clinic, especially for that long. But a break was long overdue. What about you?"

"Well, my flight home is . . . open ended."

Slater raises an eyebrow questioningly.

"I haven't booked my flight home yet. It's a bit risky doing it that way, sure. But this solo trip was kind of a last-minute decision. Maybe even a reckless one." I shift my eyes to the sand.

"I think that's really brave of you."

"You do?"

"Yeah, I mean, why not travel while you can? Do it your way. However you want to work it."

"That's what I said!" Everything inside me smiles. Slater Johns and I, on the same wavelength.

"You still never told me where you're from," he says, stroking his beard in the way I've noticed he does when he's thinking something over.

"Milwaukee. What about you?"

"Rockford."

"Ah."

A silence falls between us, and I can tell we're both thinking the same thing: that's too much distance to be considered close but too close to be considered distance.

"Maybe I'll see you around sometime. I mean, after we're rescued off this island."

"Yeah, maybe," I say, trying not to sound too hopeful.

Discussing home causes a shift in mood after the excitement of last night. Anxiety begins to swell inside me. How much longer are we going to be here? How long does a boat motor repair even take?

"Hey," Slater gently lifts my chin, turning my face to meet his. "Everything's going to be okay."

Then, with the same tenderness he showed me last night, he kisses me, holding me close as he breathes me in. He tastes salty, like a day at the beach, and once again I find comfort in his touch.

"Uh, excuse us . . ." A voice comes from behind, and we both startle.

"Oh, uh, good morning, Dave, Julie." Slater's voice is strained and breathy as he addresses them.

"Good mornin' there. See you two are gettin' on just fine." Dave laughs, shaking his head back and forth. Julie slaps his arm.

"I'm glad to see everyone made it through the night okay," she says. "Have you seen any sign of the captain yet?"

"Not yet. But they'll be coming for us today. Don't worry," Slater assures her, his tone transformed, back to business as usual.

How is it that this man, the same one I would have bet the bank on as being egotistical prick just yesterday, is the one who's singlehandedly keeping us all afloat here on this island? His assertiveness, his leadership, the way he reassures us all at exactly the right moments. I can imagine those qualities are part of what makes him a great doctor.

I watch as Julie's shoulders soften and Dave's worried expression relaxes. Whether Slater actually believes we'll be going home or not, I can't be sure. But one thing I'm now certain of is that, without him, this whole thing could have gone a completely different way.

"What's that?" Dave asks, a note of concern in his tone.

We all stop, halting all movement and silencing our voices as we listen to find the source of the noise. A deep hum emerges from somewhere in the distance. The sound grows louder and louder as we crane our necks toward the source of the noise.

"A boat!" I exclaim. "Look!"

A small vessel appears just over the horizon, speeding nearer as we all stare, using our hands to shade our eyes from the blinding sun.

"They're coming back for us!" Dave shouts, radiant with relief.

"I knew they'd be back!" Julie says, slapping Dave's knee. "I said it all along!"

Slater and I exchange a glance of overwhelming joy before erupting with laughter and embracing each other tight.

The minute we are safely seated on the captain's boat, my island-mates begin hurling questions, demanding to know why we were left to fend for ourselves for so long.

"But how could you just leave us like that! On a barren island with nothing! Overnight! We were terrified! Thirsty! Starving! Shame on you!" Julie doesn't hold anything back as she allows the fear and anxiety of the previous day to erupt.

Heated conversation is exchanged in Spanish between Slater and the captain as we sail back to the resort. This time, the fervor behind his words is nothing short of admirable. I find myself nervously fidgeting with the strap of my life vest, picking at the frayed edge with my nail as I wait for what I hope will be a perfectly logical explanation.

"He says the motor was beyond repair. It took him all day to travel into town and find a new one," Slater relays to us, though he doesn't sound convinced. "Says he tried to have someone bring him out on another boat to rescue us sooner, but the wind made it too dangerous to sail. Had to wait till morning."

When I glance back at the captain, he folds his hands and raises them toward me, offering an apologetic gesture. I return it with a flat-lipped smile, although, what I'd like to say to him wouldn't require translation.

Relief fills my soul as the resort finally comes into view. Mariachi music playing over the loudspeakers floats across the water—further reassurance that we've made it. The grand, white condominiums that tower high above the sparkling, azure pools remind me that in just a few short moments, I'll be reunited with civilization. Clearly, the paradise we left behind is alive and well, as if we'd never been gone.

The small craft pulls into a slip with a gentle thud and the captain grabs hold of a thick, white rope anchored to the dock. One by one, we exit the boat, each of us more grateful than ever to be back on land.

"What do we do now?" I ask, directing the question mainly at Slater, though everyone seems to be contemplating the answer. "Should we go to guest services and report this? Do we call the police?"

"They'll never get away with this!" Dave grumbles, loud enough that I'm all but certain the captain must have heard. "They'll be hearing about this back home, too! News stations, social media. The whole shebang!"

"Calm down, dear. Let's be grateful the man at least came back for us. I shudder to think what would've happened if he hadn't. . . ." Julie's voice trails off.

"Listen—everyone, just keep calm. I've got the captain's name. We've all seen the boat to give a detailed description. Let's just see if the captain will come to guest services with us so we can get this ironed out. I'm sure they can help us come to a practical reconciliation." Slater gives my hand a squeeze. As per usual, he's the authoritative voice of reason that we need, and all at once, it's settled.

"Let's go then. I don't know about the rest of you, but I'm starved," Dave says, nudging Julie.

VRRRAAAMMM!

Behind us, a boat motor roars to life, a heavy spray of water coating the docks in its wake.

"What the—" I start, wiping droplets from my sunglasses.

"Hey! Get back here!" Slater bellows.

"You won't get away with this!" Dave yells, waving his fist high in the air.

But it's no use. The boat is already gone, speeding back out to sea—and so is the captain.

The four of us sit, exchanging questioning glances as an officer in an all-beige uniform jots our names down on a sheet of paper.

"This sort of thing happens from time to time," the policía explains. "As hard as these resorts try to keep unauthorized people from selling their services to vacationers, it's nearly impossible to enforce. Without proper permissions, your average person shouldn't be able to trespass on resort property and claim they're offering boat-ride excursions to remote places. But the ocean is tricky territory. Technically the resort can't kick those people out of the water. The only thing we can do is warn tourists to stay on the resort, or utilize resort-guided excursions only. Many people see through the scams, but occasionally—"

"Now wait just a minute," Dave starts, a rigid scowl plastered on his face. "You're sayin' it happens from time to time that people like us get left on deserted islands? You're blaming us for this mess?" He points a finger in the officer's direction, which Julie promptly swats away.

"No, sir. What I'm saying is that, unfortunately, you all boarded an unauthorized vessel, and with that, came a terrible consequence. It is only fortunate that the man returned for you. Those small boats are not made for such long journeys across the ocean. It is no surprise he had to turn back. Ten passengers? Way too much weight for two small engines on a ship that size."

"How were we supposed to know that?" I ask.

"He had a very professional sign and everything," Slater adds. "It even had the resort logo on it, if I'm not mistaken."

"You're absolutely right, Slater," Julie interjects.

"I can promise you that we will be on the lookout for this boat. If we find it, we will be sure to investigate the situation."

"If?" Slater clenches his jaw.

"There are thousands of boats in Cancun alone, Señor. Most of them are unregistered and unregulated. We will do our best. Of course, the resort has been notified, as well as surrounding resorts, and we will do our best to alert new travelers to participate in only resort-certified excursions." The officer folds his hands on top of his desk. "Please, if there's anything else we can assist you with, you let us know."

"Slater . . ." My voice cracks.

"I know," he says calmly. "I know."

Despite my disappointment at realizing the man responsible for scamming us into a night alone in the wilderness would likely never be held responsible, the rest of the week at the resort was filled with dancing, great food, and most importantly, new friendships.

"Tomorrow is Saturday."

Slater looks at me over the rim of his margarita. "It is."

"All packed for Honduras?"

"Just about. Still a few things left to pack." His voice is somber, and I feel bad for bringing it up.

"Just don't go riding any sketchy boats across the ocean out there, okay?" I say playfully.

"Why, you don't think I can survive on a deserted island twice?" A wide grin plays on his face.

"I have no doubt that you could. But I think I might miss getting to talk to you."

His smile widens. "Me? Are you sure? Because I thought you hated me?"

"Give it a rest." I scoff.

"I'll miss you, too, Hannah."

We go back to sipping our cocktails, neither of us completely sure what we want to say next. One week ago, I was a divorcee, stepping off a plane alone in another country to prove that I could do hard and adventurous things all by myself. To prove that I didn't need Mark to dictate my life any longer. How have things changed so much in only seven days? Sitting here now, across from a man who was a total stranger not long ago, I watch the gleam in his green eyes—reflecting an understanding of a shared experience only we can fully grasp—and I realize: everything has changed. Today, my heart aches for a whole different reason. But it doesn't make sense. No one can meet a perfect stranger on vacation and fall in love just like that. Can they?

"So do you plan to stay here a little longer?" Slater asks, focusing my thoughts back to our dinner.

"Uh, yeah. Maybe. I'm not actually sure."

"Well you deserve it. Relax, read your books. I feel bad I distracted you so much this week. You hardly got to enjoy them."

"Don't feel bad," I say, blushing. "I may stay a few more days. Dave and Julie are here an extra week."

"I heard the resort comped their stay and gave them a free week for their troubles," Slater says, scooping guacamole onto a tortilla chip.

"Can't say I blame them."

"Yeah, I guess not. It's just, it didn't turn out half bad for me after all."

I smile, tucking a strand of hair behind my ear. "I could say the same."

Slater grins, straightening in his seat.

"Another drink, Señorita?" A waitress dressed in a brightly colored floral-patterned blouse holds a tray next to the table.

"No, thank you," I say, covering the top of my glass with my hand.

Slater declines as well, and eventually we make our way outside, following the pulsing rhythm of tamboras and maracas. I stop to kick off my wedges, the feeling of the sand between my toes freeing as we walk. Slater's hand brushes the back of mine before we gently lace fingers, the feeling instantly transporting me to our time spent huddled under the palm leaves.

"Hannah, if I don't see you again—"

"Don't say that," I interrupt, breaking his gaze. I stare down at the sand where my slightly chipped pink polish peeks out from the sand. An entire current sweeps through the pit of my stomach.

"No, seriously. I mean, we had a great week. I want you to know I'll never forget you."

"I'll never forget you either, Slater."

"But if our paths don't cross again . . ."

I don't need to hear anymore. I know where he's going with this. *We can still be friends, Hannah. Hit me up on the socials, Hannah.* It's nothing I haven't heard a million times before.

"I understand, Slater," I tell him, my voice sounding harsher than I intend.

"What?"

"You don't need to say it. I got it. We had a great week and now it's over. I understand. It was really nice meeting you. Thanks again for saving my butt out there. I hope you have a really awesome time in Honduras."

I do my best to paint an expression of cool indifference on my face, hoping he can't see the tears welling in my eyes. This is stupid. What had I expected would happen? We're two different people, from two totally different backgrounds. Life can't just stop after a week of vacation gone wrong.

I should have listened to what my gut instinct was trying to tell me all along. Slater Johns is exactly the type of man I knew he was. I just didn't want to see it after that night on the island.

"Yeah, okay. Well I should probably get back to my room. I have some more packing to do before I leave. My flight is at five tomorrow morning."

I nod, fearing that just one more word will push me to the edge of a tearful breakdown. Together we walk back to the lobby, the bright fluorescent lighting no doubt giving away more of the emotion on my face than I'd like. The sudden ding of the elevator call button marks the beginning of an awkward silence that settles between us.

"I'll call you. If that's okay?" Slater says, breaking the tension.

"I'd like that."

Slater nods, something unspoken hanging just beneath his breath.

"Enjoy the reefs," I manage to say just as the elevator doors open. I turn to leave, welcoming the escape as a tear falls down my cheek. But before I can cross the threshold, he catches my arm, his touch firm and deliberate as he pulls me back. His embrace fills me with a longing like I've never felt. This is really it. This is what it feels like to say goodbye to someone you've just met. Someone you've fallen hopelessly in love with.

"Come with me," he whispers into my ear. "Come to Honduras."

"Slater, I-I can't. We've only known each other for a week. My divorce has just been finalized. I'm supposed to be—"

"So what?" he interjects. "So what about any of that? I know it's fast, but you said it yourself, you haven't even purchased your ticket home yet. Your plans can still change. You could leave this resort and come to the reefs with me. We could have one more week."

His emerald eyes are pleading with me to say yes, and it crushes me to have to turn him down—to break my own heart.

"I can't, Slater. I'm sorry. I wish more than anything we had met at another time, or under different circumstances. But I have to—"

"Hey." He holds his hands out in defeat. "I get it. You don't need to explain yourself." He pauses, holding on to my gaze. "It's been a pleasure, Hannah."

For the final time, he leans in and places a gentle kiss on my cheek, the gesture seeming both sweet and irritatingly juvenile after the intense week we've spent together.

"Goodbye, Slater."

• • •

The wheel on my discount luggage vibrates as I drag the suitcase through the bustling airport. Signs point me toward customs and security, and a feeling of satisfaction settles over me as I navigate my way through: a single woman, confidently navigating the world, just as I set out to do.

"Buenos días, Señorita." A tall, handsome man at the counter greets me pleasantly as he reaches a hand out for my passport.

"Buenos dias," I respond back, handing it over with the confidence of someone who does this sort of thing all the time.

When I finally step out into the bright sunshine, a shuttle bus is waiting to take me to my destination. The driver kindly loads my bags into a stowaway compartment and motions for me to board. I choose a seat by the window in a row by myself and take a seat. An upbeat tune plays from staticky speakers overhead as I pull out my phone and open the last message I received from Slater.

Don't let one bad egg ruin it for the rest of us.
Luna Del Mar Resort
West Bay Inlet, Km 4
Sandy Bay, Roatán, Islas de la Bahía
Honduras, C.A.
Just in case you change your mind.
—S

I tuck my phone back into my pocket as the driver climbs inside and closes the doors.

"Vámonos!" He gives a thumbs-up and the bus lurches forward.

As we get closer to the resort, the beauty of the island becomes apparent. The water is clearer than I could have imagined, a vibrant teal like something off the cover of a vacationer's magazine. Palm trees thrive at every turn, their green leaves striking against the blue sky.

When the bus comes to a stop, the doors open to a perfectly orchestrated row of villas, each one overlooking the ocean, their own private docks stretching out like tiny peninsulas into the sea.

"Wow," I can't help but say under my breath.

The driver ushers us into a small, stuccoed building labeled Recepción. I take a seat on a cushioned chair, parking my suitcases beside me. My knees bounce up and down, nervous tension searching desperately for an escape.

"Can I help you miss?" the clerk asks in a thick accent.

"Yes. I'm meeting someone. His name is Slater Johns." It comes out sounding more like a question, but she seems to know right away who I'm looking for.

"Ah, Mr. Johns. One moment." The clerk picks up the phone, dials quickly, then waits, looking up at me occasionally over the mouthpiece.

Apprehension knots in my stomach. Was this the right move? What will Slater think of me just showing up like this? On one hand, he did invite me. But on the other, I did decline. What if he's already met someone new? It only took us a week to fall for each other, after all.

Time feels like it's ticking backward as I nearly talk myself out of confronting him. But before I can change my mind, a familiar voice stops my thoughts right in their tracks.

"Hannah. You came."

When I look up, I see Slater standing in the doorway, sandy legs and board shorts, a look of astonishment on his face.

"I did," I say, my own voice sounding foreign and shaky in my ears.

There's no more time for talking as he rushes toward me and wraps me in his sunblock-smeared arms. It feels as though we're picking up right where we left off, standing outside that elevator in Mexico. Right where we began on that deserted island.

It's hard to imagine what was going through my mind as I boarded that plane to Mexico—why I thought that a solo boat excursion in Cancun was a sound and sane idea. But I'll never forget that island. And I'll always be grateful for the time I spent there, for the love I found there.

"Come on," Slater says, throwing an arm around me. "We have a lot of catching up to do."

I follow him out of the lobby and into the warm sunshine of Roatán.

"You know," he starts, "I've been thinking. Rockford really isn't that far from Milwaukee."

I move my sunglasses down my nose and look at him skeptically.

"Well, I've always liked Milwaukee. Beer, cheese, Harleys. What's not to like?" He nudges me with his elbow, and I can't contain my laughter.

"Seriously? Cheese?"

"And then of course, there's you."

I'm not ashamed to say I was wrong about Slater Johns as we walk hand in hand across the second island we'll conquer together.

About the Author

C.S. Robertson enjoys writing psychological thrillers with a touch of romance. She has a deep interest in the shadows people hide behind and is drawn to stories that blur the lines between truth and deception, love and obsession. Her debut novel is set to release soon. When not writing, C.S Robertson can usually be found scrolling bookstagram, sipping hot tea, or chasing chickens in the backyard. She's a firm believer in plot twists, quiet mornings spent at home, and the kind of characters that linger long after the last page.

You can find C.S. Robertson on:
Instagram, Facebook & Bluesky: @csrobertsonwrites

You can visit her website at:
linktr.ee/csrobertsonwrites

A
SUMMER
TRADITION

A Summer Tradition

Jessica Daniliuk

Jackson,
I can't stop thinking about that one night. I know I shouldn't be, and based on how you've been, it seems like you aren't, but I can't help it. I can vividly picture your hands on my body and how safe I felt lying in your arms. This wasn't a one-time mistake for me; it's actually something I've wanted for a while now. Ever since orientation, when we talked all night into the next morning, I knew you were someone special. It's horrible to think that my happiness means Harper's misery, but I also can't keep denying the truth. I love you, Jackson. I always have. Saying this is unlike anything I've ever done before, but I have to say it. Pick me. I want to be with you, and the other night it seemed like you wanted to be with me, too. I just need to know one way or the other. Meet me by the giant oak tree tonight if you feel the same way I do. If you don't show, I'll have my answer.

—Lily

LILY BENT THE CORNERS OF the letter in her lap. She wasn't sure if the heat or the guilt of betraying her best friend was causing her to sweat; all she knew was that her new shirt had defined pit stains. Lily tried to make eye contact with Jackson through the rearview mirror but instead saw that his hand was planted firmly on Harper's upper thigh. Lily couldn't help but be transported back to a few weeks ago when she had been the recipient of that touch.

For the last major party of their senior year, the friend group had been celebrating the occasion at their favorite frat, Jackson's frat. With it being their final semester of college, Lily and her friends had been celebrating all of their "lasts." In the fall, everyone had been down to pour one out for their youth and slightly mourn how they would never again have those experiences. But after the thousandth "last," the concept lost its novelty for everyone except Lily and Jackson.

That May night, the music was turned off, and the brothers of Sigma Delta had turned the lights on, but Lily and Jackson refused to let the party end. Jackson invited everyone to go upstairs to his room for a few nightcaps and an opportunity to reflect on "the good old days" that weren't technically over yet. Mia and Nikki politely declined and went back to Mia's dorm. Charlie refused to give in to the light hazing and left ten minutes after. For those next thirty minutes, it was Lily, her childhood best friend Harper, and Harper's boyfriend, Jackson. Harper and Lily took turns trying to defeat Jackson in some racing game he was obsessed with. Lily got close once, but lost control at the very end, causing Jackson to do his little victory shake that was both charming and annoying at the same time. Others in Lily's position would leave to avoid becoming an awkward third wheel, but there was nothing awkward about their situation. It was normal to Lily; she was simply hanging out with her two favorite people: her best friend and the boyfriend who happened to be Lily's first college crush.

It had taken some time for Lily to get to a place where she could comfortably be the third wheel, though. When Harper and Jackson had first started dating, Lily had done all she could to avoid being alone with them. On one hand, she loved seeing Harper happy and, knowing Jackson, it was clear Lily's best friend was with an amazing guy. But, on the other hand, Lily had wanted to be with him more than anything. After the first few weeks of avoidance and a stream of texts from Harper asking if she'd done something wrong, Lily decided that Harper was way more important to her than a guy she never even told anyone she liked in the first place. It was a secret, so clearly it was just infatuation and nothing more. Eventually, Lily lost feelings for Jackson, and third-wheeling became a regular thing. Three years later, she had two best friends, and her attraction to Jackson was a distant memory, or so she'd thought.

Harper's eyelids fluttered as her head bobbed up and down. Lily and Jackson couldn't help but giggle as Harper begrudgingly lost her battle against sleep. Their last college party was officially over.

"Okay, I think it's time to turn in. Lily, is it okay if we pick this up another night?" Jackson put an arm around Harper and scooped her up before her head hit the pillow.

Lily didn't want to go home—she was having fun—but she knew in less than a month they'd be spending every second together at the music festival, so there were going to be plenty of chances to get drunk and nostalgic. Lily was packing up her stuff when Harper suddenly jolted awake.

"No, no, you guys stay. I'm gonna head back to my dorm." Harper got up and started collecting her things.

Jackson jumped up and put a hand on Harper's shoulder. "Are you sure? You can spend the night."

"I say this with all the love in the world, but in a few weeks, I'll be spending three nights in a bed with you, all sweaty and disgusting in the desert. I need a night in my own bed. Plus, you guys are having fun. Keep having fun. Last party, woohoo!"

Harper finished getting her belongings, and Lily slowly sat back down on the bed, unable to ignore the joy sprouting in her heart.

"Let me at least walk you home." Jackson was practically velcroed to Harper's side.

"Fine, if you insist."

Jackson smiled. "I'll be right back, Lil."

Harper waved goodbye, and Jackson followed right behind her. Lily took a sip of her warm beer but quickly placed the cup back down on the carpet. Being alone definitely harshed her buzz.

However, she was suddenly aware of the fact that she was unaccompanied in the bedroom of her best friend's boyfriend. She couldn't help but feel dirty, even though Harper was aware of the situation and had practically arranged it. Over the years, Lily was rarely alone with Jackson for more than the few minutes it took for Harper to leave the room and come back. It's not like they were avoiding each other; Harper was just always there, and Lily liked it that way. She loved spending time with her best friend, so she couldn't complain.

The last time Lily and Jackson spent a significant time alone had been right before winter break freshman year. That night, Lily decided she was going to tell Jackson how she felt, regardless of how it affected their friendship. They were at some craft event hosted by the school, one that nobody was participating in. None of the students even looked in the direction of the various tables, except for Jackson. He didn't care what other people thought and had a reputation for acting on his impulses just so he could tell interesting stories later. Sometimes this got him in trouble, but it always ended up providing entertainment for the rest of their friend group.

Jackson had grabbed Lily's hand and pulled her to a table. The craft was making friendship bracelets—very ironic since Lily had been hoping to become more than friends. Regardless, they sat down and got to work. After a few minutes of watching Jackson struggle to tie off a jumbled mess of string, it became clear that Lily had finally found something Jackson wasn't good at. She couldn't help but laugh, which she constantly did around Jackson, and she spent the next half hour teaching him how to make friendship bracelets as they traded summer camp stories.

As that night had drawn to a close, Lily's feelings for Jackson were at an all-time high, but that only solidified a harsh truth. He was her only friend at school, and the fear of losing that relationship overwhelmed the desire to confess.

A few days later, winter break started, and Harper revealed that she had been keeping a secret from Lily: she would be transferring to Lily's college in the spring.

And the second Harper and Jackson met, there were sparks even Lily could see.

Lily hadn't thought about that craft fair and their friendship-bracelet making in years and was confused why it suddenly was all she could think about. She hated herself for devolving back to a time when she had feelings for Jackson, the second Harper went home. Especially since everything she currently felt toward him was strictly platonic, the same way anyone would feel about a best friend.

Lily paced around Jackson's room, debating if she should leave and text him some excuse, promising they'd hang out again soon and do something with Harper. Lily started pulling her phone out of her pocket but stopped halfway. Her and Jackson were friends, nothing more. Lily didn't have feelings for him; she was just drunk and alone with her thoughts, overanalyzing was natural, expected even. Lily's eyes were drawn to a framed picture on top of Jackson's desk. It was from last year's music festival with Charlie smiling on the left, Mia and Nikki making silly faces on the right, and Jackson in the middle, wrapping his arms around both Harper and Lily. Every photo in Jackson's room showed him being touchy, that was just the kind of person he was. He was raised in a family that greets by hugging, and Jackson kept the tradition alive. Lily's parents were more of the handshaking type, even to their own daughter, so it had been an adjustment when she met Jackson. Lily just hoped he wouldn't be as touchy while they were alone in his room.

Lily's mind began to pull itself in five different directions. Every simple thought spiraled into feeling guilty about spending one-on-one time with the man Harper loved. Lily had a pit taking up space in the bottom of her gut, and with each second, it was growing. She needed to get out of there. Lily turned and started to make her way toward the exit, completely forgetting about the full cup of liquid next to her foot. Beer spread all over the carpet and started to travel under the bed. In an instant, Lily panicked and began tearing through Jackson's room, looking for paper towels, completely forgetting she was in the room of a boy without a single preparation bone in his body. Lily opened the top desk drawer, and in the middle of everything, there it was. The friendship bracelet from freshman year. Lily took a step back and froze, her sock a sponge soaking up cheap beer.

The door creaked open. "Oh crap, let me go grab some paper towels."

Jackson quickly returned with an entire roll, dabbing and wiping up beer while Lily remained in place. She couldn't help but look deeply into the fact that Jackson had held onto it all those years. A few minutes ago, she felt guilty for letting that memory creep back in, but apparently Jackson had returned to it time and time again. Back when Lily was coming to terms with Harper and Jackson dating, she had thrown out her bracelet, knowing that every time she looked at the string, it would be a reminder of how she'd let fear keep her from something that could've been amazing. Now, looking at the bracelet in Jackson's drawer, she was brought back to that belief. Could she and Jackson still be something amazing?

Jackson finished cleaning up the beer and flopped tiredly onto the bed as if he'd cleaned the entire house.

"Wow, beer really sets in immediately."

Lily couldn't move or speak. Part of her was afraid to. Her brain was betraying her, and she didn't know if her body would follow suit. But the desire to ask why increasingly climbed its way to the surface. Maybe if she knew why all of the other questions would subside.

"Lil, you okay?"

She turned and met his gaze. Jackson was the only person she knew with green eyes; they were the first thing she'd been drawn to.

The urge became unbearable; Lily grabbed the friendship bracelet and held it up. She was only able to push out the one word. "Why?"

Jackson's eyes widened as if he'd been caught. Lily had thought Jackson wasn't afraid of anything, but in that moment, that proved to be untrue. He looked terrified.

"You're my-my friend and you uh, gave me that. I couldn't just throw it away. Freshman memories, you know?" He stuttered over his words.

A bead of sweat ran down Jackson's forehead and splattered onto the comforter. Lily knew he wasn't telling the truth; Jackson was a horrible liar. Lily put the bracelet down on top of the desk and sat next to Jackson on the bed. Neither spoke, and their breathing alternated until it was in sync. Lily didn't know what else to say or what she wanted to hear. She expected that the only way to move the conversation forward would be to confess what she had meant to that night three years earlier. But the more she processed the more she realized, she didn't want to talk; she was finally ready to act.

Lily moved forward and kissed Jackson. As their lips met, the tornado of thoughts dissipated. Everything and everyone she should have been considering were far away; all that she cared to know was that Jackson was a really good kisser. Jackson pulled back and once again looked terrified, but this time in a different way. Lily hoped it was in a way that would lead to more kissing. Jackson put his hands on either side of Lily's face and just looked at her. In that moment, words were not spoken, but everything between them was clearer than ever. Jackson pulled her back in, and they continued kissing.

The next morning, Lily had woken up in Jackson's bed, but he was nowhere to be found. As she stared at the ceiling, the guilt she'd pushed to the side the night before began to settle in the middle of her chest. It was crystal, her feelings for Jackson had never left; they'd just been disguised as something else. Lily couldn't hide the truth from herself anymore, which meant she definitely couldn't hide it from Harper; Lily was also a horrible liar.

The weeks following, Lily did her best to avoid Harper while Jackson did his best to avoid Lily. Avoiding Harper was almost impossible, considering she and Lily typically talked every day. Lily had used every excuse she could think of: She was struggling with finals, nervous for graduation, trying to successfully transition back into living with her parents and needed alone time to do so.

The implications of their night together overwhelmed Lily's every thought to the point where she had tried to back out of their big trip. She couldn't spend an entire weekend pretending to be a caring best friend while also watching Jackson and Harper commit PDA everywhere like they normally did. She texted Harper that she wanted to back out, and a few minutes later Harper was at her door. Harper eventually won Lily over, explaining they needed to finish out the tradition they'd adopted that first summer. Lily knew she couldn't go from the biggest proponent of celebrating lasts to missing out on their annual trip without exposing the real reason why. Going to the festival was also a great excuse to finally get some answers from Jackson since he physically wouldn't be able to avoid her anymore.

So, there she was, sitting next to Charlie, who was scribbling something down in his notebook. Curious and hoping to draw her attention from what was going on in the front seat, Lily glanced at the pages but couldn't make out the chicken scratch.

"Whatcha working on?" Lily thought if she kept a positive tone, maybe she'd trick herself into being excited.

Charlie turned the notebook slightly toward himself and away from Lily's prying eyes. He seemed both nervous and determined. "Just a list of things to do before graduation."

Charlie was a year younger than the rest of the group, so he had been celebrating their lasts but still had time to experience all of his own. Lily couldn't help but worry about Charlie being alone next year after his friends graduated. She'd always seen him as a sort of little brother.

Jackson chimed in. "Oh, like finally talk to a girl?"

It was nice to know Jackson had the ability to speak. Everyone else, except for Lily and Charlie, laughed.

"Ha, ha, very funny. No, I have actual goals on here."

"Like what?"

"Like, make a difference in someone's life."

"I did that. Me and the Cleaner Earth Club stopped them from tearing down those trees near campus to put up that disgusting Burger Palace." Nikki turned all the way around to look Charlie in his eyes.

"Yeah, you made a bad difference. Think of all the late-night burgers we could've had."

Jackson glared at her through the rearview mirror. Lily tried to catch his eyes, but he looked back at the road.

"You getting to drunkenly eat a bacon burger was not worth losing one of the prettiest spots on campus. John Wilson has already torn down so much land that doesn't even belong to him to put up restaurants where the workers are disrespected and underpaid, and where the food actively harms you with each bite.

"I don't think anyone has ever hated somebody as much as Nikki hates this 'John Wilson' dude." Harper laughed while Nikki began to turn a deep shade of red.

"Yes, I do, and you guys should, too! Do you know how many poor animals are killed to supply product for just one of his stores?" Nikki lifted off her chair as much as her seatbelt would allow to try and confront Jackson and Harper directly.

"It's okay, Nikki, you can put the soapbox away."

Nikki kicked the back of Jackson's seat, causing him to giggle, which he did every time he successfully annoyed her. Being the mediator of the group, Mia grabbed Nikki's hand and changed the subject.

"What are some of the other things on your list, Charlie?"

"Do something crazy that could get me in trouble but get away with it."

Harper turned around to look at Charlie, causing Lily to look out the window. "You could've already checked that off if you didn't chicken out when we went to West Campus."

West Campus was a dorm building set up when the university first opened. Decades later, it became unsuitable for students to live in, so it had been condemned. There were all sorts of tales about how it was haunted, so in sophomore year, the group decided to find out the truth. Charlie was only a freshman at the time and had been afraid of getting expelled or arrested, so he'd stayed in his room while his friends made a memory they wouldn't stop talking about for years to come.

"That was two years ago! I'm not afraid anymore."

Nikki laughed. "Yeah, sure. Okay, on the way back we're stopping at campus and you're gonna go in by yourself."

"No, this isn't a group list. You guys don't get to decide what I do." His volume increased with each word.

"You just said you weren't afraid anymore. So, prove it."

"You suck, Nikki."

"In all fairness, you did say you weren't afraid," Mia practically whispered.

"Charlie, the rest of us are about to go into the real world, where we have to make really tough decisions. That's way scarier than some old building. If we can do it, you can do it."

Lily wondered what decisions Jackson was referring to. Was he planning on letting Harper down easy during this trip so he and Lily could finally be together? Lily didn't even know if Harper and Jackson had talked since the night of the party, but based on the show in the front seat, it seemed like nothing had changed.

"Guys, I said no. Drop it." At the end of his sentence, Charlie's voice cracked slightly.

Lily knew exactly what was going to happen next. Their friend group loved to poke fun at each other, and Charlie got the brunt of it. Something like a voice crack was bound to get mockery and laughter; even Lily couldn't help but chuckle. As expected, the entire car filled with laughter, causing Charlie to shrink into his seat and continue scribbling in his notebook.

A few hours later, Jackson pulled over to get gas. That particular station with the dark night as its backdrop looked like a horror movie poster.

"Anyone want to come with me to grab some snacks?" Harper smiled and tried to connect with Lily, who was still doing her best to stay hidden.

Normally Lily would say yes before Harper even finished the sentence, but now she couldn't risk being alone with Harper, not before she talked to Jackson and cleared the air.

After a moment, Mia responded with slight urgency. "I'll go, too. I've had to pee for like an hour."

"I'm not letting you go into the sketchy bathroom alone. I'll come, too." Nikki jumped out of the car, and she and Mia took the lead.

Harper looked disappointed as she crossed over to Jackson. Lily hated making her friend upset, but soon the weirdness would be over. Depending on Jackson's response, everything would either go back to normal with Harper or Lily would break her heart. Harper said something to Jackson that Lily couldn't quite make out from the backseat. Jackson responded and Harper leaned in to kiss him, but at that moment he turned back to the gas pump. Maybe their night had meant something after all. Lily watched Harper walk into the store and felt like she was sitting on pins and needles. This was the perfect time to talk to Jackson.

"Can I get your artistic opinion on something?" Lily had completely forgotten about Charlie.

"Um, sure."

Charlie flipped through a few pages of his notebook, showing various symbols. "So, for this year's touch football game, which logo should I go with for my team, Charlie's Angels?"

Lily spent what felt like an eternity going through the options and hearing each detailed backstory. By the time they came to a decision, everyone was back in the car. Her window had closed.

After four more hours trapped in the car, they finally made it to the motel. The festival wasn't the only tradition; they'd also been staying at the same place every year. The motel was run-down and definitely wouldn't be used in an ad convincing people to visit the city, but it was within the budget of six college students, had a shower, and was only fifteen minutes away from the festival. It also had a firepit where they'd sit around the first night and plan which artists they'd see the next day.

They got out of the car, the headlights and a few dying outdoor lights brightening an otherwise dark sky. They loved this motel, but it wasn't everyone's favorite. Like every other year, they were once again one of three cars parked in front of the rooms.

Jackson started walking toward the front desk. "You guys take the bags out of the trunk. I'll go check us in."

"I'll go, too!" Harper ran forward and grabbed Jackson's hand.

And just like that, Harper and Jackson were back to normal, as if their non-kiss at the gas station never happened. Lily craved clarity. Nikki and Mia were in the corner talking, and Charlie was still writing in his notebook, so it was the perfect time to slip the letter into Jackson's things. Lily opened the trunk and zipped open Jackson's duffel bag just enough to slip the piece of paper inside. She closed it and turned around to see Charlie looking at her.

"Woah, Charlie, you scared me." Lily tried to steady her voice but knew it was shaky.

"I don't think they'll last."

"What? Who?" Lily wanted to know the answer but feared what it meant. Did Charlie know something, and if so, how much did he know?

"Mia and Nikki. They're just so different, ya know?"

"Yeah."

Charlie reached behind Lily and grabbed his backpack. Just as Lily's heart began to settle, Jackson and Harper returned.

"Let's get this party started!" Harper seemed excited; Lily hoped it would last.

The group brought their bags in and threw them down onto the floor. The second everything touched the matted carpet, Jackson was ready to get back to tradition.

"Okay, bonfire time. And leave your phones."

"What?" Mia seemed horrified.

"I want your undivided attention. Come on, live in the moment for once."

Everyone placed their phone on the desk, Mia only finally doing so after receiving a look from Jackson. Lily walked over to her bag and started searching for her sweatshirt.

"Can't we just unpack first?" Nikki seemed more annoyed with Jackson than usual.

"No time. We're already behind schedule because Mia had to pee at pretty much every stop."

Mia said nothing but looked embarrassed. Nikki scowled at Jackson. Lily didn't know if she was projecting, but there was tension in the air. Already, this trip felt much different from the ones in years past.

"You heard me, Lil, no time to unpack."

The first words he'd spoken to her, and he'd used her nickname like they still had a close and strong bond.

"Give me a second. I'm just grabbing my sweatshirt."

Lily finally separated the garment from the pile just in time for Jackson to grab it out of her hands.

"Oh, you mean this sweatshirt?"

Jackson shook the sweatshirt in the air and held it above his head. He'd do this a lot to Lily, holding something of value far out of her reach, knowing he was already a foot taller, practically a foot and a half if he stood on his toes. At first, Lily was annoyed Jackson would resort to such juvenile games when there was still an important conversation to be had. But the more she protested, the more her smile grew.

"Jackson, seriously it's freezing!"

"Fine, if you want it, try harder."

"Jackson, please."

The pair began chuckling as Jackson contorted his body in crazy ways to keep the sweatshirt away from Lily.

"Just get taller. You clearly don't want it bad enough."

"Jackson Timmons, I will tell your mother."

For a moment Lily hated the hold Jackson had over her. She had been angry with him for weeks for ignoring her, but suddenly she was calling him his full name just so she could see his playfully annoyed smirk. They were always fake fighting, even at times wrestling, so this wasn't out of the ordinary, but once Lily tripped and her hands landed on Jackson's chest, she was reminded just how different everything was now. Lily jolted backward, trying to maintain a neutral face. Jackson brought the sweatshirt down and handed it to Lily, and for a moment their hands touched and they both lingered. Lily wondered if Harper noticed anything but didn't want to look at her to find out.

Charlie cut through the tension. "You guys go to the bonfire without me. I think that gas station hotdog is fighting back."

Both Nikki and Mia made their disgust clear through an array of noises.

Harper tried to rally the troops. "I think that means we should get the hell out of dodge. Let's go before this place becomes a warzone."

Harper and Jackson were the first to exit, followed by Mia and Nikki, and then Lily in the back. Without Charlie, she was now a fifth wheel, and without the guiding light that was her friendship with Harper, she was lost. Jackson struggled for a couple of minutes, but eventually, a fire raged in front of them. At least Lily could be mesmerized and get lost in the flames.

"Finally, I thought that'd never work." Jackson sat down on one of the stumps and put his arm around Harper.

"I didn't doubt you for a second." Harper turned and kissed Jackson on the cheek.

Now that they were across from each other and she wasn't staring at his back or through a car window, Lily could see the discomfort on Jackson's face. The couple appeared to be strong, but appearances could be deceiving. Jackson's face, whether he wanted it to or not, was telling the truth: everything wasn't okay with them, and his night with Lily had meant something. Lily now, more than ever, hoped Jackson would read her note and give her a clear answer. She wasn't sure what would happen next, if they'd tell Harper right away or have one last hoorah before their world came crashing down. All she knew was that the thought of being in Jackson's arms again or hearing him say "I love you" while looking into her eyes was enough to give her complete butterflies. She needed Jackson to just check his bag.

It was a good bet that Mia would be cold, so Lily knew a way to get them back in the room.

"Anyone else cold? I'm freezing. I think I want to head back."

"But you're wearing your sweatshirt." The corners of Jackson's lips started to curl up.

Mia spoke through chattering teeth. "Honestly, I could go back inside."

Jackson's smile faded. "Are you serious? I just got the fire going."

"And who knows what Charlie did to that bathroom." Nikki gagged.

"It's been thirty minutes. I bet things have cleared out. Come on, let's just unpack, chill, and talk inside." Lily thought she might've been obvious but was also sick of hiding the truth.

Mia shot up while the rest of the group hesitantly rose from the logs. This time, Lily was in the front, hoping to get to the room quickly so her weeks of crafting theories could finally come to an end. The closer they got to the room, the clearer it became that something was wrong.

"My car! Where's my car?" Jackson yelled out, motioning to a space that once held their way back home.

Harper ran up next to him and rubbed his arm, hoping to calm him down slightly. "It's okay, my phone's inside, I'll just go call the police."

Harper opened the door and immediately let out a scream. Jackson ran to her, and the rest of the group followed. Harper stood in the middle of an empty room. The only thing besides the motel furniture was a blue backpack on the bed. Charlie's backpack.

"Is this some kind of prank?" Nikki looked around, moving at a slower speed than the situation required.

Mia, Jackson, and Harper ran around the small room searching for any information or clues they could find. Lily's eyes were fixed on the backpack. Why would Charlie take everything that belonged to them but leave the one thing that was his? Lily walked over to the bed and zipped open the front pockets. Nothing. She unzipped and shoved her hand into the first main pocket to find a skinny slip that felt like a picture.

"He's gone," Mia yelled out from the bathroom.

"He took my phone!" Harper held a hand to her forehead.

"Mine's gone, too." Jackson seemed more angry than worried.

Nikki stopped searching through drawers to answer. "Same."

Mia made a face that insinuated she couldn't find her phone.

"Wow, great idea about 'living in the moment,' Jackson." Nikki walked up to Jackson, standing on her tiptoes so they were a similar height.

Jackson took a step closer until they were practically nose-to-nose. "Like I knew Charlie would go crazy and do this."

"Guys, please, you two fighting isn't helping. Lily, what about you? Where's your phone?" Harper sounded desperate.

Lily pulled her hand from the backpack to reveal a picture of Mia with her mom and a random man. The room went quiet for a moment, and Lily realized everyone was looking at her.

"What's that?" Nikki walked over and grabbed the photo out of Lily's hands.

Her mouth slammed shut, and all of her features melted to a state of pure detachment.

"Mia. Why are you and your mom in a photo with John Wilson? And why is his arm around you?"

Mia's face bloomed into the complete opposite of Nikki's, every emotion making an appearance in a matter of seconds.

"I-uh. He—" She couldn't get the words out.

Mia's eyes widened. Lily couldn't help but feel relieved that she wasn't the only one harboring such a detrimental secret.

"Oh my—Your mom said her ex was in food service. It was right in front of me this whole time. But—You've been lying to me all these years and pretending like you hate the guy when he's your father?!"

Tears started to well in Mia's eyes. "Nikki, please, baby, I can explain."

Nikki ran out of the room, and Mia followed quickly behind. Lily turned and made eye contact with Jackson for the first time since the night she'd gotten lost in them.

"I knew it."

Lily and Jackson turned to see Harper sitting next to the backpack, another pocket open, holding a piece of paper and crying. Lily immediately recognized the bent corners of the paper in Harper's hands.

Lily didn't know what to say but knew she needed to speak and try to salvage the friendship. "Harper, I'm so sorry."

"Both of you have been acting so weird since that stupid party. You know, my gut was telling me that something was wrong, but I didn't listen because I didn't think the two people I love most in the world would do something like that to me. I can't believe I'm that stupid."

Harper slowly rose from the bed, and everything seemed to click in Jackson's head. He ran over and tried to wrap his arms around her, but she pushed him away, shoving the letter into his chest.

"Harper, can we talk about this?"

"No, I don't want to hear it from you. From either of you."

Harper injected her words with venom and ran out of the room. As she passed, Harper shot Lily a look, one of disgust and melancholy she'd never seen before. It wasn't a complete surprise; Lily knew Harper would be hurt, but Lily still couldn't have anticipated how much pain she herself would feel.

Lily was once again alone with Jackson. Nothing was standing in their way now. Lily could just speak what was in the letter and get her answers.

"Jackson, I—"

She went to grab his hand, but Jackson was already halfway out the door, calling out for Harper.

Lily walked over to the bed and collapsed, preparing for the moment when her heart would break in two. Through her tears, she noticed the final pocket of the backpack lying beside her was cracked open. She unzipped it completely, felt around inside, and soon pulled out another piece of paper.

In the middle of the page, in Charlie's chicken scratch handwriting, the words "make a difference in someone's life" were scribbled—with a large check next to it.

About the Author

Jessica Daniliuk is so excited to work with Nicole Frail Books again. Her story "Dancing Queen" was seen in *Another Chance to Get It Right: A New Year's Eve Anthology* and her story "Strawberry Macarons" was seen in *Recipes for Romance: A Sweet Valentine's Day Anthology*. She has also recently published with Quill & Flame Publishing and Livina Press. She hopes everyone has a great summer and is able to get into the spirit with *Just One . . .*

You can find Jessica on:
Instagram: @jmdaniliuk

You can visit her website at:
jessicadaniliuk.com

VINTAGE LOVE

Vintage Love

Caz Luan

Chapter 1

Tamina

"YOU HAVE TO COME WITH me, Tams. We can visit all the vineyards, drive around, take in the scenery, eat lots of foodie stuff if you like, and drink all the wine we can possibly drink without keeling over."

"Chantelle, I don't want to go and then—"

"Let me stop you right there."

This is my best friend in the whole world, Chantelle Newman.

"I am not taking no for an answer. We had an awful semester and barely made it through exams. We deserve a little vacation. Just think: three wonderful, student-free weeks where we can literally do anything without someone telling us to be a good example."

We are both teachers at an art academy in San Francisco. We were sitting in my classroom, surrounded by wooden desks, scattered chairs, and the subtle but suffocating fog that white chalk leaves behind. I teach history, and her lessons are more hands-on, like sculpting classes.

I bite my bottom lip and consider the consequences of two young women driving around wine country, intoxicated and adventurous. It *has* been a grueling semester.

We always start with high hopes and expectations of being the best teachers ever. But by the last exam of the year, we've usually rediscovered our long-lost hobbies of day-drinking and talking each other off the ledge.

The semester is officially finished, and I have summer break to look forward to . . . if she allows me some breathing room. She wants to get away from everything; all I can think of is my bed.

Staring into her hopeful, smiling face, I feel my resolve fade. A trip could be great. I need the distraction.

I broke up with my fiancé a month ago. It's a long, experienced by most brokenhearted, story, but chivalry is truly dead and buried beneath the oak tree in my backyard.

Love should be easier than this, shouldn't it?

"Three weeks of fun. How can you turn that down?"

That is a very good question.

Chantelle has been chatting my ear off all the way down to Napa Valley. There are advantages to staying in the San Francisco area.

"So, the owner's name is Ria, and she isn't expecting us until after two, so why don't we go and grab some breakfast at the winery next door?"

We agreed to leave our worries behind when we started our journey this morning. My little purple Volkswagen Bug might be old, but there was no way we could go on an adventure without driving my trusty steed.

As we drove through the beautiful countryside, it appeared to wake up with us. We were surrounded by lush greenery and proud trees reaching for the sky. An endless valley of highs and lows stretched before us, and I couldn't help but wonder what rich history it held.

Chantelle directs me to a quaint little bistro nestled between trees, and I already feel more relaxed.

We take a seat at one of the round tables in the garden. This tiny corner successfully makes you forget about the wide world out there while the wind brings notes of abundance on the faint sea breeze.

"You know I really needed this."

Chantelle winks and places her hand over mine. "What are best friends for?"

"I'll drink to that," I say, taking a big gulp of the mimosa we both ordered.

"Just promise me you'll be open to new experiences," Chantelle begs, her eyes filled with concern.

"Of course. Starting right now, I will be saying yes to every suggestion. Let's live it up." I raise my glass in a toast, and she clinks hers to mine, a devious smile on her lips.

Chapter 2

Storm

I COME HERE EVERY WEEKEND to hide from the landlord.

Ria is driving me insane. She is a very single married woman. Her husband is an expatriate like me, yet his rotation alternates with mine. When I am at home, he is away, and vice versa.

That may be why his wife is so clingy when I am here. Or any other man, for that matter.

I work as a fire training officer on one of the biggest oil rigs in the ocean. When I come home, all I want to do is rest, take in nature, and maybe have a good time with some of my buddies. She hardly allows the latter, as she is always sniffing around me and making my dates feel uncomfortable. She acts as if she has any claim to my time and the company I keep.

My buddies always joke and say I got into drilling because I think I'm too good for any woman, but that is not the case. When you had genuine love and lost it because you were a stupid kid, you tend to be more selective.

I smile at Melissa, the waitress. She comes to take my usual order. When she walks away, I find myself pulled into memories about the woman who changed me into who I am today.

I never told anyone this, but we broke up because I wanted more. I thought seeing the world would satisfy my hunger, but it only meant that I had this collection of photos illustrating how truly alone I was in all those countries.

Now, I find myself fleeing my house every few weeks to escape my lonely existence and the memories of her. I take the time to recall how the wind blew through her long, auburn hair and how her rich, hazelnut eyes sparkled when she saw me. I touch my chest, feeling the guilt overwhelm me when I remember the tears I wiped from her cheeks when I told her I was leaving. She didn't try to convince me to stay. She calmly walked away without looking back; that was the last time I saw her, almost eight years ago.

Like a coward, I never attempted to find her, but I must have some strong, magical powers of recollection, because I swear I can hear her laughter floating by on the breeze. I scan the crowd before me . . . and find her sitting with another woman in the garden.

Tamina Moore is quite an unexpected sight, and just as beautiful as I remember. Her laughter fills the space, and the carefree expression on her face makes me ache. At least she is happy—one of us should be.

She lifts her face to the sun. The truth seems to play hide-and-seek on her face until it highlights her eyes. She is too far away to see clearly, but I could have sworn her eyes grow greener as she speaks and then smiles.

That smile could always make my walls crumble.

I glance around and see a few other men mesmerized by the two ladies at the garden table.

She stands up to get something from her handbag, and I get a great view of her body. She has turned into a beautiful woman, and regret floods my heart.

She wouldn't want to see me.

Not after all these years.

I vaguely become aware that one of my best buds is heading their way. Jeff might be a bit reserved but has never shied away from what he wants.

And I admire that.

I finish the meal Melissa placed before me while keeping a close eye on Jeff and the girls.

When I get up to leave, fate would have Tamina strolling in the same direction as me.

So, it must be her friend who has caught Jeff's eye.

Thank goodness for that. I don't think I could stand Jeff dating my ex-girlfriend.

Unintentionally, I find myself standing behind her.

Her hair seems to have caught flecks of sun, and I stare in wonderment. Could this be a sign that I need to make a move? She looks shorter than I remember. I edge closer, and she smells sweet, just as I remember. I look down and imagine my hands on her waist, pulling her closer for a kiss.

Wake up, Storm, that is never going to happen. She must despise you.

"Storm Davis, is that you?"

She has turned around, and if her shocked expression wasn't lined with so much hurt, I might actually be smiling. I hesitate and then decide to see where this goes.

What is the worst that can happen?

"Yeah. It is good to see you, Tamina. How is life?"

What am I doing? She doesn't want to talk to me. I broke her heart and abandoned her for a meager life of adventure.

"Fine. How are you? Did you find what you were searching for?"

She has always been so supportive. How could I not see how much I needed that in my life?

"I have done everything I set out to do and traveled the world, if that is what you are asking."

She tilts her head, and a sad smile forms on her lips. She could always see right through me.

"That's great. I'm so happy you're happy. It's all I ever wanted for you."

She knows I am lying. Why doesn't she call me on it?

"Well, I must get going. My friend will be wondering where I am, and I'm sure you have other things to get to. It was nice seeing you."

She swipes her card at the counter and silence envelopes us while she settles her account. When she is done, she turns to leave, and, in my stupidity, I call out to her.

"Tamina!"

She doesn't turn; she only stops and waits.

"It was really nice seeing you, too." My voice is raw.

She nods, and this time, she is the one walking away.

Chapter 3

Tamina

"WHO WAS THE GUY YOU were talking to back at the restaurant? You seemed to know each other."

We are on our way to Silvanus Winery to meet our host for this break-away, Ria.

I try to sound unaffected. "Oh, no one. He was someone from my past, but he's not important anymore."

"Well, he is a *dish*. Maybe you would want to get to know him again, if you know what I mean." Chantelle pokes my thigh.

"Not an option; he made that clear back then, and honestly, I don't know the man anymore."

Storm has definitely changed. His beautiful, bronze skin makes him look more exotic, and his broad shoulders would make any girl swoon. Not to mention, I remember what it felt like to be in his arms and to have my tears wiped away by his gentle touch.

"I thought you said you would try and be open to new things?"

I smirk at Chantelle, clearly seeing right through her pathetic attempt.

"I did, and I will. But Storm is part of my past, and I want to focus on my future."

We turn onto a long, winding dirt road, and she allows me a few moments of silence before she ruins my concentration.

"Maybe. Maybe not. Either way, he is Jeff's friend, and we are having dinner with them tonight."

My mind has been running wild the whole afternoon. Flashes of his chestnut hair and piercing brown eyes force their way from my memories. Now, he towers over me, but back then, he was just this sweet boy I fell in love with. A boy who broke my heart when he left for the unknown, making me feel like my love wasn't worth staying for.

How am I supposed to act around him after feeling so rejected?

Even though we met Ria this afternoon when she booked us into our villa, I am still stunned by her beauty as we walk closer to the estate house.

She welcomes people at the enormous wooden doorway that leads to the dining area. The details of the gorgeous estate are mesmerizing, and I am again in awe of the luxurious surroundings. Every piece is a testament to class and style.

The air is filled with laughter. The sultry night wind cooled my skin on our walk to the main house. Now I feel the flush spread in anticipation of seeing Storm again.

I am confident in my knee-length blue dress. I kept my dainty gold necklace on. Despite its small size, it always felt like armor against the world, reassuring me that somewhere someone loves me.

We spot Jeff, and we weave between tables to make our way over. Jeff winks the waiter closer and orders a bottle of wine for the table.

I can't stomach another glass of wine, so I interrupt and ask for Jack Daniels on the rocks. Jeff's shocked face turns bright red as I hear a voice behind me say, "Well, there you go, Jeff. Another person that knows that other alcohols are available in wine country."

Storm sits beside me, and I am enveloped in his masculine smell.

"Good evening, ladies. Are you enjoying our sights so far?" Storm is charming, and I press my hand to my stomach to calm the butterflies.

Storm seems pleasant, but I know he's faking. He dominates the conversation and immediately steers Jeff into reminiscing about their excursions. He completely ignores Chantelle and me, and I start to feel anger boiling beneath the surface. By the time our dinners arrive, the two of us haven't spoken a word for at least twenty minutes.

"I could have told you the steak would be a better choice."

I look up to confirm that he had, indeed, meant those words for me, and instantly I lose my temper. The nerve of this new man before me is baffling. He hasn't spoken to us in minutes and wants to judge my food choices? He has no idea who he's dealing with. I have also changed.

"Well, luckily, I don't need help making my own choices. In fact, I'll have another whiskey."

I beckon to the waiter and place my order. Chantelle looks at me with an expression of amusement and embarrassment. It's too late now. I've already started this engine, and we're ready for a few laps.

"In fact, contradictory to common belief, some women are more decisive than you will ever know."

"Is that a fact? So, you are telling me that women decide to make bad decisions knowing that it is a lousy choice."

I thrust my finger in his face. "You're one to talk."

His face pales, and I realize that that might not have been the response he sought. He rises abruptly, thanks Jeff for the invitation, and leaves the room without looking back.

"Well, that could have gone better." Chantelle looks at me with piercing eyes, and I lose my appetite. I know she still wants to spend time with Jeff. This is as good a time as any to make my departure.

I move my chair backward and excuse myself.

"But you can't walk to the villa by yourself. . . ."

She lowers her head, and her lips are pressing tight into a grimace.

"I'll be fine. Besides, it's only a ten-minute walk."

With a tense smile in Jeff's direction, I turn to leave, unsatisfied and still a little hungry.

Chapter 4

Storm

MY PHONE RINGS INCESSANTLY. I grab it from the bedside table and toss it into the laundry bin in the corner.

A hard, persistent knock echoes from below, and I curse as I toss the covers and stomp downstairs to give someone a piece of my mind.

I rip the door open, and Jeff unceremoniously pushes me aside to enter.

"Why the hell are you still sleeping? Do you think the girls will wait forever?"

I rake my hand through my hair, trying to grasp his words.

"Are you going to keep staring at me with that dumb look, or are you going to get dressed?" Jeff folds his arms over his chest with a smug grin.

"Why are you so irritating? Besides, you saw what happened last night." I was only trying to talk my buddy up, but that backfired. I flop on the couch and pick up the remote to switch on the television.

Jeff rips it out of my hands and turns the set off before he sits on my coffee table and stares me down.

"What? I went to dinner like you asked, didn't I?"

"She is the girl."

I avoid his eyes and squint at the sunshine streaming in from the open door. I came home early, but I was tossing and turning all night.

"I don't know what you are talking about."

Jeff huffs. "She's the girl you can't get over. She's why you haven't had a decent relationship the whole time I've known you."

Now my patience is running out. "What if she is? There is nothing I can do about it now, is there? She clearly still blames me for leaving."

He slaps my face, and I start to stand, but he pushes me back down.

"Wake up, man. This woman has traveled two hours to get here and has been dropped into your lap. This is your chance. You can fix this and win her heart. You did it once. What's stopping you now?"

I shamefully lower my head until I feel his hand on my shoulder.

"Happiness is only a construct until you find the one to realize it. You deserve happiness, man; you can't keep punishing yourself for a mistake you made as a kid."

"She didn't even fight me on my decision. Maybe I lost her way before I let her go."

Jeff snorts. "That's not what I saw last night. I thought she was going to skewer you with her fork. You shouldn't have left. Chantelle says it was bad because she just broke up with her fiancé. Maybe your stupid comment reminded her of that."

I never considered she could be with someone else. My heart contracts in jealousy, and my fists ball up.

"Who was this shithead?"

Jeff jumps up and punches the air.

"I knew you still had feelings for her. I saw the look in your eyes when you sat down next to her. Will you stop being stubborn and go after the girl of your dreams? Or am I going to have to slap you again? I enjoyed it, and I'll do it."

I smiled, grateful for the friend he had become.

"I guess I am going to get the girl."

I get up and walk over to Jeff to hug him.

"Thanks for looking out for me, man."

He grabs me by the shoulders and turns serious.

"Don't thank me yet, man. We have a plan. Now, to get the girl. Get dressed. We have a date."

We walked to the girls' villa. I didn't realize they were staying so close for three weeks. Deliberating how convenient this was to the plan Jeff and I concocted on the way here, I lifted my hand to knock on their door.

Tamina opens the door wearing another sundress, and my words evaporate. The green of the dress is reflected in her eyes, and a sense of possession takes hold of me. I want to make this girl mine. She has always been mine. It just took me a little longer to realize that the home I have been searching for can be found in her arms.

I reach out for her instinctively, and she steps back. Right, I have not made my intentions clear yet. Watching her skittish movements, I know I must ease her into this gently. I owe her that much.

Tamina calls out for Chantelle and leaves the door open while she returns to her breakfast plate on the table.

I look at Jeff, and he nods encouragingly.

I sit closest to her and pop a piece of bacon from her plate into my mouth.

"Can I help you with something? Maybe get you your own plate of food?"

She is at least talking to me.

"No, thank you. I like your bacon. Gives me an excuse to sit close."

She moves her chair to the other side, and I move my chair, too.

She isn't going to get away from me again.

She huffs and grabs the last piece of bacon to put in her mouth. Between chews, she shocks me.

"I am . . . sorry about . . . last night. I shouldn't . . . have said . . . what I did."

I place my arm around the back of her chair and secretly delight in the warmth radiating off her skin.

"I am the one who should be sorry. I didn't behave appropriately and would like a chance to make it up to you."

She swallows before she answers.

"No. There is no need. What we had was in the past. Besides, in three weeks, I am returning home, and your life will continue without me."

Not if I have anything to do with it. I lean closer and hear her breathing turn shallow.

"We will see about that, Santuàrio."

A twinkle gleams in her eye. She used to love it when I spoke Portuguese to her.

"You know I still can't understand you, right?"

I place my hand on her cheek and rub her soft skin with my thumb.

"Your heart knows what it means. It always has." Her eyelids flutter, and I can see the restraint etched on her face in the straight line of her pursed lips.

"We should go. Chantelle said we were going on an adventure today. We don't want to be late."

"And what an adventure it will be." I get up, help her out of her chair, but don't let go of her hand as I guide her out and lock the door behind me.

Chapter 5

Tamina

"I AM WARNING YOU, CHANTELLE. You had better stay by my side. Don't leave me alone with this man."

Her pout is ridiculous, and I playfully shove her away from me.

We were walking behind the guys, who were being very secretive about our destination. We had no idea what to expect, and after that intimate moment this morning, I felt even more in the dark.

"You said you would give this a real chance," Chantelle says accusingly.

"I said I would be open to new things. Not jump back into a relationship with a man who rejected me years ago because I wasn't enough for him."

I have stopped in my tracks, and the old familiar sadness engulfs me. It was so hard to continue without Storm. I fear I won't survive a second onslaught on my fragile heart from his boyish charm.

The guys keep walking and leave us behind.

Chantelle puts her arms around me, and my knees want to buckle. I was so close to leaning into his comfort this morning. I don't know what I would do if I found myself in a similar situation.

"You must help me, Chantelle. I don't think I'm strong enough to resist him."

She leans her head to my temple, and I sigh shakily.

"You need this. Think about it this way. At least this time, you know there's an end, and *you* are in control. Last time, you had no choice but to accept his reasoning. This time, you are the one who gets to take what you want and then walk away with your heart intact."

Last night, we'd discussed all the juicy details she could pull out of Jeff. Only we're not totally recognizing one fatal flaw:

I don't feel like the one in control at all.

* * *

Storm watches my face anxiously when we round a corner and see two substantial open barrels of purple grapes. I barely acknowledge the other people standing around and walk up to the first vat with reverie.

If we do what I hope we'll be doing, we'll be well on our way to making this vacation memorable.

We move closer to our apparent guide, Mr. Godfrey, the winemaker. Storm is talking to him and approaches me when he calls for everyone's attention.

"It is such a wonderful thing to see all of you here today. Even though it's a lot of fun, foot-stomping grapes is not for the faint of heart. To our few brave heroes today, I want to welcome you and explain a little bit of our history."

The man gives an animated speech, which I miss completely because he's barely started when Storm leans over to me.

"Are you ready for this? It could get messy."

I want to give him a fierce stare back, knowing he's messing with me. But looking into his eyes makes me come undone, and my words disappear. The best I can do is let out a wobbly harrumph before pleading with my eyes in Chantelle's direction.

She ignores it spectacularly, and I am left to my own devices.

I focus on our guide, and I only catch the last sentence.

". . . since we weren't expecting such a crowd today, seven of you go in this vat and you two in the other smaller one. Sometimes it good to keep your original equipment after upgrading, right?"

Looking around frantically, I try to evade the big sausage finger pointing straight at Storm and me.

"There's no way to avoid it, little lady. You two will be working harder than the others, so if I were you, I would flex my toes before getting in," Godfrey chuckles.

Smiling weakly in the direction of the robust man who is clearly taking pleasure in my discomfort, I step closer to the vat, which will unknowingly become my emotional drain for the next hour or so.

Storm gives me a hand after we wash our feet, and I almost trip on the rim when our fingers touch. The surge of electricity that flows between us could be enough to power a small country. Looking down, I try to maneuver myself into the grapes, but he picks me up and dumps me in without so much of a twitch.

However, those few seconds I was suspended and my body was pressed against his strong physique was enough to keep me awake for months. I could feel his muscles ripple from my weight, and there was something feral about the little growl he gave when he put me down. I have never felt this raw before.

I started stomping on the grapes as hard as I could, getting rid of all the pent-up confusion.

"I never figured you for the type."

I stop, leaning against the side, already out of breath. Why is it so easy for Storm to bait me?

"What type would that be?"

He points to the pulverized grapes beneath my feet in jest.

"The murdering kind. Just look at it. It looks like a crime scene over there. Those grapes could have been kind, good-natured grapes that never hurt anyone in their lives. Now, you are stomping the vinegar out of them. What did they ever do to you?"

I couldn't hide my smile. Storm always had a way to get me out of my head.

"I am doing as instructed. Is it my fault that your skills are lacking?"

His eyebrows pull up, and his smile reaches his eyes.

"Oh, is that what you think? Let me put you at ease. I have the perfect way to make you even more efficient." He moves closer, hands up in a threatening manner. I scramble to get out of the way but squeal in delight when he starts tickling my sides.

My gleeful cries echo over the vast vineyards. Without control over my limbs, grape juice splatters everywhere, and I can hear the surprised laughter about our antics coming from the other vat.

Out of breath and with my body completely jelly, I hang onto him for dear life. His eyes search my face, and I bathe in the warm comfortable feeling that rushes through my body.

I am definitely not in control anymore.

I try to hide that fact, but his hand brushes against mine, and the spark that transfers between us makes me jerk my hand away so quickly that I throw myself off balance and fall into the grapes.

I can't hold back the laughter as I realize what I have just done to myself.

Looking up into his eyes, filled with amusement, I strip the years of loneliness from the walls of my terrified heart.

His laughter falls in rhythm with mine.

It is a deep, playful rumble that reverberates through his body, up to his broad shoulders.

I swim closer to the edge and must look like a little drowned puppy because as soon as Chantelle and Jeff see me, they start to laugh.

Feeling light, I flick some crushed grapes in Chantelle's direction. She unsuccessfully tries to dodge the fine flying vintage.

Arms circle my waist and pull me to my feet. I want to lean back into his body, but I resist.

I look down at my dress, stained with dark red splotches.

Isn't it funny how my ruined dress brings me more joy than the man I almost married? Although, I know it isn't the dress that makes me feel this way.

"You did good, girl, although usually we only use our feet to get the job done." Mr. Godfrey gives me a hand out of the vat.

"I can't take any credit. I was used as a puppet in the process."

Storm jumps out and lands next to me. He whispers in my ear, and his warm breath sends shivers down my spine. "More like a tool, if you ask me."

Dripping wet, my tone turns to that of the scolding teacher. "You're the tool."

His wickedness becomes clear when he turns his back on the gawking audience we have acquired, essentially blocking us from their view.

"And you can use me anytime you like."

The wink is what makes my heart squeeze.

My body flushes with heat, and I push him out of the way to rejoin reality. It is far too easy to fall into the trap of opening up my heart to him, especially when the yearning to belong makes my body strum with anticipation.

Chapter 6

Storm

SLOWLY, I AM CHIPPING AWAY at the brick wall her heart hides behind.

Most days, she can withstand my charm, but more and more, I find that she engages without thinking. My cleverly set traps expose the voids in her life while proving to her that I know exactly how to fill them with love and respect.

Before we know it, we fall into the rhythm of friendly banter we had in high school. Only now there is the added element of yearning. And it is so strong that I can't ignore it anymore.

We are strolling toward Ria's dining hall hand in hand, and I indicate to Jeff to go ahead. He starts pulling Chantelle forward, and I subtly hold Tamina back.

"We're losing them."

Her voice is matter of fact with a hint of . . . excitement?

"Let them go. I need to talk to you."

I don't think she realizes, but she stops to stare at me, and the world around us fades away.

"You know I am leaving in a week. Whatever you have to say should be left unsaid."

She starts walking again, but I pull her back.

"Can't you feel it? The chemistry between us is growing too hot to ignore. You must feel it, too."

Tamina tilts her head to the side. "You are a fireman; put it out."

I chuckle but know I need to get serious.

"If it was that easy, we wouldn't be here. I have taken it slow these two weeks to give you time to adjust, but you must realize that what we have is real."

She rips her hand from my hold and steps back.

"You are *not* doing this to me again. You make me love you and use me, and when you need to leave for work, I'll be the one left behind with a shattered heart. No! You know I need to leave in a week, and this was working because I could prepare myself, but what you're asking is impossible."

I threw my hands up in the air.

"Why do you have to be so stubborn? I have tried everything I can to prove that I want you."

She turns around, and it seems like she is . . . counting. When she faces me, I can see the fire in her eyes.

"You don't understand. Let's just drop it."

She starts walking, but I call out, "If you are too much of a coward to admit you want me, that's fine. But I want you."

The force with which she turns and runs toward me to push me away is impressive.

"Get it through your thick skull. Wanting me and keeping me is not the same thing. And I will not be your toy anymore."

She storms off toward her villa, and I let her be. Eventually, she will come back, and then we will end this ridiculous notion of hers that I don't want to keep her. Because she is mine, and nothing will keep us apart ever again.

Chapter 7

Tamina

COULDN'T HE HAVE STARTED THIS fight after dinner? I'm starving.

I hear the faint grumble of my stomach and stare at the depressingly dry crackers I found on the table. I pick up my phone to see a text from Chantelle.

We are going to Storm's house. Meet us there.

Chantelle always looks out for me, but this is partly her fault. She said I would be in control, and I wasn't. When he held me back today, all I hoped for was that he would kiss me. What scares me the most is that I wanted to weave my arms around his neck and kiss him back. I wanted to feel my body melt into his and form one exquisite moment that would echo into the eternity of what would be my lonely existence when I left here in a week.

Over the past two weeks, I have surrendered to the possibility of what could be. Even though I knew it couldn't last, I wanted to feel what it would be like if he were mine. I basked in his attention, and I let myself be taken in by the notion of being in love and having the relationship be sacred for both of us.

But the reality was that this is not the case.

In a week, I will return to my mundane real life alone, and he will move on to his next conquest or return to work. I was just a distraction to him, and he only wants me because he can't have me.

I press my hand to my heart and wince at the prospect of what I have lost. No. Storm was never mine to begin with. I must remember that.

I look at my watch and quickly deduce that the kitchen at the main house will still be open for dinner guests. I dig my flip-flops out from under the table, where I'd kicked them when I came in.

Taking my handbag and an extra jacket, I psych myself up to make this trip alone in the dark.

Noises of nature surround me, and I feel my steps turn into a run. Out of breath and with a flushed face, I stumble in the door of the estate house.

"Heavens, where did you come from so late at night?"

Ria helps me to a table and gestures for a waiter to bring me something to drink.

After gulping down the whole glass, I force the words past my lips between deep breaths.

"I came . . . for . . . dinner."

Concern floods her face, but she calls over her shoulder.

"Bring us some of the Bordeaux and two chef's specials."

Everybody scurries away, and my eyes beam gratefulness at her.

"Calm down. You will be safe here, and if you want, I can call Storm to come and get you after we have dinner."

I shake my head vehemently, and she only stares in silence.

When the food arrives, I have caught my breath and feel much better. I even enjoy the deep notes of cranberry and spice in the wine.

The lamb cutlets placed before me complement the wine perfectly, and I enjoy my meal immensely until she breaks the silence.

"What did he do this time?"

I gaze at her in confusion, and she clarifies.

"Storm. Do you think you're the only girl he has paraded around the estate? He has at least three to four of them each rotation."

Three girls every rotation? How can that be? He seems so sincere.

"He wanted more from me than I was willing to give."

Her smile doesn't reach her eyes.

"You would be the first. Most girls are more than happy to jump between the sheets with him. Can you blame them, I mean? Have you seen him naked? It is truly a sight."

My fork halts midair.

"You've seen him naked? I thought you were married?"

She continues eating, unbothered by my intrusive questioning.

"I am, but I think that made me more of a conquest, if you know what I mean. It's the thrill that gets Storm off. And once he has you, he loses interest."

My mouth is agape, and I recognize the slight tremble in my hand. I abandon the last bite and place the fork back down. Ria carries on unperturbed.

"He uses vague phrases and never commits, but you always feel so damn special when you're together that you can't help but fall for him. So, I don't blame you. I've been there, and it hurts to be cast aside when he is done with you."

I hear the words, but something doesn't make sense.

"But he didn't cast me aside. He wanted me. He said so himself."

Tears form while I try to convince myself that the man Ria has described is not the Storm who begged me only hours ago to see us as more than a fling.

She puts her hand over mine and squeezes.

"Honey, he said that to every one of us."

I lower my head and let the hopelessness overwhelm me.

She lifts me from my chair, and I willingly let myself be led to her car.

"Come, I will take you home. You shouldn't be out at night in your state."

The door slams and I am consumed by exhaustion. I can barely keep my eyes open, and my head falls against the headrest, enveloped in darkness.

My eyelids feel glued together, and I struggle to open them, only to wince at the glimmer of sharp sunlight penetrating the fog surrounding my head. I lift my hand to touch my throbbing temple. I tried to recall how much wine I had, and it escapes me. How did I get home? Am I home?

I slowly force my aching body to stagger into an upright position. I take in my surroundings through slits and see something that resembles a bedroom. But everything sparkles and reveals a sense of wealth I have never seen before.

This is not my room. I close my eyes and wonder if I have ever seen opulence like this, failing to recall any incidents while I rub the expensive brocade fabric under my fingers. I am lying on a huge bed with luxurious bedding. That only means one thing: I am in a strange place and have no idea how I got here.

The door to my left opens slightly, and someone pops their head in.

"Oh, you are finally awake. Took you long enough. You really can't hold your wine, can you?"

I wince as I stand and recognize Ria, our host, walking closer with a tray filled with breakfast goodies.

"I brought you some breakfast. I need to get to the dining hall and didn't want you to starve while I was gone. The bathroom is that door, and you will find clean towels in the cupboard."

She simply turns to leave, but something in her words jars me awake.

"What do you mean starve while you're gone? I can leave, right?" My voice is scratchy, and it hurts to talk.

"Unfortunately, no, my dear. I have been waiting patiently for Storm to recognize that what we have is real. He has been fighting against it, and you only complicate things more."

She turns around but halts when a terrified cry leaves my lips.

"Wait, please. What does this mean?"

"It means you stay here until he returns to work, and then I will set you free. I won't allow an insignificant little floozy like you to come in and ruin everything I have worked for. Storm is mine, and no one will stand in our way. Now, eat your breakfast and don't make a fuss. There is no one else here to hear you scream."

"But why? I have done nothing to you." My voice is a whisper, but she still hears me.

She focuses all her wrath on me, and her face distorts into something ugly.

"Because he wanted you. He could have had me, but he wanted you. A nobody from nowhere."

The door slams shut behind her, and a deep sigh takes over before the tears drip onto my hand.

How did I get tangled up in this? All I wanted was to belong to someone again, even if only for a little while.

Chapter 8

Storm

I DIDN'T SLEEP AT ALL. I missed the feeling of her fingers weaving through mine and chastised myself for not going to Tamina's villa to check up on her.

Chantelle said she did send her a message, but she never responded. She also said that she probably needed some time to cool off and that my presence would only exacerbate the situation.

Only now do I find myself marching to her villa in the early morning hours, and I don't care if she is still in her pajamas, with unbrushed teeth and hair as wild as a bird's nest.

We are going to talk this out right now. I need to tell Tamina everything. It is the only way to make her understand how deeply I feel for her.

I knock on the door, and when that does nothing, I hit the wood with my fist and all the rage from being denied.

"Tamina, open up! There is no escape. We will talk this out, and I will not leave until we do."

Another few minutes pass, and I walk around to the back to peek inside through the window. Everything is eerily quiet, and there is no movement at all. I take out my cell to call Jeff.

"Hi, do you know what time it is?"

"As if you can talk, man. Listen, I need to talk to Chantelle. Is she with you?"

He snorts and must have handed her the phone because her voice is the next one, I hear.

"Hi, what's up? Did you talk to her?"

"No, I am at your villa, but everything is quiet, and it looks like she isn't here. Can you call her phone for me?"

I hear a scuffle on the other side, and the next moment, I hear a faint ringing sound.

"I'm dialing her now, but it rings and then goes to voicemail. Can you hear her phone on your end?"

The villa is absolutely silent, and an alarm bell goes off in my mind.

"I don't want to bother you, but I think you need to get down here and open up for me to have a look."

"I'm on my way."

The line goes dead, and I tuck the phone into my back pocket. Seconds later, it rings, and I assume Jeff has found Tamina.

"Hey, did you find her?"

"I'm standing at your front door, but no one is here. The fire is in your area so I thought I would drop by to pick you up. Where are you?" It's the fire chief of the local fire station. I am a volunteer firefighter, and they only call me in when it is an emergency.

"Are you sure you need me? I am kind of in the middle of something."

His regrets rumble through the line.

"I am so sorry, but this is a doozy. The west side of the mountain near your house has been set ablaze, and if we don't work fast and evacuate everyone, this might turn nasty. I need boots on the ground to contain the blaze before it reaches a critical stage."

I take off running in the direction of my house.

"On my way. See you in five."

I call Chantelle again and tell her to leave me a message the moment she locates Tamina.

There is no time to waste, and I prioritize the emergency on hand, but my thoughts never wholly leave the beautiful brunette who has captivated my mind and heart.

* * *

The fire is out of control. It has already spread further than any other fire in the district, and we are pulling out all the stops to try to contain it. Every able man has been utilized, and the surrounding vintners have volunteered some of their resources.

I haven't heard from Chantelle and am getting more worried by the second.

When my phone starts ringing, I hand off the hose to one of the rookies and take the call.

"I am a little busy at the moment. That is why I told you to send a message."

My tone is impatient, but we are dealing with a crisis.

"Actually, man, I thought you might want to hear this in person. We can't find Tamina. Her phone has been turned off, and she is nowhere to be found," Jeff says, hesitant about my reaction.

I freeze, and my limbs go numb.

"She left?" I whisper.

"That's the thing, all her stuff is still here. Of course, the only thing missing is her handbag with her phone."

I breathe a sigh of relief until confusion sets in.

"Where could she be if all her things are still at the villa?"

Regret filters through the line. "I have no idea, man. We've looked everywhere," Jeff states.

The rookie is trying to get my attention, and I give my last orders before putting my phone away: "Find her."

We have been hosing scorched earth for hours when our directives change.

We get the call over the walkie, and I can't believe my ears.

"Wait, you want me to let the fire ravage Ria's house? You have got to be kidding me." The disbelief is clear in my voice.

"That's what she said. I requested access to her irrigation system, and she refused, saying we needed to move on from her property."

"But that is ludicrous. Ria will lose not only her generational vineyard but also her home."

"Apparently, she said we should focus on other places. She is fine with the outcome."

That is so strange. Ria's whole identity is entangled in the wealth the vineyard brings to her name. She even made her husband sign a prenup to prevent him from acquiring her property. So why would she be so willing to let it burn to the ground when we can save it?

The red flags all point to something suspicious; all I can think of is that Tamina is still missing. But Ria's actions are too apprehensive to be ignored. Besides, even though we have had our differences, it wouldn't be right to let her lose everything when I could have stopped the fire. And what about the people she has working in her home? No one is allowed access to the mountain, but what if they were already there?

I watch as the fire jumps, and suddenly, my legs carry me toward the house I see in the distance.

Thick smoke hinders my sight, and I trip over something, going down hard. I jump right back up, pumping my arms and pushing to go faster. My lungs are screaming from the little oxygen left in the air, and I wish I'd brought my oxygen tank along, but I left it abandoned against one of the water rigs.

I see the fire closing in, and I decide to kick open the back door. It was my best chance. I know the front door is massive and solid oak. The flimsy back door splinters open, and I rush through the opening.

"Is anyone here? We need to evacuate immediately. If you need help, call out. Call out, and I will find you." Not a sound can be heard beyond the loud crackle of the fire devouring its prey on the path of destruction behind me.

"You have to give me a clue. Where are you?"

"Here." It was so soft I almost missed it.

I rush up the stairs and start kicking down the doors.

Each room is just as empty as the one before it until I get to the very last door. I kick it, and it remains intact. Locked.

I open the latch on my belt, releasing my mini axe. The others laughed at me, but I insisted it could be useful. Now is the time to prove them wrong.

I start chipping away at the area surrounding the handle, and when I deem it weak enough, I give the door another mighty kick.

The door crashes down, and there she is, lying on the floor, wearing the same clothes as yesterday.

Tamina!

I run to her side and check for a pulse.

I fight tears when I feel a faint beat against my desperate fingers.

I bend and pick her up, tossing her over my shoulder. We need to get out of here now. The wind has been blowing all the smoke in this direction, which means it won't take long for the flames to reach us.

I practically run down the stairs and plan to escape through the back door, but I skid to a halt when I see flames licking the doorframe.

It's too late. I need to find another way. The front door should be fine, as it is on the other side of the flames. I jog over, jostling Tamina, but I don't hear any complaints. My lungs feel like they are bursting, so I can only imagine what hers feel like.

I unlock the door from the inside. Never been more grateful for those people who are more trusting by nature and only install single-latch locks.

Outside, I am met by the same rookie and a medical team.

"Take her. She needs oxygen."

He immediately grabs her limp body and deposits her with EMS before he comes back and helps me out of the fire's path.

I sink down beside her and take her hand. The oxygen mask is over her face, and I see her eyes flutter.

I can breathe for the first time when she opens them. Since I learned she was missing, my life has moved at a suffocating pace.

She struggles to pull the mask away, and I gently bat at her hand.

"You need it, love, don't move it. Just breathe."

She insists, and her voice is raw from all the inhaled smoke, but I bend down to hear what she is saying.

"You came back for me."

I ignore the wetness running through the black soot on my face.

"I always will. You are my Santuàrio."

Before she can question me any further, I place the mask back over her face and put my forehead against her temple before I whisper, "My sanctuary."

Chapter 9

Tamina

IT HAS BEEN THREE DAYS since the fire wiped out half the valley.

I was taken to the hospital and stayed for one night under observation. Storm refused to leave my side and slept in a very uncomfortable-looking chair.

Ria was arrested on counts of attempted murder and kidnapping. Her husband flew back, but according to the sergeant, that was only to start divorce procedures.

Chantelle has been staying with Jeff, and I have bunked with Storm. I say bunked because he only has one bed and refuses to let me sleep alone, so we have been sharing.

At first, it was awkward to be so vulnerable around him. But I have come to thank all the bachelor gods that he never considered turning one of the other rooms into a guest room.

That leads us to this moment: me lying on the pillow, staring at him as he snores and relishing his morning breath. A loud snort startles him awake and it takes a few seconds before his eyes can focus on me.

"How long have you been awake? Do you need to go to the bathroom?"

The doctor said I suffered mild smoke inhalation but should be okay in a few days.

"You know I can walk, right? I don't need your help."

He pushes onto his elbow, and his dark hair flops over one eye.

"Is that so? Did you forget who saved you from certain death in a fiery abyss?"

I giggle because every time he describes the fire, it becomes more and more dramatic.

"You really are a tool, you know that?"

He smirks and cups my cheek in his hand.

"Yes, but I am your tool."

I lean into his warmth.

"We need to talk." He turns serious and regret floods my system. He is going to tell me he wants me to leave. I knew it was too good to be true. He moves to lean against the headboard, and I follow suit. Once he makes sure I am completely content, the words flow.

"I know we had a relationship many years ago which ended abruptly."

"Because you wanted to see the world."

He winces, and I bite my bottom lip.

Why do I always have to do that?

"Yes, because I wanted to see the world. I thought seeing the world would make me feel less . . . small."

"Did it work?"

He gives the question some serious thought.

"No, I came back the same small person. And I think I know why."

He looks at me, hopeful, but I wait to see where this is going.

"It was because I couldn't open my heart. I see it like this: I have always felt empty, and gaining experiences worldwide looked so enticing because I was chasing the dream of finding a place where I belong. I didn't feel at home in my own skin."

He watches me closely, and I try to give none of my disappointment away.

"And you found your place here."

He chuckles, and I want to slap him on the head.

"No, love. I found my place with you. I always thought it was a geographical location that would change my feelings of inadequacy, but it has always been a person. You, to be exact."

My heart is beating out of my chest, and I lift my fingers to cover the gasp that wants to escape my lips.

"Now, I have a few options here. I could deny myself the pleasure of your company and a lifetime of happiness and stay here. Option two is to confess to you that I love you with every fiber of my being and that there has never been another woman who has captured my heart quite like you. And then I pack up my shit and go home with you. Hopefully, you will allow me to make a home with you because I ain't going anywhere."

"But what about your job?"

"I talked to a buddy in San Fransico, and he said they were looking for a new fire chief at one of the stations. He has already submitted my résumé, and I have an interview the day after we return."

"You can't leave your home behind just like that."

"Let's get one thing straight. You are my home, my love, and my everything. Do you really expect me to keep renting from the woman who almost took my future from me?"

He is correct, but I haven't considered the situation like that until now. Ria is probably going away for some time, and then the vineyard would fall into disrepair, not to mention the villas and Storm's house. Then something else dawns on me.

"Santuàrio. That's what it means? It means 'home'?"

His hands frame my face, and he pulls me closer.

"Actually, it means 'sanctuary,' and that is what you are, love. You are my safe place to exist and thrive. Only with you can I be the man I was destined to be. You belong with me, and my heart is yours, to do with as you please."

I smile and feel my cheeks press against his hands.

"You are such a sappy tool."

His face comes closer.

"Yes, but I am your sappy tool to use as you please. Now, kiss the tool."

And I do. And I plan to kiss the tool for many years to come.

About the Author

Caz Luan is a South African author who has always been in love with the idea of love. Her sassiness and humor get her in trouble more often than not, and if it wasn't for the fact that she doesn't look good in prison colors, she might have had many more friends. Her dark romance, *Sweet Torture*, released in June 2025, and she is excited to collaborate with Nicole Frail and And You Press on yet another anthology. "Taste of Sin" was featured in *Craving You: A Spicy Valentine's Day Anthology* in early 2025. Caz's work also appeared in another anthology titled *Out of Bounds*, which released in May 2025. She will be releasing her two paranormal stories in August 2025. She is currently traveling around Africa with her ex-pat husband, searching for inspiration.

You can find Caz on:

Instagram: @cazluanauthor
TikTok: @cazluanauthor & @caz_luan_author
Facebook: @caz.luan

You can visit her website at:

www.cazluan.com

MILLENNIAL MAGIC

Millennial Magic

Mitchell S. Elrick

THE FIRST TIME PRESTON SWINGS the hammer down, he completely misses the stake and nicks his thumb. It doesn't help that the sun is acting like it's getting paid overtime.

"Yow! Shitballs!" he winces through his teeth as a small bead of blood forms just above his nail bed. He looks up, making sure Tana sees none of this. Thankfully, she doesn't.

If she had, she'd have let out a laugh so loud every campsite within a two-mile radius would have heard. To add insult to injury, she definitely would have a one-liner like, "We should ask for help. I'm sure there's an eleven-year-old boy scout around here somewhere." Or "Want me to call Smokey the Bear? At Uni he majored in fire safety, but I heard he minored in tent studies."

But, luckily, Tana is too busy unpacking the truck. The foldable chairs are already set up around the fire pit. The tablecloth that covers the wobbly wooden table has all their cutlery and plates ready to go. And, of course, a very tattered, very stained copy of one of those Harry Potter books is perched on the corner of the table. Preston has no idea which one it is. Of course he doesn't; it's always a different one. But what he does know is that some people carry journals. Some people carry bibles. Hell, some people carry guns to feel safe. But no. Not his girlfriend. Tana carries pages full of fictional characters. Everywhere she goes. At least one copy. And honestly, Preston's surprised she'd only brought one. There it is, though, plain as day. After a quick assessment of what is already unpacked, Preston assumes all Tana has left to do is get the coolers.

So, with the back of his hand, Preston wipes the sweat from his brow and swings the hammer down a second time, connecting perfectly with the metal stake. The only problem is that, this time, as the hammer meets the stake, the top end crumples, causing zero percent of the stake to actually dig into the ground.

Why are all tent stakes made out of the flimsiest metal?

Preston yells as he slams the hammer on the dirt. But as he does so, from the depths of the van, Tana is yelling the exact same thing.

"Fuck!"

Hearing each other's simultaneous frustration causes an eruption of laughter. When he makes it to the truck, Preston sees the problem. The spigot on the water cooler, one of those giant orange Gatorade ones, the one Preston uses for work every day, has broken clean off and flooded the back half of the truck bed. The blankets and one of the sleeping bags are soaked. And worst of all, their access to fire—the matches and the cardboard box they were in—are in the same situation as the blankets.

Tana shrugs and points. "At least the important stuff didn't get ruined."

Preston sees what she's pointing to. At the other end of the truck bed, Preston sees a stack of candy and chocolate. Next to the stack of sugar are six completely not-ruined, not soaked, very tattered, very stained books of pages filled with fictional characters.

Preston rolls his eyes. "Yeah, thankfully nothing important got soaked." Preston grabs the water-logged box of matches. "Nothing important. Only our means of light and warmth during the night!"

"It's not a big deal," Tana says. "We just need to get a lighter."

Preston rolls his eyes again. "And blankets, and a new sleeping bag." Not to mention, the nearest gas station is at least thirty minutes away. What a waste of time and gas!

Tana smiles. "The blankets will easily dry out by the time the sun goes down."

Preston raises his eyebrows, "And what about the sleeping bag? That won't dry out."

"Oh, no," Tana says, covering her mouth sarcastically. "We might have to share."

"Share?"

Tana lightly puts her hand on Preston's chest. "You heard me."

Preston pretends to consider this. He would jump out of a flying car if it led to sharing a sleeping bag with her. And, after all, they do need fire. Plus, the gas station is only about thirty minutes away; it's really not that far. "Just a lighter?"

"One lighter. That's all."

"Just one?"

"Just one."

As the truck twists and turns through the Colorado mountains, Tana reaches into the back of the truck bed and comes back with two small cardboard boxes. "Want a frog?"

At this point in their relationship, Preston is no longer weirded out by this question. It's been asked too many times. He knows what she means. Chocolate. Chocolate in the shape of a frog. Which made no sense, even when she explained it. Something about trading cards or something like that. Preston figured it must be like that Pokémon thing. He'd made fun of her the first time she offered one. But then she shoved a piece into his mouth. It was so abrupt, and the milk chocolate was so creamy it melted in his mouth. Since then, Preston no longer liked chocolate. He liked frogs. For multiple reasons. So, normally, he'd say yes to this question, but he'd already crammed two frogs into his mouth on the drive up and stuffed a third one as they were packing the truck back up for their lighter adventure.

"I'm good, thanks."

Tana frowns and reaches into the back again and comes back with a small bag. "How about some beans?"

Seemingly, another odd question for a snack, but, again, Preston knows she means something else. Jellybeans. But, not the fun, sweet jellybeans everyone gets at Easter. Nope. None of that strawberry, cherry, grape, wild berry awesomeness. If anything, it was the exact opposite of all that. In fact, Preston was pretty sure his girlfriend bought these just to torment him.

"Gross," he says right away. "You never give me a good one. Last time you gave me, Three-Headed Dog Slobber flavor."

Tana gets a hurt look on her face. But it's fake. She's terrible at hiding a smile. "That one's not terrible!"

Preston shakes his head. "One time you gave me Witch Weekly's Most Charming Smile flavor. That was the worst. And what does that even mean? It tasted like hairspray!"

Tana laughs. "Well, that's bec—"

But Tana is cut off by the loud splat of a raindrop. Then another. And another. Within a few seconds, the windshield is being pelted.

As the torrent of rain catches them by surprise, Preston rolls up the windows and slows the truck as the two trudge on for a few minutes before Tana is back at it, offering a treat to her boyfriend. "Here. This one's good. Try it."

Preston rolls his eyes. He knows it'll be terrible. But he also knows his reaction will make her laugh. And her laughter is like magic. He can't explain it. It's unignorable. Euphoric. So, hearing beats taste in this showdown of the senses.

Preston grimaces and takes the bean. "What's this one called?"

Tana smirks and says, "Ha—Wait, what's that?" She leans closer to the windshield.

"What's what?" Preston is genuinely confused. He can't see more than thirty feet in front of him. The relentless raindrops pick up enthusiasm.

Tana points to the median. "THAT!"

The "that" Tana is referring to is a car rolled over on its side. The rain and the wind have gotten so bad that Preston doesn't see it.

"That sucks," Preston halfheartedly says when he finally sees it. "I wonder how long it's been abandoned. Bunch of crazy drivers during the summer!"

But Preston doesn't actually see it. He sees the car. He sees that it's rolled. But that's it.

What he doesn't see is the slight movement coming from the vehicle. Did Tana see a hand?

Preston doesn't have to hear Tana's next words, because she's navigating the steering wheel from the passenger seat. "Pull over!!"

When the vehicle comes to a stop, Preston isn't sure what to do. But Tana is. She's already unbuckled, and the door is halfway open, ready to go save the goddamn day. Rain is spraying the interior of the vehicle when Preston says, "Wait. I'll go check it out."

He doesn't really want to, but he'll be damned if his girlfriend goes out in this weather only to get kidnapped or killed. Both of these scenarios are highly unlikely with downpouring rain and a rolled-over car on the side of a Colorado mountain. But when you're in love and danger is even possible, "worst-case" might as well be the only scenario. Plus, it'll get him out of having to eat more beans.

So Preston turns to Tana, pops the jellybean into his mouth, and says, "Just going out to get one lighter, huh?"

Tana grabs Preston by the cheeks and kisses him. "Just one." Maybe it's the kiss, maybe it's the jellybean, but Preston swears he tastes birthday cake.

Preston unbuckles his belt and pulls on his sweater. A gift from Tana, it has a picture of a green snake and a black bird right below some lettering. Tana explained it many times, something about a guy named Riddle and a stupid raven, but Preston has no idea what that means, because Harry Potter is for kids and girls. But Tana bought and gave it to him because he's her "favorite little death eater," and he also doesn't know what that means, but she smiles when she says it, and Preston will pretty much do anything to see that girl smile or laugh. So, here we are.

As he exits the truck, he's immediately smashed with weather. The drops don't feel like drops; they feel like little bits of stress. Little bits of chastity. Because that's what this is going to lead to. It'll be too dark, too late, too tired by the time they get back to the campsite. No shared sleeping bag for Preston. Of course not. Now he has to be a goddamn boy scout and pretend like he gives a fuck about an abandoned car. And to top it all off, the jellybean is definitely changing flavors. Is that sweat? It's definitely sweat that he tastes. And a whiff of wild animals wafts through his nose.

But then his mind goes blank. Because what he sees now is not what he saw from the highway and definitely not what he expected to see when he left the pickup. He wipes the rain from his brow.

The shattered windows. The engine is still holding on for dear life. Because the vehicle is rolled on the passenger's side, the driver's side wheels continue to spin, while the passenger wheels try to gain traction. But the rain has turned the earth into a bath; nothing can catch. And even though it's raining, the car smells like burning metal.

Growing up in a small town, Preston may not have learned much about wimpy wizards, but he sure as shit knows the fear of a car on fire.

Through the spiderwebbed windshield, Preston sees the woman in the passenger seat. Her head is resting against the earth. Lines of red trace the lines on her forehead like a river.

His first thought is the worst thought. A question. "Is she dead?"

But he doesn't have much time to think because he hears a man's voice coming from the driver's seat. Preston sloshes through the grassy gravel, his shoes sinking into the earth. When he gets to the man, Preston has to hold his hand over his mouth to keep the vomit down.

The man's elbow is mangled, bending in a way elbows shouldn't bend, exposing bone and spilling blood.

"Arrrgggggghhhhhhhhh!" the man screams. "Help!"

Preston climbs the hood of the car and kneels down. Luckily, the window is broken, so Preston begins to work on the man's seatbelt. But, just as he does so, he hears a sound he'll remember for the rest of his life.

A soft whimper. A cry. A child.

Preston couldn't pick the age of his own mother if you gave him four guesses. But, from the car seat and the fact that the child's head was no bigger than Preston's palm, it was obvious this kid wasn't any older than one or two.

Shooting fear rushes through him. He wants to help, but he's not sure what to do. He looks up toward the direction of the pickup but it's no use. The heavy rain, the nasty wind, and darkness beats down any hope of seeing Tana. Just the thought of not being able to see her flips a switch in his brain.

The faster I get this done, the faster I get back to her.

He slides his way to the passenger door. Since the glass of the window is already broken, he's able to lean right in. As he begins to unlatch the straps of the car seat, shards of broken glass around the window frame cut into his sweater. As the glass makes its way through the material and into his skin, he finally has the kid in his grasp. But the rain is unforgiving. Just as he pulls the kid through the window, Preston slips, and a shard slices like it's trying to hide inside his stomach. He yelps, but his sound is drowned by the rain and thunder.

He wants to lead the little girl back to his car, back to safety, back to Tana, but he can't leave the parents in the front. Despite the unstoppable rain, the car is somehow getting hotter, the fire growing.

Again. Preston doesn't know what to do. Again, he wishes Tana were here. She would know what to do.

But, as if the universe had heard Preston's predicament, he hears a voice behind him. It's a man's voice. Not the man in the car. No, this voice is bigger. Much bigger. Perhaps the deepest voice Preston has ever heard.

Preston turns and spots the biggest man he's ever seen in his life. The man is so big Preston could double, literally double, no, triple in size and still be smaller than this man.

Between the black duster, the disheveled beard, and the goggles, Preston was certain this man rode a motorcycle.

"Hi. I'm Rube—" but the wind and rain snatch the man's introduction out of his mouth.

Everything happens so fast, and everything is such an emergency, and the weather is so relentlessly wet, what happens and what is said after that is a little blurry. But the large man sweeps up the little girl and tucks her under his duster, protecting her from the rain. Without much of a word, the man walks off in the direction of the pickup. So Preston gets back to work.

When he gets back on top of the car, Preston hears voices inside. The woman has woken up.

"My baby! Where is Ariah! Where is she?!"

The man is trying to speak, but he's lost too much blood.

Preston assures them the baby is fine and begins working on the man's seatbelt. Between the man's broken elbow, the pressure of the glass in Preston's side, and the rain, he can't get leverage. If he unbuckles the man's seatbelt, he'll fall on his wife, possibly hurting her worse and wedging both of them in the burning car. If he tries to pull the man out through his seatbelt, he could drop the man. Besides, Preston knows his stomach wouldn't allow that type of maneuver.

Every route seemed worse than the last. The car is getting hotter. The car seat where the baby had been is mostly melted at this point.

But, then, Preston has an idea. It's a long shot. But it might work.

By now, the engine has stopped running and the tires have stopped turning, so if he could pull the car back on all four tires, he could easily get both the mother and father out.

"Hold on," Preston says. "I'll be right back."

"No!" the woman yells. "Don't leave us! Please!"

Preston slides down and makes his way around to the base of the car. He tries to reach up to grab the bottom panel, but as soon as he does, he's met with a shooting pain; a cruel reminder of the shard that had taken up residence in his abdomen. The pain was so bad that it takes him to a knee. At that, Preston knows his plan is worthless. He'll never be able to flip the car back on all four tires. There's just no way.

But then, Preston feels a hand on his shoulder. A hand the size of a catcher's glove.

Preston looks up, way up, and sees the bearded man. "Let me help."

The man grabs the base of the car and sets it back on all four tires like a waiter setting a plate.

The wails from the wife bring him back to reality and he gets to work. The woman mentions that her foot is pinned and she's got a gash on her forehead, but beyond that she claims to be fine. The bearded man whisks her out of the passenger seat and gently places her on a rock. With tears in her eyes, she yells, "Help my husband!"

Without thinking, Preston takes his shirt off and tries to steady the man's arm. The bearded man reaches into his duster and pulls out a very well-sanded stick. "Here, use this. I'm not allowed to use it right now anyway."

Preston has absolutely no idea what this means, and it's so insignificant that later he'll tell himself that he remembered wrong, that the stick came from the ground, not some guy's duster pocket. Who has sticks in their pockets? How absurd.

It takes Preston a minute to steady the tourniquet, but he finally has the arm stabilized when the large man hands Preston a sleeping bag. But, not just any sleeping bag. It's Preston's sleeping bag. The one he was going to try to share with Tana later because hers had been soaked earlier—not that he was thinking about that in a time like this. But, nonetheless, it was definitely his sleeping bag. Tana must have given it to the man when he took the toddler to the car.

The bearded man points to the man with the tourniquet. "It's cold. He's lost a lot of blood. Put this on the man." But he didn't say *man*. He said something else. It started with an M, but Preston couldn't tell. Seemed like a made-up word. Preston must have misheard. But he didn't have time to think. The man needed warmth. After a minute of tucking the sleeping bag around the man, Preston can hear the cries of sirens. With every breath, the sounds of EMT vehicles and firetrucks become louder and louder.

When the EMTs finally get to the scene, the rain and wind decide to stop their bullying, making room for the sun to show its face. The EMTs and firefighters take control of the situation, tending to the man and his wife. As they are being bandaged and properly cared for, a few firefighters take care of the car.

"A little longer and things could have gotten bad," one of them says as he puts out the burning front seats.

"Right!" another says, turning to Preston. "How did you take care of all three of them?"

"Oh." Preston says, caught off guard. "I, uh, had help. Without—" Preston turns to look for the bearded man. Ruby? Rube? Was that his name? Preston couldn't remember.

Preston turns left. He turns right. The bearded man was nowhere to be found. How could a man THAT big just disappear?

"Are you cut?" a medic noticed Preston holding his side.

As the medic works away at the wound, Tana walks over with the toddler. The kid is smiling, holding a book. Take a wild guess at the title.

"Babe, I'm so glad you're okay!"

Preston smiles at Tana, trying to hide his pain as the medic stitches him back together. "Did you see where the big man went?"

Tana cocks her head. "Big man?"

"Yeah," Preston says. "The one with the big trench coat. And the beard. And the goggles."

Tana's face is nothing but confusion. "What?"

Preston shakes his head, annoyed. "The big man. Like a small giant. Like eleven feet tall? The one that brought her to you." Preston gestures toward the little girl.

"Preston," Tana says. "You brought her to me."

Preston shakes his head. Tana must be confused. "No, no. He brought her to you. Then you gave him the sleeping bag. The one we were going to . . ." But Preston decides it's best to not continue.

Tana's look of confusion turns to concern and she glances at the medic. "Preston, you brought Ariah to me. Then you asked for the sleeping bag. You said you needed it to keep the man warm."

Preston doesn't know what to say so he says the same thing anyone says when they're confused. "What?"

"Babe." Tana kneels down so she's face to face with her boyfriend. "You brought Ariah to me. You told me to keep her safe. You asked for the sleeping bag. You saved those people."

Preston shakes his head but the medic interjects. "Yeah, that woman—" The medic points to Ariah's mother, the one that was wedged in the passenger seat. "She said you pulled her daughter to safety then pulled the car back on all four wheels."

This makes Preston laugh. He's five-foot-nine, one hundred and eighty pounds soaking wet (literally). There's no way he pulled the car back to all four wheels. "I couldn't have done that. Look at me."

The medic raises their eyebrows. "I've seen and heard of crazier shit. Were you scared?" Preston scoffs. "Obviously."

"Yeah," the medic says, a little too nonchalantly. "Adrenaline's fucking crazy. You probably blacked out. But it's a good thing. You saved those people. You're a hero."

The words are nice, but Preston doesn't feel them. What about the giant man? He's the one who really saved those people.

When they are finally alone for a couple minutes, Preston recounts the event to Tana exactly as he remembers it. When he finally finishes, he's out of breath, holding his side where his stitches are, and his girlfriend is smiling.

"What did you say his name was? This man who helped you."

Preston tries to close his eyes and remember. "Rube? Or Ruby? Rubis? Shit, I couldn't really hear him. The wind and rain were crazy."

Tana smiles. The type of smile that makes Preston know she's holding more back than she cares to tell. "What?!" he demands.

"So a man," Tana begins. "A giant man. Over ten feet tall, you say, was wearing a black duster, had a mangy beard, motorcycle goggles, and some sort of stick, the perfect size for a tourniquet, hidden in his duster? And he just casually set a two-thousand-pound car back on all four wheels. As if by . . . magic?"

Well, put like that, Preston knows just how crazy it sounds. The car thing may have been exaggerated. Preston may have helped. He can't really remember now. And the stick. Well, that probably came from the ground. And, maybe he was forgetting going all the way back to the truck to drop off Ariah and get the sleeping bag. After all, adrenaline really is a crazy thing. And the gash in his side. He did lose a little bit of blood. Maybe he was feeing a little loopy. Loopy people see crazy things.

Preston sheepishly looks at his girlfriend. "It does sound kind of crazy."

The medics take care of all the patients. The family is headed to the hospital. The man has a long recovery, but Preston and Tana are told the family will make a full recovery. The firefighters take care of the car, thanking Preston again for his quick thinking. The police, when they finally arrive, ask Preston for his statement. To be honest, he really wants to get back to his weekend in the mountains, and if he tells them about Rube or Ruby or whatever that man's name was, perhaps they'll ask more questions and that will just take too much time. So Preston decides to leave the parts about the bearded man out of the story and just recalls what he remembers doing and what he was told he did.

Which is smart, because Preston and Tana are back in the pickup in no time. But, just as the couple are pulling away from the scene, Tana sees a group of cops. Some of them are pulling stuff from the burned car, some are cataloguing, some are standing around, not doing much.

So, for the second time that day, Tana tells Preston to stop the truck. She gets out.

Preston tries to ask her where she's going and what she's doing, but all she says is, "I'll be right back." Tana walks up to the group of officers and Preston witnesses a conversation of some sort. The officers nod and hand Tana a small bag. When she returns to the truck, Tana hands the bag to Preston. He can hear metal clinging and right away he knows what it is.

"Stakes! The good ones, too." Preston laughs.

"Yeah," Tana says. "Saw your little situation this afternoon. Think we could hire a boy scout? Don't want you to break a thumb."

A sheepish look covers Preston's face. "How'd you get these?"

"They're from the car," Tana said. "The tent was mostly burned through, but the stakes were good. The officers said they were going to be thrown away."

Preston nods. "Well that worked out."

"And while you were giving your statement to the police," Tana adds, "the medics tried to tell me we should just go home so you can rest. You shouldn't even be driving!"

"Fuck that," Preston says with a snort.

Tana rolls her eyes. "I told them you'd say that, so they gave me a thousand pounds of gauze and ointment and bandages for your cut. And, like twenty blankets. So, we don't need your sleeping bag."

A smirk begins to creep over Preston's face. "So, you're saying . . ."

Tana rolls her eyes even harder. "You're forgetting the whole reason we left our campsite this afternoon."

Preston furrows his brow. Then it hits. A lighter!

"Shit!" Preston groans. "We still have at least twenty minutes to the nearest gas station. If it's even open."

A tired helplessness hits Preston. All of a sudden, the pain in his side seems to feel worse. But then, a mischievous smile crosses Tana's face. She holds something up. A lighter.

"Where did you get that?" Preston laughs. "Did the medic give you that, too?" Tana smiles. "No, Ariah did."

"What?" Preston is even more bewildered. "How did a two-year-old have a lighter?"

Tana's smile gets bigger. "When the medics showed up, I took her to them. She wanted to walk, so I put her down and we walked. She found it. On the ground, like twenty feet from the pickup."

Preston frowns. "Does it actually work? There's no way it survived that rai—" But before Preston finishes his sentence, Tana flicks the starter and voila—fire. He can't help but laugh, but then stops, because laughing hurts.

Tana tosses the lighter to Preston. "Read what it says."

Preston fumbles it, but when he finally gathers it, he holds it up to the overhead light of the pickup. It has two sides.

He reads the first side. "Just A Spark of . . ."

Then to the other side: "Magic."

About the Author

Mitchell S. Elrick is a middle school English teacher living in Denver, Colorado, with his wife and son. When he isn't teaching, he's reading, writing, or making up wildly mediocre songs that somewhat entertain his son and fully annoy his wife. With the happy family lives a cuddly cat and a lunatic guised as a black lab. It has been confirmed the cat and the dog aren't fans of the songs, either.

Mitchell is the author of the short stories "Polka Dots," "MJ's Jersey," and "Lewis," all available from Attic Ebooks.

You can find Mitchell on:
Instagram: @mitchellselrick.author

SENT BY APHRODITE

Sent by Aphrodite

Rowen Burrows

Prologue

George

"BUILT AROUND THE THIRD CENTURY BCE, this is all that remains of the temple of Aphrodite, goddess of love and beauty, here in Symi Square," announced the tour guide, Daphne. Waving a hand at the ruins, she invited the group to step closer and have a look. "Did you know Aphrodite was worshipped in port towns as she was also a goddess of ports?"

No, George had not known that. As he continued to listen, he stepped closer to the ruins. There really wasn't much left, and it was surrounded by a small fence.

He loved topics linked to religion and history. As a teacher, he spent a lot of his life teaching these subjects. During his summer vacations, he made sure to travel to different places so he could learn more himself. And simply because he enjoyed it.

Greece had always been his favorite country, and he had visited Athens, Kos, Zante, and Crete. Now, he was visiting Rhodes and had booked a walking tour so he could find out more about the area.

Clapping her hands together, Daphne said, "And with that, we have come to the end of the tour. Thank you all for joining me today. I do hope you have enjoyed it and learned something new. I will be here for the next few minutes for any last questions. Have a wonderful day."

Planning to thank her, he hung back to let a couple ask her questions. While he waited, he placed his hands on the little fence and took his time surveying the temple. How would it have looked in its prime?

"Aphrodite, goddess of love," he whispered to himself, smiling softly. No one was paying him any mind as he looked around, so he continued, "Many people would have come here in the past praying to you for love, and I could really do with some right now. Everything else I have tried has not worked. I am not sure what to do."

He had tried going on blind dates, and used dating websites and apps, but nothing seemed to click. He'd felt no spark. The one relationship he'd had that lasted longer than a few months fizzled out, and that was the end of that. Many thought he was boring, didn't want to travel so much, or didn't respect his job. They didn't understand the passion he had for teaching, or the hours he put in.

What could it hurt voicing his wish to the goddess of love herself?

Looking up at the sun, he added, "Just one. All I want is just one man that would understand and accept me."

Sighing, he looked at his feet. He didn't want to be alone, and he knew lots of teachers who had found that perfect balance of love and work. He simply hadn't yet.

Would he?

Just as he let go of the fence, intending to talk to Daphne, a small gust of wind whipped past him. Pink dust was picked up and thrown in his eyes.

"Ow!" Starting to rub them, he stumbled back.

"What the . . .?" a deep voice said behind him.

A body collided with him, knocking him to the ground. Still unable to see well, he stayed where he was for a moment to clear his eyes.

"Uncle Hugo! You pushed someone over." That was a little girl, and she sounded shocked.

"I'm well aware, Ellie," came the stressed reply. "And do you need to say it so loud?"

No doubt the man was mightily embarrassed, and her loud voice would only attract more attention.

The girl laughed. The type of laugh children had when they knew they were being a pest and found it to be the funniest thing in the world. "You had dust in your eyes, so since you can't see, I was making sure you knew."

The man snorted. George could hear the affection in his voice when he said, "Well, thank you."

"See, I *am* helpful." The girl then gasped, and George heard her footsteps as she rushed off. "Oh, no! My flowers!"

No longer distracted by Ellie, Hugo focused on George. "Oh, man! I'm so sorry. Can I help you up?"

Dazed, George nodded. Blinking his eyes open, the dust was gone. The man beside him was rubbing his eyes with one hand. The dust must have gotten him, too. His other hand was held out to George, so he accepted it, letting him pull him up.

"Wow." Hugo squinted, testing his eyes were clear. "Just one gust of wind and the dust got us both, huh?"

Just one. The very words George had used a moment ago.

Hugo smiled, but his blue eyes showed worry. "I saw it get you and tried to step around you, but it changed direction and got me, too. I'm so sorry I bumped into you; I couldn't see a thing."

"No problem at all," George stuttered. "It happens. Thank you for helping me up."

"Anytime."

For a moment, their gazes locked, but it didn't last long.

"Uncle Hugo! Look, we discovered a temple," Ellie shouted with excitement. The flowers were clearly forgotten.

As Hugo beamed at his niece, George took a second to stare. Not only was that smile mesmerizing, but the way the sun glowed around his red hair gave him a halo.

"Again, I'm so sorry." Their eyes met once again. "Are you sure you're okay?"

"I am absolutely fine. No harm done." Dusting himself off, George inclined his head. "Have a great day."

Don't go. What an odd thought.

"Uncle Hugo!" a little voice shouted, breaking their trance again. "You have to see the temple!"

Chuckling, George peered over his shoulder to see the girl. Clinging to the fence and staring at the temple with wide eyes, her utter joy put a smile on his own face. Little red pigtails bounced as she turned to face her uncle, beckoning him over. She couldn't be more than five or six.

"You better go. She looks ready to climb in."

Alarmed, Hugo checked. Sure enough, she was now reaching through to touch the stone.

That was when George saw some flowers blowing across the temple floor. The same gust of wind must have claimed them, like an offering to the goddess herself.

Heading toward her, Hugo asked with genuine interest, "Oh, wow, Ellie.

Which one is this? And how about we move away from the fence, instead of reaching through?"

"Okay, Uncle Hugo." The girl skipped back straight away. "Let's read the sign. That will tell us what temple it is."

"It is for Aphrodite," George blurted.

Ellie squealed with glee and clapped. "My favorite! Did you know she's the goddess of love and beauty?"

Shaking his head, Hugo patted her shoulder. "No, I didn't know that."

"She is also the goddess of ports," added George. He really needed to mind his own business, but he couldn't help it. It was a moment to teach.

"That's so cool!" Ellie turned to him in awe.

Hugo raised an eyebrow, impressed.

"I learned that from the tour guide," George admitted, blushing as he avoided Hugo's eyes.

Thirty-four and blushing. Wonderful.

Remembering why he was still there, he glanced around, but Daphne was gone. Such a shame.

"Thanks! I learned something new today." Grinning, she grabbed her uncle's hand. "Let's go, Uncle Hugo! We have so much more to see, and the others will be waiting. Sorry my uncle pushed you over!"

The excited child led the way whether Hugo wanted to go or not. Hugo's eyes met George's one final time, remaining focused on him right up until they disappeared around the corner.

"Huh." George stared at the temple, dumbfounded. Was meeting Hugo a sign?

Chapter 1

Hugo

THERE! AN EMPTY TABLE WAS *right there*!

He had timed getting a drink very badly; it seemed everyone at the hotel was enjoying the outside bar, soaking up the sunshine at the end of the day. Having waited at the bar for a table to relax, now was finally his chance. Hugo gently moved through the crowd, sipping his drink as he went, his eye on the prize. A small table by the pool right in the sunshine had his name on it.

Just as he was about to reach for the chair, someone stepped in front of him, grabbing the same seat. Unable to stop his momentum, he slammed into the back of them. His drink went all over him, his shirt getting the worst of it. The man's drink dropped and landed on the floor with a smash of glass.

Conversations went quiet around them as people stared and laughed. After a few seconds, they turned back and carried on with their day.

Unfortunately, that didn't solve the problem for Hugo. Closing his eyes, he sighed.

Why me?

Opening his eyes again, he had to deal with this accident. "I'm so sorry!"

"What the . . .?"

The man turned around, and Hugo was stunned. Dark brown eyes met his, looking rightfully frustrated. His glasses were a bit wonky after the bump. Straightening them, the man glared at Hugo, who cringed back.

"We should really stop meeting like this . . ." Hugo tried to joke.

The man's jaw dropped, confused for a moment. His mouth was moving while he thought of how to respond.

Well, fancy that. The man Hugo had knocked over two days ago happened to be at the same hotel. And Hugo had bumped into him. Again.

Well done, genius!

Confusion turned into a small smirk. "You, again."

Well, didn't that just make Hugo's stomach flutter. The man wasn't mad. Hurray!

"If it makes you feel better, dust did not get in my eyes this time. I just wasn't paying attention."

The man chuckled. "Or perhaps it was deliberate. That *is* twice now."

Fake sobbing, Hugo pleaded, "Don't remind me."

"I am assuming this happened because you were waiting for a table like I was, spotted this one, and came over?"

Hugo nodded, then swept his hand out. "But, of course, the table is yours. I'll let the staff know what happened and I can happily grab you another drink for your troubles. What can I get you?"

The man's lips quirked. Hugo should really stop paying attention to those lips, so he looked at his eyes instead. Big mistake—they were full of mischief.

"A beer is fine."

Looking at the label on the broken bottle, Hugo made a note of what to get. Snapping his fingers before making finger guns, he replied, "Coming right up!"

Why? Why? Why?

Could this get any more embarrassing?

"Oh, your shirt is wet." The man's eyes were glued to the wet patch, making it slightly see-through. Were his eyes darkening?

Well, well, well. Someone likes what they see.

Which made him blush. The stranger was definitely his type, as he was slightly taller than Hugo, dark-eyed and dark-haired. The light blue glasses were super cute, and his shorts, sandals, and short-sleeved shirt showed off some lovely, tanned skin.

Without thinking, Hugo whipped his shirt off. Many around the bar were shirtless since it was by the pool. It was also warm, so he didn't mind. Using it to pat his chest before tucking it into the back of his shorts, he shrugged.

"I'll dry off soon." Checking the man's clothes, he asked, "Did I get any on you?"

Amused, he responded, "Why? Hoping I will take my shirt off, too?"

"I'm game if you are."

Why, oh, why am I not thinking before speaking?

The man's jaw dropped, and he went a beautiful bright red.

"Please forget I said that," he begged. His voice had gone higher in panic. "I'm going to go now. And get your drink. And then leave you alone."

Turning around, he nearly bumped into someone else. Oh, goodness gracious.

Apologizing *again*, he rushed off. It didn't take long to admit his accident, get some more drinks, and return to the table. A member of staff had followed to clear the mess away, which started another round of apologizing. Luckily, they just laughed it off.

At the table, the man was now seated and watching Hugo, as if waiting for his return. Gulping, Hugo put down the beer like it was on fire.

"Right, I'll leave you alone now. I'm so sorry, again, and I hope you have a great evening."

Attempting to turn around to do just that, a hand grabbed his arm. "Wait!"

Turning back to look at him, Hugo was confused.

"Why not join me?" the man asked, looking just as shocked as Hugo felt.

Hugo hesitated. He wouldn't mind sitting with the cute guy, but they hadn't had such a great start. "Are you sure that's a smart idea? I might accidentally knock you over again."

"I am sure we can risk it."

"Then I'd love to join you." *And embarrass myself even more.* "Thank you."

Slowly, he sat down, giving the stranger time to change his mind. He didn't.

Taking a sip of his beer, he watched Hugo peeling a label off his own bottle. Suddenly going shy, Hugo had no idea what to do or say.

At least he was sitting at a table now. Success!

Thankfully, the man knew what to do. Holding out his hand, he said, "You have taken your shirt off, so the least I can do is introduce myself. I am George Braxton."

Shaking it, he responded, "Hugo MacIntyre, and it's lovely to meet you. What brings you to sunny Rhodes?"

Sitting back, George closed his eyes as the sun hit his face. It made him glow, showing a golden tint to his hair. Well, at least Hugo wasn't staring at his lips and eyes anymore. Just all of him.

"I came here for a vacation," George answered. "I love to soak up the sun, eat local food, and learn about the history. You?"

"Nice. I'm doing the same and came with my whole family." Feeling a bit more relaxed, Hugo got comfortable and took a sip of his drink. "My parents, my brothers and their wives, and my niece. We take a family trip every year and have done it for as long as I can remember."

"That is really lovely." George sounded wistful as he opened his eyes, meeting Hugo's. "No partner of your own?"

George choked on his drink, obviously not meaning to ask that. Hugo grinned.

"Nope, no partner. I have my wingman, though. Ellie certainly keeps me on my toes." Tilting his head, he watched George. "What about you? Who are you traveling with?"

Shrinking a little, George took some time to answer. It made Hugo feel guilty and want to take the question back. Clearly, it was a sore spot.

"I am on my own. I do not have any family. No partner either, and my friends all have lives of their own. Traveling with me in the summer is expensive, especially as I can only go during school breaks. I am a teacher, you see. So, better to go alone than not at all."

Hugo's heart went out to him. "I'm sorry to hear that."

Shrugging, George took another drink. "It is what it is."

Wanting to lighten the mood, Hugo changed the subject. "It's cool that you're a teacher, though. I'm a teaching assistant!"

That bit of information caught George's attention. "Oh, wow. What do you teach?"

"I'm in primary education, currently with fifth grade," he answered proudly. "I help teach a little bit of everything, but my favorite is geography. I just finished my first year."

"That sounds challenging." George pouted in thought. "I cannot imagine working with younger children. I work in secondary education teaching history and religion."

Hugo scrunched his nose up. "I can't imagine working with teenagers."

George chuckled. "It has its moments, but I love it."

"There you are!" a voice interrupted them.

A shadow loomed over their table, blocking out the sun and making it cold. Hugo scowled at his oldest brother, Cristian.

"We were expecting you back by now, so I came to find you. . . ." Cristian stared at George, then looked at Hugo very confused. "Why are you shirtless?"

"It's hot, duh," Hugo retorted. Unfortunately, Cristian knew him well and waited for the real answer. "Fine. I bumped into this lovely gentleman while trying to claim the table and threw my drink over myself."

Sighing, Cristian glanced up to the sky. Probably praying for divine intervention to smite down his baby brother.

George didn't help. "And threw my drink all over the floor."

Closing his eyes in despair, his brother replied, "You're a walking accident. Honestly, this is the second person you've knocked into since we got here."

Hugo smirked. "If it makes you feel better, it's the same man."

Cristian's eyes were open again, this time with disbelief, then he grimaced at George. "Ah, so you're the man my idiot brother mercilessly tackled to the ground."

"I did *not* tackle him to the ground!" Hugo responded indignantly.

"That's not what Ellie said," Cristian crowed. "She said you knocked him over and wrestled him to the ground."

She hadn't. Cristian was just being a butthead.

Concerned, George responded, "I assure you I was just knocked over. No wrestling involved."

"And I'm sure my brother is very disappointed by that."

Hugo had been taking a drink but ended up spitting it out in surprise, covering his brother. Some of it even came out of his nose. Very dignified.

"That's gross!" Cristian snapped.

"Serves you right for being a butthead."

Rolling his eyes, Cristian tried to goad him. "You're twenty-four, come on, be a bit more creative." His brothers were always pushing him to use "big boy" words, finding it hilarious that he never did.

"Some of us work with children so we need to mind our language."

Watching their bickering, George got another word in. "I apologize. It seems I have delayed you for something."

Beaming, Hugo focused on the man he wanted to look at and talk to. "We watch sunsets together as a family."

The longing on George's face did it.

"Why don't you join us?" Hugo asked.

Surprise flittered across George's face. "But I am a stranger."

That had never mattered to Hugo, nor his family. They all made friends easily. "Everyone's a stranger until they meet. How else do you make friends?"

Looking unsure, George asked Cristian, "Would you mind?"

"Of course not," he answered. "Say the word and me and our brother, Dylan, can beat him up for you, or share embarrassing stories about him. Consider it his penance for knocking into you *twice*."

Ever so happy, George nodded. "I would love to join you."

Cristian snorted. "You say that now, but my daughter hoped to see you again. She has *questions*."

A whole massive list of them since he seemed to know about Aphrodite, and she wanted to know what he knew.

"I do not mind."

"Come on, then." Standing, Hugo offered his hand to pull him up. This was almost becoming a habit. "Let's go watch a sunset."

George looked absolutely ecstatic as he took it. And Hugo's heart skipped a beat.

Chapter 2

George

GEORGE HAD COME TO RHODES expecting to explore the island alone, just like he always did whenever he traveled. What he had not expected was to meet a family four days into his trip that basically claimed him as their own. And he was completely thrilled by it.

Meeting Hugo at the temple had left him hoping to see him again, already drawn to the other man. Being bumped into that second time had been frustrating, until he'd seen who was behind him. It quickly turned to surprise as his silent prayer to see him again was answered.

An invitation to see a sunset with the MacIntrye family had started as an apology but had quickly turned into something more. Sitting on that beach beside Hugo had started a friendship.

That same evening, the family had found out he was on a few of the same excursions as them and asked if he wanted to join them instead of exploring alone. Originally, he'd said no. Feeling awkward, he hadn't wanted to intrude. But when they ended up at the same place to eat, or the same shop to buy souvenirs, they had absorbed him. Eventually, he had agreed. It felt good being part of a group.

Seeing Hugo for the majority of the past few days sent butterflies through George's body. Starting to crave seeing Hugo's smile and hear his voice, it was like they had never been strangers. A few times, George had caught Hugo staring at him, his eyes darkening. However, other than talk, nothing had happened. Was it too soon for anything more?

What did Hugo think of him? Anything romantic?

George certainly thought of Hugo. Knowing Hugo was ten years younger had made him hesitate, but it didn't seem to bother anyone else. It never came up, which helped him relax and consider future possibilities.

It also helped that Hugo was a teaching assistant, so he understood George's workload. He was funny, and kind. Welcoming. Everything George had ever wanted.

It had been the loveliest few days, having people to talk to and travel with. How he had missed having someone with him, seeing new places and sharing those memories. Then sadness crept in, reminding him he wouldn't always have this. Once he returned home, reality would return. That meant no Hugo, or Hugo's family. He was going to make the most of their company while he could.

"George! Look at my photographs!" Ellie said, patting his shoulder.

Feeling queasy, George opened his eyes to smile at her. Plonking herself down on the seat beside him, she put a photo album in his lap containing printed photos of the family's adventure in Rhodes, and the first photograph he saw included him, looking happy.

"Mummy and Daddy bought me a camera that prints pictures so I can make my own album this year," she told him, leaning on his arm so she could see them with him. "I have an album for every holiday I have been on, so I'll always have memories. I was too little to remember some of them."

What a lovely idea. "Where have you been?"

"Barcelona when I was a baby, then Lake Como, Berlin, Florida, Rome, and now here!"

"That is amazing!" George replied.

It was heartwarming that they chose somewhere as a family and created memories together. George had never had that as he was an only child, and he had lost his parents when he left college.

Kicking her feet up and down, she asked, "Where have you been?"

"Lots of places," he answered. "I have been to Florida, too, as I wanted to go to the beach. I went to Toronto to see a hockey match, then Machu Picchu in Peru. I think you would all like Athens. You can go on a bus trip to the temple of Poseidon at Cape Sounion to watch a sunset there."

Her eyes lit up, and he knew exactly what she was going to say to her parents. She loved Greek temples and had spent many hours talking to him about mythology. No doubt she would want to go, which is why he'd suggested it since they all loved sunsets.

"I want to go!" Just like he'd thought. "Was it your favorite place?"

"It was," he admitted with a bob of his head. "Until I came to Rhodes, met all of you, and got the chance to talk to a fellow historian."

Ellie giggled, realizing he meant her.

Every morning, she had a list of questions, and he had thoroughly enjoyed answering them. Some of them required research, meaning he learned new things, too.

The young girl laughed in delight. "This has been my favorite vacation, too. We got to meet you, and you've made my Uncle Hugo really happy. You're our friend." His heart swelled at her words. Ellie poked him, changing the subject. "We haven't looked at my photos yet. You're supposed to start at the beginning."

"Of course. I am sorry."

Closing the book gently, he opened it like he was told. Together, they looked at photographs of the family at the airport. The hotel. There were some trips they had gone on including a boat ride to Marmaris in Turkey, then the Valley of the Butterflies, and Rhodes Town. The place they had met was captured forever in her photo album.

After that, he started appearing in the photos, and he held back happy tears.

The first picture with him was when he reached the beach with Hugo and Cristian. Hugo was running off in the background to grab a hat from the sea.

Feeling nervous, George followed Cristian and Hugo. The family spotted them and waved, then peered behind them to look at George.

"And who's this?" a man asked. George could only assume he was Dylan since he looked exactly like his brothers.

"That's the man Uncle Hugo knocked over!" Ellie shouted excitedly. "He found you again! Yay!"

"Yeah, and get this, he knocked into him again and took out his drink," Cristian gloated. "I just found them at the bar after Hugo's accident. So, we invited him to watch a sunset with us in hopes he forgives our dear brother."

Dylan laughed. "Say the word and we throw him in the water!"

Smiling, George shook his head. "Thank you, but I assure you it is not needed."

Dylan pouted, disappointed.

"Anyway!" Hugo clapped his hands. "Introductions! Everyone, this is George. George, you've met Cristian and his daughter, Ellie."

Ellie waved, so George waved back.

"The woman with the blonde hair is Cristian's better half, Denise." Hugo pointed as he went. "That's Dylan. Next to him is his better half, Monica. As you can see, all three of us take after our dad, Oliver."

The older man chuckled proudly. Hugo wasn't wrong; all three sons were red-headed and blue-eyed, just like their father.

"And then there is our beautiful mother, Opal."

A woman with silver hair approached him to shake his hand. "Welcome, George."

"Thank you for having me."

Monica's hat got caught in the wind, ripping off her head and rolling across the sand. Predictably, it ended up in the water. Her dark hair whipped around her face.

"Dylan, my hat!"

Dylan stared at it and waved as it got pushed about in the water. "Bye, hat!" His wife was not impressed. "Fine, I'll go save the hat, but if I get attacked by sea creatures sent by Poseidon, that's on you."

Ellie laughed hysterically at that.

"I'll get it," Hugo offered, running toward it. "Looks like I'm going in the water after all."

The next photograph was taken during the sunset, the sun proudly shining in the background. George was sitting beside Hugo on the beach, looking out at the sea. Both of them were laughing without a care in the world.

"Have you ever watched a sunset before?" Hugo asked, splashing his feet in the surf.

"A few times," George responded. "But I have never made a habit of it. Why do you all enjoy them?"

Hugo gazed at his family fondly. "We do this to make sure we have quiet time at the end of the day. Time to reflect and realize how lucky we are. We are all together, on vacation, seeing the end of another day. Each moment is precious and never promised."

After that, George knew he would appreciate them more.

George had loved watching them all together, noting how at ease they were. There was so much love in this family, and he had been blessed to be included for a short while.

"Next page, George! Go! Go!" Ellie prompted, poking him to hurry up.

George chuckled, enjoying the memories this brought on. On the next page, it was a trip to Kalithea Springs that George didn't go on, as he had his own plans that day.

The next one of him was at Prasonisi Beach, standing with Hugo in front of the sea.

Practically doing jumping jacks on the sand, Hugo shook him enthusiastically. "I've wanted to come here for so long. Did you know this is where the Aegean Sea meets the Mediterranean? Isn't it beautiful!"

Hugo looked more excited than a child at Christmas. Running into the water, he laughed with his arms raised into the air.

"Come on, George, join me!"

George was definitely more into history, and when he talked about it, the family listened. It was the same for Hugo. When he talked about geography, and his other passion, geology, everyone was drawn to him. George could listen to him all day.

Next was the Acropolis of Lindos. It had been a scorching hot day, and the group photo showed everyone in thin, long-sleeved shirts and trousers to protect their skin. George was in the center, looking like he belonged.

Standing in front of the temple of Athena Lindia, Ellie squealed in excitement. "Another temple! Quick, we need a group photo!"

"I can take a photograph if you want?" George asked, wiping sweat from his forehead. "I can make sure you are all in it."

Ellie looked offended, and Hugo was trying to hide a laugh. "Don't be silly. I can ask the nice tour guide. You have to be in it, too!" Looking unsure, she asked. "Unless you don't want to be in it?"

Not wanting to upset the girl, he explained, "This is a precious family moment. I do not want to intrude."

Oliver patted his shoulder. "You're not intruding at all."

Pleased that was sorted, Ellie ran over and asked. The tour guide was more than happy to do it.

Hugo stepped close to him and winked. "Can't get out of it that easily." Pointing at the camera. "Smile!"

That was when he felt Hugo's arm wrap around his shoulders and Ellie's arm around his leg. George had never smiled so wide.

The last page of photographs were from when they walked around the area of the hotel, Faliraki. They'd gone shopping and sat on the beach. Not once did he look awkward, and not one of them looked annoyed with him there. They had wanted him there.

With the back cover closed, George breathed to hold back happy tears. Such wonderful memories.

The family spent most of their days outside the hotel, exploring new places. Sometimes they split up to do different things. However, they always made sure to watch the sunset together at the end of the day, eating dinner and relaxing. Family time was important to them all, and George had been included. It meant the world to him.

Today, they were on a ferry on the way to the island of Symi, which was why George was feeling unwell. Never having been on a boat before, he'd just discovered he was prone to seasickness. Ellie was doing her best to distract him.

"They are lovely photographs, Ellie."

Beaming up at him, he couldn't help but smile back. He could see a thought cross her mind as her eyes went wide. "Before I forget, these are for you."

Fishing in her bag, she pulled out some loose photographs. He owned no photographs of himself on his travels unless they were selfies. These showed various bits of his adventures with the family, many including Hugo.

"These are amazing, thank you so much. Are you sure I can have them?"

Nodding enthusiastically, she answered. "Yep! So you remember us. Mummy said that because you met us at Aphrodite's temple, it's a sign you're a good person. The goddess wouldn't send anyone mean."

George's heart fluttered, pleasing him to know they trusted him and were gifting him these precious moments.

"I will treasure them forever."

Walking over, Hugo looked concerned as he handed George a bottle of water. "How are we feeling?"

Considering George had nearly thrown up on him before Hugo managed to hand him a bag, he had every right to be concerned. Though talking to Ellie had really helped.

"Better now that Ellie is distracting me."

She clapped. "Yay!"

Slumping in relief, Hugo said, "That's good." The boat had stopped and everyone was starting to disembark. "Time to get off. Hopefully that will help even more."

Rising, George's legs wobbled. He still didn't feel so good. He didn't bother to take in his surroundings as he got off the boat; instead, he took deep breaths once he got on land. Not one of them laughed at him. They waited patiently.

Once his stomach settled, he opened his eyes to stunning blue water and sweet little buildings. It was truly breathtaking, and well worth the discomfort to get there.

Nodding to signal he was ready, they explored the beautiful little island together. Ellie was up ahead, taking her photographs. Hugo stayed close, chatting away.

"The island is around twenty-two-point-four square miles with just over two-thousand-six-hundred inhabitants. Symi Town is also known as Gialos," he told them. "There are a few beaches on the island, including one called Agios Emilianos Beach, named after a nearby chapel. Something of interest for the historians of the group: there are remains of a venetian castle overlooking the harbor."

George couldn't take his eyes off him. Ellie was already searching for the castle.

It saddened him. With only today left of his vacation, he would miss them tomorrow. Hugo most of all.

George was falling for this man. So quickly, too, that it was almost unbelievable. He wouldn't change it for the world, but would he ever see him again once he left? Maybe he would if he was brave enough to tell him how he felt.

Turning to him, Hugo smirked. "What are you thinking about?"

"I do not want to leave tomorrow. I am scared I will not see you again."

There, he'd said it.

The smile he received in return was so sweet. Hugo's fingers brushed against George's as they walked. It had been no accident; Hugo was seeking permission.

Blushing, George met Hugo's gentle gaze with his own. Feeling emboldened, wanting more of a connection and to seize the moment, he clasped Hugo's hand so they could walk side by side.

"Is this okay?" Hugo asked quietly.

Bumping his shoulder, George leaned into him. "This is absolutely perfect."

Squeezing his hand, Hugo tugged him along. His family saw but made no comment. No, they acted like it had been expected.

"Good. Because tomorrow doesn't have to be the end. I don't want to say goodbye, either."

Chapter 3

Hugo

"GEORGE! I HAVE MORE QUESTIONS!" Ellie shouted once she sat down, patting the seat beside her to prompt George to take it.

Sniggering, as he knew all too well what it was like to be on the other end of Ellie's questions, Hugo took a seat across from them and leaned back to relax.

Symi had been wonderful to explore while holding George's hand. Seeing how George looked at him, he'd taken a chance, and it'd paid off. His hand had been warm in his, comforting. It was meant to be there.

They had only known each other for a few days, but it felt enough time to know. Hugo wanted to be with George. His family had accepted him, and everything felt right with the world.

Now they were heading back to Rhodes on the ferry. George hadn't looked so good on the way here, and Ellie had handled it like a pro. Now, she was doing the same thing, keeping George distracted.

Hugo enjoyed watching them. Ellie was excitable and chatty and loving, and George accepted that with no issue. He listened to every question and answered it like it was the most important thing in the world. Questions he didn't know the answer to, he would be sure to have an answer for her by the end of the day. Ellie had someone to talk to about history, and George had become her hero.

Hugo should have felt replaced, but he didn't. It was amazing to see her so happy.

George was meant for this family. Hugo knew it, and he had every intention of keeping him in his life. Today was George's last day in Rhodes, while Hugo still had six more before they headed home. That wasn't forever, but he would make every second count until George got on that shuttle to the airport tomorrow. He wanted George to want to see him once he was back home, not just think of him as a summer romance.

George was leaning forward on his chair to look at the list of questions Ellie had. "Go for it."

Hugo smiled at the two together with their heads down. Preferring geography, Hugo had never really been interested in history. Listening to George, and the way he taught it, he had absorbed so much. It now fascinated him, just to hear George talk about something he was passionate about.

"Who is Aphaea?" Ellie asked.

"A goddess of agriculture, worshipped on the island called Aegina." There was no hesitation with that one.

"Who is Socrates?"

"A philosopher who came from Athens," George responded. "I have a book about him at the hotel I can show you if you would like."

Ellie nodded. "When was the Parthenon in Athens built?"

George squinted at that one. "I want to say the fifth century BCE, but I will need to double check."

Ellie loved being able to tick off her questions and write down the answers.

These were all small historical things Hugo would never have known, and now those facts were seared into his mind.

Before he knew it, they were back at the port and getting off the ferry. George's hand had slipped into his own as they walked to the bus that would take them back to their hotel.

"Go to dinner with me," George said as they stepped into the vehicle.

Hugo paused on the steps, holding up the line. His heart beat quickly as he met the other man's eyes.

"Just the two of us," George added.

Hugo stared, absorbing what he had just said.

"Holding up the line, little brother! Get moving!" Dylan shouted.

Behind him, the crowd laughed.

"I'd love to," he answered.

Flustered from being in the way, he turned around and fell up the steps. George chuckled and caught him, pushing him back upright and led him to a seat. Sitting together, Hugo leaned into him. Their hands were still interlinked. George was looking out the window, but his finger gently rubbed Hugo's wrist.

So comforting, and so natural.

Once they departed the bus at the hotel, they all headed straight to the restaurant. His family were nearby on a different table, but it was far enough away to feel like they were on their own.

On a date.

Laughing, they talked and ate. They shared food from each other's plates, and George's mouth closed over Hugo's finger to accept a morsel. Hugo held back a groan while George's eyes danced with mischief.

Naughty man.

Hours passed, and it was time to head their separate ways for bed.

Unable to let him go yet, Hugo held his hand to George's room. At his door, George let go of his hand to cup Hugo's cheek. His fingertips were warm. Giving Hugo a second to get with the program, George slowly leaned in. His lips claimed Hugo's in a sweet kiss. Pulling back, George assessed his reaction. Waiting. Looking ever so hopeful.

Hugo's eyes moved to George's lips to watch him lick them.

This time, Hugo leaned in, desperately wanting more. This time it was harder, longer. Possessive. Hugo's hands reached for the back of George's shirt to hold on and pull him closer.

Fumbling with his pocket to pull out his keycard, George managed to get the door open and pull him into the room with him. The door closed as Hugo's back hit it. George's lips were relentless, and soft, and sweet. All Hugo could think about were those lips on his.

Breathing hard, George pulled away. His eyes were closed in bliss.

"Stay with me tonight," he invited. His voice sounded as breathless as Hugo felt.

Hugo nodded without hesitation. Looking into the room, he winked.

"Oh, no. Only one bed . . ." Hugo swiped George's lip with his finger, making sure their eyes met. George's stare seared him with so much heat. "What are we to do? Share?"

Snorting, George gently petted his chest. "I think it is too soon for more, but I would like you to stay with me. I want to spend all the time I can with you before I leave tomorrow. We may have only known each other a few days, but I do not want to lose you."

Placing a single kiss to George's lips while holding his chin, Hugo said softly, "Then as you wish, I'll stay."

Happiness flooded through his veins, wanting this as much as George did. Taking his hand, George pulled him further into the room so they could remove their shoes.

"So how do you want to do this?" Hugo asked, eyeing up the bed.

There really was only one, and there wasn't a sofa. If Hugo stayed, it would be in bed with George. He needed to make sure they were truly comfortable with it.

"If we're sharing a bed, we kind of need to know what the other does to sleep."

George frowned, not understanding.

"Do you prefer the left or the right?" Hugo asked, then added with waggled eyebrows, "Do you sleep naked? Snore? On your back?"

George laughed. "Very wise questions. I prefer to sleep on the left."

"Excellent! That works for me as I have no preference." Hugo went to the right bedside table, putting his phone and sunglasses down.

George watched, clearly liking Hugo's things in his space. "I sleep in pajamas. It is warmer here, so I sleep in just shorts."

Which meant Hugo would get to see his chest. Delighted, he responded, "I sleep in boxers."

"Since I have seen your chest many times already, I think I am more than fine with that." George looked dreamy.

He wasn't wrong. On the beach, Hugo was almost always shirtless. There was also that time at the bar. Now it was Hugo's turn to see George, and he looked forward to it.

"And as far as I know, I do not snore. I also sleep on my side," he added.

"I do snore," Hugo answered. "I'm also a cuddler."

George's grin got bigger. "I can cope with that."

Getting ready for bed, they passed each other like they'd done it a thousand times. Side by side in bed, Hugo's head rested on George's bare chest while his hand lay over George's heart. George played with Hugo's hair.

"You are sunburned," George said. His fingers brushed over the sore skin.

"It happens." Snuggling in closer, Hugo had no intention of moving.

Rolling his eyes, George went to the bathroom, ignoring Hugo's protests, and bought out a bottle of after-sun care. "Would you mind if I put it on you? It will not be easy for you to reach."

Sitting up, Hugo nodded. The sooner George was happy, the sooner they could get back to cuddling. George's hands felt so good on his back, his shoulders and neck.

Hugo groaned and leaned forward, giving George more space to work. "That feels really good."

"Good, but you need to take care of yourself. Sunburn is bad."

"I know. Sometimes other things get priority."

"Like snuggling with me?" George called out as he washed his hands.

Coming back out, he leaned on the doorway, looking so good in just his shorts. His bare chest was on full display, and his hair was spiked all over the place from Hugo's hands. The smirk really added to the sexy vibe.

"Exactly."

Walking closer, George leaned forward and dropped a kiss on his lips. "Good thing I like taking care of you then."

Holding out his arms, Hugo invited him back into bed. "Then it's only fair I get to take care of you. Come on, you have a long day tomorrow. You need to get some sleep."

Getting the hint, George kissed Hugo's forehead. "Thank you for staying with me."

Climbing back in, he wrapped his arms around Hugo and tugged the sheet over them both.

Completely relaxed, Hugo fell asleep. It was the best night's sleep he'd ever had.

"Promise to call me when you land?" Hugo asked.

Negative emotions were creeping in, and he had to hold them back a bit longer or saying goodbye would get harder. And involve tears. He was already struggling to keep it together.

George was leaving. The bus was right there behind them, ready to whisk him away.

Sensing his worry, George stroked his cheek. "I promise. As soon as I am off the plane."

Mollified for now, he stepped aside to let his family say goodbye. They'd had breakfast together to send George off properly. His family had noticed them coming into the restaurant together, but they hadn't said a word or judged. Ellie had cried, and George had cuddled her to make her feel better.

Now, she was much cheerier as she handed him some photographs. "See you soon, Uncle George."

George's whole face lit up. "See you soon, El."

Hearing George being called "uncle" made Hugo's insides twist. It was real. George was in his life and wanted by his family.

Giving them space, the family backed off a bit. Nearly everyone was on the bus now, so they didn't have long left.

Hugo gently kissed him. "I will see you soon."

"You bet." George's expression was goofy as he got on the bus. At least he could go up the steps without falling over.

Just like that, he was gone.

Hugo watched the vehicle disappear, feeling a presence beside him.

His mother's hand rested on his arm. "Oh, Hugo. My boys may look like their father, but you all take after me for love. You've all fallen hard and fast."

"Is it too fast?" Hugo asked.

Shaking her head, she answered, "The hearts knows, sweetheart. Sometimes, time is irrelevant. George is wonderful for you." Pulling him into a hug, she comforted him. "He will call when he lands. We can send him photographs, and we can videocall him to watch sunsets together. Just because he is not here physically doesn't mean we cannot include him."

"I miss him already." It felt like half of him had gone with that bus.

"I know, but a few days isn't long. Perhaps he can meet you at the airport when we land." Pulling him, she led the way back to the others. "Come on, he would not want you to miss him. He would want you to have adventures to tell him about."

Looking at his family, he knew his mother was right. He couldn't be glum and ruin the rest of the vacation; he simply had to look forward to the future.

"Okay, Mom. Let's go make some memories."

"That's my boy." Patting his cheek, his mother added, "And you never know, George may be with us on our trip next year."

Wouldn't that be amazing. The thought put a smile back on his face.

Chapter 4

George

FINGERS TAPPING NERVOUSLY ON HIS legs, George waited in the lobby.

Hugo and his family had caught an early morning flight, meaning he'd had to leave his house super early to beat them to the airport. The cup of coffee he had bought over an hour ago had gone cold. He'd thought he'd need it to stay awake, but once he'd gotten to the airport, the anticipation of seeing Hugo had left him a ball of nerves.

The arrivals screen was right in front of him, telling him Hugo's plane had landed. Soon, they would be together again.

Ever since he'd stepped on that bus to come back home, he'd felt torn in half. The photographs and videocalls made it better, but it hadn't fixed everything. The only way to do that was to see Hugo again. Hold his hand. Kiss him.

Now his leg was nervously tapping. Knowing he wasn't far made him twitchier. His eyes moved from the screen to the arrivals' door.

When a crowd started walking through, his pulse picked up as he stood, hoping to get a better view. Spotting Hugo the moment he stepped through the door, George headed toward him. Hugo's eyes scanned the room, and their eyes met. His smile lit up the whole world, and just like that, George felt at peace.

"George!"

Hugo bounded toward him at high speed, dragging his suitcase behind him as he dodged other travelers. Only, in his enthusiasm, he took a wrong step, and the suitcase took out the back of his legs. Thankfully, George anticipated that and caught him.

Taking a moment to hold him close, George whispered, "You are so clumsy."

Winking at him, Hugo responded, "Only around you. You clearly make me weak at the knees."

Laughing, he answered, "Or, maybe it is because you know I will be there to catch you."

Hugo sighed happily. "Yeah."

"UNCLE GEORGE!"

Ellie was next through the door, pulling her little suitcase and also tripping over her feet.

"Family thing?" George raised an eyebrow.

"Don't know what you're talking about."

"Uncle George! I missed you." Plowing into his leg, she held on tight as she giggled.

The little girl's joy at seeing him made his heart full. He loved her already, well and truly.

"I missed you, too, El."

"I have questions. Lots of questions. I wrote them down before I forgot." She was already waving the sheet of paper at him.

"El." Cristian rolled his eyes as he appeared with Denise, picking up his daughter while she squirmed in a fit of giggles as he tickled her. "How about we give them a moment, then you can ask as many questions as you want in the car." Cristian paused, raising an eyebrow at George. "Assuming you're grabbing a lift?"

George blushed. "If that is okay? I got here by train."

"You're always welcome," Cristian replied, walking off to the side with his daughter to give them space. Denise smiled at him as she followed, collecting her daughter's suitcase on the way.

"You can sit next to me, Uncle George!" Ellie called out.

He got such a thrill being called *uncle*, never having been called that before. This family had well and truly accepted him, and he felt loved. Most of all by the man in front of him, clinging on to his hand like his life depended on it.

The rest of the family trickled through. Oliver shook his hand, while Opal kissed his cheek. Monica waved at him, only to turn around in alarm as Dylan came through and bumped his shoulder on the doorframe, then hit the frame with the suitcase.

Ecstatic, Dylan came over to pat George's shoulder. "Am I glad to see you. You can stop this one—" He pointed at his brother. "—from constantly falling over."

Hugo scowled.

Worried, George asked, "What happened?"

"He slipped in a puddle and fell in the pool."

Hugo nodded as he cringed. Yep, it looked like he'd definitely done that.

"Nearly landed on Cristian, it was hilarious," Dylan added. "Then he fell off a big rock."

"Hang on! You *pushed* me off the rock," Hugo retorted.

"You still fell," responded Dylan.

"How about you . . ." Hugo breathed deeply, containing his annoyance. "Just go away."

Rubbing his hands, Dylan saw a chance to wind up his brother. "Come on. Use your 'big boy' words."

Hugo glared, so George pulled him close and changed the subject. "I noticed the clumsiness is a family thing?"

"Oh, yeah. We get it from Mom," Dylan answered. Their mother nodded unapologetically. "But we all have our loving other halves to save us. Which is why Hugo needs his knight in shorts and flip-flops around."

The family laughed, and Hugo squeezed his hand tighter as he leaned against his shoulder.

"Well, he is here now and has already saved him from a suitcase," George reported.

"Good job!" Oliver clapped. "Now let's head home."

Starting to walk away, the family headed to the parking lot.

Finally alone, well, as alone as one could be with people everywhere, George met Hugo's gaze.

"You came," he said, almost like he was dreaming.

"Of course I did," George assured him. "I did not want to be without you any longer."

Hugo's lips brushed against his and it was heaven. Divine. George could have this as much as he wanted, and he never wanted to let him go again. The past few days had been painful.

He'd known Hugo for mere weeks and already he was integral to his future.

"I love you," George blurted out as heat rushed to his face. Was that too soon?

Hugo's face softened as he cupped both of George's cheeks. "And I love you, too."

Those words made his heart soar.

Taking his hand again, Hugo was almost skipping as he swung their arms. "We better find the others. Ellie has *questions*."

Snorting, George responded, "I would not expect anything less."

When they reached the cars, they found family waiting. Each of them had a happy expression as they glanced at their clasped hands. Ellie was cheering.

Finally, he belonged. And it felt so right.

Epilogue

Hugo

Three Years Later . . .

"ANY REGRETS?" HUGO ASKED, BRUSHING wind-blown hair from George's face.

He highly doubted George did, but he wanted to tease him. Today had been a long day of sightseeing, temper tantrums, and a whole lot of questions.

Once done with his hair, his husband wrapped his arms around him from behind and kissed the top of his head. Clasping their hands together, George played with Hugo's ring, which he'd had specially made with a rose quartz. Proof that this rockhound was all his.

Hugo was playing with George's ring, too. Taking the time to choose something special, Hugo had been so excited when he'd found this one. George loved his rose gold ring, the color of a sunset, with the Greek key design as a reminder of how they met.

Before them was the sunset George had told Ellie about years ago. The temple of Poseidon at Cape Sounion was truly captivating.

"Coming back to this area?" George asked, confused. "No. Being with you all makes it so much more special, and I have been to places I did not see last time."

Shaking his head, Hugo turned so they were facing each other. Their arms were still wrapped around the other. He winked as he continued his teasing. "No, being with me and marrying into this family."

Searching the crowd, they located each member of the family. George smiled fondly at all of them, showing how much he loved them.

Cristian and Denise were talking to Ellie, who was holding a notebook and making lists, just like she always did. Her parents smiled at her with such pride.

"So, what is on the itinerary, El?" Denise asked.

"Tomorrow we're going to Delphi to see the temple of Apollo," Ellie responded. "Then the next day is the temple of Zeus and the Parthenon!"

Her love of history was still as strong as ever. In fact, it was stronger now that she had a history teacher for an uncle.

Monica and Dylan were trying to take a stick off their eighteen-month-old son, Daniel. He'd found it on the ground and had claimed it. Any attempt to remove it made him scream and run.

Hugo's parents were holding each other as they sat on the rocks, watching the sun go down over the beautiful blue waters.

"Let me see, do I regret having a family?" George narrowed his eyes. "Moving my whole life so I could work closer to you, which got me a job I really enjoy? Having people to travel and explore the world with?" George cupped Hugo's cheek and leaned in for a kiss. "Do I regret moving in with you before marrying you, the love of my life, and taking your name? Never. You were sent by Aphrodite herself, and I will never regret meeting you."

Hearing those words sent joy zipping through Hugo's veins. He couldn't possibly love this man more.

"Sent by Aphrodite?" Hugo asked with a raised brow.

"Did I never tell you?" George replied, and Hugo shook his head. "The day we met, I had just made a plea at Aphrodite's temple, hoping she would send me love. As soon as I did that, that dust cloud appeared, and you collided into my life."

Could it be possible that the goddess herself had intervened? He would thank her every day for doing something so wonderful.

"I didn't collide . . ." Hugo retorted. Although, that was exactly what he had done. "It was a gentle stumble."

"I ended up on the ground," George reminded him.

"Details!"

Rolling his eyes, George kissed Hugo's forehead. "Anyway, I asked for love, and love was sent to me. *You* were sent to me."

"Sent by Aphrodite herself," Hugo added, feeling ever so pleased. There was no joking, just absolute love in his statement.

"Exactly that, in that big cloud of dust." Leaning closer so only Hugo could hear, George whispered, "I will thank her every day and hold on to this treasure forever. I am never letting you go."

"Good, because I've no intention of letting you go, either."

Kissing him deeply, George only stopped when they needed to breathe. They turned back to face the view they came to see. The sun disappeared, and the sky turned pink, as if Aphrodite were blessing them once again.

About the Author

Rowen Burrows was born and raised in Warwickshire, UK, and currently lives with her husband and miniature poodles. She has a background in museums. Her main focus is paranormal romance, but she has recently delved into contemporary romance, as well. She is currently working on three series titled The Wing Mate Series, The Legends Series, and Sweet Christmas Standalones, as well as short stories for anthologies. Rowen started her writing journey at a young age, but in 2023, at the age of thirty, she decided to push herself and share her stories with the world.

You can find Rowen on:
Instagram & Facebook: @rowenburrowsauthor

WHEN LIGHTNING STRIKES

When Lightning Strikes

Melissa Cate

STEPHANIE SIGHED AS SHE WATCHED Lexi hurry around the hotel room, grabbing her clothes from random places and throwing them into her suitcase.

"How are you this messy when you travel? Your office is like neat freak city, but this room has been a disaster all week."

Lexi laughed. "I have to be orderly at work. My private space at home, though? Always chaos. Traveling for work is a mix, so more like . . . organized chaos."

"Now that you mention it, I remember Dani complaining about that a few times growing up." Stephanie raised an eyebrow. "Does Nicholas know this about you?"

Lexi bit her lip as she shoved the last thing—a pair of shoes—in her suitcase and zipped it shut. "He knows that I'm messy. Thankfully, he's like my brother—all neat and tidy. Nice complement to me, don't you think?" She grinned. "Can you believe he drove here to surprise me? I mean, it's not unlike him, but I'm still stunned. And his plan to drive up to Chicago for a couple of days? I get to see the Fourth of July fireworks in Chicago! I bet they're so much more amazing than Portsmouth's. The ten minutes from Stansville to Portsmouth is more convenient, though."

"No doubt." Stephanie slumped onto the chair in the corner of the room. "I just have to ride home with Doctor San—Toby—by myself." It was difficult to call the pediatric oncologist by his first name, as he'd requested, but she was trying.

Lexi stopped and sat down. "Are you okay with that?"

Stephanie put her hands over her face. "I'm just so embarrassed!" She peeked through her fingers. "You know I can barely carry on a conversation with him."

Lexi giggled. "Is that all?"

Stephanie stood. "Is that all? Is that *all*?!" She started pacing the room. "When I first met him at karaoke, I had to leave because I seemed to forget how to form words around him." Stephanie held up her hand when Lexi tried to interrupt. "Then, on the way to this conference, you made me sit up front while he drove. You talked more to him from the backseat than I did sitting next to him! What are we going to do for a nearly seven-hour drive from Peoria to Stansville?!"

Lexi wrinkled her nose. "Radio?"

Stephanie threw a pillow at her.

"Really, though, Steph, the man is interested in you. Just be your normal, awesome self."

Stephanie groaned. "There's no way he could still be interested after hearing my incoherent babble on so many occasions. Maybe knowing that will take the pressure off this ride home."

"There you go, then." Lexi smiled. "Nicky's waiting for me in the car. I told him I was just grabbing one more thing." She brought her voice to a whisper. "I didn't tell him it was my whole suitcase." She hugged Stephanie. "Have a fun trip. I'll see you in the office next week. Give Micah a squeeze for me."

Stephanie's face softened as she thought of her three-year-old son. "I will. You have a good trip, too, boss."

Lexi squealed and hurried out.

"Might as well grab some breakfast."

Stephanie grabbed her keycard and slid it into her pocket. As she waited for the elevator, she thought about everything she'd learned at the conference. Lexi's instincts had been spot-on when she asked her to join her; there had been plenty of sessions for her to attend as the business manager. She was anxious to put her notes together and couldn't wait to talk to the practice doctors about what she'd learned.

The elevator dinged just before the doors opened. She started to walk inside when she realized Doctor Sanders—*Toby*, she told herself—was in there. She turned, content to make a beeline for the stairs, when he spoke. "Stephanie? It's just an elevator. You don't have to talk to me if you'd rather not."

She bit her lip and stepped back inside, noticing he was also headed to the main floor. She gave him a small smile, but she noticed his eyes seemed sad.

Before she had time to ponder why, the elevator dinged again, and the doors opened. He held out his hand, "After you."

She murmured her thanks and rushed down the hallway to the breakfast room, hoping he was headed elsewhere. She quickly filled a plate before finding a table. *Apparently, everyone wants breakfast at the same time today*, she thought as she sat at a small table near a window with her back to the door. She whispered a prayer of thanks for her food and took a bite. She gazed out the window, people-watching, when she felt someone brush her arm. The tingling sensation that came with it caught her off-guard, and she lifted her head.

"Mind if I join you?" Since first meeting him, she'd thought Toby's voice was soothing, and that his voice alone could calm the savage beast. It had a melodic tone to it and felt comforting. This morning, though, his voice had a gravelly quality to it that she found incredibly appealing. She gestured for him to have a seat across from her. They ate in silence for a moment.

"Stephanie—"

"Toby—"

They laughed. "You go first," he offered.

She tilted her head. "Are you okay today? I mean, you seem kind of sad. I'm not sure that's the right word. Maybe melancholy?" She frowned. "What I'm trying to say is that you don't seem quite yourself."

"I'm okay. Thank you for asking. Most people don't take time to ask the doctor if he's okay."

Stephanie set down her fork and stared. "That's awful."

"I guess it depends on how you look at it. I wouldn't expect patients to check in on me, of course." He shrugged. "My staff is great, but I'm not friends with them—not like you and Lexi. And most of us doctors don't check in on each other, even if we should."

"Well, when we get back to Stansville, I'll check in on you whenever I need to call your office."

He smiled, wider than she'd seen the whole conference. "Will you now?"

She studied him before answering. "Yes, I will." She hurried on before she lost her nerve. "Or if you need to talk, you can always call Lexi's office and I'll be there, willing to listen." She took a drink of water to hide the blush creeping up her cheeks.

"I might hold you to that." He winked.

They finished their breakfast, and Toby spoke as he stood. "I think I want to take a walk before we leave. I heard the riverfront is a beautiful place to walk. Would you like to join me?"

"Sure. It's a beautiful day for a walk. We certainly have time. Dani's not expecting me to pick up Micah until this evening."

Outside, they found their way to the riverfront. Their pace was slow, and Stephanie relaxed in the quiet as they listened to the sounds of the city waking up, mingled with the birdsong and the river's hum. They stopped at a lookout spot and watched some boats on the water. Toby turned. "Stephanie?"

"Hmm?" she asked quietly, not wanting to disturb the moment.

"What's Micah like?"

She threw her head back as she snickered. As they started back toward the hotel, she tried her best to capture her son's personality. "He is a very precocious three-year-old who is fearless and happy and silly. He makes my hard days better and my good days brighter. He wants to know everything about everything, and if your explanation isn't good enough in his eyes, he'll ask someone else." She dropped her voice to a whisper. "I'm so glad he doesn't know about Google yet."

"He sounds pretty awesome."

"He really is." She thought for a moment. "He loves superhero anything and anyone who can fix things . . . you know, Bob the Builder, Handy Manny, Doc McStuffins, the Octonauts, Team UmiZoomi."

"His mom, too, am I right?" He bumped her with his elbow.

Amusement danced in her eyes. "You *know* I'm his favorite."

"I would imagine so."

Stephanie tilted her head as she turned to study Toby. "This walk seems to have done you some good. Your eyes seem lighter."

He grinned. "Maybe it did."

She smiled as she contemplated his words. For the first time, she wondered if Lexi and Dani were right about his interest. She decided to try to be a little more open—and not be so intimidated. *Surely, he's not perfect*, she thought.

●　●　●

Stephanie hummed as she entered her room. She couldn't believe she'd just had an *actual* conversation with Doctor—*Toby*. Maybe the drive home wouldn't be so bad after all.

She walked over to the nightstand, grabbed her water bottle, and took a quick glance around the room to see if she or Lexi had forgotten anything. Amazed, she realized Lexi had somehow managed to pack everything that had been lying loose earlier that morning. She walked to the front of the room to the small, doorless closet to grab her suitcase and stopped cold when it was empty. She scanned the shelf. Nothing. *Oh no, no, no.* She searched under the beds, by the television stand, and under the table. She even checked in the shower, knowing it was hopeless, but trying it anyway.

She picked up the phone and called the front desk. "Hi, this is Stephanie Aldridge in Room 212. I stepped out for a bit this morning, and when I returned, my suitcase was gone. Is there any chance someone thought we checked out?" Her hopes fell as the clerk informed her no one would be in today until after the 11 a.m. checkout time. "Okay, thank you."

She grabbed her cell phone and tapped Lexi's name. The call went to voicemail. "Ugh! Hey, Lex. It's me. Did you happen to grab my suitcase accidently? Like, in addition to yours? I can't find it, and I have no idea where it is. Let me know. Thanks."

She paced the room as she waited. When her phone buzzed in her hand, she jumped and dropped it on the bed. Shaking her head, she answered it on speaker, closing her eyes. "Hey, Lex."

"Hey, Steph, sooo—we just stopped in Rockford for brunch and Nicky mentioned he couldn't believe that I had packed two suitcases for a three-day conference." Lexi tried to keep her voice light.

"You didn't pack two suitcases."

"Correct." Stephanie could hear Nicholas mumbling on the other end. "He says he's really, *really* sorry. He thought it was my bag and tossed it in the trunk. When I came down, I waved him back in the car and put my suitcase in the backseat."

Stephanie rubbed her temple. "It's okay. It was an accident, and at least I know where it is now."

Lexi let out a breath. "Are you sure?"

"Yeah. I mean, I'll be home tonight, so when you get back in a few days, I'll get it from you then. No biggie."

Lexi's voice dropped to a whisper. "Nicky really is very sorry. He feels bad."

Stephanie whispered back. "Tell him it's totally okay, as long as it comes home in one piece."

Lexi giggled. "It better! I'll talk to you soon. Have a nice ride home with Toby. Byeeee!"

The phone call ended before Stephanie could chastise Lexi for pushing her toward Toby. Stephanie rolled her eyes. Her phone buzzed again. She opened the text that had come. Her heart swelled at the picture of Micah that Dani had sent to her. *Only a few more hours, sweet boy.*

She glanced at the time and gave a yelp. She didn't wait for the elevator but ran down the steps to the front desk to check out. Toby walked up as she was finishing. His voice rumbled as he whispered, "You travel light."

She turned toward his voice, realizing too late how close to her ear he had leaned. She swallowed hard and licked her lips as she felt his breath against her cheek. "Long story. Well, not really, but I'll tell you on the way home—well, to Stansville."

He pulled away slightly and smiled. "I can't wait to hear it."

A few minutes later, they were loaded into his minivan with the sun shining brightly on their faces as they headed east.

"So, what happened with—"

"I still can't believe—"Stephanie nodded toward him. "You first this time."

"So, what happened with your suitcase?"

"Oh—Nicholas thought it was Lexi's when he came up to help her get her stuff. She didn't know he had it until they were nearly two hours away. He mentioned that he was surprised she packed so much for a three-day conference."

"Oh, man. Shall we detour to Chicago?"

Stephanie put her hand to her chest as she declined. "No, it's fine. They'll be home in a couple of days. I won't need anything I don't have before they get back." She touched his arm. "Thank you for offering. It's kind of you."

He turned his head slightly. "It's not a problem."

She noticed a blush creeping up his neck as he gave his attention back to the road. She realized she'd seen very few men blush and decided she liked it on him. She took a moment to study his features. He was so unlike her late husband Ryan, and yet, she was drawn to him. His strong jaw, sandy hair, athletic build, and oh—those gorgeous green eyes. No wonder she was always flustered around him: the man was too attractive for her. The first time they met, she had just finished singing karaoke with Dani and Lexi. She didn't say much, but she did snort at a funny comment before escaping to the bathroom. Lexi knew him and insisted later that he'd come over because he was interested in *her*—widowed, single mom, exhausted, not-in-great-shape Stephanie. But there was no way. Not with him looking like that and her looking like—well, a tired mom.

She blinked out of her thoughts when she felt his hand on hers. Awareness shot through her, and she bit her bottom lip. She realized he was waiting for her to say something. "I'm sorry, I think I zoned out for a minute. Did you ask me something?"

His eyes twinkled. He patted her hand before putting it back on the wheel. She realized her hand was still on his arm and pulled it away. "I was just wondering what you still can't believe."

"Huh?" She wrinkled her nose. "Oh!" She giggled. "I still can't believe you drive a minivan."

"What can I say? Coaching youth sports has me doing all sorts of things sooner than I expected."

"What do you mean?"

"Teaching little kids how to be good sports. Tying little shoes. Hauling sports equipment. Buying a minivan. I always thought I'd be a husband and dad before any of that happened." He shrugged. "Wasn't in the cards to happen that way."

"Well, you have been busy becoming an oncologist." She smiled at him. "I'm pretty sure that took up a lot of time."

He gave her a wry smile. "You could say that."

"At least you have time now, right?"

"Yes, but now the problem is finding the right type of woman." He grimaced. "The sports moms find out I'm a doctor and want to set me up with their sister-cousin-best friend-niece-aunt-neighbor, and not because they know anything about me besides I'm a doctor and coach their kid."

And that you're an 11 out of 10, she thought. "That makes sense." She tilted her head. "What else do you think they should know?"

His brow furrowed and he thought for a few minutes. "I think they should know I work hard and play hard. I go all-in on things. I love my parents. I love my sister and her family. Being Uncle Toby is the best. Holidays are my jam, but I sometimes get called away for a patient. Fun-i-days, which is what my parents called them, are a blast."

"What are fun-i-days?"

"Oh, you know, the holidays that aren't actual holidays like Fourth of July or Labor Day but are really an excuse to have fun? Like Halloween, St. Patrick's Day, Mother's Day, Father's Day." His dropped and he leaned toward her. "Valentine's Day."

She felt her face heat as she wondered what it would be like to be loved by a man like him. *Maybe not* like *him*, she thought. *Maybe him.*

He sat back up. "We go all out on those days and include everyone in the family. Family costumes. Matching St. Patrick's Day shirts. You get the idea."

"That is *awesome*." She beamed.

"I think so, too." He groaned. "I guess there is one more thing they should know. It's a bit embarrassing, though."

"You don't have to tell me."

"I'll tell you." He pointed at himself. "I go all-in on things, remember?"

She tapped her chin as she considered this. "You *do* have me curious."

He focused on the road in front of him, pursed his lips, and took a deep breath. Everything came out in a rush. "I'm-a-Potterhead-I-love-all-things-

Harry-Potter-I've-been-to-Wizarding-World-four-times-and-am-going-again-in-September. Most people think I'm in one house because I'm a doctor, but I'm loyal and hard-working, soooo . . ." He trailed off as he saw her bite her lip out of the corner of his eye. "It's okay. You can laugh."

"Wouldn't dream of it." She swallowed a giggle that tried to escape.

"It's okay, really. I know it's weird for an adult to like Harry Potter."

"That's not what made me laugh. It was the delivery." She couldn't stop herself. "It was so cute and funny, like you hoped that I wouldn't know what you're saying if you said it super-fast."

His eyes widened. "Cute, huh?"

She waved him off. "I'm a Potterhead, too. Unashamedly." He eyed her with a wary expression. "Promise. I also get guessed in the wrong house. I'm fiercely loyal and protective but love to learn, which landed me blue." She sighed. "I've never been to Wizarding World. One day, though. When Micah is older and can appreciate it. Dani indulges me with an occasional Potter night, but she's not nearly the fan I'd need for Wizarding World."

"I get that. I usually go by myself. I can't wait to take my nieces and nephews when they're older."

"I bet Uncle Toby is well-loved."

"I'm their favorite. Don't let anyone ever tell you different, especially my sister." His voice dropped conspiratorially. "She thinks because she's Mom that she's the favorite, but I'm pretty sure it's me."

Stephanie smirked in disbelief. "Yeah, right," she said as she closed her eyes. So far, the drive was better than she'd been expecting.

Stephanie blinked and tried to figure out where she was. *Toby's car.* "I fell asleep?!"

Toby smiled. "Yeah."

"I can't believe I fell asleep. I've never been able to sleep in a car." She moved around in her seat, trying to find an exit sign or some indication of how long she'd been sleeping. "Where are we?"

"Heading around Cincinnati now."

Stephanie's jaw dropped. "There's no way." Just then they passed an I-275 sign, and she gasped. "Crazy." She squinted as she inspected the horizon. "What's that?"

"A storm. It shouldn't take us long to get past it since we're heading south, and I heard on the radio it's moving north."

Stephanie's stomach growled. "I think I need some food."

Toby chortled. "I think that's an understatement. Let's pull off and get something. Stretch our legs. Bathroom break. All the things. Is that okay?"

"Sounds great. Do you mind if we dine in somewhere? I hate fast food on road trips. I want time to savor my food."

Toby nodded. "I think that sounds great."

As they were leaving the restaurant an hour later, they noticed the sky had darkened considerably. Stephanie deflated. "I hope this passes quickly."

Toby's face blanched, but then he smiled and turned to her. "You know how Midwest storms are. They come on fast and hard, then float away like nothing happened."

"Meanwhile, everyone's drenched because no one thought they'd need an umbrella." Stephanie nodded. "You're right. It'll probably be gone quickly."

Toby reached out his hand, and Stephanie stared at it, confused. "Would you like to drive?" He opened his hand, revealing the keys.

"Nope, no thank you. You're doing great. I have no desire to drive, especially with a storm."

"If you're sure . . .". His voice trailed off.

"It's kind of you to offer, but I'm more of a navigator than a captain."

"All right then, let's get goin', Owen." He facepalmed and turned away.

"Did you just say, 'let's get goin', Owen'?" She stifled a giggle, knowing he was already embarrassed. She got in the minivan to give him a moment to recover.

He slid into the driver's seat and shut the door. He turned to her.. "I'm around kids a lot. Patients, sports kids, nieces, nephews, kids' church. They're everywhere. I say silly things to them. Things that I usually wouldn't use in normal conversation with an adult. I'm sorry."

Stephanie stilled as she wondered if that meant he didn't think of her as a potential date. "It's okay. I get it. 'Let's hit the road, toad.'" She tried on a small smile.

Toby reached for one of her hands, and she felt the heat of his touch flow through her. "Stephanie," he said, holding her full attention. "I want to be very clear that I do not think of you as a kid or some random person. I don't know why I said it unless it's because I'm so comfortable with you. I need you to understand that I don't pursue anyone lightly. I take relationships seriously."

She swallowed hard as she stared at his beautiful green eyes—*no way are his lashes naturally that perfect*—and realized he was watching her watch him. "I-is that, um." She licked her lips nervously and his eyes flickered to them before coming back to hers. "Is that what you want? A-a relationship? Wi-with me?"

"Stephanie, since karaoke, I've been captivated by you. Watching you perform that night, with so much life—you weren't doing it to impress anyone. You were just yourself. I was like a moth to a flame. I couldn't *not* come to the table to meet you."

"Really?" She could barely breathe, and it came out as a whisper.

His hand cupped her face, and she leaned into it, allowing the electricity between them to flow freely. "Really." He slid his hand down her arm and held her hand again. "Maybe when we get back to Stansville, we could go out sometime?"

She nodded. "I'd like that."

He lifted her hand and pressed his lips to it. "I can't wait. Let's get back."

"Me, either."

He started the minivan and pulled out, making his way back to the highway. They hadn't gone far when the rain started. With the rain pouring down and the dark sky, visibility was not great. "I think I'm gonna pull off to the shoulder until this passes." A bright flash filled the sky, and a thunderclap echoed through the minivan.

"Good idea," she agreed. "It shouldn't be long."

Just as Toby started to drive onto the shoulder, there was another bright flash and thunderclap, nearly at the same time.

"Did you hear that?" asked Stephanie.

"How could I not?" he replied, gritting his teeth. Toby seemed to be having trouble steering.

"Not the thunder. The loud pop." She scrutinized the dark dashboard. "Toby?"

"I'm sure it's nothing," he said, his jaw clenched. He slid them to a stop on the side of the road and put them in park.

She could tell he was stressed and trying not to worry her, which worried her. "Why aren't there any lights on? And the radio stopped." She fought to keep the panic out of her voice. "What's going on?" The downpour nearly drowned out her question. "Please tell me what's happening." She put her hand on his, giving a small squeeze when she felt his stress.

"Thanks." He turned his hand over and laced his fingers through hers. He leaned over and bumped her shoulder with his elbow. He closed his eyes and turned off the ignition before turning to her. "I think—and I don't know for sure—but I *think* we just got hit by lightning."

"What are the odds of that? Like one in a million?" Stephanie started typing into her phone.

"Probably. I'll check the van when it stops raining."

"So not one in a million." She turned her phone to him. "One in a hundred thousand. Apparently, it happens a lot, but still good odds." She flipped the phone back to her. "It also says not to get out for at least thirty minutes."

"Then by all means, I'll wait at least thirty minutes," Toby agreed.

Stephanie grinned. "Please do. I'm gonna call Dani." She reached out her hand to give his a squeeze after she tapped Dani's image. "It'll be okay."

"What'll be okay?" Dani's voice was loud over the phone.

"Hey, Dani." Stephanie kept the phone on speaker and talked with it in front of her. "Toby and I are near Cincinnati somewhere."

"So just a couple of hours to go?"

"Well—"

"Well, what? Wait, are you and Doctor Sanders—"

"Both on this call? Yes." *Great*, thought Stephanie, *she's in matchmaking mode.*

"Hey, Dani." He sounded weary.

"Hello, Doctor Sanders." Dani practically sang his name. "Are you guys in a tunnel? Or the ocean? You two sound like there's some weird stuff happening around you, but I can't figure out what."

He pressed his fingers to the bridge of his nose. "There's a thunderstorm." Another flash of lightning. More thunder.

"Ahh, I hear it now."

"Anyway, Dani, I'm not sure what's going on, but there was a flash of lightning and a loud popping sound." Stephanie took a deep breath. "And then the car died."

"What? Are you guys okay?"

"Yeah, we're physically fine, just a little shaken. It was weird. I've never heard of that happening."

"Wild." Dani paused. "Do you need me to keep Micah another night?"

"Honestly, I have no idea yet. Most likely?" Stephanie raised her eyebrows at Toby, who shrugged. "I'm guessing we won't be able to find a mechanic who can work on it tonight, and I don't know how long it will take once we get it in. Are you okay with that? Or should I try to get a rental?"

"Take your time. Have some fun. Be silly. Talk to adults who aren't patients' parents. Or at least one." Stephanie heard the smile in Dani's voice, and she risked a side-eye at Toby, who started coughing into his hand. She saw his grin anyway.

"Are you sure?"

"He's doing great, Steph. I'm hanging out with Josh and the kids tonight, so he'll come along with me, if it's okay with you?"

"As long as Josh doesn't mind," worried Stephanie.

"Nope. He'd fill the house if he could." Dani's voice was full of warmth. "Do you want to talk to Micah?"

"Please."

"Hi, Mommy."

"Hi, Micah-saurus!" Stephanie smiled broadly.

"Aunt Dani is siwwy."

"What did Aunt Dani do that's so silly?"

"She makes siwwy faces."

"She's good at that. Hey, Micah-saurus?"?"

"What, Mommy-sauwus?"

"I'll be home in just a few more sleeps, okay?" Stephanie wiped away a tear starting to fall.

"O-tay, Mommy-sauwus."

"Have fun. Be good."

"O-tay. You, too."

"Love you."

"Wuv you."

Stephanie put her hand to her chest.

"Steph?" Dani was on the phone again. "Take me off speaker, please." Stephanie turned off the speaker and put the phone to her ear. "Have a little fun the next few days. Don't go *too* crazy but at least get to know the man you're sidelined with. You never know what you might find."

"I'm working on it," Stephanie whispered.

Two hours later, they were at a hotel in Mason. The state trooper who helped them insisted the "best auto repair shop ever" was there. The bonus is that the owner kept it open every day that Kings Island was open, with a happy staff who could fix nearly anything, at least according to the trooper. Toby called and the mechanics said they'd see what they could do to help him out.

The line to check in seemed long, and Stephanie hoped there would be a couple of empty rooms. Suddenly, the lobby cleared. Toby stepped up to the counter as the clerk turned to him. "Checking in, sir?"

"I hope so."

The clerk gave him a blank stare. "You don't have a reservation?" When Toby shook his head, the clerk continued. "It's a holiday weekend, sir, I don't think I have anything."

"Would you mind checking?? That storm just killed my car, and until we get it back, we're stranded here." Toby used his soothing doctor's tone, and Stephanie wondered how anyone could deny him anything. He leaned in for a glimpse of the clerk's nametag and must have realized he recognized her. "Lena?"

"I can, but I don't want to get your hopes up." She peered at him over the top of her glasses. "Wait. Doctor Sanders?"

"Yes?" Toby smiled as he tilted his head, like he couldn't quite place her. Stephanie knew that, as a medical professional, he would never divulge that he knew someone who had come into his office for help.

"It's Lena McGann. You treated my daughter, Brooke, two years ago. She is doing so great now! Thank you so much!" She hurried around the desk and hugged him. He patted her back as his face flushed. She stepped back and spied Stephanie. "Oh! This must be your wife. Let me see what I can find the two of you." She rushed back around the corner and started typing. "Mrs. Sanders, you are married to a lifesaver!" She waved a hand. "But you know that already."

Stephanie smiled. "He's pretty great." She enjoyed watching him as his face reddened even more.

"Ah, yes!" Lena beamed at them. "I have a room with a king; it also has the in-room jacuzzi." She winked at them. "I was going to give it to the late check-in, but they can have the suite with two queens." She kept typing.

Toby's eyes widened as his head jerked toward Stephanie for help. "Umm . . ."

Stephanie took pity on him. "Lena, we'd prefer the two queen beds, if you don't mind. We'd rather not mislead you. We're not married, just riding together on the way home from a conference."

"Oh, dear. I'm so sorry." She wrung her hands. "I am so embarrassed." She studied them. "You'd make a lovely couple, though."

"Thank you," replied Stephanie, saving him from a response.

Lena finished checking them in. As they walked away, Lena called out, "My niece is beautiful, kind, and *available*." She sang out the last word.

Toby smiled at her. "That's very thoughtful of you to think of someone for me, but I am pursuing a beautiful, kind woman already. Thank you."

Stephanie stopped and gaped at him, her jaw dropping as she processed what he'd said.

Lena watched Stephanie's reaction. "Ohhh." She nodded her approval and winked. "Good luck."

"Thanks."

They made it to their room and walked inside. "Wow!" exclaimed Stephanie.

"I've never stayed in a suite before. I can't believe how much room we have, complete with a living area and kitchen."

"Me either. This is great. Maybe we can grab some groceries in a bit and make our own dinner here?"

"Oh, you want me to cook for you, do you?" teased Stephanie.

"Actually," Toby paused and took her hand. "I was thinking I'd cook for you."

Stephanie swallowed and bit her lip. "Okay," she whispered.

He squeezed her hand. "Great." He let go of her hand and walked to the bedroom door. He stopped, his hand on the doorknob. "Stephanie? Would you be more comfortable if I sleep on the couch?"

She blinked. "What?"

"Sharing a room while we're sleeping feels . . . intimate to me, and I don't want you to be uncomfortable."

She refused. "No, it's fine. I trust you." Her eyes flew to his. "Would you feel better if I slept out here?"

"No." His eyes grew large. "I would never ask you to sleep on a couch."

"I mean, would you prefer us to not sleep in the same room?"

"I'm okay with it if you are."

"Then we just need to figure out who gets what bed, and then get some groceries."

"Any ideas on what you want for dinner?" Toby asked as they wandered Stafford's Market, the only grocery store in walking distance.

"Nothing too heavy, please. I need something light."

"Sounds good."

They meandered to the produce section, adding grapes, bananas, and tomatoes to their cart. "Tomatoes?" asked Toby.

"I love tomato wedges as a snack. Yum."

"Mkay," chuckled Toby. He picked up an orange bell pepper. "What do you think about bell pepper nachos for dinner?"

Stephanie wrinkled her nose. "Never tried 'em."

"Just like nachos, but we'll use bell peppers as the chips. It's pretty easy and light."

"I'll try anything once. Let's do it," agreed Stephanie.

Toby gave her a side hug. "I love that you're so easy."

Stephanie nearly jumped out of the hug, ready to tease him. His face was the color of the red pepper he'd put in their cart.

"I mean, easygoing. I wasn't trying to say, I mean, you've just been so chill, so easy—*no!* So relaxed and go-with-the-flow about everything. I stress about everything, even if I don't show it. To be around someone who doesn't let my stress elevate theirs is a treat. I think it's helped me be calmer, too."

Her expression softened as she touched his arm. "You've been stressing?" He nodded and she wrapped her arms around his waist, hugging him. "I'd never have guessed. You've not let on at all." She frowned. "You don't have to hide it."

He let his arms relax and surround her. "I'll try not toto. I've had anxiety forever, but you can't show it in med school, or anything that comes after. The anxiety comes when the stress gets to be too much. I often use different breathing techniques but didn't want to freak you out with weird breathing." His shoulders dropped with relief. "Somehow, you've eased all of it for me." He stepped out of the hug and held her hands. "Thank you."

Stephanie winked. "No problem." She pushed the cart and peeked over her shoulder. "What else do we need?"

They finished shopping and strolled back to the hotel, sharing laughter as they put the food away. Toby preheated the oven before washing and cutting the bell peppers.

Stephanie sat at the bar of the kitchen, enjoying the view as she watched him in the small space. "Are you sure I can't help with something?"

"You're helping by keeping me company." He slid the peppers in the oven and moved to the next step.

"I can't believe I'm eating dinner at nine at night, but there was no way I could have eaten earlier." Stephanie stood and stretched. She took her hair out of the messy bun she'd had it in most of the day and ran her fingers through it.

"Same. I meal-prep for the week so I can fix dinner quickly during the week. I usually have business work hours, but sometimes I stay late with a pa—" He turned and stared. "Uh." He coughed and fumbled for a glass.

"Are you okay?" She massaged her head with her fingers, then shook them through her hair, oblivious to his reason for feeling parched.

"What?" Toby blinked. "Oh. Yeah, I'm—" He licked his lips. "Fine." He reached to set the glass on the counter and missed.

Stephanie moved quickly around the counter, cringing as the glass hit the floor and broke into several pieces. "At least it didn't shatter into tiny shards?" She squatted down to pick up the pieces, nearly falling into Toby as he did the same.

The near fall was enough to knock Toby off-balance, and he fell, his hand landing on a sharp fragment of glass. He sucked in a breath through his teeth as he glared at his hand.

Stephanie finished collecting the remnants of the glass and tossed them in the trash. "Is it bad?"

"No, not really. Surprised me is all. Small cut. Do you mind getting me a band-aid?"

"Sure." She ran to the bedroom and came right back out. "My first-aid kit is in my suitcase." She hung her head. "Which is in Chicago." She thought for a moment. "I can probably get one from the front desk."

"There's a kit in the front pocket of my suitcase."

"There is?" Her voice matched the shock on her face.

He grinned and pointed to himself. "Doctor, remember?"

She covered her face with her hands. "Duh. I'll be right back."

A moment later she knelt beside him. "Do you want to rinse it off first?"

He stood and cleaned off his hand. When he finished, she carefully took his hand and held it up by her mouth. He watched as she gently blew on the cut, and he closed his eyes.

"Is that better?" She peered up at him through her lashes, their hands together between them. She glanced at his hand and noticed the prickling of goosebumps along his arms. She held her breath as she felt her feelings for him grow and brought her eyes to his.

He nodded and glanced at her lips. When she let go of his hands, he slid his hand behind her and pulled her close as he lowered his head to hers. She closed her eyes in anticipation. He hesitated before kissing her cheek and pulling away.

She opened her eyes, wondering what happened.

Before she could ask, he put up his hand. "Stephanie, you are a gorgeous, compassionate, amazing woman." He took a breath. "I told you, I take relationships seriously. For me, that means no kissing until I'm in a committed relationship."

Her brows furrowed, and her mouth was tight as she took in his words.

"It's just, well, take Lena downstairs, for instance. She offered to set me up with her niece. This happens with some of the soccer moms—and patient moms and my neighbor lady—who think they know 'exactly the right woman' for me. If I go out with half of those ladies and then half of those ladies expect a goodnight kiss, then I've kissed way too many women without any intention of seeing them again. No judgment on those who do that, but that's not who I am." He frowned. "Does that make sense?"

"Yes," she whispered. "It does. Thank you for telling me."

He offered her a soft smile. "Shall we eat?"

"We shall," she declared.

Toby plated the peppers and sat next to her. He reached for her hand

and bowed his head. "Thank you for this food. Please bless it and our time together. Amen."

Stephanie elbowed him playfully. "Thanks."

He nudged her back. "Of course."

Stephanie took a bite and moaned. "This is really good."

He raised an eyebrow. "You sound surprised."

"Well, if I can be honest . . .". " She trailed off.

"Please. Always."

"How did you learn to cook?"

"This is the only thing I can make."

Stephanie fought to keep her face neutral but failed. "Really?" she sputtered.

Toby chuckled. "I'm kidding. My mom and dad both love to cook. We had family cooking nights at least twice a week. That way my sister and I could each pick a meal to plan."

"That's pretty awesome."

"Yeah. They are."

"I love that you're so close to your family."

"What about you?" asked Toby, as he took a bite. "Are you close to yours?"

"I was an only child, but my parents were awesome. They had me later in life and weren't able to have more. They still are awesome, but I don't see them often. I grew up in Stansville—that's how I know Dani and Lexi—but my parents moved to Florida about five years ago to retire." She blinked back tears. "They try to come up every summer."

"Have they been up yet this year?"

"They usually come in August, just in time for the fair. We always go."

"That sounds fun. I've not been to Scioto County's yet. Maybe this year." He winked at her.

She stifled her own grin. "I bet you'd have a lot of fun."

"I bet I would."

● ● ●

Toby yawned. They were sitting in the living room of their suite, the glow of the television set lighting the room.

"Don't do that. It makes me—" Stephanie's mouth stretched into a yawn, and she pointed to it. "This." She made a face at him.

"Sorry." He checked his watch. "It's almost eleven?! No wonder I'm so tired."

"I kept you up late. I'm sorry."

"I didn't mind. I've not seen *Sherlock* before. That was fascinating."

"I've always thought so," agreed Stephanie. "I used to go to bed early, but now that I'm working, I stay up late after Micah goes to bed so I can have some quiet time, or TV time."

"That makes sense."

Stephanie gasped.

"What?"

"I just remembered I don't have a suitcase." She frowned and rubbed her hands down the jeans she'd been wearing all day. "There's no way I can sleep in these. I'm too tired to drive." Her eyes widened. "Not that I have a vehicle to drive. Crud."

"I'm pretty sure I have some extra clothes in my suitcase."

Stephanie raised an eyebrow. "I'm barely five-three. You're what? Six-two? Six-three?" She shook her head. "I don't think anything would fit."

Toby stood and pulled her up. "Come with me." He led her to the bedroom and fished through his suitcase. "Here you go." He handed her a small pile of clothing. When doubt flittered across her face, he smiled. "Just try something there. You can take the bathroom and change. I'll change out here."

Stephanie sighed. "'Kay. Knock when you're done so I know it's safe to come out." She shut the bathroom door behind her and groaned. "Seriously, Stephanie? Could this day be any crazier?" *Great*, she thought, *I'm talking to myself.*

She saw herself in the mirror and wondered, not for the first time, how Toby could possibly find her beautiful. She knew she wasn't ugly, exactly, but she thought she was average. She'd never lost the last of the weight she'd gained while pregnant with Micah, so she had more curve to her figure than she'd had five years ago, even with the yoga and dance she did on a regular basis. She pinched a spot on her waist and grimaced. She put her hand on her chest, feeling for the necklace under her shirt. She closed her eyes and thought of Ryan. *You always thought I was perfect*, she thought.

She washed her hair and rinsed off her face, thankful she hadn't put on makeup that morning. She undressed and went through the pile of clothes Toby had offered: some shirts, a pair of sleep pants, and some shorts she thought might be boxers. She hoped not. She pulled on the longest shirt he'd given her and noticed it nearly hit her knees. "Almost a nightgown," she mumbled. She drew in a deep breath, inhaling the scent that was distinctly Toby's. *Mmm.*

There was a knock at the door. "Stephanie? I called the front desk, and they brought up a toothbrush and toothpaste for you. Should I lay them on your bed?"

She opened the door a crack and reached her hand out. "Thank you," she mumbled as their hands met. She closed the door and leaned against it, touched by his thoughtfulness.

A few minutes later, she heard a knock and opened the door. "Okay. I think I'm ready."

Toby was sitting on his bed, reading, when she walked out. He laid down his book and walked over to her. He rubbed her cheek with his thumb, and she leaned into his touch, craving it. "You are so beautiful."

She disagreed but whispered, "Thank you." Even if she didn't believe it, her mama taught her to thank someone for compliments.

He noticed the necklace she'd forgotten to put under her shirt. He slid his fingers underneath the tags hanging from it. "Will you tell me about these?"

Stephanie closed her eyes and nodded. "Let's sit, though. You need to hear the whole thing." She reached for his hand and pulled him back to the living room. She sat on one end of the couch and pointed to the other end as she turned to face it.

"This must be big," said Toby, hoping he was wrong.

"It is. Are you sure you're ready for my backstory?" When he murmured his agreement, she continued. "These dog tags belonged to Micah's dad, Ryan. The ring was his wedding band. He died shortly after we found out I was pregnant with Micah."

"I'm so sorry, Stephanie. That had to have been so hard."

She nodded, willing herself to hold the tears in a little longer. "It was. Dani stayed with me for several months after it happened. My mom lived with me for a while after Micah was born. Ryan's mom lived nearby and visited me daily for nearly a year after my mom left. I was a mess, grieving my husband while welcoming our son. I don't know what I would have done without those three women." As a tear slid down her cheek, Toby grabbed the box of tissues on the table behind him and set it between them. She stared at the box as she wiped the tear away.

"How did you meet Ryan?"

She lifted her head to study Toby. "Most people ask how he died first. Like that's the most important part." She barked out a laugh. "But he had a life before that. Thank you for seeing it." She closed her eyes as the memories washed over her. She took a breath and opened her eyes. "We were high school sweethearts. We met in junior high, and I couldn't stand him. I thought he was immature and rude and all the things that junior high boys are through no fault of their own. In high school, though? Whoa, he changed. It was like one day, a switch flipped. He became this caring man who loved people—everyone, no matter who they were or what they were like. His affection turned toward me. I was a goner. I felt cherished by him every day of our relationship. Even when we fought. Even when he decided to join the Army. Even when he felt a million miles away in Iraq. Even when he was dying."

"Iraq?" clarified Toby.

"Yes. In Balad." Her watery smile was fragile. "That was one of the worst places he could be, apparently, and he was there for two tours."

"Balad? W-was he—"Toby stopped, unsure how to ask what he was anxious to know.

"He wasn't killed there, if that's what you're wondering." She pursed her lips, and she focused on her hands in her lap. "About a year after he returned, he started having a hard time breathing. He couldn't run anymore. He left the Army, brokenhearted that he could no longer serve."

"Burn pits." It wasn't a question.

Stephanie's head shot up, surprised. "You know about the burn pits?"

"One of the doctors I worked with during my oncology fellowship had treated some veterans who had all sorts of problems from there. He shared some stories with me, teaching me that sometimes what appears to be an easy diagnosis—like asthma, COPD, or lung cancer—is far more complicated."

"Sounds about right. He was given lots of different diagnoses before they finally performed a lung biopsy and discovered all sorts of garbage there. By then, though, the disease had progressed so much that he needed a transplant. We were unable to find a match in time. Micah is truly our miracle baby, only here because of Ryan's foresight when he first started having problems breathing. That's a story for another time, though."

"I'm so sorry you lost your high school sweetheart." Toby sighed. "That's so much for one person to go through. You have been—"

"Please don't say strong. Everyone says that, like it's a badge of honor I should wear. I don't think I'm strong. I simply did what I needed to do to stay alive for Micah. Ryan's mom would have been devastated to lose all of us. She's been a second mom to me. She's the one who called Dani and my mom to encourage them to stay with me. She was grieving, too, but she loved me and wanted me to be cared for, even if she didn't have the bandwidth to do it at that time." Stephanie's eyes were burning from the tears she was trying to hold in. She reached for a tissue and dabbed at her eyes.

Toby's Adam's apple bobbed as he swallowed hard. He put his hand over his mouth. "You have been, and continue to be, resilient, Stephanie. Those last few years couldn't have been easy. I'm guessing you were Ryan's primary caregiver for much of that time?" When she nodded, he continued. "No wonder you don't let anything like a missing suitcase faze you. Resilient."

She warmed at his words. "Thank you." She thought for a moment and scooted across the couch to be closer to him. He turned so she could relax into him. She rested her head against him as he put his arm around her and closed her eyes. "I think I like resilient. It makes me sound tough."

He rubbed her arm and tilted his head to hers. "You are tough," he whispered.

Stephanie stirred and sat up, taking in her surroundings. She sucked in a breath. *Oh, great. He probably thinks I'm a headcase, half-sleeping on him all night.* She stood and stretched before remembering she was only wearing his T-shirt. She winced, afraid to turn around. "Sorry," she mumbled before running to the bedroom and closing the door.

She silently banged her head against the wall. She eyed the stack of clothes Toby had thoughtfully chosen for her the night before. *I'll get something after we figure out the car.* She slipped out of the long tee, smelling it one more time before tossing it onto the bed. *Sandalwood, orange, and cinnamon, so yummy.* She eyed the pajama bottoms, trying to decide if she should tie them snug around her waist, before deciding to try the shorts. Independence Day in Ohio usually means humidity and that means shorts. She pulled them on, happy to find them longer than she'd expected. They were loose, so she rolled down the waistband. *Passable. At least they won't drop to my ankles today.*

There was a knock at the door. "Stephanie?"

She opened the door with a smile and walked out.

"Oh." He gaped at her as she walked past in his clothes and his face reddened. "I'm glad you found something to wear today. It's supposed to be hot."

"That was my guess."

"Harmon's Auto called earlier. My minivan is fixable, but they can't get to it until later today. They said I should be able to pick it up around ten tomorrow. I already called the front desk, so we have the suite again tonight."

"So, one more day?"

"One more day."

"Today's a holiday!" Stephanie couldn't believe it.

"Right? I guess the Harmon family realized a long time ago that having it open during Kings Island's season could be good for business." He paused. "Speaking of, what do you think of going there today? We're not far."

"Kings Island?! I haven't been there since I was a teenager! I used to love roller coasters." She frowned. "How would we get there?"

"I was thinking about that. I could get a car for the day, although that seems silly, since it'd be parked. Then I thought I'd try Uber? We can try that out, if you want. I've not used it before, but it's probably cheaper."

"Sounds like a plan to me."

"Um." His eyes darted to her legs. "Do you want to shop first?"

Stephanie shrugged. "I think it'll be okay." She bit her lip. "Unless you want them back now?"

Toby cleared his throat. "Nope. I'm good. I have some other things."

"Do you know what time the park opens?"

"Ten. We have about two hours or so, although they'll probably be super busy. We might want to get there early."

"Go get ready then, so we can get breakfast." She made a silly face and laughed. "I'll call Dani so she knows when I can get Micah."

Two hours later, Stephanie grabbed Toby's arm and squealed. "I can't believe I'm back here. It's been so long. What should we ride first?"

Toby opened the map he'd picked up as they entered. "Um, I have no idea. What do you think?"

"Definitely The Beast. Seriously and for real. Maybe Invertigo? I rode it when it was Face/Off." She pointed at one other. "I've heard Diamondback is crazy. I love water rides, but with your cut, we should probably skip them."

"Whatever you want. I'm all yours. Lead the way."

Stephanie tugged his hand and pulled him toward the closest coaster. She marveled at how far they'd come in twenty-four hours. After meeting in the elevator the day before, she thought he'd give up. She wouldn't answer questions and found ways to escape being near him. Here she was, just one day later, chattering about roller coasters. She was still surprised she had opened up to him about Ryan.

As he trailed behind her to their fifth coaster, she turned, smiling broadly. He smirked at her. "You're an adrenaline junkie."

"It took you four coasters to figure that out?" asked Stephanie, laughing. "I blame Dani and Ryan. When we came in high—never mind."

He drew her to him and peered down at her. "I would love to hear about your high school days. Ryan included. He's a part of your story, part of who you are. I would never deny that."

Stephanie's voice caught. "Okay." She nodded. "Okay. When we came in high school, they started me out on the baby coasters, the easy ones, you know? Then Dani convinced me to try 'the next step up,' at least that's what she told me. Ryan had gone off for a couple of rides with friends. When he caught up to us and learned she'd taken me on The Beast, he was livid."

"Because he'd wanted to take you on it?"

Her mouth lifted in a smile at the memory. "No. Because he knew that she'd skipped all the middle coasters. He was worried that it was too much for me." She sighed. "I was a little mad at Dani, but only for a bit. It was scary, but it was so. Much. Fun. I rode it again that night as the fireworks went off." She stepped back and took his hand. "Let's go!"

Toby threw his head back as he followed her. "Do you ever slow down?" he laughed.

That evening, as dusk fell over the park, he whispered in her ear. "My turn to pick." She shivered and leaned into him.

"That's really not fair," she said. "I can't do that to you. You're too tall."

He leaned down again. "You do plenty." Halfway through the day, she'd woven her fingers between his. He lifted their intertwined hands now and kissed her knuckles.

He led her to the Eiffel Tower, where they entered the elevator.

She raised an eyebrow.

He winked and whispered, "I'm going for a different kind of thrill right now."

Her lips formed an O,, and she swayed into him, off-balance. He smiled as he caught her.

When they made it to the top, Toby found a quiet corner, and she followed him. They surveyed the park from their vantage point for a moment before Toby stepped in front of her.

"Stephanie, we agreed on a first date when we get home." He licked his lips as his eyes searched hers. He continued. "I-I feel like we've moved past a first date in the past day and a half."

Stephanie's gaze dipped to his lips as she nodded and took a small step closer. "I think so, too."

Toby closed his eyes and took a deep breath. Stephanie seemed to recognize his anxiety and squeezed his fingers. He let out the breath slowly, bringing his hand up to her face. "You see me, Stephanie. Not as a doctor or a coach, but as me. You aren't afraid to be yourself in front of me, or anyone. You are you: this amazing, caring, beautiful woman. You seem to see the best in people, even if they're not on their best behavior. I want to date you, Stephanie. Just you. Is that okay with you? Because—"

She put her finger on his lips. "Yes. I'd love to see what we can have together."

He kissed her finger, and she drew it away. He brought his hand up to her hair and smoothed it away from her face. He traced her lips with his thumb, and she gasped. She focused on his mouth, and he pulled her to him. He brought his lips to hers, gently at first, then with more urgency as she responded to him. She pulled back for a moment as the fireworks began over the park. "Oh, we don't want to miss the fireworks."

His eyes lingered on her, taking in her slightly swollen lips and mussed hair. He reached up to tuck a stray hair behind her ear. "We could make some of our own," he whispered, his voice thick as he leaned in.

"Even better," she murmured, her lips against his.

About the Author

Melissa Cate has always been a storyteller— her mom would record the bedtime stories Melissa would tell at night and type them up for her. After thirty years of mostly academic, devotional, or biographical writing, she jumped headfirst back into fiction in October 2023 and was a Write on the River winner in the spring of 2024. She has finished three women's fiction novels she is preparing to query. Melissa currently lives in the Pacific Northwest with her family but is a Midwesterner through and through.

You can find Melissa on:
Instagram: @melissacatewrites

You can visit her website at:
https://www.melissacate.com

CHAPPED
LIPS

Chapped Lips

Katherine Rea

THIS RAFTING TRIP WAS THE worst idea ever, but I couldn't say no. I was barely able to get the time off work. They'll probably put me on a performance improvement plan for missing a week during our busiest time of the year, but Ashley's fiancé just dumped her for a girl he met on his bachelor's party trip to Puerto Vallarta. I had no choice.

Ashley and I have been friends ever since the day in AP Chemistry when we were partnered up for an experiment and I knocked over our beaker, spilling half of the solution before we could even add all the ingredients. We ended up getting a D on the assignment, but Ashley couldn't stop laughing about it. We bonded over that (and our hatred of Mr. P, who refused to give us a better grade even after we explained the situation), and we've been inseparable ever since. But we are *total* opposites.

Ashley is a hippy-dippy hiker chick who moved out to Boulder, Colorado, for college, whereas I stayed in San Francisco. I love everything about living in the city: the dim sum, North Beach bars, fog-swept trail runs over the Marin Headlands. The only downside? No eligible men. I mean, none. Not that I'm really looking, anyway. I'm too busy with work.

"Are you excited?" Ashley asks me, looking over the steering wheel in my direction. We left our hotel in Sacramento at 5 a.m., and I'm still bleary-eyed and wary of what's to come. Ashley, however, is in her element, and I don't have the heart to tell her that I'm more anxious than excited.

"Yep," I say, plastering a smile on my face. "I can't wait," I say out loud. But I finish the thought in my head: . . . *for it to be over.*

She glances at my face, and I can tell she's not buying my fake smile.

"I really appreciate you doing this for me," she says. "I know it's not your thing, the great outdoors."

"It's fine," I say, my tone a bit more tense than I would have liked. "It'll be good to do something different. Something out of my comfort zone."

But even as I say it, the words feel hollow. I hate being out of my comfort zone. Why would anyone *like* going outside of a comfort zone? The hint is in the name. And I've done very well for myself thus far, staying nice and comfortable, mostly indoors, where I know exactly what to expect.

Ashley shakes her head. "Try to keep an open mind today, yeah? This is our chance to get away from it all and have a bit of a reset. That's why I wanted to do it."

"Okay," I agree. "Definitely. Do you think they'll have strong enough WiFi that I can check my Slack when we get there?"

Ashley groans and rolls her eyes, but it'll only take me a few minutes to respond to anything urgent, so I don't know what she's so upset about.

We arrive at our meeting place just before seven, and I wish I'd bought another coffee when we stopped for gas. Ashley parks the car, and we pause for a moment to take in the gorgeous view of the American River snaking through the valley below us. It's clear that there won't be any WiFi here.

I open my door and take a breath of the fresh mountain air. "Is there even any cell reception here?" I mutter, waving my hand around fruitlessly as I step out. But the one tiny bar I have refuses to be joined by the others to complete the little staircase indicating service. Great. There goes my Slack check-in.

I realize Ashley has already bounded off to meet some of the other folks who will be on our trip, and I sigh and start to change from my platform heels into cheap flip-flops.

"I hope you're not planning to bring that on the trip."

I whirl around, nearly tripping over both pairs of shoes, and find a tall, scruffy man behind me. He wears a sun-faded baseball cap and a wide grin. The deep dimples in his cheeks give me goosebumps, but I shake them off.

"Sorry," I stammer. "Bring what?"

He crosses his arms, and I can see the muscles in his shoulders beneath the thin cotton of his long-sleeved hoodie.

"I meant your phone," he drawls with a smile. He looks me up and down, taking in the platform heels, the flip-flops, and my super-cute bikini top.

"First rule of rafting: don't take anything you'd be upset to find at the bottom of the river." He pauses, and glances down, his eyes flicking between my heels and flip-flops. "Do you have any better shoes? Something close-toed?"

I blow some air through my lips in annoyance.

"I'm Noah, by the way," he says, putting his hand out to shake. "I'm one of the guides on your trip today."

I grasp his tan, callused hand and notice that it swallows mine up completely.

"Claire," I say, taking my hand back and trying to refocus. "I'm here with my friend, Ashley." I gesture vaguely in her direction across the parking lot, but his eyes don't leave my face.

"Sure," he says. "Glad to have you. Get some better shoes before we get on the water."

Suddenly, he looks past me and whistles loudly through his teeth. It's all I can do not to jump in surprise. But before I can say anything, he's gone, jogging over to where they're tying boats on a trailer, leaving me staring after him.

"Who was that?" Ashley asks, suddenly at my side. She bumps my hip with hers. "He's cuuuute," she teases.

I wave her off. "No one, just one of the guides," I mutter. "Apparently I have the wrong shoes and I'm an idiot to think I could bring my phone with me."

Ashley laughs. "I could've told you that. What do you think happens if you fall out?"

I stare at her. "You didn't say anything about falling out. I might fall out?!"

Ashley gives my arm a little squeeze. "It's all part of the experience. Now come on. Let's get fitted for our life jackets."

● ● ●

Thank goodness I'd brought some running shoes for the hotel gym. I hadn't counted on sacrificing my brand-new Hokas to this experience, but the alternative was duct-taping my flip-flops to my feet, so here we are.

I feel like a dork in this faded orange life vest, matching all the other people on this trip, listening to the safety talk. You can't even see my top with it on. But at least my butt still looks cute in these shorts.

The guide up at the front of our group is droning on about how you should never stand up in moving water and something about sunscreen. The other guides are standing in a little group nearby, pretending to listen. But I can see one picking at his nails with his river knife, another staring off into space. Noah catches my eye and mouths "nice shoes," giving me a thumbs-up. Is he patronizing me? I respond with a half-smile and thumbs-up back and hope that I'm not on his boat.

"Alright," says the head guide. "That concludes the safety talk. Everyone get on the bus. We'll drive down to the put-in site and get on the water pronto."

The group gives a little whoop of excitement, and I act like I'm excited, too. I tromp onto the converted school bus with Ashley and smoosh into one of the benches near the back with her, waiting while everyone else files on.

I can hear the guides checking the boats on the trailer, and then the back door of the bus opens, and they slide into the few remaining seats behind us.

The head guide is counting us at the front of the bus, and then the bus driver starts the engine, and we're off, bumping down the dirt road to the riverbank.

"Hey," I nudge Ashley. "Do you have any chapstick? It's the one thing I forgot to pack."

"Uhm . . ." Ashley feels through her pockets. "No, sorry."

"I've got some chapstick if you need it," says a familiar voice.

I turn around to see Noah holding up a tube of chapstick with a smile.

"Oh wow, you have an extra?"

"Nah, just mine. I only have one."

I pause and look into his hazel eyes. It should be illegal to have such naturally long eyelashes.

"Oh, I . . ."

"You afraid of cooties?" Noah asks.

How am I the one embarrassed when he's offering me used chapstick? I feel like I'm six years old again on the playground. At work, this would never happen. As a project manager, everyone listens to me. I love the power that comes with that—knowing you won't be questioned or teased. But out here is a different story. What's cool in my regular life is not cool here.

"Nope," I say, feigning all the nonchalance in the world. "Not at all." I take the chapstick and smear it on my lips, then hand it back like it's not a big deal to use a complete stranger's chapstick. I can feel Ashley's eyes on me, but she doesn't say anything.

We fall into silence for the rest of the ride, looking down at the canyon walls and river getting larger as we wind our way closer to put-in. I feel like I've passed one small test, but the bigger ones are yet to come.

When we get to the put-in site, the guides hop out the back immediately and start untying the boats and topping them off with air.

The head guide gives a loud whistle, and we all gather around him. It's much colder down here closer to the water. You can see the steam of our breaths, and I wonder how cold the water is.

"We'll break into groups for our boats now," he says, his thumbs casually hooked under the shoulder straps of his life vest, which is much sleeker and more compact than the clunky orange ones we have. "The Monroe family will go with Casey, the Lee party with Aspen, I'll take Nancy, Bob, Brittany, and Alex, and everyone else is with Noah," he says, pointing to me, Ashley, and an older father with his son who looks about sixteen years old.

I don't mean to betray anything with the look I give the head guide, but maybe he senses that this is not the boat assignment I wanted.

"You're in great hands with Noah," he tells me with a smile. "He's one of our most experienced guides."

I look at Ashley, who grins and does a little dance.

"I can't wait to get on the water!" she practically squeals.

"Grab a paddle," the head guide continues to the group, strapping on his helmet. "And use the bathroom if you need it. Last chance before the bivvys."

"The bivvys?" I whisper to Ashley. I must have zoned out during that part of the safety talk.

She giggles. "The portable toilets. There's a plastic bag, and you—"

"Nope!" I say, making a beeline for the bathroom. No matter what else happens on this trip, I will not be squatting over a plastic bag in the woods.

Once I'm out of the bathroom, I walk over to our boat, where Noah is lashing down an extra paddle with some nylon cam straps over the big tubes in the middle of the boat.

Ashley and the other two people assigned to our boat, the father and son, are already there. The older man has gray hair and a neatly trimmed beard. He nods politely at me and Ashley. "I'm Daryl, and this is my son, Bear." Bear is all gangly arms and legs with a smattering of acne and the beginnings of his first mustache. He does an awkward little wave, and I wonder if this kid has spent his whole life trying to live up to his namesake. I get the feeling that Bear might have been coerced into coming on this expedition like I was.

"I'm Ashley," says Ashley gregariously, sticking out her hand and offering a firm shake.

"Claire," I say with a half-wave.

Noah pops up from the boat and grins when he sees us all making introductions. "Alright, where does everyone want to sit?" he asks.

Ashley jerks her hand in the air like a know-it-all in class.

"The front, the front! Please please please."

"Well, you're eager enough, I'll give you that," he says, cocking his head to one side, considering her candidacy. "Are you a strong paddler?"

"Yes," she says. And she's not wrong. Ashley is not just a Pilates and cardio girl like me. She actually lifts weights.

"Okay," says Noah, seemingly convinced. "We'll have you and Bear up front with Claire and Daryl behind."

I give a sigh of relief that I don't have to join Ashley in the front.

"Now that's settled," says Noah, "let's get this boat on the water."

Shocked, I realize we're all supposed to carry this huge rubber raft the final dozen yards or so to the water's edge.

"On my count," says Noah, "One . . . two . . ."

We heave the boat up on "three" like a massive suitcase, and my gosh it's heavy. I feel like my fingers are gonna get pulled off my hand from the weight. We all shuffle forward toward the water.

"How much are we paying to do this?" I mutter to Ashley, who waves me off with her free hand.

"Quit whining," she chides good-naturedly.

When we get to the water's edge, I hesitate. I don't want my shoes to get wet!

"Keep going," says Noah from the back. "Right into the eddy."

I gasp as the water seeps into my shoes and instantly soaks my socks. No one else seems to mind as much, or they're better at hiding it. But soaking-wet socks before 9 a.m.? I can't.

"Snowmelt," Noah says by way of explanation, gesturing toward the Sierra Nevadas in the distance. "Alright, everyone in!"

We scramble in, and I feel relieved to have something solid between me and the water. Noah gives us quick instruction on how to paddle—how to brace our feet in the bottom of the boat and lean our whole bodies into the paddle strokes. And we're off.

"This first rapid is called Cold Cup of Coffee," Noah yells from the back of the boat over the roar of the whitewater. I can see an undulating wave train ahead, and I start to turn back and ask why it's called that, when Noah calls, "Forward!"

I turn around to paddle just as a huge wave washes over the side and soaks me from the neck down.

It's so cold that for a second I can't breathe and forget to paddle. I hear Ashely laughing maniacally, as she's also soaked.

"Yrrrrrreeee!" she trills, like a battle cry, and Bear gives a little scream of delight as well.

The sun hasn't quite risen over the side of the canyon walls, but I can see blue sky and the edges of bright morning light dancing on the water up ahead.

"Everyone awake now?" Noah laughs, somehow (annoyingly), still dry at the back of the boat.

Now that the shock has passed, I feel more than awake. I feel *alive*. As we make our way through the next set of rapids, and the next, Noah expertly steers us from the back, and we work as a team to navigate around obstacles like whirlpools and boulders.

After an hour or so, the sun starts to warm up more. As I finally feel a bit drier, I must admit, I'm starting to have a good time.

"We can stop and swim here if you like," Noah says, pointing with his paddle toward some flat water up ahead. I can already hear the laughs and shrieks of the other guests splashing into the water from the boats in front of us.

I glance at Ashley, but of course she's game. She throws her paddle down at the bottom of the boat and jumps off the side like a little kid.

"Last one in is a rotten egg," Noah winks and somersaults backward from his seat at the back of the boat.

With that, I jump in, too. By now, it's mid-morning. Even though the water is freezing, the sun warms my face, and the life vest buoys me so I can simply float and enjoy.

After ten or fifteen minutes, the guides start to corral everyone back into the rafts, and I swim to the side and try to pull myself up. Noah pulls himself up out of the water and back onto the raft in one swift motion, making it look easy. It is not easy. It is damn near impossible. Ashley, giggling, finally gets a lift from Daryl, who heaves her up by the life vest lapels. As he pulls, Ashley kicks in the water and propels herself the rest of the way into the boat. Then she turns to help me. Try as I might, I cannot do the little kick that Ashley did. The angle is too awkward, the boat is in my way. Ashley and I keep collapsing into peals of laughter each time she tries and fails to haul me back in. Finally, she pulls me up all the way with so much momentum I land right on top of her, and we're both flopping around on the bottom of the boat like two fish. This gets us laughing harder than anything, and Daryl and Bear and Noah all join in too.

"Alright," says Noah finally, wiping a tear from his eye. "Let's regroup.

Coming up, we've got our biggest rapid of the morning: Kanaka. This one's got drops, rocks, bumps, and waves, so I need all your focus and teamwork as a crew."

I get into position and start to dial in to Noah's commands as we get closer to the rapid. I can hear the whitewater rushing louder, the tone in Noah's voice getting tenser and louder. I can feel him lining up the boat with little micromovements, telling us to stop, then forward, left, then one stroke right. And then we're in Kanaka.

"Forward, forward!" Noah yells. We paddle madly, but I can feel the boat listing slightly to the right. I see the boulder before we hit it, but I barely hear Noah roar—"Get down!"—before I feel the impact.

We don't just graze the boulder; we hit it like a pinball, and the ricochet is much stronger than I expected. Before I can even think, much less get down, I'm over the side and in the water.

"Claire!" I hear Ashley yell before a giant wave washes over my head. Even with my life vest, I feel like I'm in a washing machine. I try to orient myself so I can swim back to the boat, but I can barely even keep my eyes looking downstream. The rapids are so much stronger than they look from the raft.

I go under another big wave. I'm struggling to breathe. *This is it*, I think. I'm going to get thrashed all the way to the end of this river, if I don't drown first. And that's when I feel something, someone, lift me up and out of the water.

I look up from the bottom of the boat to meet Noah's gaze, his eyes full of concern, all the teasing gone. And I start coughing violently, the back of my throat full of bile and river water.

"Forward!" Noah yells to the three others, guiding our raft through the last little bit of the rapid.

"Are you okay, Claire?" he asks once we're safely through. I feel his hand on my shoulder and wish I didn't look so pathetic in this moment.

I give one more cough and nod, realizing my paddle is long gone. I must have let it go in the water. Noah is already pulling out the spare, which he hands to me.

I'm embarrassed and soaking wet but also extremely grateful. He saved me.

"Thanks," I say. Noah gives my shoulder a squeeze.

"Could have happened to anyone," he says. "I've swam that rapid myself many a time. Now, you're practically a veteran."

That makes me laugh, and I feel a lot less stupid about having fallen out. I'm not used to being this bad at something. At work, I'm the go-to person. I have everything under control. Maybe that's why I didn't want to go on this trip—not because I dislike the outdoors, but because of the lack of control.

We're in a flat section again, and Noah is calling commands with less intensity now. I notice he's leveraging his body, pushing the boat along the current by leaning all the way back, then prying the blade at the end of the stroke. His shirt is wet now from Kanaka, and I can see his lats flexing as he draws the paddle forward and back. I involuntarily shiver (probably because I'm cold), when Ashley breaks my thoughts.

"I thought you were a goner," she says with a wink. "You okay?"

"Honestly, I'm more okay than I would've thought."

"Really? 'Cause I thought this might spell the end of our friendship," Ashley says with a smile. "That you'll never come on another trip with me again."

"We'll see. Maybe I'm not as uptight as you think."

Ashley's eyes widen in mock surprise. "Okay! I like this new Claire."

"We'll break for lunch here," Noah interrupts, gesturing toward a beach on one side of the river.

The other boats have already pulled over, so we join them. Everyone takes off their life vests and hops out onto the shore. I try to walk from the back of the boat as gracefully as I can, but I've given up on even trying to look like I'm cool, calm, or the least bit collected out here. Noah offers a hand to help me off the boat, and I take it.

"M'lady," he jokes, pretending to doff a cap.

"Sir," I joke back. I feign a curtsy and nearly slip off the rubber tube, splashing into the water again. We both crack up at this, and he grabs me under the arms to steady me. My breath catches in my throat at the feel of his hands on my ribs, and finally, Noah is the one who looks embarrassed.

He flushes a little and mumbles, "Sorry, just instinct. Want to make sure you don't fall."

I wave it off. "Don't worry about it. Thank you for saving me again."

He chuckles drily before wandering off to the other guides, who have already gotten tables out and have started prepping lunch.

Ashley has gone to chat with other guests, so I have a little time to myself. I watch everyone from a distance and wonder if I look spectacularly silly, flirting with my guide. After all, he probably sees women like me all the time—women looking for a break from metropolitan dating life, desiring men who have calluses on their hands from work, who don't just stare at a screen all day.

I walk along the river's edge, relishing the feel of the sun drying my hair and clothes, wiggling my toes lightly in the little waves breaking on the sand. I'm so lost in my own thoughts that I don't hear anyone come up behind me.

"Claire?"

I whirl around to see Noah.

"Sorry," he says immediately. "I didn't mean to startle you."

I smile and put a hand on my chest to steady myself. "No, not at all," I say. "You must think I'm wound tight as a drum. I promise I can be fun sometimes."

Noah laughs, and his eyes twinkle mischievously. "I don't doubt that at all. Do you mind if I join you? I just want to make sure you're okay after that swim."

I nod and let him fall into step next to me. My left shoulder is almost touching his side, and I have the sudden urge to lean into him.

"I'm fine," I say. "I know I'm a little out of my element here. At work, everything has to be done perfectly and finished yesterday. I feel like I've built this persona around delivering on those expectations, but I'm not sure it's who I really want to be. Maybe it's just what I'm comfortable with."

I'm rambling, I know, but for some reason I can't stop the words from coming out.

"I understand," Noah says. "I lived that life myself, for a little while. I was an associate at PwC the summer after I graduated college."

I stop and turn to look at him: his toned, lanky figure, the shaggy bleached hair. "You were an accountant?"

He laughs. "Is that so hard to believe?"

I laugh, too, and continue walking. "Yes!" I say. "Yes, it is."

He shrugs. "Well, maybe you're right, because it wasn't for me. I realized pretty fast that I was chasing someone else's dream."

"I always thought I loved living in the city," I say slowly. "And loved being good at my job. But now that I'm out here, I'm realizing there's a lot I'm missing out on. That feel of sun and water . . . you don't get that working a nine-to-five."

Noah smiles, and I can see those crater-like dimples again. "No, you do not," he agrees.

"The only downside," I continue coyly, "is there's a lot of wind out here. And it makes your lips really chapped."

Noah looks down at me and stops walking. "Claire, are you saying you'd like to borrow my chapstick again? What about the cooties?"

"Well, that's a good point. Do you go around lending your chapstick to every city girl who makes her way out to the river?"

"Nope."

"Every girl who falls out of your boat?"

"Nope."

We're looking right at each other now, and he pulls out his chapstick slowly, brushing his thumb against my cheek with the other hand.

"Claire, I solemnly swear that the only cooties on this chapstick are mine and yours, and that I don't go around lending it to just anyone."

I smile, and I swear he's about to lean down and kiss me, when I hear a loud whistle from down the beach.

"Ayo, lunchtime, you two!" yells one of guides.

We pull back from each other, and the moment passes. I take the chapstick and apply it before handing it back.

"Thanks," I say softly.

"Anytime," Noah says.

And we make our way back to the group for lunch.

That afternoon, I focus on the water and make it a personal goal not to fall in on a rapid again. I keep my feet planted and learn to feel the movement of the boat, to anticipate how it will hit each wave. It's thrilling, and I realize that rafting isn't giving in to a total lack of control at all; it's controlling what you can and letting nature take the wheel for the rest.

When we stop at another flat-water section to swim, I'm the first one in the water, no holds barred. I even try to somersault in backward, like I saw Noah do before Kanaka, and even though I end up bellyflopping, I can't stop laughing.

Before I know it, the trip is over, and we're all getting out at the dam, dragging the heavy boats from the water so that the guides can load them back onto the trailer. It's not any more fun lugging the raft out of the water than it was carrying it in this morning, but at least I have a bit more appreciation for our boat, and I'm already soaking wet. I stopped noticing my squishy wet socks hours ago, which I would've never thought possible at the beginning of this trip. Even more surprising, I haven't missed my phone for the last couple hours.

As we're waiting for the buses to come pick us up and shuttle us back to our cars, I watch the guides stack the boats on the trailer and lash them down. Noah scrambles to the top of the pile and directs the guides below. As he hops down, I catch a bit of his conversation with one of them.

"Yeah, but you know how it is," Noah is saying. "These people have one good day on the water and go back to their high-power jobs. I live out of my car. It's not a good fit."

I feel my ears get hot and avert my eyes before either of them can catch me eavesdropping. Is that what Noah really thinks about me? That I'm that su-perficial?

I ride the shuttle back in silence, and Ashley notices I'm quieter than usual.

"You were having such a good time by the end of the day. What hap-pened?"

I shrug. "Nothing. I'm just tired." I lean my head against the window and try to swallow my disappointment.

When we get back to the parking lot, I change into my dry clothes and try to avoid everyone else, even as Ashley is exchanging numbers with Bear and Daryl to stay in touch. I just want to go home. I was right to think this trip wasn't a good idea. I was silly to think that Noah saw me as someone different, to think that what we had could be special. Maybe he's right; we just aren't a good fit. I don't even want to check my phone for messages. I just stare at the river, now far below us, soaking in one last view before we go.

I'm sitting in the passenger seat, waiting for Ashley, when I hear a knock on the window. I jump and see Noah at the window, smiling and holding up his tube of chapstick.

I open the door uncertainly and get out.

"I think you forgot this," he says.

"No, it's yours."

"What's mine is yours," he murmurs, pulling me close.

But I push back and look up at him. "I thought we weren't a good fit."

He looks at me seriously. "It depends," he says. "How much do you care about sleeping in the back of my pick-up truck? Are you willing to take a chance on a river guide like me?"

I take the chapstick from him, but instead of using it, I toss it away.

"I'll take a chance on you any day," I say, and I pull him down to kiss me, finally.

About the Author

Katherine Rea is a writer from Saratoga, California. She currently lives on California's Central Coast with her husband, two children, and an orange cat. When she's not writing, she enjoys reading, spending time outside, and traveling.

You can find Katherine on:
Instagram: @katherine_rea_writes
Twitter: @katierea17
BlueSky: @katierea17

You can visit her website at:
https://www.katherinerea.com

STARTING AGAIN UNDER THE SUMMER SUN

Starting Again Under the Summer Sun

Elizabeth Baizel

THE LIGHT STREAMED THROUGH THE cracks in the window, waking Lillianna. It wasn't fair; she had *just* fallen asleep. Their plane had arrived late, or early, depending on how you looked at it. Either way, the sun had been high in the sky when they'd reached their hotel, and Lillianna's mother had been exhausted after the trip. When they arrived, they were greeted by another crisis. Lillianna's mother was supposed to have booked two adjoining rooms, but somehow the hotel said they'd booked a suite with two beds, not separate rooms. Too tired to argue, Lillianna took the room and helped her mother to bed before falling into a deep sleep.

Now, with bright sunlight hitting her directly in the eyes, there would be no getting back to sleep. Having fallen into bed at six, still in her travel clothes, there was no need to wake her mother to search for a fresh outfit. She grabbed her phone before creeping out of the room. Her mother stirred in the next bed, rolling over and away from the light.

Downstairs, a complimentary breakfast was laid out with a variety of the usual items found at hotels, such as eggs, bacon, and rolls. However, there were also a few items that seemed unique to Iceland, including blinis (some with fruit and some more savory), skyr, and cured fish. Lillianna reached for some coffee before grabbing a pastry and a small scoop of skyr to go with a fruit blini.

She had eaten on the plane but wasn't entirely sure that what they'd served her would qualify as real food. The blini she was eating, on the other hand, was delicious. Lillianna had never had a blini in her twenty-three years on this planet and was very disappointed that this was her first. Where had they been all her life?

She put her coffee down at a small table and went up to get several more, only to stand by as a tall man with short, cropped, black hair and a blue sweater took the last one. She watched, displeased, as he walked back to his table and sat down across from a beautiful redheaded woman with sparkling blue eyes and a million freckles. He cut the treat and shared half with the woman as she giggled and slapped at his hand but took the breakfast.

She approached a staff member. "When will there be some more of those delicious blinis?"

The woman with a name tag reading Anna looked confused before registering Lilliana's question. "I'm sorry, Miss," she said in a thick accent. "But there are no more, breakfast is over soon."

Lillianna looked surprised before checking her watch. It was almost 10 a.m. Icelandic time. She sighed heavily. Thankfully, her mother had planned for today to be a recovery day. "Do you mind if I take some things up to my mother? We had a long flight, and she'll need something to eat with her medications when she wakes up."

The woman nodded and even helped Lillianna put together a small plate for her mother. As Lillianna walked out of the breakfast area, the last blini-eating man stared at her. In admiration or admonishment, she couldn't decide. She didn't care either way. She was going to take care of her mother, for however long she had left.

Back in the room, Lillianna debated waking her mother with the plate of food or letting her sleep more. She gently tapped her mother's shoulder.

"Five more minutes," she mumbled before rolling to the other side.

That answered Lillianna's question. She placed the plate in the small mini fridge and left her mother a note saying she would be in the lobby or just outside the hotel if she needed her.

Lillianna made sure to grab her bag and hoodie before once again sneaking out of the room. Back in the lobby, she remembered this morning's debacle and approached the front desk. "Excuse me," she said.

A tall, pale, blonde woman with startlingly blue eyes and a name tag stating Ingrid emerged from behind the partition.

"Can I help you?" she asked sweetly.

"Yes," Lillianna started. "Earlier this morning, my mother and I checked in. We were supposed to have two adjoining rooms; however, when we checked in this morning, they had the reservation mixed up with another Jones, or at least that's what I was told. I'm not entirely sure what happened. But the end of it is that my mother and I are sharing one room instead of having two separate rooms, which we need."

The woman nodded in agreement but said nothing. Lillianna had never been one for confrontation, but this situation had to be cleared up. She couldn't imagine having to share a room with her mother for the next ten days.

"I'm sorry, Miss, but the reservation here says it's for two adults, one room with queen-sized beds," Ingrid said from behind the counter as she stared at her screen.

Lillianna was starting to feel frustrated. She hadn't had enough sleep to continue arguing with the woman behind the counter, so she pulled out her phone. "I have the reservation here," she said, pointing to her confirmation, which clearly stated two adjoining rooms.

The woman looked at the reservation and saw Lillianna was correct, two adjoining rooms. She nodded in agreement. "I see that, Miss Jones. Let me check the system."

She started to type quickly, staring hard at the computer in confusion and disgust. She typed and clicked for several minutes before looking back at Lillianna. "I'm sorry, Miss Jones. I see you are correct. I don't know what happened. It appears a change may have been made a week ago, but not from your end. There are no notes. I'm very, very sorry."

Lillianna took a deep breath. Now she was getting extremely irritated. "I appreciate the apology, but what can we do to fix it?" she asked, trying not to vent her frustrations on this woman.

The woman typed again, the frown lines on her face deepening. "I'm sorry, Miss Jones, but we don't have any adjoining rooms available at this time. The hotel is completely sold out for the next several weeks."

Lillianna took another deep breath; this woman couldn't be serious. "Can you check again? Considering we booked this months ago, I can't imagine what happened. Maybe you can ask your manager?"

The young woman looked back at her computer and typed some more before excusing herself and disappearing behind the partition. Lillianna heard the woman speaking to her manager in Icelandic. A few moments later, the blonde woman returned with another older woman in a blazer and a badge that read Elizabet.

"I'm sorry, Miss Jones, but we don't have any adjoining rooms. We are fully booked for the next three weeks. I can't imagine how this situation occurred, but we can look and see if any other hotels have the space and move you there. Or we could discount your stay here with us."

Lillianna had had enough difficulties with the luggage and her mother already. There was no guarantee that any of the other hotels would have anything better. Their current suite was lovely and had a fantastic view with a balcony, from what she had seen last night. She thought for a moment. It didn't matter how it had happened; they were stuck together, so they would have to make the best of it.

"I guess we'll stay," she answered, reminding herself it would be for less than two weeks. "Please credit the account on file."

Elizabet nodded and typed a few things into the computer. She printed a new receipt for Lillianna and handed it to her. "Thank you for your understanding. I hope you and your mother enjoy your stay."

Lillianna nodded. It wasn't this woman's fault she and her mother had at what could be, at best, described as a strained relationship.

"Thank you," she said before walking over to the coffee bar and pouring herself another cup. This was going to be a long trip.

As she was pouring the milk, the dark-haired man from breakfast came in. He reached for a cup as Lillianna was discarding a sugar packet and knocked over her coffee. The steaming, black liquid spilled everywhere, and Lillianna had only a moment to jump back before it reached her shirt.

"Oh my god. I'm so sorry," he said apologetically in a thick Irish accent as he began grabbing napkins and trying to soak up the mess.

"It's the day, it would seem," Lillianna answered sarcastically, picking up her cup and some napkins and throwing the mess away.

"Let me get you another," the man said, still sopping up the mess on the counter.

"I've got it," she replied, reaching for a fresh cup. She poured another and added her milk and sugar, this time unaccosted, and then retreated to a large, overstuffed chair to read her book.

The man poured himself a coffee then sat down across from her. He looked around the room as if searching for someone, but not finding them, changed his gaze to the book in her hand.

Lillianna looked over the top to return his stare. "Can I help you?" she asked, annoyed at the interruption.

He smiled. It was the smile of a man used to being told he was handsome, who reveled in the attention of women. "I'm Liam, and I'm sorry."

Lillianna wasn't used to his forthright approach. She lived in an apartment complex where she only knew her neighbors' names because they had exchanged keys in case they got locked out. She knew some of the people in her program, but only because after five years of classes with the same people competing for top grades, you couldn't help but learn something about them.

"Hi," she said tersely, returning to her book. Wasn't reading the universal sign of *I'm happy on my own*?

"This is usually the part where you tell me your name," Liam suggested.

"Why do you want to know?"

He laughed a little.

"Because I feel bad. First, I took the last blini, and now I've overturned your coffee. Let me make it up to you by taking you to the best coffee place in Reykjavik," he replied in earnest.

"Lillianna," she said, still annoyed by her stolen breakfast. "And maybe another time. I'm waiting for someone."

He glanced around the empty lobby quickly, with the subtlety of a hammer in a glass factory, before asking, "A boyfriend?"

Lillianna shook her head. "My mother. We got in very early this morning, and she's still in bed. I don't want to go far without her knowing. Strange country, you know."

Liam smiled and nodded. "Maybe some other time." He stood up and crossed the lobby, and Lillianna saw the redhead waiting at the door.

Lillianna smiled slightly, then opened her book as he walked away.

An hour later, her mother emerged, tired but dressed and with her make-up flawlessly done. Lillianna was sure it was to hide her sallow skin, made worse by fatigue. She headed straight to the coffee bar. "Good morning, hon," she whispered as she poured the coffee.

"Good afternoon, Mom. How are you feeling today?"

Her mother walked over to where Lillianna was sitting, taking the chair next to her. "Just a little tired, honey. How are you this morning?" she asked in her thick Long Island accent. The rasp that usually preceded the coughing fits was missing, and Lillianna was hoping for a good day, or what was left of it. "Have you had a good morning, honey?"

"Mom, if we're going to be able to enjoy this vacation, please stop with the sweet nicknames. You gave me a perfectly good name, please use it."

"I'm sorry, hon—I mean, Lillianna, it's just, well, whatever you want. It's got to be close to lunchtime. Do you want to explore a little and maybe find a cute café or something?"

Lillianna refilled her coffee then wrapped her thin fingers around the warm mug. She knew she should cut her mother some slack about the name thing, but she couldn't help but feel she was too old for such platitudes. She was adding some cream to her coffee as her mother looked at several brochures advertising local areas of interest.

"Why don't we just walk around and see what strikes our fancy?" Lillianna replied, placing a to-go lid on her cup.

"Sounds good. Let me grab my sweater, and we can get going," her mother replied.

Back in the lobby and prepared for the summer weather, the ladies exited the hotel and turned left to explore the shops. They peered into windows and enjoyed the cool, Icelandic day.

An hour later, they found a tiny café at the end of a lane that didn't seem to be crowded. They entered to find a case full of beautiful pastries along with a menu of enticing sandwiches. They ordered a large sandwich to share, two coffees, and a pastry each before sitting at a small table near the window.

Lillianna and her mother chatted about their flight and their first day in Reykjavik. As Lillianna sipped her coffee, she glanced out the window to see Liam approaching. He waved at her through the glass before entering.

"You found the perfect coffee spot all on your own, I see," he said, pulling up a chair to join them at their table.

"Good afternoon," Lillianna's mother started. "Lilli, aren't you going to introduce me to your friend?"

Lillianna sighed. Where does he get this level of confidence, and does he really think this type of behavior is endearing? "Mom, this is Liam. I met him in the lobby this morning while you were sleeping."

Liam held out his hand to Lillianna's mother. "Liam Reagan. You must be the sleeping beauty your daughter told me about."

Lillianna rolled her eyes. Any cheesier and they would change his name from Liam to Limburger.

Lillianna's mother giggled a little. "Christina. Nice to meet you, Liam," she said, placing her tiny, bony hand in his.

He smiled broadly, and Lillianna had to give him credit: he had a very nice smile. "And what brings you to Reykjavik?" he asked as he signaled to the woman behind the counter, requesting three more coffees. The woman nodded and brought a cup for Liam and some fresh coffee for the ladies.

While Lillianna wanted to tell him to leave, that she was having lunch with her mother, it was clear her mother had been charmed by this Irish rogue, and he must not have noticed Lillianna had spotted the redhead earlier. Instead of arguing, Lillianna poured milk into her mug before bringing it to her lips, blowing slightly, but said nothing.

"Well, if you really want to know, we're going to elf school," Christina told him. "I always wanted to search for elves, fairies, leprechauns, all the fey."

Liam gave another smile. "Really? Why?"

Lillianna looked at him closely for a hint of mockery or sarcasm, but he just stared at Christina with genuine interest and listened closely as Christina described the difference in the fairy folk from several countries.

"What made you so passionate about the wee folk?" he asked.

"My mother came from Ireland and used to tell me stories of leprechauns, fairies and pixies. Old tales. I was fascinated. I would make leprechaun traps and fairy houses. But then I grew up. I became an accountant, and while it paid the bills, it didn't leave any room for fantasy. So now I'm retired and going to learn how to find elves."

Lillianna had to suppress the urge to argue that her mother's explanation was a highly sanitized and abbreviated version of the story. Liam smiled, one that reached his deep blue eyes and had probably melted a great many hearts, but Lillianna wasn't entirely sure of this good-looking, smooth-talking Irishman who seemed to be taking an interest in her and her mother, yet had a mysterious redhead on his arm almost everywhere he went. Her ex, Gareth, had smiled like that to her face while he was sleeping with her frienemy Melanie. She knew she should get over it and that not every man on the planet had the morality of a street dog, but still, what were his motives?

"So, when are you attending the elf school?" he asked.

"We have signed up for the Friday class, and I have a special session scheduled for Monday," Christina replied with excitement. "Lillianna's birthday present to me. You should join us. It was the last one with availability, or at least that's what Lilli told me."

Lillianna glared at her mother. Why was she inviting this perfect stranger? This was supposed to be their getaway. But her mother ignored her.

"We had planned for a friend to join us, but that fell through, so we have an extra ticket."

The friend her mother was referring to was Lillianna's ex-boyfriend. Lillianna had booked the tickets months in advance, only to have Gareth cheat on her, hence her original desire for separate rooms.

Liam smiled again. "That would be lovely." He glanced out the window to see the tall, gorgeous woman with long, red hair pointing animatedly at her watch. "Now, if you'll excuse me, ladies, I am being summoned." He stood up and placed his mug on the table. "It's been a pleasure meeting you, Christina, Lillianna. I look forward to seeing you again soon."

He left, but not before paying for their lunch. The door chimed as he exited. Lillianna watched as the woman hugged him tightly and they walked away down the cobbled streets.

Lillianna and her mother spent the rest of the afternoon window-shopping, enjoying the bright sunshine. By late afternoon, her mother's energy was fading, and they returned to the hotel for Christina to rest before dinner.

She helped her mother sort out her medications before getting her settled in bed. There was a lot she wanted to say to Christina, but it would have to wait until later. Her mother was so fragile, mentally and physically, and Lillianna didn't want to rock the boat. Not on their vacation. With her mother settled in bed, she left the room with her laptop, hoping she could get some of her schoolwork done while her mother rested.

She headed down to the business center, opened her laptop, and connected to the Wi-Fi. She had ten unread messages in her email. Two were from her classmates regarding an assignment due at the start of the fall semester. Two were from professors checking in and making sure she was still going to be able to be a lab assistant next year. The rest were just junk, except for one from Melanie. Lillianna clicked on her email, intrigued by what her former friend would want to tell her after all this time, but didn't want to send her via text message.

Lillianna read the incredibly long missive in which Melanie went on about how bad she felt, about how Gareth had said they were broken up. About how she was drunk, and that it didn't mean anything. She rambled on about how she didn't want it to damage their friendship and how she was really sorry. It had been almost six months now since Lillianna had caught them in bed together, and it still hurt that she had been so naïve. Her first impulse was to delete, but in the end, she decided to save it to respond to later, maybe when she wasn't so jet-lagged.

She worked in the business center for about two hours before deciding it was time to wake her mother up to go to dinner. She placed her laptop back in her bag and was just about to leave the business center when she bumped into Liam in the lobby. "Good evening, we meet again." He smiled, stepping to the side to let her pass.

"Hi. We do seem to keep meeting strangely. I have to go. My mom and I should get some dinner and then try and get over the jet lag," she said, sliding past him toward the elevator.

"Well then, good night. Maybe breakfast?"

Lillianna let herself smile a little. "Sure, see you at breakfast."

He winked as the doors closed, and she felt the elevator rising along with her heart rate.

Lillianna was able to get her mother to wake up, but the medications were doing their jobs a little too strongly, and she was in a daze. "Room service, then, Mom?"

Her mother nodded and stumbled to the bathroom. Lillianna was worried about her in there. It wouldn't be the first time her mother could be hurt in the bathroom. She wished she could stop worrying about her mother, but a lifetime of practice isn't easily broken. Things hadn't gotten better with Christina's diagnosis.

Ten minutes later, Christina exited the bathroom looking paler than when she had gone in.

"Room service? What do you want, Mom?" Lilianna said, handing her mother a laminated menu of the hotel's offerings.

Christina looked over the menu before picking a soup dish and some toast. Lillianna tried some savory blinis and a grilled chicken salad. The food arrived, and as Lillianna was helping set up her mother's tray at the tiny desk, her mother asked, "What do you think of Liam? He seems so nice and sweet. He reminds me of your grandfather with that accent."

Lillianna snorted, not forgetting about the redhead. "Mom, I'm not looking for romance. Besides, I think he has a girlfriend."

"Really? What makes you say that?"

"Mom, just drop it. Men aren't your strong suit."

Christina let the subject drop, and they talked a little bit more about their next day's plans before her mother fell back to sleep, snoring softly. Lillianna opened her book and read until the words started to swim on the page. She turned off the light, then snuggled into the pillows and was asleep in minutes.

* * *

The alarm went off at seven. Lillianna reached to silence it, knocking it off the stand. The sun was shining through the crack in the drapes again. Lillianna looked over to see her mother still snoring softly. They didn't have a lot planned today—a trip to the caves, or a light hike to the church Lillianna had been hoping to see but it wasn't on any type of timetable. She crept out of the room and down to the lobby for breakfast.

At the head of the buffet line, she spotted Liam with a plate of blinis. His eyes twinkled, and he had a big, goofy grin on his face. "Don't worry, there are plenty left," he said before walking over to sit at a table with the tall redhead from yesterday afternoon.

Lillianna made her way through the breakfast line, filling her plate and putting several helpings of the blinis on. When she emerged from the breakfast nook, all the tables were filled with other guests. She looked around for a spot, but the only unoccupied chair was next to Liam and the strange woman. She scanned around for another chair when Liam started to wave to her. "Come on over. You can sit with us," he called, pointing to the open seat.

Lillianna continued to search, hoping someone was about to get up, but no such luck. She reluctantly walked to Liam's table and set her food down with a polite "thank you" before turning to grab a coffee. Liam followed her, refilling his own cup.

"Sleep well?" he asked, passing her the skyr. She declined and reached for the milk. "You really should try the coffee with skyr. It adds a richness milk can't."

She nodded but continued to pour the milk. "Yeah, I slept okay. Mom always snored, but it's worse when she's really tired."

They headed back to the table where the redhead was finishing her fried potatoes. "Good morning," she said with an accent as thick as Liam's. "I'm Saoirse." She held out her hand. "Liam's sister."

"Sister?" Lillianna said in surprise, taking Saoirse's hand. "I thought maybe you were his . . . well, never mind. Nice to meet you, Saoirse."

She sat down at the table more relaxed than she'd been in several days. She hadn't noticed all the tension she had been holding in with the travel and her encounters with Liam until it had resolved. But as they talked, she felt her opinion shift. Maybe he was a genuinely nice guy, and her mother was right, for once. At breakfast, Lillianna learned that Saoirse was not only Liam's sister, but she was also engaged to a banker from Bristol named Brian. She and Liam were on a vacation as a last hurrah before she tied the knot.

As Lillianna was finishing up her breakfast, her mother shuffled in. "Good morning, Mom," Lillianna said, rising to help her make her way to the table. "Are you okay?"

Her mother nodded before collapsing into the chair and going into one of her coughing fits. Liam went and got her some water while Lillianna sat next to her, timing her fit. If they lasted more than three minutes, she had to get her mother a special inhaler. But it was over in less than a minute.

"Are you okay, Christina?" Liam asked.

She nodded. "Just a cough." She smiled, taking the water. "Lilli, dear, maybe we should hold off on the Hallgrimskirkja church today."

Lillianna nodded. They had kept things fluid because of her mother's illness, but she was disappointed that, given the walking required, they might have to forgo the church altogether.

"You should go to Perlan. It's a beautiful museum and has some lovely geothermal hot springs. Just what that cough needs," Saoirse chimed in.

"What a wonderful idea," Christina replied, trying to clear the tickle still in her throat.

"Mom, can I get you some breakfast?" Lillianna asked, standing up.

"I'm perfectly capable of getting my own breakfast, Lilli. I just need a minute to collect myself," she said, stubbornly standing and immediately falling back into her chair. "Well, maybe this once."

Lillianna rolled her eyes but kept her comments to herself. This would not be the first time she would be getting her mother breakfast, nor the hundredth time. She felt like she had been her mother's caretaker for much longer than the months since her diagnosis. She had nursed her through her depression and drinking since she was twelve. This was nothing new.

Lillianna started to make her way to the buffet, spooning a little of everything but the pickled herring onto a plate and claiming the last blini for herself. Liam saddled up to her as she was getting some coffee for her mother. "If your mom's too ill, Saoirse and I were planning to see that church today, maybe we can go together."

Lillianna smiled. It was kind of him to offer, but she hated to be a third wheel. "I'm sure she'll be fine after some breakfast."

But she wasn't. After picking at a few things on her plate, Christina excused herself to go back to their room. Lillianna followed.

"I'm tired, dear," her mother started. "I don't want to ruin your vacation."

"Our vacation, Mom, not mine, ours."

"Liam and his sister seem nice. Why don't you spend the day with them? I can stay here and maybe go out on the balcony to read after a nap."

Lillianna didn't point out that she had just gotten up. There was no point in arguing with her mother; she was the most stubborn person she knew. "Okay, if you're sure? I'll have my phone on me if you change your mind," she said before grabbing her bag and sweater.

Liam and Saoirse were waiting in the lobby. "You really didn't have to wait for me. I wasn't even sure I was going to come."

Saoirse nodded knowingly, and Liam just said, "No trouble, we're not in a rush."

They headed out the door toward the church. There was a significant climb, and Lillianna doubted her mother would have been able to do it. At the top was a magnificent, tall, white church that looked over the whole of Reykjavik. They stood there admiring the view before going inside. Saoirse began to tell them everything about the building, better than any tour guide would have, and they all agreed to go up to the tower.

From there, the view was even more stunning, and Lillianna felt grateful they had let her tag along. She was staring down at the city when she felt a hand at the small of her back. She turned slightly and saw that Liam had gently placed his hand around her waist. She thought about telling him off but found she enjoyed the physical contact. She and her family were always reserved and rarely hugged. It had been one of the reasons she had been attracted to Gareth: he was always so open and affectionate. A little too affectionate, it turned out. Saoirse headed down the stairs before either of them, and, meeting them at the bottom, stated they were having a service shortly and that she wanted to stay and experience it.

Liam looked at Lillianna. She had never been religious and didn't relish the idea of sitting through a service she knew nothing about in a language she didn't know, but she didn't want to appear rude.

"I think I'll pass. Unless you want to," he said to Lillianna.

"I'm good. Are you sure you don't want us to stay?"

Saoirse smiled and shook her head. "I'm good. Besides, Liam and I need a break from each other. Too much togetherness can be smothering." And with that, she wandered off to join a group of practitioners.

Liam and Lillianna left and made their way into historical Reykjavik. They walked around until Liam suggested lunch. He guided them to a small café off a side road, similar to the one she and her mother had enjoyed the day before. "You have to try their Plokkfisheur."

"God bless you," Lillianna said, half joking, not having any idea what a Plokkfisheur was.

She let Liam order for them both and found that Plokkfisheur was a delicious, creamy type of fish stew. They enjoyed their lunch, and Lillianna allowed herself to have traditional Icelandic beer, as her mother wasn't there to be tempted. They talked for a while about their journey so far and the amazing architecture they were seeing. Eventually, Liam asked her, "Is your mother okay? She didn't seem well this morning."

Lillianna put down her spoon. How does one tell a relative stranger that their mother is dying? Her mother wouldn't even admit it to herself, but Lillianna had talked with the doctors, and the cancer was inoperable and spreading despite the radiation and drugs. They estimated a year, maybe eighteen months at the most, which is what had prompted Lillianna to take time away from her studies to plan this trip. It had been almost nine months since the diagnosis, and up until three weeks ago, her mother had seemed healthy; you wouldn't have known she was even sick. But the disease was now progressing, and she didn't know how long she would have.

"No, she's not. She's been sick for a long time. The doctors don't give her much more than a year. That's why this trip is so important to us, our final hurrah," Lillianna said, tears welling up in her eyes.

She and her mother had always had a strained relationship. It had gotten worse when her father had left to find someone less drunk and needy. She didn't blame him for leaving; she blamed him for not taking her with him. She had been left to care for her mother and herself. She had made the dinners, kept the house clean, gotten to school on time, all while her mother partied or slept it off. It wasn't until she went to college that her mother thought to clean up her life.

Liam nodded in understanding.

"Do you think we should go and find Saoirse?" she asked, changing the subject.

"No, she'll find us when she wants to. How about we check out some of the hot springs?"

"How about not. I don't have a swimsuit. Besides, I think my mom and I have passes for Saturday."

"Then a walk around Tjornin, it is," he said. "We might meet up with Saoirse then."

They didn't find Saoirse, but Lillianna got some beautiful photos to show her friends online. They were just passing the other side of the lake when Lillianna got a text from her mother; she was awake and wanted to go to dinner soon. They headed back to the hotel, where they found Saoirse sitting in an armchair and scrolling on her phone. "Where did you guys go?" she asked with the smallest hint of annoyance in her voice.

"Around the lake. How about you? Did you enjoy the service?" Liam asked, giving her a big, brotherly hug.

She nodded. "Brian said he was going to call tonight, so you're on your own for dinner."

He nodded and followed Lillianna to the elevator. She thought about inviting him to join her and her mother. But after spending most of the day with her, he must be getting tired of her company, so she thanked him for a lovely day and then went to her room. There was her mother, her hair neatly done and in much better spirits than the morning. "I found the perfect place to go to dinner. Get changed and let's go."

Lillianna hopped into the shower before changing into a clean pair of jeans and a chunky knit sweater. "Okay, Mom. Let's go."

They grabbed their bags, and her mother directed them to the restaurant. The hostess greeted them warmly. "Do you have a reservation?" she asked with a slight haughty accent.

Christina and Lillianna looked at each other with slight confusion. They had never considered needing a reservation. "I'm sorry we don't have one," Lillianna said.

"I'm sorry, but we have an hour or so wait. You can stay in the bar until we have a table ready."

"Mom, we don't have to stay. We can go somewhere else," Lillianna said, afraid for a moment. Bars and her mother didn't mix well, but Christina didn't seem to mind.

"We'll wait over there until it's ready," she said, heading to a tall table in the bar.

Christina looked at a menu and then spoke to the bartender. "Can I have a virgin margarita?" she asked.

Lillianna let out a sigh of relief; her mother was staying true to her promise. "I'll have a Mysa," Lillianna added.

"You don't have to not drink on my account," Christina said, holding up her five-year chip. "Five years, not a drop, don't even miss it."

Lillianna nodded. "I know, but I've never had a Mysa. It looks interesting, something different."

An attractive young man with the blondest hair Lillianna had ever seen placed the drinks in front of them. Lillianna reached into her wallet. "No, Miss, compliments of that gentleman over there."

They looked down the counter to see Liam lifting a glass to them. Christina waved him over, and Lillianna found she was excited to see him. He had also changed his clothes and done something to his hair, but it was his kind smile that seemed to warm her from the inside. "Good evening, Christina, Lillianna," he said, reaching down to give Christina's hand a light kiss.

"Fancy seeing you here," Christina said.

"You did call me to say that you would be having dinner here tonight and that I could join you?"

Christina blushed as Lillianna stared at her mother. "I guess I did. Well, since you're here, you must have dinner with us. I insist."

Liam smiled, and Lillianna found she couldn't be annoyed with her mother for inviting him. They enjoyed their drinks and chatted about the elf school class the next day until the hostess came to collect them.

"Follow me," she said, leading them to a small table in a corner. She gave them each a menu before placing a basket of bread on the table and returned to her station.

"So, what do you do, Liam?" Christina asked.

"For work, you mean? I'm in finance. I work from home, mostly chained to the computer."

"Really, finance? Lilli isn't that interesting?" Christina said, picking apart a roll from the basket.

Lillianna nodded noncommittally. Looking at Lillianna with his deep blue eyes, Liam asked, "What about you?"

Christina spoke up. "Well, I told you at lunch yesterday that I was an accountant, and now I get to be a world traveler. Lilli is in graduate school. What is it you're working on again? Something in medicine or something."

Lillianna let out a sigh. "Cognitive psychology, Mom. I'm studying how people think, specifically how we read."

Christina let out a little laugh. "That's right, though, why we need to know that, I can't fathom."

"Because it will help with teaching and especially those with different learning abilities."

Christina nodded in confusion, but Liam leaned closer. "Go on. How do you study reading? Is it different in different languages, like Chinese or Arabic?"

Lillianna's face lit up; she loved discussing her research. The server approached and took their orders before Lillianna could launch into her favorite subject. They talked all through dinner, with Christina chiming in here and there with her personal opinions. The restaurant slowly emptied around them as they ordered desserts and steered the conversation to their favorite books and movies. Several hours into the meal, Christina started to slump slightly in her chair.

"I think your mother is fading fast," Liam said. "Maybe we should wrap this up."

Lillianna looked over at her mother, who was looking very tired. "Sure, Mom, are you ready to go?" she asked.

Christina nodded. Liam paid and helped them back to the hotel, where Lillianna took over and put her mother to bed.

● ● ●

The next morning was elf school day, and Christina was up before Lillianna. "Just a few more hours until school," she said with too much energy for seven in the morning.

Lillianna got up and dressed quickly; maybe Liam and his sister would be downstairs. She and her mother were both ready in less than half an hour and headed straight to the lobby, Christina to fuel up for class and Lillianna to see if Liam would be there with his sister. Neither of them was disappointed. The hotel had a beautiful buffet with make-your-own waffles, and Lillianna was happy to see Liam standing there looking better than the blinis.

"What time is elf school?" Liam asked, placing three blinis on Lillianna's plate.

"Eleven. I'm hoping to get there early. I can't wait," Christina said excitedly, finding a small table for them.

Liam and Saoirse joined them with coffee and their plates, and to Lillianna's pleasure, Liam sat next to her, their legs brushing under the small Formica table. "Are you still going to join us today?"

"Join you?" Saoirse questioned.

"I invited Liam to the elf school session with us today. Maybe you can come, too?" Christina said, sipping some coffee.

Saoirse looked a little confused. "I thought we might be—"

Lillianna felt Liam kick his sister under the table.

"You don't have to come if you don't want to, SeeSee. But I, for one, have never learned how to track an elf. A skill that I feel may be holding me back in life."

Lillianna was impressed he'd been able to speak those words with a straight face. Saoirse looked around the table and returned her brother's stare with a smirk. "Okay, elf school it is." She smiled slyly while nibbling her toast.

By ten thirty, Lillianna, Christina, and Liam were outside the school. Christina was vibrating with anticipation, and Lillianna was starting to get a flutter in her stomach when Liam looked at her. Ten minutes before class, Saoirse appeared, and Liam seemed surprised. "You decided to come."

"Well, no education is complete without learning about elves," she said, placing a coffee in her brother's hand.

The instructor called the class of thirty-five students to follow him into a small clearing. Lillianna was surprised to see so many older adults; she had thought her mother unusual in her interest in elves, but over half the class was her mother's age or older. Lillianna accepted a workbook from a small gray-haired woman old enough to be her grandmother and went to sit in one of the chairs behind her mother. Christina sat up front and started chatting animatedly with a dark-skinned German man and his wife, telling them how she had gotten her Certification of Ordination from the Church of Gnome two months ago and was hoping to complete the Fairy Trail in Ireland by the end of the month. The couple nodded politely, then spoke to each other in German. The class began with a brief history of elves, and while Christina took notes and listened with rapt attention, Saoirse, bored, pulled out her phone to check the time. Liam, on the other hand, divided his attention between the lectures and stealing glimpses at Lillianna, giving her sly smiles when she caught him looking at her.

The class continued for several hours, and afterwards, Christina held the instructor up to ask further questions. Lillianna had to rescue the polite man from her mother's interrogation by reminding Christina that they had a private session scheduled for Monday, and she could ask all her questions then. Following the class, Christina suggested dinner, but Liam and Saoirse had other plans. "Will we see you tomorrow?" Christina asked.

Liam assured her they would before he and his sister walked off and away from downtown, while Lillianna and her mother made their way back to their hotel. The sun was still high in the sky when they reached their hotel. Lillianna checked her watch; it was dinnertime. She didn't know how anyone got used to the sun being out at all hours here.

Back in the room, Christina collapsed on the bed. Lillianna helped get her mother's shoes off before wrapping her in a blanket and then escaping to the balcony with her book to enjoy the cool evening. She put her book down and watched the clouds drift across the sky.

Unable to concentrate on her reading, though, she went back into the room. Her mother was sleeping peacefully, which meant she was on her own for dinner. She grabbed her bag and headed downstairs. There was an outdoor patio with several different firepits and chairs spread about. Lillianna sat in a chair near an unoccupied fire and tried to read again, but after skimming the same paragraph three times, she gave up and watched the flames. She wasn't usually like this; she was always in such command of herself. She hadn't even been angry when she found Gareth cheating. She called him up, said it was over, and left his things on the lawn after changing the locks. No anger, no tears, just a quick, decisive action, and she'd moved on.

She tried to read again, only to look up and see Liam standing over her with a coffee in each hand. "Milk and two sugars. Right?" he asked, handing her a mug.

"Yes. Thanks. That's me." She smiled, taking the cup and motioning to the chair next to her. Liam took a seat, and Lillianna stored her book away.

"Where's Saoirse?" Lillianna asked, taking a sip of her coffee.

"She's on a call with Brian. The wedding is in six months, so they have a million decisions to make. Honestly, I zone out when she talks about colors or place settings."

"So, a big wedding?"

"Not really. My dad passed a few years ago, and we don't have a lot of family. Brian's family is pretty big, though, and apparently, there are lots of weird family dynamics making everything interesting. Not fun interesting, just *interesting* interesting."

Lillianna nodded in understanding. "I'm sorry to hear about your father. It must be hard."

"It is at times, but mostly it's okay. It's part of why Saoirse and I are so close. Our dad was sick for a long time, and it took a lot out of our mom, so it was often just the two of us. We're each other's best friends," he said nonchalantly.

"Sounds nice. To have someone close for something like that. It's just me and Mom," Lillianna said. "It has been for a long time now."

Liam nodded, waiting for her to continue, but she let it go. It was in the past; she needed to stay in the now.

"So, what are you reading?"

Lillianna held up *The Count of Monte Cristo*, and Liam took the volume, then handed it back. "I've heard it's good. Lots of revenge."

Lillianna smiled. "I know, I've read it like ten times. It's my favorite."

They talked for an hour or two about movies, books, elf school, and their families. They were talking about the British *Office* versus the American *Office* when her phone pinged. It was her mother; she was hungry and wanted to know about dinner. Lillianna checked her watch. Ten o'clock.

"Oh my god. I'm sorry, I have to go, Liam. It's my mom."

He stood as she got out of the chair to head back into the lobby. "Tomorrow then?" he asked.

Back in the room, she and her mother ordered room service, and Lillianna listened as her mother talked animatedly about the elf school classes they had attended earlier in the day and were about to take go back again on Monday. Lillianna nibbled at her dinner as her mother continued to talk. She felt herself nodding off as her mother prattled on, only to have her mother rocking her gently. "Lilli, time to sleep," she whispered.

Lillianna nodded before curling up in bed.

The next morning, Lillianna woke up to the sun on her face, and when she looked at her watch, it was just past eight. She looked around to see her mother's bed empty. Panic rose in her throat, but she was put at ease when her mother emerged from the bathroom. "Mom, you scared me."

Christina smiled. "Now you know how it feels. Breakfast?"

Lillianna hadn't eaten much of her dinner the night before, and the thought of blinis with Liam was delightful. She dressed quickly and joined her mother in the lobby. Liam was sitting at a table waiting for them. "Good morning, ladies. Coffee?"

He stood as Christina sat down. "Where's your delightful sister?" Christina asked.

"She had to leave last night. She had forgotten she had made plans with Brian and the minister on Sunday, and she wanted to make sure she was home in time."

"Oh. you didn't mention it last night. I didn't even get to say goodbye. She's super sweet," Lillianna added.

"Well, you know, once you're married, your time is never your own. I guess it works the same for engagements," Liam said

They all enjoyed the breakfast and each other's company while drinking coffee and discussing their plans for the day. Christina and Lillianna had tickets for the Perlan and baths starting at noon. Liam was befuddled; he didn't have any plans for the day at all now that his sister had left but might try to join them later.

Having finished their breakfast, Lillianna and her mother returned to their room to get the things they would need for Perlan. Everything neatly stowed away in Lillianna's bag, they returned to the lobby. They helped themselves to some more coffee and sat in the large, overstuffed armchairs.

As Christina was sipping, she swallowed wrong, which started a coughing fit. Lillianna quickly got her some water, but it wouldn't stop. After two minutes, she raced upstairs to their room to grab the rescue medication, and when she returned, Christina was still coughing. Lillianna forced the medication into her mother's mouth before handing her another inhaler. Her mother was able to force the liquid down her throat between coughs and then took a long drag on the inhaler. Lillianna crouched next to her, hoping her breathing would settle. They had purchased travel insurance in case her mother got sick on the trip, but she didn't want to test it.

Fortunately, the inhaler seemed to be doing its job, and her mother's breathing settled. "Mom, maybe we shouldn't go. "

Christina shook her head violently in disagreement. "No, I've always wanted to. I know my hair won't do that crazy ice sculpture thing like in the winter, but they're supposed to help with healing."

Lillianna rolled her eyes internally; her mother was way beyond the abilities of a hot spring to heal her cancer. But the coughing fit had subsided, so she didn't argue. They waited outside for the next tour bus and made their way to Perlan. The ride to the museum was short but bumpy, and Christina was tired and nauseous by the time they arrived.

Lillianna got her a cup of herbal tea at the entrance before they started their tour. Neither of them was surprised when they found Liam standing outside the entrance to the springs in purple water shoes, a red-and-white flowered pair of swim trunks, and a Hawaiian shirt opened at the front. Lillianna tried not to stare at his very well-maintained physique. He may claim he is chained to a desk, but his abs would say otherwise. He had the thick, muscular legs of a bicyclist with calves bigger than Lillianna's thighs. His chest was tanned, and she noticed a tattoo hiding under the sleeve of his right bicep.

"Are you going to take the waters?" he asked in much too serious a tone for Lillianna not to giggle.

Christina didn't even try to hide her admiration. "Why of course, Mr. Reagan. Will you accompany us?"

They both needed to lay off the Jane Austen for a while. Lillianna smiled and bit her lip to keep from laughing. "Let's get changed first. We'll meet you out here in a minute."

Christina and Lillianna ducked into the women's locker room to change. Lillianna had never worried much about her appearance, especially since the breakup, but after seeing Liam in the hallway, she was very grateful she hadn't slacked off on her marathon training. She removed her jeans and chunky knit sweater to replace them with a tasteful two-piece tankini of blue and yellow. She grabbed the purple cover-up she had purchased in Hawaii two years ago with Gareth then went to collect her mother.

Christina had always been a petite woman, but her illness had made her tiny and too thin. Even her lavender-skirted one-piece, which she'd bought two weeks ago for their trip, was hanging on her tiny frame. She took the matching cover-up Lillianna offered and followed her outside.

It was summer, but it was a Reykjavik summer, and they both shivered as they followed Liam to a hot spring. They took several steps into a bath, and the springs' warmth enveloped Lillianna up to her waist. It was warmer than she had imagined, and she was grateful she had remembered to bring a water bottle for herself and her mother. They floated at the edges of the springs for an hour before Christina had deemed herself sufficiently pruned and wanted to get out for a little while.

As they got out, Lillianna caught Liam staring at her runner's legs appreciatively. She took her time putting on her cover-up, making sure he could enjoy the view a little longer. But the cold summer air demanded she wear something to break the wind. They approached a small eating area; Lillianna ordered the lamb soup while her mother tried the Plokkfiskur. The ice cream looked tempting, but instead they went with coffee and a traditional tea for her mother.

Liam told them he would bring it over when it was ready, so they left to find a table near a heater. Liam arrived with their drinks and promised a staff member would be over soon with the soups. "You are going to love the Plokkfiskur, Christina; it's not as good as the place Lillianna and I went to the other day, but it's good."

"Thursday? Was that while I was napping?" Christina asked, raising a thin eyebrow.

Lillianna blushed a little. "Yes, Mom, you said to go out and enjoy myself, so I did."

Liam seemed to be enjoying the interaction and added, "Lillianna was the perfect companion. We enjoyed the church as well as a tour of the Tjornin. Maybe tomorrow we can take you to it if you are feeling up to it."

They ate their lunch and then returned to the springs. This time, Liam was even less subtle as he ogled her getting into the spring, to the point where Christina suggested a picture might last longer.

"I'm sorry," he apologized, turning his gaze onto anything but his companions.

"It's fine. I don't mind," Lillianna said, finding for the first time in her life she didn't mind being the object of a male's gaze, especially since the gaze was Liam's.

They stayed another hour, but the heat and the water, while refreshing, were also draining, and Christina asked to go back to the hotel. They returned to the locker rooms to shower and change, then met Liam outside. He continued to avoid Lillianna's gaze, something her mother had no problem picking up on and teasing him about.

The bus ride back to the hotel was just as bumpy, though Lillianna didn't seem to mind it as much with Liam sitting next to her, each bump bringing his knee into contact with hers. Back at the hotel, Christina needed help to get back to the room, so much so that Liam carried her, much to her enjoyment.

"I haven't been carried by a man in decades. Lillianna, do you see this? His muscles aren't just for show."

"Don't mind my mom. She says things when she's tired," Lillianna protested, ashamed and stunned by her mother's behavior. She was used to her mother lacking tact, and finding joy in teasing Lillianna about any part of her life she could, she just wasn't usually quite so obvious in front of others. She must be exceptionally tired.

"It's okay. She's right. When I'm not chained to my desk, I help my friend Toby at his gym. It's similar to your American CrossFit. Never know when you need to help a damsel in distress." He smiled broadly.

There was that Irish charm again, Lillianna thought. Ever since she'd shared breakfast with him and his sister, she had started thinking of him as a possible vacation romance. She was even starting to find his cheesy one-liners somewhat endearing.

"It's okay. I can walk the rest of the way," Christina said as they reached their door.

Lillianna swiped the key and said goodnight to Liam. As he lowered Christina gently to her feet, he bent down close to Lillianna. So close she thought he might kiss her, and she was in the frame of mind to let him. But instead, he straightened up and said he might be back on the patio tonight if she would like to join him. Lillianna nodded noncommittally and helped her mother into the room.

She got her mother changed into warm pajamas. "Do you want the window blinds opened or closed, Mom?" she asked.

"Open, please. I may go out on the balcony later. It's so beautiful outside," she said, plopping onto the bed. "It's early, dear, why don't you and that nice young man go out. Maybe see some of the sights."

"I feel bad leaving you. You seem so tired. What if you have another coughing fit?" Lillianna protested meekly.

"I'm a grown woman. You've spent most of your life taking care of me. Now go off and have fun before it's too late," her mother stated with more strength in her than Lillianna had thought she possessed.

"What do you mean, Mom?"

"You know exactly what I mean. You've had to shoulder too much, and you know it. I know it. This is just the first time I've admitted it. It wasn't fair to you."

Lillianna tried to object, but Christina continued. "It wasn't fair. I see that now. I've known it for a long time; it's just here you can't run away from me like you do at home."

"Mom, I—"

"No, I know you don't mean to run away from me, but you hide at school and work, in your research. I don't blame you. But you need to stop hiding from life. That young man down there is the sweetest thing I've ever met, and if I were twenty years younger, I would hop on that train so fast—"

"MOM!" Lillianna interjected.

"It's true, but here you are. Hiding with me. Go, go have fun. Enjoy the vacation. I'll be here for a little while longer, and watching me sleep can't be that entertaining. Enjoy your life. It's yours."

Lillianna stared at her mother in amazement. Was this really her mother, the woman who had spent most of her childhood in a stupor or so hungover she couldn't remember the day? Is this the same woman who called her on her first day of college, asking for a ride to the doctor's and reminding her they were out of cereal? The woman who had interrupted half her dates in high school to have Lillianna pick her up at a bar or boyfriend's house after the relationship had gone south. Here she was acknowledging her and her sacrifices in a hotel room in Iceland, of all places.

Lillianna rushed to hug her mother, her bony frame fragile in Lillianna's arms. Her mother returned the hug, their first real deep and meaningful hug in years. Tears welled up in their eyes when Christina gently pushed her daughter away. "There now, no need for dramatics. I need my rest, and there is a nice young man downstairs who I think is waiting to buy you a drink."

Lillianna smiled and wiped her eyes. "Okay, Mom. I'll go; you get some rest."

Christina nodded and snuggled into the bed, rolled over, and closed her eyes. Lillianna crept quickly out of the room, shutting the door noiselessly behind her.

Outside on the patio, Liam waited with a craft beer, sitting in a chair by the fire, reading a copy of *The Count of Monte Cristo*. She walked up to him. "Good book?"

He smiled back. "The best. Can I get you something?"

She nodded and they walked to the bar. She joined him in a beer and they went back to the fire. He started by saying, "I'm sorry about today. It was rude of me to stare—"

"Thank you, but I actually didn't mind it, at least not then. It was actually sort of nice to have someone even look," she interjected.

"You were just so radiant, so vibrant." He leaned in close.

She could smell the hops and malt on his breath but didn't pull away. He gently caressed her lips with his, and she met him with passion.

He pulled away slowly and stared at her breathlessly, and she returned his gaze. He reached out a hand to stroke her hair gently before drawing her closer for another kiss. They remained out on the patio in the cool night air, watching twilight descend and then the summer sunrise again.

About the Author

Elizabeth Baizel has been writing stories and tales since she learned to write but has only recently begun sharing them with the world. When she isn't writing, she is running marathons or taking her dog, Watson, for walks in her beautiful Upstate New York town. She enjoys sushi, reading, biking, and gluten-free double chocolate cake.

Elizabeth's debut story, "Misery on the Bounty," was featured in *Recipes for Romance: A Sweet Valentine's Day Anthology*, and her story "Help Wanted" appeared in *Emerge Magazine*.

You can find Elizabeth on:

Instagram & Facebook: @elizabethbaizelwriter

THE TURN AT CROOKED CREEK

The Turn at Crooked Creek

Dan Houston

IT WAS A PLEASANT DAY in Crooke City, a small town in Montana at the base of the Bear Tooth Mountain Range. Dakota Steele was driving his 1977 Chevy Silverado pickup along the twenty miles of two-lane highway leading into the thriving metropolis of downtown Crooke City. He had his window down and his left elbow hanging outside, enjoying the drive. The big 454 engine's deep, throaty sound put him at peace.

Dakota was meeting his lifelong friend, Marcus Longfeather, the owner-operator of Middle Rockies Outfitter, serving the Bear Tooth Mountain Range area. Marcus had asked Dakota to guide a VIP client for him as a personal favor while his leg continued to heal. The client, Alex, was coming in from Bozeman to get outfitted for the trek up to the high country the next day. A climate researcher for Montana State University, Alex was going to place several high-tech sensors across the mountain range. They collected real-time weather data for an experimental new weather predicting algorithm.

Marcus was going to be the guide, but due to his recent accident, he was no longer able. Dakota typically didn't take on new clients without vetting them himself. But he could tell this was important to Marcus and decided to bend his otherwise rigid rules to help his friend.

Dakota's Silverado rumbled into town, headed down the main drag that divided the town in half. Marcus's outfitter shop was just on the other side of town, next to a gas station with a garage service.

Dakota drove around to the far side and parked. At fifty-five, he was in great shape and considered by most to be ruggedly handsome. He dressed like a typical cowboy with a white button-down brush popper, faded blue jeans, and buckskin cowboy boots. He wore his 44-magnum revolver holstered to his right hip and a bushcraft fixed blade knife on his left. As he walked inside, he was greeted by Marcus with a big smile, a handshake, and shoulder pat. Marcus was on crutches, and his leg was in a cast after the accident he had a couple weeks ago.

"Greetings, Cheveyo!" Marcus said. "Thank you for doing this, my friend. I owe you one."

Cheveyo was the tribal name given to Dakota when he married his Cheyenne wife, Archisa. Very few people called him by that name.

"I expect Alex to get here any minute now," Marcus stated. "Can I get you something to drink?"

"Well, I wouldn't say no to a cup of Nia's coffee," Dakota said, smiling.

Marcus turned toward his wife Nia, who was behind the counter. Nia smiled and nodded, then disappeared back into the kitchen area. "Let's grab a seat while we wait," Marcus said.

As they got settled around a small, round table with sturdy wooden chairs, Dakota said, "So tell me a little more about this Alex fella. When is he supposed to get here?"

Marcus, unable to look Dakota in the eye, said, "Any minute now."

"What are you not telling me?" Dakota asked with a stern tone.

Marcus stuttered a bit and started to answer when the bell over the door rang, drawing their attention to a woman crossing the threshold. With a beaming smile, she walked over to Marcus, who was struggling to stand up, and gave him a big hug and kiss on the cheek.

"Marcus! It's been far too long!" she said, stepping back and looking at his injured leg. "How's the leg doing? Where's Nia?"

Marcus was about to answer her when Nia entered the room carrying a tray holding a coffeepot and cups.

"Alex!" Nia said, smiling broadly. "It's so good to see you! How have you been? You are looking very good!"

"I'm great, thank you! It's so good to see you, too. I've missed you both."

After the excitement of the initial greeting subsided, Alex noticed Dakota sitting at the table across from Marcus. Looking eager, she asked, "Is this my guide?"

Dakota pinned Marcus with a glare, raising a single eyebrow. "Guide?"

Like a little boy caught with his hand in a cookie jar, Marcus stammered, "H-Hey, Dakota, meet Alexa Lockhart. Alexa, meet Dakota Steele."

Nia's eyes narrowed as she poured coffee into cups for everyone. She smacked Marcus on the shoulder. "Oh Marcus, tell me you told Dakota *ALL* the details about Alex!"

Dakota stood. "I can answer that for you, Nia. The answer is *no*. Marcus failed to mention a few details."

"Wait a minute," Alex said. "You *are* my guide, right?"

"No, ma'am," said Dakota. "It seems there's been a misunderstanding. I'll be on my way. Nia, thanks for the coffee." He tipped his hat and headed for the door.

Marcus called out, "Dakota, wait! At least let me explain!"

Dakota kept walking.

Nia rushed out the door after him, heading straight for Dakota's truck and climbing in just as he was shifting into reverse. "Dakota, please!" Nia pleaded. "Hear Marcus out. He would never put you in this situation if it wasn't very important."

"Marcus should have known better," he said angrily. "I can't guide a female alone in the mountains!"

"Why not? It's been ten years, Cheveyo. Archisa wouldn't want you to live like this."

"Live like what?" Dakota said, his expression one of disbelief.

"Like a hermit," she replied. "Like your life ended with hers. Living as if Archisa was a shield surrounding you and keeping you from feeling anything real."

"That's not how it is," he argued.

"Then prove it," Nia dared him.

They sat in the cab of the truck, silently staring at one another and waiting to see who blinked first. Dakota jumped when Marcus knocked on the driver's side window.

As Dakota rolled down the window, Marcus said, "Look, Cheveyo. I know you feel betrayed, but I didn't know how to approach you with this. I apologize, my brother. I wish I'd done things different, but I'm stuck between a rock and a much harder rock."

Dakota stared his friend down. "Well, at least we agree on that!"

"I'll leave you two to sort this out," Nia said. She placed her hand on Dakota's arm. "We both love you." She smiled warmly at him, then slipped out of the truck and walked back to the store.

"You got a good one, Marcus," Dakota said without looking at him.

"She is the best part of me, and I sometimes wonder how I got so blessed. I couldn't tie my shoes without her," Marcus joked. "Listen, brother. Alex and I go way back to when I was deployed in Afghanistan. She's a combat field medic and as solid as they come. She found me after I was wounded, patched me up while holding the insurgents at bay, then dragged me to the exfil. I owe her my life, and it kills me that I can't do this for her," Marcus said, lowering his head.

"Why can't the trip be postponed until after you heal up?"

"The deadline to demonstrate her weather prediction model is November this year. Those sensors have to be deployed now in order to get enough data from the summer storm season to prove the model's accuracy."

Dakota sat there quietly, his mind reeling, staring through the windshield, but seeing nothing. "It's not that I don't want to help you. You know that. It's just that I can't be alone in the mountains with a female. It just doesn't feel right," he continued. "I mean, in my heart, I'm still a married man! What would people say?"

Marcus shook his head. "Brother, you know I loved her just like you do. But she's been gone ten years now. Do you think she would want you to live your life this way, still clinging to the past? If she were alive right now, she would tell you to take this job, and you know it."

Dakota remained silent.

"I don't know what else to say," Marcus sighed. "Whatever you decide, brother, just know that you are family, and you have my respect and love."

With that, Marcus turned and walked away.

Nia sat down across the table from Alex, who was nervously bouncing her heel.

"I don't understand what the problem is," Alex started. "Marcus has already trained me, and everything has been planned for months. I'm not some helpless female who needs a man to protect me. I'll go up by myself if I have to."

Nia attempted to reassure her. "He doesn't see you as a helpless female."

"I've had to put up with that chauvinistic crap my entire life and I'm sick and tired of it!" Alex snarled back.

Nia chuckled.

"Why is that funny? I certainly didn't expect you to take his side."

Nia calmly leaned over, taking Alex's hand. "You are both very much alike. Headstrong, fiercely independent, and you both spend far too much time worrying about what other people think."

Alex started to object, but Nia raised her hand.

"I'm not finished. You have both allowed fear to dictate how you live your lives. It breaks my heart to see Dakota close himself off to the possibility of another love because he fears it will tarnish the memory of his departed wife. It also breaks my heart to see you close your heart to the possibility of loving another man. After that two-faced devil broke your heart, you fear all men will betray and hurt you. Both of you need to open yourselves to the possibility you are wrong and start living again. He hides himself at his ranch, and you hide yourself in your work. It's not good for your souls."

Marcus hobbled back inside, joining them. Dakota was notably absent. Marcus leaned his crutch against the wall and awkwardly sat down with a sigh.

"I spoke with Dakota. I wish I had good news, but I have nothing."

"What does that mean?" Alex asked.

"It means he needs time to think things out. If I try to pressure him any further, it's a guaranteed no. I've known Dakota my entire life—we grew up together. He has saved my life more than once, and there is no one on this Earth I trust more, but we need to just give him the time he needs. Nia has your cabin ready if you want to go unpack. After dinner, I'll go over the route with you again, and we can check the weather reports and go through the gear one more time."

"Plan for success," Alex smiled.

Marcus grinned. "It's the only way!"

Alex paused for a minute, her expression changing to one of concern. "I hear what you say about Dakota. I can appreciate the respect you have for him. You always told me to know your limits when it comes to hiking in the mountains. Does he know his limits? I'm not trying to be mean, but he looks a little bit long in the saddle to still be guiding in the mountains. Do you think he's physically strong enough for the task?"

Marcus looked straight at Alex. "Who do you think carried my sorry ass off the mountain two weeks ago?"

Alex's eyes went wide. "He's the one who saved you?"

"Yes," Marcus nodded. "When Dakota heard what had happened, he went out at night, by himself, breaking all of his rules and risking his life to find me. He tracked me in the dark and somehow managed to carry me up the ravine, plus the two-hour hike back to basecamp. So, yes, I think he's up to the task."

"Understood," Alex said in a matter-of-fact tone. "I'll accept that he's up to the task physically, but with the way he reacted when he looked at me and stormed out . . . is he emotionally capable?"

Marcus was quiet for a moment. "Many things in life are about timing. I know he's capable of doing this job, but I can't guarantee the timing is right for him."

"Timing for him how? What are you not telling me?"

"For that, we need a drink," Marcus said with a smile. "Something a little stronger than coffee."

Nia arrived right on cue with a bottle of Crown Royal, a bottle of 7Up, and three glasses with ice. She joined them at the table and poured the drinks.

In a solemn voice, Marcus said, "Dakota met Archisa, the love of his life, when he was fifteen years old working on his father's cattle ranch. *Archisa* means 'victory' in Cheyenne. She was the daughter of a Cheyenne shaman, Ma'taa'e'e, and Ten Bears, the tribal leader. Dakota was out by himself rounding up strays when a snake spooked Dakota's horse, and he was thrown. The snake bit Dakota, and he was miles from any help.

"Archisa and her mother were out collecting medicinal roots and herbs along the river when they found him dying from the wound. They treated Dakota and looked after him for three days, camped out along the river while he recovered. During that time Dakota's heart was lost to Archisa.

"When Dakota turned twenty-five, Ten Bears finally give him permission to marry Archisa even though he had asked for her hand every year since they met." Marcus smiled. "They had a tribal ceremony, and Dakota was given his Cheyenne name of Cheveyo, meaning 'Spirit Warrior.' I have never seen a couple more in love with each other."

Alex took a drink of her crown-and-seven. "What happened to Archisa?"

Nia continued the story. "It was about ten years ago. Archisa wanted to forage the high mountains for specific plants and herbs. Even though she knew the mountain as well as him, Dakota insisted on guiding her. They climbed up to Froze to Death Plateau, where she thought they would have the best chance of finding what she needed. That first night at camp, Archisa surprised Dakota with news she was pregnant. Dakota was overjoyed, but also very overprotective, as I'm sure you can imagine. He wanted to go back home the next day. But Archisa insisted since they were over halfway up to Tempest Mountain, they should continue. Dakota never could say no to her.

"As the trail became more difficult, Archisa started cramping and began to bleed. The scent of her blood must have attracted a cougar that started stalking them. They stopped for a rest. She walked just a few feet away to pick some herbs when the cougar attacked. Dakota killed the animal within seconds, but Archisa's wounds were fatal. All he could do was hold her and their unborn child in his arms and try to comfort her during their last moments."

Everyone sat quietly for a few minutes, absorbing what had just been said.

"Thank you for sharing that with me," Alex whispered. She cleared her throat. "So now more than ever, I need to know if you think he is emotionally ready to take another female up the mountain alone."

Marcus and Nia looked at one another, hoping that the other would have an answer, but both remained silent.

The next day, Alex decided that if her trip was going to happen, it was up to her to convince Dakota to agree to be her guide. She was determined her general distrust and bias against men would not prevent this from happening. But in her defense, with very few exceptions, men had always let her down; an abusive high school sweetheart, an inappropriate college professor, and finally, the fiancé she'd caught in bed with a neighbor when she returned home from her last tour in Afghanistan. She pushed her emotional baggage aside, climbed into her rented SUV, and drove to Dakota's family ranch, about twenty miles east of town.

Driving into the sun, Alex enjoyed the peaceful drive, her road trip playlist thumping through the SUV's speakers. Oddly enough, she wasn't very nervous given the gravity of her situation. She had learned much about Dakota and how respected he was in the community, and for some reason, that was a comfort to her. Even though he came off as a cranky old bastard, in reality, he was a man of worth.

She pulled up to the rustic, single-level log home, admiring the picturesque view with the mountains as a backdrop. Dakota's Silverado was parked in front of a barn, so she parked beside it and hopped out. On the way up to the house, a yelping beagle dog came running up to greet her. Alex stopped, quickly assessing whether the dog was protecting the homestead or just damn happy to see her. Based on the rapid tail wagging, the lack of a snarl, and the nature of the breed, she decided on the latter. She bent down, smiling, and held out the back of her wrist to let the dog sniff her.

"Hello there, sweetie. Are you a good doggie?" Alex asked playfully.

Dakota stepped off the front porch, barefoot and carrying a shotgun. "RUCKUS!" he yelled. "Leave her alone! I apologize, ma'am. He doesn't mean to be rude, he's just excited to have company."

Alex laughed. "He's adorable. And not nearly as concerning as being met by somebody with a shotgun." She smiled, pointing at the Mossberg 500 12-gauge that Dakota was carrying.

Realizing how it must look, Dakota treated her to a Clint Eastwood–style crooked grin. "My apologies again for the appearance of being inhospitable. Whenever Ruckus throws a fit, you never know if it's a snake, coyote, wolf, bear, or a visitor. I find it's best to be prepared for any contingency."

He stood there for a moment, sizing her up. At 42, Alex still had the athletic body of her military days. She was wearing military-style BDU pants, a long sleeve white thermal undershirt, with a worn blue jean jacket and her favorite pair of tactical boots. Her dark brown hair was pulled back into a ponytail, and a pair of aviator sunglasses concealed her blue eyes. As usual, her EDC knife was sheathed to her waist. She wondered what he made of her appearance.

Finally, Dakota spoke. "If I were a betting man, I'd wager you have a pistol concealed in the small of your back. And if so, I'm pleasantly surprised."

Alex ignored how his praise warmed her. "I'm Alexa Lockheart," she said, extending a hand. "Everybody calls me Alex."

Dakota accepted her hand. "Why on earth would they do that? Alexa is a beautiful name. Why shorten it to make you sound like a man?"

She blushed. "Sounding like a man has its advantages when you work around men. Plus, I got tired of all the Amazon jokes."

Dakota looked confused. "I don't have a clue what you're talking about, but I'll take your word for it. Have you had any breakfast?"

"Just some of Nia's coffee."

"I was just getting ready to fry up some bacon and eggs for Ruckus and me. You're welcome to join us if you're into that kind of food."

Alex smiled. "Who doesn't love bacon and eggs?"

Dakota invited her into his house and set about making breakfast. She sat at the kitchen table and watched as he stoked the fire on his antique cooking stove.

"How do you like your eggs?"

"I'm not a big fan of runny eggs, but I'm also not too picky, so however you normally cook yours is fine with me."

"I usually break the yolk and cook mine well done in the bacon grease. They're not pretty, but they taste damn good."

"Sounds perfect." Alex grinned.

Surprised, Dakota nodded. "Dirty eggs it is. How hungry are you? Do you want two, three, four?"

"Two will be plenty."

Ruckus was whining and looking up impatiently at Dakota.

"Alright, buddy. I'll give you just a sample to tide you over." He broke off a small piece of bacon and pitched it toward Ruckus, who eagerly caught it in his mouth.

Alex smiled as she watched Ruckus devour his treat, wagging his tail and looking very excited.

"I have a fresh loaf of sourdough that Mrs. Guthrie brought over a couple days ago if you're interested in some toast?"

"That sounds wonderful," Alex commented. "It's been ages since I've had some real sourdough."

"Well, it doesn't get more real than Mrs. Guthrie's. I think you'll like it."

Dakota brought some plates, utensils, and cups over to the table. He then brought a platter with the bacon and the eggs. Another trip delivered sourdough toast and a bowl of fresh-churned butter. He poured her a cup of coffee and asked if she took sugar or cream.

"I got used to drinking it black in the military," she replied, "and it's still my favorite way."

"Me too. If you get too much milk and sugar and other crap in there, it's not really coffee, is it?"

Alex took a sip, and her eyes went wide. "Damn, this is good coffee! What's your secret?"

Dakota shrugged. "I learned to make coffee from Moses."

"Okay, I'll bite. How does Moses make coffee?"

Dakota lifted his cup, took a sip, sighed, and said, "He-Brews it."

There were a few seconds of silence before Alex finally cracked. "Not bad," she laughed. "It's been a while since I've heard a decent dad joke. How long have you been waiting for an opportunity to say that one?"

Dakota took another sip, hiding his grin behind the coffee mug. "It's been a while," he admitted, earning more laughter from them both.

Ice broken, they finished breakfast and made polite get-to-know-you conversation while Dakota slipped Ruckus nibbles of bacon beneath the table. *This man is not at all like I thought he was*, Alex realized. Dakota was still rough around the edges, and he no doubt believed that women had their place at home, but there was a sincere kindness and a respectful quality about him that naturally lowered her guard.

After breakfast, Dakota walked her around the ranch. By the time they finished the tour, Dakota had brought them back to her Bronco, and they still hadn't discussed the uncomfortable subject of whether he was going to be her guide.

Dakota turned his attention to her SUV. "It's a damn shame what they've done to this truck," he commented. "A Bronco used to be a real man's rig, tough and dependable. Now they've gone and completely emasculated it."

Alex was a little bit shocked at his comment. "Well, I happen to think it's a great little vehicle, and it gets me where I need to go. Plus, it was the only SUV they had available to rent in Billings. So, if you have that big a problem with it, instead of harassing the driver, maybe you could go complain to them."

She waited to see how he responded. Dakota looked a little surprised at her comments as well.

"Wait . . . was that a test? Were you trying to get me mad?"

Dakota served up another Eastwood grin. "I need to know that you will listen to me out there if it gets serious, even if you don't agree. So yes, that was kind of a test to see how your temperament is."

"So, how did I do?"

"Well, you didn't punch me, so there's that. But if I'm being completely honest, I just don't know yet. Look, I get it. This is very important to you. And Marcus has told me about you saving his life in Afghanistan, and Nia thinks you walk on water, so it's not really about you at this point. It's more about me."

Alex placed her hand on his shoulder. "I think this trip will test both of us. But I give you my word, you will be in charge. I'll listen to you, and leave the attitude behind. I can't do this without you. Please, Dakota. Will you guide me?"

Dakota met her eyes. He nodded.

Alex was overcome with happiness. "Thank you." She laughed as she reached forward and gave him a friendly hug to seal the deal. She stepped back, smiling from ear to ear. "Just think of this as our summer vacation!"

Dakota and Alex left basecamp at daylight, beginning their working vacation. The pace was brisk but sustainable, and they made great progress. Alex was able to deploy six sensors and then confirm they were transmitting using a satphone to speak with her research assistant back in Bozeman. With the daylight fading, they stopped at a location Dakota knew to be a safe campsite. They each pitched their own tents and settled in for the night.

The second day started out similar to the first: getting an early start and heading deeper into the wilderness. Their pace slowed somewhat as the terrain became more difficult, but they continued to make good progress by the time the sun was setting. As they relaxed and ate their meager dinners, they talked only enough to discuss the next day's destination and the best route to get there.

Dakota seemed distant, and Alex was concerned about how he was dealing with everything but didn't think it was a good idea to bring it up. She instead focused on her work and kept her worries to herself.

"It's going to rain tonight," Dakota noted. "We need to make sure to anchor the tents good and point the openings downhill. Hopefully it won't be a toad strangler and slow us up too much tomorrow."

With the camp set up to Dakota's satisfaction, they bedded down for the night. Later, Alex was awakened by a loud clap of thunder as the rain rolled in. She typically enjoyed sleeping in the rain, but this time it was different, and she didn't get much rest. By morning, the slow drizzle made tearing down camp interesting. Dakota passed by her, carrying his pack.

"Some vacation, huh?"

Alex noted his sarcastic grin as she finished packing her gear and followed Dakota back to the trail.

The light rain continued steadily. Dakota gauged their visibility at a hundred feet or so. This made the last few sensor deployments a lot slower, and Alex was having difficulty getting a clean signal on the satphone.

Dakota had a feeling they were being watched. He hadn't seen any bear sign or any other evidence of predators, but the rain was making it more difficult to tell.

When they deployed the last sensor, Alex tried to confirm it was online, but the signal kept dropping. She informed Dakota they needed to find a better spot for reception. Their trail ran alongside the Crooked Creek River, and Dakota knew of an outcropping of rocks that formed a scenic overlook area ahead that might do the trick.

Antsy, Alex outpaced Dakota, and the distance between them increased. Instincts on high alert, Dakota was convinced something was hunting them and stopped to scan the surroundings. Up ahead, he spotted a huge mountain lion, stalking its way down closer to them.

In that moment, Dakota realized that Alex had traveled way too far ahead of him. He shouted to Alex, but the rain, the roaring river, and the distance prevented her from hearing. He had to close the gap!

"Come on, old man," he said to himself. "She's not dying on my watch!"

He dropped his pack and charged up the slick path, his heart pounding out of his chest and his lungs burning. Moving on pure adrenaline, he closed the distance just as the big cat took up position, crouching on a ledge above where Alex was preoccupied with the satphone. The predator introduced itself with a blood-curdling scream.

Startled, Alex looked up and locked eyes with the mountain lion. She turned to find Dakota, her mouth opened, but no sound came out. She was paralyzed with fear, Dakota realized. He watched her turn back to the big cat just as the beast launched itself toward her in a great arch. It screamed out midjump with jaws open wide, baring vicious-looking fangs.

With no time to stop and take aim, Dakota leaped with all his strength, covering the remaining distance and intercepting the animal midair. Dakota felt the monster's teeth plunge into his left shoulder as one of its claws shredded through the flesh on his back. The pain was excruciating, and Dakota thought he might lose consciousness.

But instinct took over. Dakota pulled his gun and felt the familiar recoil of his 44-magnum as a round penetrated the beast's chest cavity, exploding its organs and exiting through the spine, leaving a fist-sized hole. Still entangled, Dakota and the mountain lion collided with Alex, sending her backward. Dakota hit the ground hard, cat on top, knocking the wind out of him and momentarily stunning him. Painfully, he shoved away the cat's carcass. With the weight removed, he collapsed back onto the ground, trying to regain his breath. Slowly, things started to come back into focus and . . . Alex! Where's Alex?

Panic took over for a second, giving him the strength to stand. He looked around, desperate, in search of her. She couldn't have gone far. She was standing right there next to the . . . riverbank!

He ran toward the rushing water, sliding down the embankment and splashing waist-deep into the frigid water. He quickly spotted her pack about fifty feet away, hung up on some rocks. Half running, half swimming, he raced toward it.

"God no! *Please*, God, no!"

He finally reached her, underwater and unconscious, held in place by the strap on her pack. The current was strong, and he knew his body would quickly go numb from the cold temperature so he had to move fast or they would both be just as dead as if the big cat had finished the job.

He straddled the rocks and pulled her partially out of the water. She was pale, her lips tinged blue. A trickle of blood began running down the side of her head.

The panic, the cold, the pain, and the fear were almost overwhelming. Dakota's mind was wandering, thoughts racing. Memories of what happened to his wife and unborn baby. Rage! Anger! Defiance!

"Not again," he screamed. "You hear me? This is not happening a second time! I won't allow it! Red Rule Number 1!" he shouted out loud. "Don't panic. If you stop thinking, you die." He repeated the rule to himself until old habits fell in place, like his body knew what to do even as his mind still reeled.

Dakota carried Alex out of the river and up the embankment then began to breathe air into her lungs. Her skin was cold as ice, and his fear was growing again.

"Breathe, Alex," he pleaded. "Come on and just start breathing. Please!"

He repositioned again and started performing chest compressions. He alternated back and forth between compressions and mouth-to-mouth for several minutes. He realized her core body temperature was the problem. She was in hypothermia, and it was making it damned difficult to jumpstart her. Dakota pushed on, clinging to hope.

Finally, Alex sputtered and coughed up water. Dakota spun her over so the water would drain out easier.

"That's it, Alex. Fight for me! You got this!"

Miraculously, she started breathing on her own again, but she was still unconscious and needed to be warmed up immediately.

Dakota removed her pack, then gathered all his remaining strength to pick her up and position her over his shoulders. He almost fell as he tripped over her pack, sending it tumbling down the bank and into the river's current, out of his reach. Dakota sighed as he watched it float away.

"One shit at a time," he snarled, concentrating on putting one foot safely in front of the other with Alex draped across his now throbbing shoulders.

Dakota knew he was on borrowed time before his body staged a strike and walked off the job. *Don't panic*, he thought to himself. *Assess the situation, prioritize, and solve the damn problems*. His first priority was getting Alex warmed up.

Dakota looked around. Everything was soaked from the rain. No way he was going to get a fire started. Then he noticed the dead cougar lying over by the trail. He cocked his head.

"It worked for Luke Skywalker, so it's worth a try."

With his knife, he slit across the lion's belly and splayed it open just wide enough to position Alex, back first, into the cavity. He then broke off a few branches from a nearby bush and stacked them in front of her. As much as he wanted her to be okay, he was actually thankful she wasn't conscious for that experience.

He found his 44-mag close by, then retrieved his pack. He made quick work of setting up his tent and unrolling his sleeping bag. Alex was still unconscious but breathing well, and her color had returned somewhat back to normal, so Dakota moved her out of the carcass and carried her to the tent. He removed her wet and bloody clothes, placed her shivering body in the sleeping bag, and zipped it up.

Now, he had to take care of himself. Dakota found some flowering weeds he recognized growing along the river and grabbed a handful. He cut bark from a familiar tree and scooped up some clay by the riverbank while topping off his canteen. Next, he removed his shirt and cleaned his wounds as best as could. He rinsed the blood from their clothes, gathered everything, and headed back up to the tent.

Once inside, he checked on Alex again. She was still breathing, steady and slow, and her color had improved. Allowing himself to feel some measure of relief, Dakota went about hanging up their wet clothes to dry. He pulverized the stems of the weeds and mixed it with some clay and a handful of tobacco he kept in his pack to make a poultice. He winced as he applied the mixture to his wounds. Strips cut from his wool blanket served as bandages to cover his wounds as best he could.

He fetched his camp bowl and placed the tree bark and the flowers from the weeds in it, covering them with water. It would be best for the tonic to boil for maximum strength, but without a fire, he would have make do with a cold brew. In a few hours, it would help with the pain and fever, but for now, he needed rest.

Beyond weary, he unzipped the sleeping bag and started to climb in . . . but froze. A very naked Alex was in there. Terrified of what was about to happen, he knew there was no other option if he wanted them to survive.

Dakota closed his eyes. "Please forgive me, Archisa." Then he settled inside next to Alex.

Alex slowly became conscious, surprisingly aware of the fact that she was somehow still alive. It felt like her head was about to explode from the inside, and she had something dried and crusty on the side of her face and in her hair. Her chest ached for some reason. Her breathing felt off, as well. She tried to open her eyes, but the daylight was painful.

Why was her head in so much pain? She pulled her arm up to block the light and try opening her eyes again. As her arm traveled up her torso, her hand brushed across her breast. She held her hand across her eyes and forced herself to open them.

She was surrounded by an eerie light-green glow. Her vision was blurry. She gave it a minute, and slowly her eyes started to focus, and . . . wait a minute. Why were her breasts bare?

She pulled her hand back down and grabbed one. Yup, bare titties. She slid her hand down further, and . . . yup, she was completely naked.

"What the hell is going on here?" she rasped.

Alex tried to roll onto her back, but something prevented her. She reached her arm around to see what was stopping her and suddenly froze. It had been a while, but she definitely remembered what a male body felt like. Specifically, a naked male body.

Feeling a bit panicked, she wiggled around, trying to get out and, in the process, caused the naked male in the sleeping bag with her to moan out in pain.

Dakota! What the—This can't be happening!

Alex managed to turn around enough to see Dakota lying there, asleep on his side. He was wrapped in some kind of makeshift bandage, but otherwise, he appeared to be buck-ass naked, as well.

The zipper for the sleeping bag was on the other side of Dakota, and there wasn't enough room inside the tent for her to shimmy out. She tried to wake Dakota, but he was dead asleep. Her only alternative was to crawl over Dakota to reach the zipper.

She awkwardly started to spider crawl over him, trying not to touch him. After a minute, she gave up and sat right down, straddling his hip. She leaned down, practically laying on top of him to reach the zipper and open the bag.

Once free, she crawled away to sit up for a moment and collect her thoughts. Being vertical made her head throb worse, but at least she could breathe better and think. Sitting in the chilly tent, she realized she had been staring at Dakota's naked butt for the last several minutes and snapped out of it. She closed the sleeping bag to cover him up.

Alex noticed their clothes hanging around the tent.

"Thank God," she murmured, reaching for the nearest article and starting to get dressed. Then she checked on Dakota, trying to wake him. He grunted and tried to roll over but winced in pain.

"What can I do to help?" Alex asked.

He tried to speak but wasn't able to talk. Dakota rustled an arm from under the sleeping bag and pointed at his canteen. Alex picked it up, unscrewed the lid, then held it up to his mouth. He swallowed several times, then stopped to breathe. His eyes met Alex's, and he nodded his thanks.

Alex smiled. "Anything else I can do to help?"

Dakota pointed over at the camping bowl with what looked like a sad pesto ground into the bottom.

She picked up the bowl, peering inside. "Is this what you want?"

Dakota nodded. She brought the bowl to him, and with a little assistance, he was able to take a few sips of the bitter concoction.

"What is it?" Alex asked.

"Cheyenne medicine," Dakota croaked.

Alex placed her hand across his forehead. He felt a bit warm. "Can you tell me what happened last night?"

He pointed to his backpack, and she brought it over to him. He pulled at one of the zippered pockets and reached inside to reveal a map. He unfolded it and pointed to a spot marked *Crooked Creek Gorge*.

"Is that where we are?"

Dakota nodded, then moved his finger over to another spot, indicating the location of the Sage Creek Ranger Station. In a barely audible voice, he whispered, "Go get help."

Alex was confused for a minute. Then, shaking her head, she said, "No! I can't leave you here unattended. You could die!"

Seeming to summon what little strength he had left, Dakota raised himself up and pulled at her collar. "You have to, it's our only chance." He held the stare for a moment, then he fell back down, collapsing back onto the sleeping bag, unconscious.

"Dakota? Dakota, stay with me!" Alex said, shaking him softly.

When he did not respond, she held her ear close to his lips and confirmed he was still breathing. She sighed with relief and checked his pulse. He had a strong heartbeat and seemed stable, despite somewhat shallow breathing. At that moment, she felt a little panic settling in and tried to come to grips with their situation. She hadn't felt this kind of fear since her combat tour. Her anxiety spiked as adrenaline flooded her body, making it next to impossible to think rationally. She had to calm herself somehow.

Dakota was unconscious, and she was on her own. She fought back tears that were filling her eyes as she left the tent and stood outside in the brisk morning air. She surveyed the area, looking for signs of danger. When nothing jumped out at her, she was able to calm herself somewhat, but her mind was still racing and unfocused. She needed to shock herself back into the present.

She went back inside the tent to check on Dakota again, then started taking her clothes off. She put her boots back on, grabbed Dakota's revolver, and went outside. She walked naked down to the river's edge and scanned the area once more. Satisfied there was no immediate danger, she stepped out of the boots, placed the barrel of Dakota's pistol into one of them, and walked into the freezing water.

The cold plunge was exactly what she needed. Alex's breaths became short and rapid, and her body tensed up as the cold therapy worked its magic. She estimated she'd been in the water about five minutes by the time she started to feel a stinging sensation on her skin.

The walk back up to the tent felt stiff and clumsy as her body grew warm again. She surveyed the forest to see what, if any, food was around, unsure how long she and Dakota would be stranded there. Though she had plenty of experience surviving in the desert, the forest was largely unknown to her. She had no idea what might be safe to eat.

Back at the tent, her pack was nowhere to be found. Alex went through Dakota's bag to inventory what they had to work with. She found some typical survival gear, more ammo, several more maps, and six leather-wrapped bars of what turned out to be pemican. She had read about the wonder food—that Native Americans and settlers used to live off the meat-and-fat bars for months at a time back in the days before refrigeration—but had never tried it.

She opened one of the pouches and found what looked like the love child of a protein bar and beef jerky. She took a small taste. *Surprisingly decent*, Alex thought. She was really needing some calories and finished the bar in no time.

Feeling calmer and in control, Alex knew it was time to assess the predicament they were in and decide on their next step. She retrieved the map and studied the locations Dakota had pointed out. She had never been a scout, but thank goodness the Army had trained her to navigate using maps. It was a rusty skill she never had to use during her two tours because she always had GPS tracking equipment available, but she was able to recall the basics as she calculated the distance from their current location back down to the Ranger Station.

Alex estimated the trip at about sixteen hours if she didn't stop or run into trouble. Then, she didn't know if anyone would be there, or if there was a way to call for help. Plus, the travel time back to Dakota was going to be too long and, in her opinion, too risky.

She noticed a small note on the map, marking a spot labeled Ten Bears's cabin. She estimated about a three-hour hike to get there, but she had no idea what kind of provisions or help that would be either. As Marcus would say, she found herself between a rock and a much harder rock with more questions than answers.

More rainy weather was a concern, as well. Frustrated, she leaned back and rested her head across Dakota's legs. He moaned and adjusted himself inside the sleeping bag. Alex raised up, not wanting to make him uncomfortable. She noted he was sweating across his brow and touched his forehead, confirming that his fever had returned. He was running out of time.

Alex made her decision and started to gather supplies. She decided that she would drag Dakota to Ten Bears cabin on a makeshift travois, a one-person litter used to move the wounded off the battlefield. Even though the military now uses lightweight aluminum stretchers in the Army, she had seen villagers use something similar while in Afghanistan. The basic construction consisted of two branches about eight feet long with a cot suspended between them. Using broken tree limbs and the remains of Dakota's blanket that she had found tossed to one side of the tent, she constructed the travois and dragged Dakota's heavy frame out of the tent and onto the litter.

Alex packed up their camp and put the gear at the foot of the travois by Dakota's feet. Even though Alex was very fit and stronger than most women her age, she knew the second she picked it up, her grip would not last if she had to support the weight and pull it up the trail. Using the last vestiges of the blanket roll, she made a makeshift harness that fit over her head like a Pancho, cutting slots to hold the two branches so that the weight was supported across her shoulders. Her hands were then free to stabilize and drag it along.

With everything loaded and the canteen full, Alex started up the path. Dakota's revolver was tucked securely into her waist at the ready. The uncertainty of exactly where the cabin was, or what they might encounter along the way, made her worry if she was making the right choice. Regardless, they were both committed now. Second-guessing her decision was useless. Alex plodded along at a steady but maintainable pace, focusing only on continually putting one foot in front of the other.

Alex was never happier than when she'd trudged Dakota's unconscious body over a rise and around a large tree, catching her first glimpse of the tiny log cabin. It was getting dark, and the temperature was dropping. She had been trekking for the last hour in a light rain, so she had stopped along the way to cover Dakota with their tent.

Alex was plenty warm thanks to the exertion of dragging Dakota along, but she worried that he might be getting too cold. She brought him into the dim cabin, disconnecting from the travois and settling him down as gently as possible. Alex gave her shoulders a minute to relax as she took stock of the cabin's interior.

She spotted a lantern and checked to see if it had oil in it. It was about half full, so she removed the globe and looked for a match. Fortunately, she found a box of wooden kitchen matches close by. Once she had the lamp going, she had better light to look around the small cabin.

There was a rustic wooden table with two matching chairs that looked like they were hand carved. A potbelly stove across the room stood in a corner. On the opposite wall, there was a platform bed with a few blankets laid over the frame to make a mattress.

After all the exertion from the hike up to the cabin, Alex did not have the energy to wrestle Dakota's heavy, unconscious body onto the platform bed, so she decided for tonight that they would sleep on the floor. It wasn't fancy, or even comfortable, but they were inside, dry, and safe for now. After rolling out their sole sleeping bag and managing to stuff Dakota into it, she found enough wood beside the stove to build a fire and chase the chill out. Exhausted, Alex removed her damp clothes and crawled in next to him. His body was very warm. His presence felt comfortable and somehow safe to her as she snuggled close to him and fell asleep.

The next morning, Alex woke up, still cuddled next to Dakota. His skin was hot to the touch, and she realized with dread that his temperature was too high. Alex pulled the sleeping bag down to his waist to help regulate his temperature. She quickly dressed, grabbed Dakota's gun, and went outside to look around and see what resources were available.

She found more wood chopped and stacked up against the side of the cabin. She carried some in and hoped it wasn't too wet to burn. She stoked the embers from last night and added some wood. Back outside, she didn't see much that would help them, but after a moment, she heard the sound of running water.

She walked around the back side of the cabin and noticed a trail leading out into the woods. It led her to a nice little creek. Heading back to the cabin, she located a few pots, pans, and dishes, along with an assortment of other kitchen supplies. She brought water up from the creek and set it on top of the stove to boil. She ate another bar of Dakota's pemican and washed it down with the last of the canteen water.

She moved the boiled water off the stove to cool and went over to check on Dakota again. His breathing and heartbeat seemed okay, but his haggard expression was pinched in pain. Alex then remembered the homemade tonic the Dakota brewed. She had almost tossed it out to reduce the weight she had to carry, but since the camping pot had a tight-fitting lid, she'd kept it just in case.

She opened the lid, cautiously sniffing to see if it had spoiled. The smell reminded her of an herbal tea. She had no idea what it was or what it was used for, but it's what Dakota had brewed and what he requested in his brief moments of lucidity. So she raised his head slightly and gave him a few sips.

He partially came to but kept his eyes closed. "Water," he croaked.

Alex returned with some of the boiled water and took a sip herself to make sure it wasn't too hot before allowing him a few more sips.

"Dakota," she said. "If you can hear me, I need to roll you over so I can look at your injuries."

He did not respond. She unzipped the lower half of the sleeping bag and pulled it open, fully exposing Dakota's naked body. She tried to remain professional but had to admit—seeing him like made her breath quicken, remembering how it felt to sleep pressed against him all night.

"Come on, Alex. You've seen a lot of naked men before," she said to herself. "Quit acting like a teenager and take care of him."

It was a bit of a chore, but she managed to roll him over. The blanket strips he used for bandages were matted down with blood and dark, mud-colored stains. She carefully removed them and, for the first time, looked at the deep cuts across his back and the puncture wound on shoulder. They were packed over with some sort of dirty-looking paste.

First order of business, she decided, *clean out the wounds.*

This took several minutes, and Dakota moaned in pain several times but did not appear to wake up. Alex was glad he was not fully conscious for the next part. She needed to stich up his cuts, and the only thing she could find was a small fishing kit from his pack. She selected the smallest hook he had, deciding that the nylon fishing line would have to do for the sutures. She also found a pair of needle nose pliers and boiled everything to minimize the chance of contamination and infection.

Once again calling upon her Army training, she used a continuous-purse-string style of suturing to pull the two sides of the wound together before tying off the stitches. When the last stitch was tied off, she relaxed and straightened from her crouched-over position. She stretched her arms and leaned back, realizing how tense she had become. She was no stranger to treating serious wounds, but using a fishhook and fishing line in dim light was a first.

She was sitting there silently beside him for a minute when Dakota grumbled, "Took you long enough."

Startled, Alex jumped. "Holy crap! I didn't know you were conscious! How did you stay so still? That must have hurt like hell!"

"It wasn't a picnic," Dakota replied sarcastically. "But thank you."

"You're welcome. . . . You have to be the strongest man I've ever known."

"Not really," Dakota said. "Don't confuse strong with tough."

"Isn't it the same thing?"

Dakota slowly rolled over, groaning a bit, and looked up at her. "Being strong means you can lift heavy things or punch someone hard enough to do some damage. Being tough means you can take that hit, then turn around and whip his ass."

She chuckled. "Well, you're definitely a tough ass!"

He looked at her with a shocked expression and urgently asked, "Wait a minute, you didn't stitch up my ass, too?"

She laughed out loud. "No, but I have enough fishing line left over if I need to."

"Thanks, but I'll pass."

Alex was relieved to see him smiling. "You should do that more often."

"What?"

"Smile."

Their eyes met, and for just a second, there was a connection that surprised them both. For the first time since they met, they felt they possessed a mutual respect for each other. She was no longer just a pain-in-ass city girl with no business hiking into high country. He was no longer just a cranky old widower with no social skills and a sexist attitude.

At that moment, their defenses were obliterated, allowing them to see past the outward persona they each used to deal with the pain in their lives.

Dakota was first to break the silence. "Well, before this gets any more awkward, I better stop smiling before you imprint on me and start following me around like a stray kitten."

Alex smirked. "Is that how you see me? A helpless little stray kitten?"

"Not anymore," Dakota said, looking straight into her eyes with a sincere expression. "Thank you for saving my life."

Alex's grin softened. "Thank you for saving me first."

Dakota sat up, taking in their surroundings for the first time. "This is Ten Bears's cabin. How did you find it?"

Alex showed him the map, pointing to where it was marked. Dakota stared at the map for a moment and shook his head.

"I'll be damned. Ten Bears was Archisa's father, and this was his private cabin. Nobody else knew about it, and it isn't on any map, except this one. That's Archisa's handwriting." He leaned back, looking up as he fought back the tears welling in his eyes. "After all this time, she's still looking after me."

Alex was moved to tears by his revelation. "Maybe I should give you a little privacy," she said, standing up.

Dakota reached for her hand. "No, please stay. I'd like you to stay with me if you don't mind."

Wiping her eyes, Alex sat down beside him and leaned over onto his chest, settling under his raised arm.

"That day on the mountain, when she and our child were taken, my soul died. Nia is right. I've been going through the motions, but not really living. This experience with you has changed that forever. I understand now that Archisa would never want me to live like I have been for all these years. It's high time I get out of my own way and start living again. But I'll be honest with you—it's the scariest damn thing I've ever faced, and I don't have a clue how to start."

Alex gently wrapped her arms around him. "That's okay. I'll be your guide."

That night, they made love to one another. It had been years since either of them had been with someone, and it was slow and careful, for the sake of Dakota's wounds, but it felt effortlessly natural, as if they had known one another for years. The next day, they woke in each other's arms, transformed into better versions of themselves.

"Good morning, Alexa," Dakota smiled.

Hearing him say her full name put an answering smile on her face. She really didn't care for Alex anymore, she decided.

Alexa kissed him. "Good morning, tough-ass. How did you rest?"

"That was the best rest I've had in years," Dakota teased.

"What now?" Alexa asked.

"Now, we send up the Bat Signal."

"I can't wait to see that," Alexa giggled.

Dakota, with more than a little help from Alexa, put together a signal fire. The column of white-gray smoke rose up above the mountains, easily seen for miles around.

"I don't know if Batman will come," Dakota commented, "but the Rangers from Sage Creek Station will definitely see it and send up a helicopter to check it out. We just have to kick back and wait for the cavalry to arrive."

They stood arm in arm, watching the horizon and waiting for help to arrive to deliver them from their vacation.

Six weeks later, in her office at Montana State University in Bozeman, Alexa was busy getting ready for the first of several demonstrations of the new weather model algorithm. She had just arrived and was busy checking emails and reviewing the day's appointments.

Her mind wandered for a minute as she took a bite of her drive-thru breakfast bagel, wishing it was sourdough with bacon and dirty eggs. Since being rescued and returned to civilization, she and Dakota had gone their separate ways. They still talked from time to time, though.

Thankfully, Dakota was a fast healer and was already back to his somewhat normal routine of taking care of Ruckus and the ranch. She had had second thoughts about returning to her life in Bozeman, worried she should stay and help him recover. But Dakota had convinced her that she owed it to herself to see this project through.

Alexa had already submitted proposals for a satellite research wing in Crooke City, with her in the role of director, of course. She was just waiting on the military contract to be approved.

Peggy West, her undergraduate research assistant, walked in. "Good morning, Alex. Do you need anything before we set up for the demo?"

"Good morning, Peggy. And please—it's Alexa now."

Alexa started to ask about catering for their guests when a sudden wave of nausea sent her running for the trash can behind her desk. After a solid couple minutes of unscheduled retching, she sat back in her chair, closing her eyes and breathing deeply.

Peggy came around Alexa's desk, tissue in hand. "Are you okay?" she asked. "I guess you're more nervous than I thought."

Alexa accepted the tissue, nodding her thanks and wiping her mouth with some embarrassment. "I don't feel nervous at all. In fact, I'm pretty excited for these demos."

Peggy looked concerned, but said jokingly, "Maybe you caught something trapezing around the mountains with Paul Bunyan and it's just now manifesting. I swear, I always get sick coming back from vacations!"

Alexa managed a smile, still feeling somewhat nauseous as she considered whether she could have been exposed to something.

Laughing nervously, Peggy offered, "The only other thing I can think of is morning sickness, but—"

Peggy paused, midsentence, staring intently at Alexa, who was looking back at her with a shocked but elated expression, tears beginning to well in her eyes.

About the Author

Dan Houston is an aerospace electrical engineer who, after thirty-five years in the industry, got tired of writing technical documents and decided to explore other forms of fiction. He began his writing career by penning bedtime stories for his two daughters, sharing only one page at a time during their goodnight calls while he traveled for work. Though he still writes for his two daughters, Dan is ready to expand his audience to fans of western, action, and science fiction genres with stories that emphasize traditional values and strong characters.

You can visit his website at:
https://linktr.ee/danhoustonauthor

WHEN YOU KNOW, YOU KNOW

When You Know, You Know

Caroline Baccene

"GET OFF MY COUCH."

Groaning and hoping the television had mysteriously turned on during my nap, I twist my head away from the person practically yelling in my ear and press my face into the couch cushion.

"Dottie. Seriously, get up."

Unless my sister's television has become anthropomorphic (thank you, word of the day calendar), it must be Megan pushing at my shoulder and annoying me.

Shoving my face deeper into the pillow, I moan, "Go away."

"It's been a month. No more wallowing. I'm going on vacation, and you're coming, too."

My neck creaks as I turn slowly to face her, checking to see if she's playing some awful joke on me. Her dark brown hair, usually so similar to my own, is pulled up in a slick ponytail, not at all like mine at the moment, which is knotted with frizzy chunks plastered to the side of my face. And I'm pretty sure there's some dried chocolate ice cream in there, but it's hard to say. Could be ramen noodle broth.

To my astonishment, Megan's face is serious, some might say even annoyed, like she's the one being shaken awake.

"Vacation?" The word has barely left my mouth when she rips the blanket off my body and the air-conditioner's breeze hits my bare legs, making me curl into a tighter ball.

"Paul and I are going to the beach, remember? A romantic beach house for a week, no responsibilities, sandy beaches, ocean waves—"

"Perfect. Sounds like the three of us would have a blast, but I'll just stay here. Thanks."

"Yeah, except I'm not leaving you here alone. Who knows what my apartment will look like when I get back? You're coming, too."

"No way. A week of watching you and Paul doing it sounds like hell."

"We'll 'do it' behind closed doors. Besides, he's bringing his brother, too. Everything is already arranged."

Thinking about Paul, I groan as I imagine what his brother must be like. Skinny, with a small jaw and even smaller forearms. It's not like Paul is unattractive. He's fine, I guess, if you like older bankers, which I don't.

As I sit up, I ignore the crumbs that fall from my shirt and say, "You are *not* trying to set me up one month after I caught my boyfriend cheating on me."

Megan snags the pillow off the couch before I can return to my fetal position. "No. He just went through a breakup, too. He's not looking to date anyone."

"Well, good."

Although then I'm stuck having to hang out with a stranger while my sister and her boyfriend splash in the waves and kiss under the stars. Or whatever happens in all those romance movies she watches. I wouldn't know since I refuse to subject myself to that torture ever since my *first* boyfriend cheated on me. And yes, this has now happened to me multiple times.

"Wait, no. Not good. I'd have to be polite. And shave my legs. And wear a bra. No way."

"You have two options: come with us or go back to your apartment."

Megan knows good and well that my apartment is currently housing my jerk of an ex-boyfriend since he convinced me we should move in together just last winter. Even though there are still a few of my belongings there, I've decided to abandon them in the name of freedom. Or maybe dignity. Whatever word that means I don't have to show my face to Andrew again.

"You know if I'm there, I'll just complain and make everyone miserable. Plus, I'd eat all the junk food you bring."

"Exactly why one of my suitcases is filled only with snacks."

Seeing the steel behind her eyes, I know I have no choice. I'm going on vacation.

At least my sister gives me time to shower and pack a bag before she shoves me out the door and into her Jeep. And I breathe a sigh of relief when she tells me that Paul and his brother are meeting us there so we will have two cars, because there's nothing worse I can imagine right now than if I had to sit in the backseat for three hours with someone I've never met while Megan and Paul sing showtunes from the front with the windows down the entire way. Again, I'm assuming based on those romantic comedies.

So, instead, Megan and I drive in comfortable silence with the windows down, listening to the alternative rock station on the radio, and with my huge, dark sunglasses on and baggy sweater, I can almost pretend I'm still curled up in the dark living room in my own ball of misery.

The beach house is worse than I'd imagined. I'm pretty sure I'm going to disown my older sister, if that's even possible. I know Paul and Megan aren't rich, but when I heard *beach house*, this isn't what I expected. The house is on the beach, but that's the only positive thing I can say about it. The entire thing, from ceiling to floorboards, needs painting. And the furniture is so old, I wouldn't be surprised if there were fifty-year-old cobwebs under the chairs. There's a couch, but sadly, I don't think even my petite frame could stretch out in it, which is fine with me since I don't plan on staying in the living room often to socialize. The biggest bedroom, which will be Megan and Paul's, is in decent condition with an attached bathroom. The other two bedrooms are just big enough for a double bed and dresser in each. There's a tiny bathroom connecting the two rooms.

The main problem I really have is the entire house is small. If it were just my sister and me staying here, it wouldn't matter. But to share this house with two grown men, only one whom I've met and don't really know anyway, for an entire week? Maybe all the sugar and trans fats finally got to me, and I am in hell.

Since mystery brother and Paul haven't arrived yet, I take the bedroom that's facing the ocean so at least I have a view while I hide the entire time. The window is open already when I enter, and the sound of the ocean waves coax me into closing my eyes and leaning out a bit to feel the wind on my face. This, I could get used to. This is what beach vacations are all about. I'm almost in a state of tranquility when the sound of car doors slamming and men's voices reach me, causing my eyes to open and my mood to plummet again. I guess I should be social and greet the brothers. Ugh.

When I make it to the "cozy" living room (positive thinking works, right?), the front door is open, letting in that pleasant breeze, and Paul is kissing my sister in a way that I hope I never have to see again. My sister notices me and backs up a step but keeps hold of one of Paul's hands as she gestures to me.

"Paul, you remember my sister, Dottie."

I keep my position across the room, leaning against the wall, and we exchange an awkward wave. It's not that I don't like Paul. He's alright. We haven't spent much time together since they started dating a year ago. My sister likes him, so I guess that's all that matters. He's older than her by a few years, and since she's older than me by seven, that makes him probably ten years older than my twenty-five. He's got a respectable job as a banker, and he owns his own home. He's good to her, she says. She could do worse. She could've spent the last couple of years of her life with a cheating, mooching, stupid excuse for a man. But my sister has always been the smarter of the two of us.

Paul smiles and pulls Megan in front of him, wrapping both arms around her waist. "Dottie, excited to be at the beach?"

"Thrilled." I don't mean it to come out sarcastically, but I think ever since the breakup, my brain has decided to be as unpleasant to everyone as possible. Maybe I have a hormonal issue.

Thankfully, Paul doesn't seem to notice my attitude, and I ignore my sister's narrowed eyes as he continues, "Oh, me too. Nothing like it, am I right?"

Seriously, I'm trying to be nice, really. So I even surprise myself when that sarcastic voice speaks again as I say, "A week of hot air, sand, and you guys. What's not to like?"

"That's what I've been saying," a deep voice says from across the room.

My head turns to my right, and I see a man entering the open front door carrying a duffle bag and taking off his sunglasses. This cannot be Paul's brother, because Paul's brother can't be over six feet tall with muscles that I can see even through his thin T-shirt. And he looks to be only a couple years older than me. He's practically the opposite of Paul with his tanned skin and blonde hair.

Not-Paul's-Brother makes his way to Megan, giving her a side hug that clearly shows she knows him. Then the threesome turn to me, and I manage to keep my position against the wall as my sister introduces us, even though I'm regretting my choices to come here since the last thing I need is to be paired with this underwear model for the next week.

"Michael, my sister Dottie."

While I'm perfectly content to exchange another awkward wave, apparently Michael doesn't agree. Instead, he crosses the small space in probably three of his giant steps and then he's in front of me with his hand extended. As a twenty-five-year-old that was, until recently, employed professionally, I do know how to shake someone's hand. So, there's no excuse for what I do next, which is to reach my hand out like I'm a monarch waiting for her hand to be kissed.

The only reasonable explanation: I'm still recovering from the last month of nonstop sugar, barely any social interaction, and British television shows.

At least one of us is thinking clearly, because he just turns my petite hand in his huge one before shaking it and releasing me.

I'm quick to shove my limp hand between my back and the wall, swearing I'll never put myself in a position to greet someone again.

"Dottie, I've heard a lot about you. Nice to put a name to the face."

Since I didn't know Paul had a brother until four hours ago, I can't say the same. And suddenly I'm speechless, just staring into Michael's light blue eyes, trying to come up with something eloquent to say. Because I've seen those eyes before, only one month ago. On a night I had hoped to forget.

"What's the celebration?"

The man sitting at the bar next to me is barely audible with the club's loud base and drunken voices all around us.

Looking down at the two shots and two large drinks in front of me, I reply, "My newfound freedom. But these aren't all for me."

He nods and wipes a bit of sweat off his upper lip, looking around as if he might puke at any moment. He's on his second beer, unless the bartender has already come and cleared the evidence of his inebriation away. I look over my shoulder again but only manage to see the back of Andrew's head from my position as he moves his hips in time with a woman who is definitely not me or the sick friend he's supposed to be visiting right now. We've been together for two years and he's never taken me to a club, and now I guess he never will. Glancing at the stranger next to me and seeing him wipe his forehead with a napkin, I ask, "How about you? Celebrating?"

He shakes his head and looks around again before replying, "Proposing to my girlfriend tonight."

At least one of us will have a pleasant evening. Pushing one of my shots of vodka his direction, I tell him, "I'd say you need this more than me, but that's definitely a lie."

He accepts my drink with a slightly confused nod, and we clink glasses. Just before I look forward again to down the alcohol, I am drawn in by the bright blue of his eyes. Why couldn't I have met this guy two years ago instead of my soon-to-be-ex? Speaking of, as if he can hear my thoughts, Andrew looks to his right, notices me, and freezes like a deer in headlights.

"Freedom?" Blue Eyes says next to me, but my eyes are locked on the jerk who still has his arms around the tall blonde with legs up to her shoulders.

"Huh?"

"You said you were celebrating your newfound freedom?"

From across the room, Andrew has the gall to look embarrassed, like he got caught with his fly down at work instead of practically fornicating on the dance floor. Suddenly, I see red, and before I realize what I'm doing, my feet are on said dance floor, carrying me toward Andrew while one of my drinks is clutched tightly in my hand.

When I reach him, there are so many things I want to shout, so many names I want to call him. But, really, there's nothing worth saying, not since I got a text from one of my old coworkers saying she saw him with another woman here, at a club I didn't even know existed. So, instead of telling him anything, I throw the cold liquid in his face, turn around, and head back to the bar, where I grab my purse and slide my remaining drink to Blue Eyes, who is staring at me like I've lost my mind, which maybe I have.

"Here. Turns out I only needed the one." Then I make my way out, hoping to forget this night by drinking a bottle of red wine on my sister's sofa.

Glancing at Megan as I turn away from Michael, or as he was known previously, Blue Eyes, I breathe a sigh of relief when she cuts in. "Michael, I think the first room on the left is yours. We were talking about walking down the beach to this seafood place for dinner in a couple of hours. It's super close and supposed to be delicious."

He nods and leaves us to unpack, and I don't think he remembers me, which is overall a relief. I'm quick to make my exit as well, shutting my bedroom door and making sure the attached bathroom I have to share with Michael is locked. Within a few minutes, I've shoved my bed across the room so it's against the open window. And shortly after that, I'm lulled to sleep with the breeze on my face and the waves roaring in my ears with just one question on my mind: What happened to Michael's fiancée?

"Get up, Dottie."

Maybe everything was a dream, and I'll open my eyes and be in my sister's apartment, curled on her couch, and this time, there's no way I'll agree to go to the beach with her, Paul, and his attractive brother that was witness to the most embarrassing moment of my life.

Cracking one eye and seeing my sister at the foot of my bed, I groan as I shove my pillow back over my face. "No, thanks."

"Dinnertime. Seafood. Beach. Let's go!"

There are many reasons to stay in this bed. The first being I'd have to change into nicer clothes than my oversized sweatshirt and blue jean shorts. Another being I'd have to actually be social, which is something I don't think I'm up for today. And the third, although maybe most important, beachfront seafood restaurants cost money. A lot of money. Money that my bank account cannot afford since I've been unemployed for a little over a month. In fact, I'm pretty sure if my sister hadn't been buying groceries and letting me stay at her apartment, I'd be bankrupt by now.

Keeping my sprawled position across the mattress and my pillow almost suffocating me, I reply, "You guys go ahead. I'll hang out tomorrow."

Megan sighs, but, for once, doesn't pester me any further. I hold my position until I hear voices in the living room and then the front door closes. Alone at last. Although now I'm awake and hungry. Thanks, Megan.

I make my way into the kitchen, search the cabinets, and find a large bag of potato chips that I silently pray my sister brought. I open it and pop a chip in my mouth, closing my eyes and moaning at the salty, crispy goodness that coats my tongue.

"Those must be some chips."

My eyes fly open and find Michael making his way into the kitchen, where he pulls himself onto one of the counters and just sits, like he isn't interrupting me and my sweet, sweet carbs.

Swallowing the half-chewed chip in my mouth, I lean against the counter across from him, not trusting them enough to hold my weight like Michael has, and hold the bag in his direction. He accepts my offering, reaching into the bag and extracting one. He chews it quickly and swallows, and I know I should say something, but, just like earlier, I seem to have lost the ability to speak around this man.

He doesn't seem perturbed by my silence, instead saying, "Didn't want seafood?"

Finally finding my voice, I reply, "Getting dressed up to eat overpriced shrimp isn't my thing."

"Me either. Want to go get a burger?"

This stranger wants to eat burgers? I mean, of course I always want fast food. And he's not technically a stranger, I guess. Although maybe that's worse, since he doesn't seem to remember we've met while it's all I can think about.

Even though I have every intention of turning down the offer, the words that exit my mouth are somehow agreeing to go get hamburgers. The next thing I know, I'm pulling my hair into a tighter knot on the top of my head and following him out the door.

As I pick out all the onions on my hamburger, even though I said no onions, Michael says, "Pickle juice instead of creamer in your coffee, or onions on your hamburger?"

Once my burger is finally clean of the foul-tasting vegetable in question, I answer, "Easy. Pickle juice. No doubt."

Michael takes a bite of his burger as we sit at an outdoor picnic table by the restaurant he picked, a fast-food place that I've never heard of but he says is a chain. I question this since there's no way I don't know every unhealthy, greasy chain restaurant that exists.

"No doubt?"

Shrugging, I eat a fry and reply, "I like coffee. I like pickles. How bad could it be?"

He looks at me in a way that's similar to how he looked at me a month ago when I threw my drink on Andrew, as if I'm one second from screaming and running down the street naked. But really, *he* asked *me* the ridiculous question.

"What? Have you ever tried pickle juice in your coffee?"

"Can't say I have."

"Then you can't judge it, can you?"

He smiles, and it does weird things to my stomach as he says, "Touché."

The burger is good, but I have to believe so many people come here for the view. Even though the water is far away, I can still make out the waves as they break the surface.

Michael leans back a bit as he asks, "So, what do you do?"

Taking a sip of my soda, I reply, "Besides regularly eat foods that clog my arteries?"

He nods as he takes a massive bite of burger.

"Unemployed for the last month. Human Resource Manager for a company that went out of business."

"Dang."

"What's crazy is they made me fire so many people before they told me they were going out of business. Worst week of my life. Although that could also be due to the fact that I caught my boyfriend cheating on me, too."

"That is a terrible week."

I'm silent, lost in my thoughts, until Michael asks, "Twizzlers instead of noodles in spaghetti, or Nerds instead of salt on a baked potato?"

We finish eating our burgers as we sit on the bench and look out toward the nearby ocean while we ask each other bizarre food-related questions, and it is the most fun I have had since my world exploded a month ago.

If you told me before arriving at the beach that I'd be spending the next four days hanging out with Paul's brother and actually enjoying myself, I'd have called you a liar and you'd have been in danger of one of my infamous eyerolls. But here we are, sprawled on the floor of the living room playing Gin Rummy. Why the floor? Because we discovered quickly that the chairs are in danger of breaking even under my petite weight and the couch is so uncomfortable that neither of us could use it for more than ten minutes. It's pretty sad when the floor is a better option than the couch. I'd suggest we sit on a bed but that seems a bit too intimate.

"Jumping into a pool of sharks or wrestling an alligator?"

Taking another card from the stack between us, Michael doesn't hesitate to say, "I'm assuming the pool is saltwater and the sharks are alive."

"Assumption correct."

He discards a three of clubs as he answers, "Alligator."

Giving him a shake of my head, I take his discarded three and say, "Ridiculous."

"There's only one alligator! There's a pool full of sharks!"

Matching his energy, I reply, "The alligator is attacking you! The sharks will probably let you swim out of the pool!"

"Keyword being *probably*!"

My sister passes us as she walks to the kitchen, lifting one of her eyebrows and looking down at us in what I'm going to choose to believe is a look of affection. Although the next words out of her mouth make me question my assessment immediately.

"Are you two really arguing over something this dumb?"

"We're not arguing," Michael and I both say simultaneously as we examine the cards in our hands.

"You're literally yelling at each other."

Michael looks up at me for a moment as he says to Megan, "It's a heated discussion in which your sister is sorely mistaken."

"Says you." But I'm smiling as I win the game.

The next day, I'm lying by the ocean. I've got my sunglasses and hat covering most of my face as the waves slowly creep their way closer to my knees.

It won't be long before I'll have to decide whether to move further up the beach or finally go inside. Based on the pink hue my skin is turning, I should probably go inside, but it's so peaceful here in the late afternoon that even the sizzling of my skin doesn't motivate me to move.

What does encourage me to finally want to leave my position in the sand is the dark shadow that covers me. Squinting up through my sunglasses, I see my sister looking down at me.

"So, this is where you've been hiding all day."

"Hiding? I'm literally lying on the beach within walking distance of the house."

Megan exhales loudly as she takes a seat next to my horizontal position in the sand. While she stares out at the ocean, I close my eyes and let the sun continue to pleasantly roast me. It's only a minute before she breaks our silence.

"You seem better."

My eyes still shut, I respond, "Do I?"

"You're not lying face down on the sofa surrounded by candy wrappers and crying over the Cooking Channel."

"What can I say? Watching people cook Italian food really gets me. Besides, have you been on that sofa in there? It's not fit to lie on."

"Mmhmm."

"What?"

"A certain brother doesn't have anything to do with your improved mood?"

Wiggling my shoulders and trying to press myself deeper in the sand, I say, "We don't have a brother."

"Dottie."

"What?"

I can feel Megan staring at me and I imagine her face full of judgment.

"Michael?" I grunt. "Ugh. No."

"He's no Paul, I'll give you that."

Sighing, the words just come out. "You can say that again."

"What's that supposed to mean?"

"Nothing."

My answer must have been too quick, because Megan loudly replies, "Paul's a great guy. You'd like him if you got to know him. But that would mean you'd actually have to spend time with him, which you seem adamantly against doing for some unknown reason."

"I'm not against hanging out with Paul."

"Have you even talked to him since we've been here?"

My silence makes her eyes glint with a disappointed satisfaction. "Exactly."

Feeling shame for some reason, I respond a bit too harshly. "Why would I want to hang out with one of your boyfriends?"

"He's not just one of my boyfriends! He's *the* one."

We both pause, and she seems to be more shocked than even I am by her admission. Finally, she looks back out at the water and exhales as she says, "Oh, crap. Paul's the one."

"You've got it bad."

Then we both laugh quietly, and I know our fight is over. Megan sighs and stands up to go back toward the house.

"Megan," I say.

She turns back and raises her eyebrows in question.

"I'll try to get to know Paul. Since he's your 'the one' and all."

"Only one day left here. Better hurry."

She smiles at me and heads to the house while I remain on the beach, wondering what it would be like to find the one, since I'm certain I've never had that feeling before. I stay there until the ocean water reaches the backs of my thighs and the sound of thunder interrupts my thoughts, much too loud for comfort.

By the time I make it back into the house, the rain is almost painful with how hard it's falling, and I'm only slightly exaggerating when I say I practically get struck by lightning three times. At my bedroom door, my cover-up and my hair dripping water, I stop and let out a weird, high-pitched groan when I see my bed.

Megan is suddenly at my side and peers through the open doorway, where my bed is currently getting drenched in rainwater from the open window.

"Shouldn't have left your window open, I guess."

If I were a violent woman, my sister would be regretting those words, because yes, obviously I should have shut my window this morning.

Still staring at the rainwater soaking my entire bed, I say, "This doesn't help the situation, Megan! I can't sleep there tonight!"

Her voice carries to me as she makes her way down the hall. "Sucks to be you."

She is so lucky I'm not prone to punching. And she's absolutely right; it does suck to be me. There's no way anyone would deny this as I lie on my back later that night with my feet squished against the end of the couch. There's a crick in my neck already from just lying here for the past thirty minutes, and no matter which way I position myself, my back hurts. This couch is the worst thing ever invented, and I'm starting to wonder if the owners use this place as a torture chamber during the off season.

The storm has finally settled down, which is why I can hear the near-silent steps of someone as they make their way through the house. Since it is past midnight and everyone went to sleep hours ago, there's only one conclusion my exhausted mind can come to: someone has broken in through the back door and is going to attack me.

When a man's shadow appears from the doorway of the hall, I scream. The shadowed man jumps and falls backward. I take this opportunity to rush to the light switch, expecting to see a robber chasing me when the light appears.

To my embarrassment, it's Michael, still in his position on the floor, looking perplexed at the entire situation. Grateful he's not a masked murderer, I rush over and stretch my hand out to help him up as I whisper loudly, "What are you doing?"

He takes my hand and pulls himself up as he replies, matching my volume. "What am I doing? You're the one trying to wake everyone up. Why are you screaming?"

Deciding not to tell him about my thoughts running wild, I say, "I was trying to sleep and then I saw your huge shadow!"

"Sorry for thinking I was allowed to get a glass of water!"

Going back to the torture couch, I reply, "Apology accepted. Turn off the light when you're done."

Michael moves to the kitchen, and I can hear the squeak of the kitchen cabinet as he gets a glass and then the faucet as he fills it with water. By the time he makes it back into the living room, I'm already shifting positions, trying to get comfortable, before I finally give up and toss the throw pillow on the floor, getting to my feet.

Still whispering, he leans against the doorframe of the kitchen and asks, "What are you doing?"

"Trying to sleep." I look around my feet and decide the floor is clean enough before I lie down and drape the afghan over me.

"Why aren't you in your bed?"

"Left the window open."

He pauses before asking, "And you're scared to close it?"

"No. My bed got soaked, and before you judge me for my stupidity, I tried to close it tonight when I got home and it doesn't shut. So, take that, Megan!"

Michael glances behind him before he replies, "You do realize it's just the two of us in here, right?"

"Never mind. Goodnight." Rolling onto my side, I can feel my shoulder already ache from lying on the hard, barely carpeted floor. Squeezing my eyes shut, the reality of my situation makes me sigh and almost sob. It takes me a moment to realize the lights are still on.

As I roll over and sit up, preparing to get up and turn off the light, I startle at the sight of Michael still leaning against the frame.

"What?"

He clears his throat. "You can sleep in my bed if you want."

"If I can't fit on that couch, there's no way you'd be able to. And trust me, this floor is awful."

Shrugging, he turns to leave. "I'm sleeping in my bed. I was just offering you the other side. If you change your mind, I'll be in my comfortable, dry bed."

It only takes me three minutes of shoulder pain before I'm following quickly after him. When I get to his room, he's already lying on his back under the covers.

"Fine. I accept your invitation. Scoot over."

He manages to shift the slightest bit so just the edges of our arms are touching when I slide into bed next to him. We lie there in silence for a couple of minutes, and I'm hyperaware of his body next to mine, of every breath he takes, and I'm starting to regret deciding to sleep next to him.

As if he can tell how awkward I feel, his voice is barely a whisper as he says, "Want to know a secret?"

My heart starts thundering as I reply, "Okay."

He's quiet for a moment before he says, "Paul's proposing to Megan tomorrow."

My head whips right to see if he's serious, but I can only make out a dark profile looking up at the ceiling. "No way."

The faceless head next to me nods. "Way. He's been wanting to for a while now."

"They've only been together like a year."

"I guess when you know, you know."

Turning my head so I'm facing the ceiling as well, I hesitantly agree. "I guess so."

"Think she'll say yes?"

Megan's words from the beach earlier run through my head. "Oh, she'll say yes."

Michael is silent for a moment before his voice, even quieter than before, says, "That's why I didn't go through with it, that night at the club. I was so nervous, but not in a good way. I felt like I was going to throw up."

Sitting up abruptly, my voice is louder than it should be as I exclaim, "You do remember me!"

Chuckling, he keeps his voice quiet as he says, "Hard to forget a woman who throws her drink at a man and buys me one."

"I bought you two drinks."

"True."

If he had made this declaration that he remembered me the first day we met, I'd have been mortified and probably hidden in my room the entire week. Now, I'm shocked to find that I'm mostly amused. In fact, thinking about the night I saw Andrew with another woman doesn't send the sharp stabs through my chest like it used to. Weird.

Thinking back to our first encounter, I say, "You did look pretty pale and sweaty that night."

"I'm going to assume you mean that I looked pretty, as well as pale and sweaty."

"Obviously."

"Just a guess but the guy you dumped a gin and tonic on was your boyfriend?"

"It wasn't a gin and tonic. That's what I was going to drink before I gave it to you. He got the cheaper cranberry vodka. Plus, I was hoping the cranberry juice would stain his expensive shirt."

"Diabolical and practical."

"That's what my Tinder profile says." Since apparently he seems okay discussing that night, I ask, "So, why were you so nervous?"

Michael sighs and moves the arm that's not touching mine, putting it under his head before replying. "We'd been together a couple of years, and it felt like everyone was pressuring me to marry her. Her parents. Her brother. Then she got offered a job across the country and told me she was going to take it if I wasn't serious about her." He exhales loudly as he continues. "Bought the ring, had a speech, and then I watched you throw your drink on a guy, and I thought to myself, 'If my girlfriend were here dancing with some other guy, I wouldn't be mad enough to do that. In fact, I'd be relieved.' Decided right then that she was not the one."

Repeating his earlier words, I quietly say, "When you know, you know."

Neither of us talks the rest of the night, but it's a comfortable silence. And, eventually, his slow breaths and warm body next to mine lull me to sleep.

It's later than it should be. This I can tell from the light coming in through the window, hitting my closed eyelids. My sister and Paul's loud voices moving through the house also tell me I've slept too long, since I'm always awake before Megan. Snuggling deeper into my pillow, it's so comfortable that I'm hoping I'll somehow be able to stay like this for just a few more minutes, but Paul's voice shouts in the hallway just as he opens the door. "Get up, man! I'm getting—Oh. Uh, sorry."

My sister's high-pitched giggle approaches from the hallway. "What's wrong—Ah! Sorry!"

Then she slams the door, leaving me and Michael still in his bed, somehow with his arms wrapped around my waist. And what I thought was a pillow my head had been comfortably resting on was his chest. Dang it. This'll be hard to explain.

Once we're up, I'm more nervous around Michael than I have been since the first day here, so I quickly escape his room and head into the kitchen, which is strangely quiet after all that yelling that was happening just a few minutes ago. Finding my sister and Paul standing in the kitchen whispering, I interrupt them as I start a pot of coffee.

"It's not what you think. Can we not discuss this so early?"

My sister's eyes are wide and too innocent-looking. "It's not early. And we weren't thinking anything."

"Mmhmm."

She fans her face. "Is it hot in here?"

"About the same as it's been all week." Which, since the house's air conditioning is only partially reliable, it's always been slightly warm.

Continuing to move her left hand slowly in front of her face, she says in an exaggerated voice that confuses me, "Seriously. It. Is. So. Hot."

That's when I see it. A beautiful diamond wrapped in a silver band on her ring finger.

"Oh my gosh." Forgetting the coffee, I run over and examine the piece of jewelry, releasing a high-pitched squeal that is very much not like me. Although I guess it could be when my sister gets engaged. "When did this happen?"

She squeals right along with me as she says, "This morning! Paul took me to get breakfast and proposed on the walk back, right on the beach."

"Aww." Glancing at the man, I see Paul blushing slightly as he looks proudly at his new fiancée, and it makes me like him. Anyone that looks at my sister like that has to be a stand-up guy. "You did good."

Michael enters the kitchen and makes his way to the coffee pot, pulling two mugs out from the drying rack as he says, "Finally. He's been wanting to propose practically since you two met."

Michael goes to the fridge, but I'm distracted from staring at him by Paul, who doesn't look even slightly embarrassed as he smiles at Megan. "He's not lying."

And the way Megan is beaming at Paul, I am so happy for her it takes my breath away.

"Here." Looking to my right, Michael is there with a cup of coffee held out to me, which is definitely new. I guess we're sharing beds *and* making each other coffee now.

Taking the offered cup from him, I smile as I take a sip and immediately spit it out all over the floor as the taste of something awful hits my tongue.

"Dottie?" My sister's anxious voice barely registers as I start chuckling while I wipe my mouth with my sleeve and look at Michael, who's wearing an amused expression.

"You did not."

He takes a step back with his hands up. "It was an experiment."

"Pickle juice?"

"You said you'd like it!"

"You are so dead." Before I even start moving, Michael is already rushing out the door, and I chase him through the sand until we reach the beach, where I shove him into the water. But he manages to grab my hand and pull me in with him.

When we come up for air, both laughing as my sister and Paul watch us from the back door holding hands, it's the happiest I've been. Maybe ever.

One Year Later

My sister smiles at me when our eyes meet, looking more beautiful than I've ever seen her, as she dances with Paul on a makeshift dance floor next to the ocean. She went with a simple white sleeveless silk wedding dress, and I have to admit that Paul looks pretty good, too, in his tan pants and white button-up. Although, everyone on this beach can see it's not what they are wearing that makes them so stunning; it's the obvious love and devotion when they look at each other.

A familiar figure steps up to my side as I watch them, and even without looking, I know who is next to me. He passes me a drink as I ask, "Have you ever seen anything so beautiful?"

"No."

When I glance up at him, Michael isn't looking at the happy couple dancing in front of the seemingly endless ocean as the sun sets. No, he's looking down at me with that smile of his that might be my favorite thing about him. Or maybe my favorite thing about Michael is the way he holds me when we're alone, making me feel safer than I've ever felt. Or the way he makes me laugh, which I do all the time now. Although, if I'm honest, there's no way to pick one favorite thing about the man next to me, because I love everything about him. When you know, you know.

About the Author

Caroline Baccene is the author of the novels *Breathing in the Fog* and *A Beautiful Lily*. She grew up in the middle of nowhere, South Carolina, where she developed a love of reading, writing, acting, gardening, and caring for all types of animals. Caroline graduated from the University of South Carolina with a degree in Early Childhood Education and was a teacher for five years. She currently resides in South Carolina with her husband and son.

You can find Caroline on:
Instagram: @caroline_baccene
Facebook: @carolinebaccene

You can visit her website at:
https://www.carolinebaccene.com

DO THE STARS EXIST?

Do the Stars Exist?
A Charleston Harbor Short Story

Desi Stowe

Chapter 1

Corey

THOUGH THE DARK, OMINOUS CLOUDS of the night sky obscure the stars, on some level I know they still exist, even if I can't see them. A steady constant of the night sky despite whatever complete and utter nonsense we decide to do on Earth. As sure as those stars exist, I love my wife. A dark cloud covered my entire life six months ago. Rebecca had stood by me when my life hung in the balance, teetering between living and the beyond due to blood loss. It seems so simple: blood loss. Not like it's something that can annihilate your very existence. She'd held my hand and sent up desperate prayers to the heavens. Rebecca had comforted my mom, who'd thought she was losing her only child, while she herself dealt with the distinct possibility of losing me.

Rebecca had stayed by my side when my medical team decided to save me, even if it meant I lost my leg. She'd sat stoic by my hospital bed, those dark, expressive eyes baring into my very soul as the surgeon told me they took my leg, they'd had to. She'd willed her unshakeable strength into me, to keep fighting through my recovery, even as my own strength waned. She never left my side through the surgeries, the pain, physical therapy, prosthetic fitting, and the drastic changes to my career as I went from a hands-on general contractor to being sidelined to an office.

Fortunately, I can still work; I've been able to pull in some kind of an income for the past couple of months. Though my mobility is much improved, no one wants me on a jobsite. But I'm good at sales. My customer service skills are strong. My company kept me on as a customer liaison and, for liability reasons, has kept me and my one good leg off of construction sites.

I hate being sidelined to the office.

The love I have for my wife has never faltered. But I can't say the same of hers for me. My near-death and its subsequent fallout has been too much for Rebecca to handle. The endless medical bills, the numerous appointments with my medical team, and my general displeasure with life. She's such a strong woman, but everyone has their limits. The knowledge that I'm the one who is pushing her to those limits fractures my heart.

Though I've never been brave enough to ask her if she still loves me and how she feels about us, the doubts circulate through my mind in a haunting rhythm. Every single day, I hate myself for the hell I put her through. Hate that the spark of those beautiful brown eyes is gone. But most of all, I hate that I've become little more than a chore to her.

Each night I lie awake here in the guest bedroom, the barracks I've been assigned since I came home from the hospital. Initially it was so that Rebecca wouldn't bump into the tender skin of my incision as she slept by my side, but that's healed now. It's been healed for weeks. I've not been invited back to my bedroom, and I've not swallowed my pride and asked. Instead, I spend restless nights alone, lying on my back and searching a ceiling that holds no answers. Wondering if the stars still exist.

I forget I don't have a leg. That's what starts the final spiral away from marital bliss to what may very well be the fatal blow. I hear a loud noise outside, or maybe I dream it. Naturally, I stand up, rather quickly, to see what's going on, assuming I have two good feet. In my half-awake, groggy state and with my imbalance, I fall into the dresser, bruising my ribs. On the way down, I hit our wedding picture, cracking the glass of the frame in a symbolic representation of my future.

"Corey! What? What happened?" Rebecca scans my room, landing on the broken picture. Not that she says anything. Just looks at me with disappointment in her eyes. She can school most of her features into obedience, but I can always read her eyes.

"Becs. It's not like that. I fell and hit the dresser, knocking the frame over." Is it like that, though? Do we inevitably end? I can't bear the thought of it, but my wife deserves someone better. Someone *whole*. Someone who hasn't saddled her with the debt of medical bills and lost wages. Someone normal.

She picks up the broken pieces of the shattered frame, setting them back on the dresser. "Here, let me help you." She takes a step toward me.

My voice is grumbled and filled with more venom than I intend. On some level, I know exactly none of this is her fault. She's taken the brunt of the anger and frustration that's built up inside me over the past few months as I've developed a new normal. I hate my new normal. "Don't coddle me. I can manage."

I've built enough strength to balance on one foot and use my triceps to lift me to the bed. Now that I'm eye level with her, full of embarrassment and shame, I see the hurt in her eyes. The hurt that I put there. I pat the space on the bed beside me.

She sits next to me with reluctance. Her spine stiffens when I try to put an arm around her. My mouth is dry, and I can't form the words I want to say.

I miss you. I miss us.

Chapter 2

Rebecca

"I CANNOT BELIEVE HE FELL asleep in the meeting!" I link arms with my bestie, and I grab my umbrella as we head to lunch. Looks like more rain is in the future.

She laughs. Our coworker is well known for dozing off, but neither of us expected him to fall asleep in a meeting our boss was leading. With commendable diligence, I avoided Morgan's gaze for the entire meeting, knowing that if we'd made eye contact, our professional composure would be lost. "Does he have narcolepsy that needs to be treated?"

I shrug. How does one fall asleep on the job and be able to remain at that job? I file it under a mental file of life's greatest mysteries. "You got me. How's non-work life? The renovation going smoothly now?"

She holds a hand over her heart. "One day, I will have a functioning kitchen back. One day!!"

Chuckling, we make our way down to the little restaurant next to our office as the wind picks up around us. Morgan's kitchen has lived in disarray for weeks now.

"I wish Corey could've taken your job." Saying his name pinches my heart. It doesn't hurt, but it also doesn't feel great. Corey's only recently returned to work since the accident. Since the day that changed everything and the world around me crumbled. I've been struggling, in vain, to find my footing ever since.

She sends a sympathetic smile my way. She'd sat with me as I'd waited to hear if Corey would even survive. When I learned they had to amputate his leg. "He's getting some work now, yeah?"

"He is, but they won't let him on the jobsite. He's doing desk work, and I know he hates it. But it pulls in a decent paycheck. Right now that's more important than job satisfaction." Maybe. *If I could only push happiness or even a lowkey contentment into my husband, I'd do it in a heartbeat.*

Morgan shoots me a look. I'm sure she doesn't agree with me; she'd probably say Corey needs to find something fulfilling to pull him out of the post-traumatic event pit he's in. She's kind enough not to argue her point. She sees beyond practicality to a fulfilled life. She's always been that way, finding meaning and purpose while the rest of us swim upstream in survival mode to make it through the day.

We enter the small diner and order salads, because it's the responsible thing to do. *I'm nothing if not responsible.*

My fork pushes food around, but I barely eat. My best friend Morgan is looking at me, waiting for answers to questions that I've been not-so-subtly avoiding. She brushes her long, blonde hair away from her face, and she's dressed to the nines in a blazer and skirt. But it's not her outward appearance I envy, not today anyway. It's her unfathomable level of patience. Her outlook on life. Her general aura. Morgan's patience wears me down, and I start unloading all my fears. "Corey and I, well, he—"

Despite my incoherence, Morgan motions for me to continue.

"We live together. As roommates. We don't fight, that would almost be welcome. It would be *something*. I know he's hurting, and I can't imagine what all of this does to a person." I put my fork down and shake my head. "I've tried giving him space to process things, to take his time returning to normal life."

Morgan raises her eyebrows. "But?"

"But, in giving him space, I think he realizes he doesn't want me in his life anymore." The last words are choked as I swallow the lump of fear in my throat that seems to have taken up a permanent residence. Everything is so hard and I'm drowning in the current.

My friend eyes me thoughtfully. "I've always thought that you and Corey were endgame. If anyone could make it, it'd be the two of you."

My eyes close as I try hopelessly to stop the flood of emotions. "Yeah, me too."

Morgan squeezes my hand. "Do you want advice, or do you want to vent?"

I giggle. Morgan's husband tries to fix everything—always. He's a fixer by nature, and it grates on Morgan's nerves to no end. They've implemented a policy: do you want to vent, or do you want me to fix it? It cracks me up that she's using it with me, though I fully appreciate the gesture. Laughing feels good. Almost normal.

"I'll take advice if you've got it."

She levels me with a look I can't read, and I find myself fidgeting in my seat. She loves Corey like a brother and his accident hit her hard. I've never seen my tough-as-nails friend cry, but she cried with me as we waited in the sterile confines of a hospital waiting room. So much waiting happens when disaster strikes. I push my lunch away; I can't deal with food today.

She points her fork at me. Her tone is no-nonsense. "Your relationship with Corey has always been easy. You fell in love without the normal drama. You get along with the other's family for the most part. You've had a very smooth road. Until now."

I blow out a breath. Corey fit into my life nicely. He always has. She's not wrong. I don't really believe in love at first sight; it seems too much like a fairy tale. But there was a *something* at first sight, a strong something. From day one, I never doubted my relationship with Corey.

She hedges, considering her words. She's blunt but kind. "Do you have any idea how rare that is? Do you want to throw that away now that things are hard? That kind of relationship is not easy to find."

I press my lips together, resolved. "No, no I don't. But I also don't know how to navigate where we are right now. I'm afraid he's going to leave me." The last sentence is a strained whisper, an audible confession of my deepest fear. "I'm not planning on leaving."

She eats her salad and I long for French fries. "Have you talked to him about it?"

I shake my head. "No, I'm terrified of what he might say. I can't deal with that. What if he's ready to let go? I'm not ready to let go, and I'm definitely not ready to hear those words."

She squeezes both my hands, and she delivers the hard truth I don't want to hear. "Living in limbo is not good for you. Nothing is more terrifying than the unknown. Not for you, not for Corey."

"He lashes out at me, he won't let me help him. We both work late so we don't have to have a meal together. We're barely roommates at this point." I rub my temples to see if I can eliminate the headache of the last six months. "Maybe he resents me for helping him in the beginning. But what was I supposed to do? Watch him suffer and laugh at his pain?"

"No, of course not. But sometimes people are the most unlovable when they need love the most," she says as she gathers her things.

Work calls, and it's something we can't avoid. We work in office equipment sales and have the possibility of a sizable bonus if we can land this contract. While no part of me has the bandwidth for a huge work project, Morgan and I agreed to team up and tackle it. Both of us could use an influx of cash.

Maybe Morgan is right, though, and Corey's gruffness and distance is more to do with the fact that his needs are unmet. He needs extra love right now, so maybe I can shift my focus toward meeting that need. Maybe I can save my marriage. As we leave the diner, a faint shimmer of sunlight breaks through and I put my umbrella away.

Chapter 3

Corey

"TEN MORE REPS AND THEN you're done." my physical therapist, Eugene Spinner, has put me through the paces, challenging my strength and my balance. But I'm grateful for it. I feel good. Physically. Physically, I feel *good*. Which is odd because the reflection in my mirror shows how physically flawed I am. After the awkwardness of falling yesterday evening, and the emptiness of having no connection left with Rebecca, I've never felt so completely lost. So flawed.

"Here ya go." Eugene throws me a towel. "Today can be your last day of physical therapy. You're doing well and have more than accomplished your initial goals."

I give him a half smile as I stretch my hamstrings.

I feel him studying me, expecting more from me. "This news is good news, a reason to celebrate. What's going on? Do you have doubts about managing things on your own?"

"No, I feel great physically, and in some ways I'm stronger than I was before the accident." Eugene set me up on an upper-body workout to compensate for my leg loss during some activities with upper-body strength, like getting up from the floor. My arms have never been this defined. Minus half my leg being chopped off, I look *good*. On the outside. Inside, I'm a trainwreck.

"So, ending therapy is a good thing." He searches my face, trying to read me.

"Hopefully the wife agrees." I pinch the bridge of my nose. "That is a strong, stubborn woman."

Eugene laughs. "I know the feeling. My wife is the same." He looks off into the distance as if he's remembering the extent of her stubbornness.

"My wife, she—" My words stop short. What can I even say? I switch to stretch the other leg.

Eugene chooses his words carefully, as if he knows they're important. Somehow, he understands his words may one day be my lifeline. "When a trauma happens, the partner has to be stubborn, has to be strong. No other option is on the table. But as the dust settles, maybe it's harder to hold on to that."

Wordlessly, I finish my stretching, but his words nestle into my mind.

Before I go, Eugene hands me a packet of mental health resources and encourages me to check them out. I nod, considering it.

"Sometimes people need a safe space where they don't have to be strong anymore."

Sitting in my car, I look at the resources Eugene gave me. I even pull out my phone. But I don't' make the calls. I can't stomach the idea of yet another appointment. More co-pays. More missed work. More hassle.

Instead, I stop by the grocery store and pick up a few items for a stir-fry. I'm no chef, but this is one dish I can manage. Rebecca and I used to cook together—and by cook together, I mean she bossed me around and did all the actual cooking while I chopped and cleaned. I loved it. Cooking a single dinner is a far cry from repaying the debt I owe her, but it's something.

"Corey?"

"In here, Becs. Hungry?"

She eyes me warily. "Don't you need to be off your feet?"

Inwardly, I cringe at the assumption I can't stand long enough to make a simple dinner, but outwardly I try for peace. "I sat most of the day." That's most definitely a lie. My leg is killing me right now after a day on my feet helping a couple pick out cabinetry and then physical therapy.

So, some couples are picking out kitchen cabinets and doing normal life, and we're . . . whatever this is right now. At least we're speaking.

She sits at a barstool at our counter and nearly smiles at me. The dark circles of sleepless nights show, but she's still beautiful. Sometimes I wonder if she's slept since the accident. She tells me she sleeps fine when clearly she's not.

"Are you trying to make up for breaking our wedding picture?"

I separate the stir-fry into two plates. "I mean, that was an unfortunate accident."

She smirks. "What happened?"

Do I go with the truth here? I've lied once already, and I'd rather not make it a habit. With a self-deprecating laugh, I stick to honesty. "I forgot I only had one leg."

Her response is deadpan. "You forgot."

I grin. "Well, I did spend thirty years with two legs." I tap the metal of my prosthetic. "This is a new development." I'm hoping it's a joke, but she doesn't laugh.

"Are you hurt? From falling?" she asks me between bites. She's eating quickly. "This is good, I'm starving."

My ribcage is a little bruised, but that's it. "Mostly my pride."

She smiles at me and takes the last couple bites of dinner. I grab our plates and bring them to the sink.

"Oh, I can wash up. You did cook, after all."

I agree but only because my leg really does hurt. "I finished physical therapy today." Our conversation feels first-date forced, but it's something.

"Finished? Really?" Her tone holds a hint of judgment but mostly surprise.

"Yeah." I prop my fake leg up to remove the weight of it from my knee. The surgeons said they fought to save my knee because having that joint makes life easier. Comparatively speaking. It's not that I'm not grateful, I am. It's just a weird vibe to be thankful for a knee when I used to have an entire leg. "I have exercises I'm supposed to continue indefinitely. I've been doing most of them at the office between clients."

She loads the dishwasher with an expert precision that makes me smile. It's such a Rebecca thing to do. It's on the tip of my tongue to say that—to say something meaningful. How much I miss the way things used to be. How she's my everything. But the emotion floods my mind, and picking out one phrase seems impossible, and I remain silent. She kisses my cheek. "I'm proud of you. I need to shower and go to bed early. I've got a meeting first thing tomorrow."

With that, she walks away. I get ready for bed, but wonder if I should tell Rebecca good night. Or something. We've made progress tonight and it feels like the next natural step. I'm about to knock on her bedroom door, our bedroom door, when I hear the sound of muffled sobs. Broken, I go back to my bedroom and look out the window at the cloudy night sky. No stars in sight.

Chapter 4

Rebecca

"YOU'RE TURNING DOWN THE PROMOTION?" my boss eyes me with confusion and a hefty dose of disappointment.

Crossing my legs and taking a deep breath, I try to find peace and not a complete mental breakdown before I speak. A year ago, I would've jumped at this promotion. That was then, and things are far different now. The promotion involves traveling once or twice a month. Can I leave Corey that often? He's doing really well, he's back at work, and we even shared a meal last night.

My mind goes back to the hospital, the night he woke up missing a leg and in pain from the extensive surgery. Reeling from being in a high-speed crash with a drunk driver. He looked at me, radiating despair, and said, "I don't know that I want to live like this." His words loop through my memories in a haunting mantra. Making my nights restless and setting my days on edge.

"As you know, my personal life has been challenging. I'm not sure I can handle the travel."

His brows furrow. "Do you want to think about it? Talk it over with Corey?"

Before the accident, I'd have discussed it over with Corey during a celebratory dinner. He's always been proud and supportive of my career success. I know he'd tell me to take the job now. But I don't know if I can take it. "No, it's too much right now. I'd love that job, don't get me wrong. But the timing doesn't work."

My boss furrows his brow and frowns, but he can join the ever-growing list of people I've disappointed, including my mother. Other than Morgan, everyone thinks I should be better now. Not still spinning from a life-changing experience. Corey's alive. I should be grateful and move on with life. I am grateful, so very grateful. It's the moving on part that gets me. My mind is stuck in that hospital room, haunted by Corey's suffering and my inability to do anything about it.

Corey and I are supposed to spend a few days at this resort a couple of hours away for my cousin's wedding in a couple of weeks. An event that should've been a perfect summer vacation. Last night I called my mom to back out of it—but the deposits have been paid and she's insistent "we need this." She expressed her disappointment that I would even ask to skip the event. A disappointment that my marriage continues to struggle in the months following the accident.

The conversation with her left me sobbing as I mourned the loss of a normal life. Corey and I would be in the same room, sharing the same small space. It feels like we're being dropped into the perfect circumstances for this house of cards to fall. So many things have been left unsaid between us. So many questions that I don't want the answers to.

But maybe nights like last night are what we need. Almost like dating again. His accident changed both of us and we can get to know each other again. If I'm being honest, that's the root of my fear. What if Corey doesn't like the woman I've become? I certainly don't. Not many people do. The existential dread weaving through the tangled tapestry of my life has changed me into an anxious mess.

Walking down the hall, I do my best to chase away the intrusive thoughts and focus on the mundane work ahead of me. Morgan and I agree to a quick walk after work. I tell her that Corey made me dinner, but I leave out the turned-down job promotion. She'll likely hear about it through the work gossip chain. I'd like to tell her first, but I can't do it now. Maybe tomorrow.

"That's better, right?" She beams at me. She is the happiest of people. I love/hate that about her.

"I don't know, Morgan. Since the accident I've been anxious and unsettled. You want to know the truth? Yeah, I've been avoiding him."

"Let's unpack that. Why?" Morgan gives me a stern look. She's not going to let me avoid this conversation.

Forcing myself to take a deep breath, I consider the question, though I know the answer already. "Corey was in a very dark place after the accident."

"Right. Anyone would be." Morgan gestures for me to continue, knowing I've left things unsaid.

"It scared me. I thought he might give up the will to fight, the will to live, especially when things were still precarious." I fought, though. I fought for him when he couldn't fight. Begged him to eat. Begged him to get out of bed. Begged him not to slip away.

She stops walking to look at me, concern etched in her features. "Is he in a dark place now? Are you worried?"

"No, I'm not exactly worried. I'm exhausted. I'm mentally and emotionally drained. I love him so much and I gave him all my strength, all my everything so he'd stay with me. So he'd fight to recover and now, I-—" My words cut off as a large lump forms in my throat. *Again.*

"Rebecca, you're amazing in a crisis. Always have been. That's your core strength, and kudos for you because not many people have that strength. Remember when my favorite aunt died? It was a smaller scale situation, sure. But you did the same for me. I didn't have the strength to face the funeral or the idea of life without her. *You did the same for me.* Stood by my side and gave me your strength. Willed it into me." She throws an arm around me, giving me a squeeze.

We walk in silence for a few minutes as I absorb her words. Then she continues: "You are not great at dealing with the fallout. The aftermath. You shouldn't be. You've already given your all during the crisis. You've played your part."

My hands gesture wildly and my voice matches. My walking pace increases to brisk, and Morgan matches my stride. "So I give up?"

"No. You let Corey be the strong one. Give him purpose. Let him take the reins and pull the two of you back together. It sounds like he's already trying." Her smile is soft and compassionate, devoid of judgment.

"What if he doesn't like me anymore? Doesn't love me? Resents me for pushing him when he was in pain?" Six hundred more questions rise to the surface, but I squash them down.

"Then we deal with that. But you can't keep swimming in the what-ifs. Those will drown you." We've reached the parking lot and she gives me a fierce hug. "Whatever happens, happens. You've got me. You've always got me."

The muted rays of light disappear into the sunset as I drive back to my home. The exhaustion of my mind is unable to stop the swarms of what-ifs and worst-case scenarios. But in that storm, a tiny inkling of hope appears, and I clutch it tightly.

Chapter 5

Corey

PULLING OUT MY PHONE, I text Rebecca that I'm working late. Yet another lie, but the thought of going home causes an array of conflicting emotions. I'm lying across the couch in the employee breakroom, resting my leg and debating my dismal options. Work finished about half an hour ago and I'm even caught up on the oppressive task of answering emails.

Bottom line: I've broken my wife. That's the truth I can't escape, not after hearing her sobs after we shared a meal together. While I love her with everything in me, while I had dreams of growing old with her and rocking on our front porch watching grandchildren play, while it absolutely *destroys* me, I need to let her go. I'll not burden her with my disastrous life. While I can do most things with my prosthesis, I'm always going to have some level of limitations, the need for prosthetic adjustments, and the expense of ongoing care. That kind of life is not what she signed up for when we married.

Staring at the breakroom ceiling, I consider the "for better or worse" part of the marriage vows. The "for worse" part must have limitations, like losing a limb three years into marriage is a get out of jail free card. I'm certain of it. This burden is mine to carry.

Leaving the office to walk to the car, slipping further into despondency, I sit in the driver's seat with my head on the steering wheel. For the first time since the accident, since my choices started being made by the inebriated driver that changed my life, I scream into the void around me and let the tears fall.

Leaving Rebecca so she can start over is necessary, but I need some time to do it. I want to make sure she's not financially strapped for cash on her income alone. My medical debt is already in my name. I can take that with me. Earlier today, I set up our bank account so a percentage of my income goes directly into our joint savings account—money I'll leave with her for unexpected expenses. I also have some things I can sell off and leave her the cash.

I drive back home in the same dull routine, but I'm bolstered by the knowledge of having a plan. Knowing Rebecca will be taken care of, at least financially, offers some comfort. My mind shifts to doing the honorable thing by leaving. The incomprehensible loss in my life that will enter with her absence fills me with dread. Sadness mixes with purpose as I pull into our driveway. A light rain trickles down from the cloud cover above me on yet another starless night.

Chapter 6

Rebecca

THOUGH COREY TOLD ME HE was running late, I made spaghetti and garlic bread. I'm letting it simmer on the stove when he comes in. The aroma of comfort food surrounds me, and I bask in it.

He looks awful. Dark circles sit beneath his swollen eyes. Is he sleeping at all? I miss him in our bedroom, but he seems content in the guest room. "Are you okay?"

He ignores my question. Instead, he pulls me into a hug, an affection that feels so foreign to me, yet I crave it. We've not done affection. Not in months. "You made dinner? You didn't have to do that."

My head lays on his chest, listening to the steady beat of his heart, and he absently runs his hand over my hair. "You did the same for me, just yesterday."

He pulls out of the hug, and I make us both plates. "Yeah, but you've done so much for me. I'm forever indebted to you already."

My eyes meet his as I consider his words. "I don't see it that way. We're a team."

We eat in a semi-awkward silence while I overthink everything. Though my family is pushing our upcoming vacation and my cousin's wedding, I want Corey's input, too. He may not feel up to it. "My cousin's wedding is coming up in a couple of weeks. Do you want to go?"

He pauses and looks at me for a long time. As if I asked him to divulge the secrets of the universe, not a simple vacation question. Though I'd be the first to admit this vacation has me on a razor-thin edge. He agrees to go, and I'm both relieved and terrified.

For the next few days, everything stays about the same. We eat dinner together some nights. Occasionally, a hug or a platonic kiss on the cheek. But Corey looks worse and worse, fatigued and with bloodshot eyes. I ask him what's going on, but the only response is a tight hug and the words, "I'll never be able to repay you for what you've done for me, but I'll try."

I never asked for, never wanted repayment. I only want my husband back.

Chapter 7

Corey

NO PART OF ME WANTS to go to this wedding. Normally, I love Rebecca's family's events because they always have an insane amount of food. Good food. Everyone is happy because we're too full for fighting. Or mostly happy. Rebecca's family is a loud, boisterous crew, while my wife is more thoughtful and reflective. On occasion, that causes some friction, and I then pull her away to a quiet place. I agreed to go, though. We had planned it before my world exploded, and I can use this vacation, these final memories before I say goodbye.

My car is electric and equipped with a camping mode. I book a campsite about a half hour from the resort in case I need to sleep elsewhere. I have a mattress and window shades for my car and can sleep well enough in it. I don't want Rebecca to feel forced to sleep next to me.

Though I've been funneling money into our accounts, it doesn't seem like it's enough. But too much money and she might notice, and then I'd have to play my card sooner. I decide to take the risk and transfer a larger chunk of funds. She's an independent woman and makes enough to live comfortably. But I don't want her to have to want for anything, not after all I've put her through. She's much too proud to ever agree to alimony, so I've got to do this now.

I've not been able to pull the trigger on calling a lawyer, though the contact is saved in my phone. My mental state has been relatively stable as I've been going through preparations. But hiring a lawyer seems so *final*.

Last night we had dinner again, and this time the conversation flowed much more fluently, like our natural relationship. Sitting on our porch last night, I began to doubt my plan. What if I could be enough for her? Could we make this work? But at the edge of my doubts was the unshakeable feeling that she deserves better. The dark clouds of a summer rain covered the sky as I mourned the last days I'll spend with the woman I love more than anything.

Chapter 8

I'M SATISFIED WITH MY APPEARANCE of a simple tank top and denim shorts as reflected in the mirror. The outfit choice is cute, sending the message that I want to have fun and not worry about all the things. That message is totally for me. I grab my suitcase and bring it outside to where Corey has already packed his things. I wish he'd let me pack the car. But I'm trying not to *coddle* him. Because this trip is about fun. Yes. I can will the fun into existence if I have to.

"Ready? I can drive."

I smile at my husband and sit in the passenger's seat. The surgeons told me how lucky we were that he injured his left leg and will easily be able to drive. Lucky they could save his knee. Lucky he's alive at all.

Well, getting T-boned by someone who should've never been on the roads isn't exactly *lucky*. Pushing those thoughts away, I focus on the scenery around us, the clouds and sun competing for dominance in the late afternoon sky.

The ride feels almost normal. I turn on some light music. We chitchat, nothing much. It's easy. It feels nice. "Oh, I got paid today. Our cost-of-living raise should have gone into effect."

"Weren't you up for a promotion?"

His question makes me wince, and I don't want to answer. I do, though. "I turned it down. It was too much travel."

I watch his profile as he frowns. "You didn't want to leave me?"

Yes, exactly. "The timing doesn't feel right, it's too much to take on right now."

In almost a whisper, I hear his fears. "Because of me."

I wave my hand dismissively. "There will be other promotions. I do want to see how much my annual raise helped, though."

As I'm pulling up my bank balance, Corey asks me to do it later—nearly begs—but it's already up. "Do you know why we have so much money in our savings account?"

He seems extremely focused on the road. After the accident, he had a hard time driving again. "Uh, I moved some money around."

"This is a lot of funds. Why?" Usually we discuss financials. Of course, we also discuss possible job promotions. A feeling kind of like regret has been hanging around me ever since I told my boss I'd pass up the promotion.

"Becs, let this go. We can talk money after we get back home."

Letting things go has never been a core strength, so I press for more. And oh boy, do I wish I'd have left well enough alone. Story of my life.

"I didn't want to get into this yet." He grabs my hand and squeezes it before returning it to the steering wheel. "I'm setting you free."

"Free?" Why is this man speaking in riddles? Why is everything so hard?

"You deserve better than this broken-down model." He gestures to himself.

"Corey. What are you saying?" My heart stops beating for a second or two.

"I think we should get a divorce."

An early evening rain splashes against the windshield as my heart shatters into a million little pieces.

"What?" The word is nearly inaudible. Hadn't things gotten better? If he'd said divorce a few weeks ago, honestly, I wouldn't have been all that surprised. I still would have said no, but the thought wouldn't have been as shocking.

"Becs, it's for the best. I can take my medical debt with me, I've set you up with extra cash." He rubs the back of his neck.

"What if I say no?"

"Come on, Becs. Do you really want to live with me? Like this?" He taps the metal of this prosthetic.

Silence surrounds us as I look out the window, tears trailing down my face. In the darkest moments since this whole ordeal began, I've never wanted to leave Corey. Now he wants to leave me? I've never hurt so much in my entire life.

"Becs—"

I love when he calls me Becs. No one else does. It's our thing. "Shut up."

"Yes, ma'am."

I consider an SOS text to Morgan, but typing the words seems like more than I can handle. Besides, what would she say? What is there to say?

The wind picks up to a terrifying violence and so does the rain. Corey lays a gentle hand on my arm. "We're not going to be able to make it to the resort tonight." He turns off on some random side road.

The weather is getting awful. I hate storms, hate them. We've always lived in Charleston, and my family will ride out every hurricane that comes for an unwelcome visit. They loved it, threw hurricane parties while I sat in the corner and cried.

"What options do we have?"

"Earlier this week I booked a place at this campground. Let's stay here tonight, or at least until the storm blows through. Then I can drop you off at the resort."

We're driving deeper into the woods, and the crackle of thunder sounds close. Staying in a car sounds like a bad idea, but visibility is absent and neither one of us is willing to risk driving.

Corey pulls into our assigned camping site. "Stay here."

He nearly hops out of the car, plugs it in, and pops the trunk open. He kneels to lower the backseats and sets up a mattress he has that fits the back half of the car perfectly once the seats are folded down. He has a pillow and a sleeping bag and blankets, too. I've never car-camped with him. He used to go. *Before.*

Part of me thinks that I should be helping him, but I'm in awe of how well he moves along a gravel surface, in pouring rain, with only one leg. I've not seen him in action, only around the house. I've forgotten he dropped the "D" word for just a few minutes and am completely mesmerized.

He hands me privacy shades for the front windows as he puts shades up in the back. No one is near us, but I'm happy for the privacy. Under the shelter of the raised trunk, Corey peels off his wet clothes and climbs in, wrapping himself in a blanket. He reaches out a hand and helps me crawl between the front seats to the back where he's sitting. He sets the car in camp mode, keeping us in a comfortable climate. We're alone in a small space and surrounded by a deafening silence until thunder cracks again, making me jump.

"Becs." He reaches out a hand to comfort me, and I crawl to him and lay my head on his chest. No part of me wants to end things, but I can't think of how to convince him that his heroic plan to save me from him is stupid. Part of me is almost flattered. The other part is hopeful. These are the actions of a man in love. Stupid actions, sure. But he loves me.

He still loves me.

Chapter 9

Carey

REBECCA NEARLY CLIMBS IN MY lap at the sound of thunder, sitting between my legs with her head on my chest and making me rethink my declaration of divorce. Her body curls into mine and instinctively I wrap my arms around her. She's terrified of storms, always has been.

"It's okay, we're safe in here." I run my fingers through her long, beautiful hair, wondering if it might be the last time.

Her body is tense, and I can feel her anxiety. "Becs. You're such a strong person. You've been so strong for me. What if, even just for tonight, you let that go. Let me be the strong one."

She breathes deeply and then she starts to sob. Clutching the blanket I have wrapped around us, her body shakes as she lets go of everything she's been holding on to for months now.

Tears coat my own face as I hold her tightly. My heart feels like a knife is wedged in it. "It's okay, I've got you."

Is it minutes? Hours? Days? What is time when your heart is breaking? Her tears start to subside. Still holding her close, I shift a bit and reach forward to detach the metal part of my body, rubbing my thigh for relief. Her hand follows mine, landing on my leg.

"Is it tender?"

Even now, she thinks of me. It's so much more than I've ever deserved. "You know how you come in after a long day insisting you need to take your bra off? I imagine it's similar to that feeling."

She laughs, but it quickly shifts to a sullen quietness. "You never moved back to our bedroom."

"I wanted to, but I didn't know if you wanted me. The night after I made you that stir-fry, I came to your room, but I heard you crying. I knew then that you'd be better off without me." She's still wrapped in my arms, but my grip around her has loosened enough where she knows I want her there but I'm not forcing it. My physical actions entirely contradict my words and it's safe to say I'm sending mixed messages.

She leans up and punches me in the arm. Hard. I probably deserved that. "I was crying because mom insisted we come this week. I thought we were making progress but that this trip might be too much. I would've gladly welcomed you back to our room that night." She lays her head against my chest again. "Any night."

Exasperated, I throw my hand up. "Why didn't you say something!"

"Why didn't you?!"

"Because you're better off without me. I come with debt and injuries. We wanted kids! A family! A full and complete life. This changes everything. My accident changed everything."

I know Rebecca feels caged in, she likes to pace in a fight, if she doesn't run away. She's trapped in here, and it's likely driving her crazy.

She whips around at a surprising speed, kneeling in front of me and sitting back on her heels. She cradles my face, her hands pressing into the stubble of my jawline. Her red-rimmed, expressive eyes search mine. "Do you still love me?"

My jaw clenches shut, but I swallow hard and go with honesty, though I'm afraid to. "I love you. I'll always love you."

She shakes her head. "Then I don't want a divorce."

My hands cover hers. "Let me do this for you. Let me set you free. Let me release you of this burden."

She frowns. "It's not a burden to love you."

"Becs, please."

"We can fix this. We can fix us. I love you, Corey. You're my home. No one else can fill that void. Only you. I love you. I don't care that you're missing part of a leg." She smirks. "I've never been all that attached to your shins anyway. Especially not the left one."

I laugh, a full, genuine, and happy laugh. But fear lurks around me.

"I don't want a divorce."

"No, but you need one so you can move on to a complete and full life." My eyes close as I imagine my life without her.

"No."

"No?" *Stubborn woman.*

She sits back and folds her arms across her chest in defiance. "I mean no. You don't get to decide what I want. I want you. I don't want a divorce. The past few days have shown me that we can crawl our way back to happiness. I *know* we can. Please believe that we can do this!"

"Believe what? That you can live with me? The accident didn't just change my body. It affected my mind, too." I run my hands through my hair. I hadn't realized that was true until right now. My mind is a bigger mess than my body.

She repeats her words, a hopeful mantra. "I don't want a divorce."

I sigh. "I never wanted one."

"Where does that leave us?" A sea of emotions fills her eyes, and this time they're unreadable.

Where *does* that leave us?

Fear and hope compete for headspace. Can I really walk away from Becs? Knowing that she wants me to stay? I'm in no position to promise her forever; I won't give her what I'm not sure I can even manage. I opt for compromise.

"One year. We fight for us, to restore us for the next year. We come back here and decide if we keep going or walk away. I'm too broken to offer forever. I'll give us a year. If it doesn't work, we walk away."

"One year?"

I pull out my phone and book a campsite, this exact campsite, for one year from today and show her the confirmation. "Yeah. For the next year, we try to find our way back to us. To a healthy relationship. If we can't, then we both agree to walk away."

"One year. I can agree to that."

Will I regret not walking away now so she can have the life she deserves? Do I have a shot at forever with this woman? Something like hope grips into my chest.

"Would you go to counseling with me? Eugene gave me some resources when he released me from physical therapy. He probably thought my head needed more work than my body."

She smiles. "Yes, but I think I need individual counseling, too."

I lay my forehead against hers. "Not as much as I do."

She chuckles. "I don't think it's a contest."

I laugh and pull her into a tight hug. Then she kisses me like she's absolutely starving for it. Without breaking the kiss, I use my arms to reposition us until I can lower down to my back with her on top of me. She looks at me a bit startled that we've changed positions. "You know my leg may be gone but the rest of my body works pretty well. Works great, actually."

She laughs and then gives me a most wicked grin.

Later that night, with our minds eased and our bodies satiated, Becs rolls to her back, tucked in next to me. "Oh I love having the sunroof! You can see the night sky."

My vision looks upward. The cloud cover has blown away, and I see the clearest of nights.

Twinkling in the heavens above are countless stars.

Epilogue

Carey

THE NEXT YEAR, REBECCA AND I returned to the same place. After both finding peace mentally and learning how to reframe our more negative thoughts, we'd shifted back into a second honeymoon phase of marriage. Each year, we'd return to the same campsite, recommitting to each other and our life together.

Despite being down a couple of body parts, I did anything I wanted. I coached my daughter's soccer team. My son bragged about his pirate dad with a peg leg. We did family hiking trips and museum visits. At times I had to pace myself, but I managed.

We lived a life full of laughter and love, intermixed with the inevitable hard times. After forty-two years of returning to our spot together, I returned to it one last time, alone. Rebecca fought and lost her battle to cancer. My final words to her were, "You don't have to be strong anymore." She slipped from this world and into a peaceful rest. Her absence left a void and endless beautiful memories for all who knew her.

I returned to our favorite place to honor the woman who taught me that love isn't found in grand gestures and greeting cards; it's found in the one who clings to you in the darkest of nights. The nights when you question the existence of the stars. Though tonight the clouds have rolled in, signaling a summer storm on the horizon, I know somewhere beyond this darkness, the stars are waiting.

*"Do the Stars Exist?" is a standalone short story that exists
in the world of the Charleston Harbor Series by Desi Stowe.*

About the Author

Desi Stowe officially started writing in early 2022, however, she'd been developing her scaffolding as a writer for many years. She had a way with words and a love of stories.

Writing was a natural next step. She also found that writing was a wonderful escape into a fictional world, even if that world mirrors real life.

She worked to combine her experience in healthcare and her love of writing into her first novel. In February of 2024, she published *Done*, her first novel of the Charleston Harbor Series. In 2024, her second novel *Shadows* and a short story *Seeking Sanctuary* were new additions to the Charleston Harbor Series world.

In June 2025, she released her first psychological thriller, *Red Gate by the Bridge*.

She lives in Raleigh, North Carolina, with her husband and two children. During the day, she works as a physical therapist. Her writing has been in sporadic spurts while juggling other responsibilities. Desi often finds herself daydreaming about plot progression and character arcs while working out or washing dishes. The characters of her novels have a special place in her heart and hopefully yours, as well.

You can find Desi on:

Instagram: @desistowe

You can visit her website at:

https://authordesistowe.com

CONTRIBUTORS' LIBRARY

Please also look for these titles, which were authored by, published by, or feature the authors in this anthology.

Northern Woods
Amy Hepp

Ripple Effects
Amy Hepp

Strawberry Macarons
Jessica Daniliuk

Includes "Figure Eights"
Jessica Daniliuk

Includes "Sinister Debt"
Caz Luan

Sweet Torture
Caz Luan

The Taste of Sin
Caz Luan

Lewis
Mitchell S. Elrick

MJ's Jersey
Mitchell S. Elrick

Polka Dots
Mitchell S. Elrick

Coffee, Dogs and Christmas Lights
Rowen Burrows

A Chance at Christmas
Rowen Burrows
Coming Soon!

Welcome Home
Melissa Cate

A Beautiful Lily
Caroline Baccene

Breathing in the Fog
Caroline Baccene

The Charred Grape
Caroline Baccene

Done
Desi Stowe

Shadows
Desi Stowe

Red Gate by the Bridge
Desi Stowe

Seeking Sanctuary
Desi Stowe

&You

Another Chance to Get It Right
A New Year's Eve Anthology

9 Stories

As the Snow Drifts
A Cozy Winter Anthology

9 Stories

Anthologies

Craving You
A Spicy Valentine's Day Anthology

12 Stories

Recipes for Romance
A Sweet Valentine's Day Anthology

19 Stories

Nicole Frail has been editing fiction and nonfiction books for adults and children for sixteen years. Between 2012 and 2024, she worked as an acquisitions and project editor for a traditional publisher based in New York City while simultaneously working with independent/self-publishing authors via her small business, Nicole Frail Edits.

In mid-2024, Nicole switched gears and decided to take her "side gig" full time, expanding the services offered through Nicole Frail Edits, LLC. Shortly after, she formed her own small press, Nicole Frail Books, LLC, to publish anthologies born out of short story contests as well as ebooks and other projects still to come. NFB now has three imprints: And You Press, Attic Ebooks, and InkBridge Books.

Nicole lives just outside Scranton, Pennsylvania, with her husband, three little boys, and two Tuxedo cats.

You can find Nicole Frail on:

Instagram & Facebook: @nicolefrailedits & @nicolefrailbooks

And visit her websites at:

www.nicolefrailedits.com
www.nicolefrailbooks.com

Acknowledgments

A massive thank-you to the following for all of the support, trust, and excitement they've shown me throughout this process.

To the authors who submitted to the short story contest, thank you for finding the prompt enticing enough to want to write about and for sharing your enthusiasm for it!

To the authors featured in the anthology, thank you for your patience while I, once again, pushed the boundaries and the deadlines. My ADHD thanks you for being understanding and supportive, as well.

To Olivia Anderson and Giovanni Sariti, my Spring 2025 interns, who went above and beyond the semester's requirements to ensure that this anthology was in readers' hands for Summer 2025. Olivia had a role in choosing the stories and offering feedback I delivered to the authors, and Gio designed the cover and provided elements featured in the interior. It's been wonderful working with both of you.

To Plunge Into Books Tours, for putting up with me. ;)

To the NFB Street Team, for being adaptable, enthusiastic, supportive, and overall awesome. We're growing, little by little, and I appreciate you all.

To the local NEPA readers who continually show up at craft fairs and vendor events and are eager to get their hands on these anthologies: you make my day every time you stop by to say hi. *heart hands*

And, as always, thank you to my family—Matthew, and our boys: Cooper, Travis, and Eli—just for being you.

And You Press, or &You Press,
is an imprint of Nicole Frail Books, LLC,
an independent ("indie") publishing
company located in Avoca, Pennsylvania.

And You Press was created to release the anthologies built from the short story contests that launched NFB in the fall of 2024. The name reflects the requirement that every book published under this imprint will have multiple collaborators so that every title released brings multiple voices to each project.

These titles may be additional anthologies, novels with two or more authors, author and illustrator teams, or something else entirely. As long as the work has multiple creators who will be credited equally for the work they've put into it or will put into it, it may be appropriate for this imprint.

To learn more about submitting a query to And You Press, visit www.andyoupress.com.

Readers!
Join the NFB Street Team for exclusive first reads and swag from And You Press!
www.nicolefrailbooks.com/street